Rachel Harriette Busk

Sagas from the Far East

Or, Kalmouk and Mongolian traditionary tales

Rachel Harriette Busk

Sagas from the Far East
Or, Kalmouk and Mongolian traditionary tales

ISBN/EAN: 9783337070809

Printed in Europe, USA, Canada, Australia, Japan

Cover: Foto ©Andreas Hilbeck / pixelio.de

More available books at **www.hansebooks.com**

SAGAS FROM THE FAR EAST;

OR,

KALMOUK AND MONGOLIAN

TRADITIONARY TALES.

WITH HISTORICAL PREFACE AND EXPLANATORY NOTES.

BY THE AUTHOR OF "PATRAÑAS," "HOUSEHOLD STORIES
FROM THE LAND OF HOFER," &c.

LONDON:
GRIFFITH AND FARRAN,
SUCCESSORS TO NEWBERY AND HARRIS,
CORNER OF ST. PAUL'S CHURCHYARD.
MDCCCLXXIII.

" It singularly happens that the Sagas of the ancient Indians are preserved to us in much fuller measure than their authentic history, which is scanty enough.   Moreover to them their *Sagas* served as actual statements of facts, so that we can neither form a right conception of their mind, nor arrive at any knowledge of their history, without studying their *Sagas.*"

LASSEN, "Pref. to *Ind. Alterthumskunde,*" p. vii.

" The Mongol is candid and credulous as an infant, and passionately loves to listen to marvellous myths and tales."

HUC, " Travels in China and Tibet," vol. ii. ch. xii.

PREFACE.

THE origin and migrations of myths have of late been the subject of so much sifting and study, the elaborate results of which are already before the world, that there is no need in this place to offer more than a few condensed remarks in allusion to the particular collections now, I believe, for the first time put into English. Translations of some chapters of the "Adventures of the Well-and-wise-walking Khan" have been made by Benj. Bergmann, Riga, 1804; by Golstunski, St. Petersburg, 1864; and by H. Osterley, in 1867. Of "Ardschi-Bordschi," by Emil Schlaginweit; by Benfey, in "Ausland," Nos. 34—36, and the whole of both by Professor Jülg, 1865-68; of these I have availed myself in preparing the following pages; I know of no other translation into any European language except one into Russ by Galsan Gombojew, published at S. Petersburg in 1865-68 *.

---

* The few notes I have taken from Jülg's translation, I have acknowledged by putting his name to them.

The first thirteen chapters of the " Well-and-wise-
walking Khan " are a Kalmouk (¹) collection, all the
rest Mongolian ; and though traceable to Indian sources,
they yet have received an entire transformation in the
course of their adoption by their new country. In
giving them another new home, some further alterations, though of a different nature, have been necessary.
However much one may regret them such transformations are inevitable. It seems a law of nature that
history should to a certain extent *write itself.* We
know the age of a tree by its knots and rings ; and we
trace the age of a building by its alterations and repairs
—and that equally well whether these be made in a
style later prevailing, utterly different from that of the
original design, or in the most careful imitation of the
same ; for the age of the workman's hand cannot choose
but write itself on whatever he chisels.

It is just the same with these myths. They cannot
remain as if stereotyped from the first ; the hand that
passes them on must mould them anew in the process.
You might say, they have been already altered enough
during their wanderings, give them to us now at least
as the Mongolians left them. But it is not possible,
most of them are too coarse to meet an eye trained by
Christianity and modern cultivation. The habit of mind
in which they are framed is in places as foreign as the
idiom in which they are written ; I have, however, made
it an undeviating rule to let such alterations be as few

and as slight as the case admitted, and that they should go no farther than was necessary to make them readable, or occasionally give them point.

As I have said these stories have an 'Indian' source, it becomes incumbent to spend a few lines on defining the use and reach of the word*.

The words Ἰνδος and ἡ Ἰνδικὴ occur for the first time among writers of classical antiquity in the fragments that have come down to us of the writings of Hecatæus, B.C. 500. Herodotus also uses the same; from these they descended to us through the Romans. They both received it through Persian means and used it in the most comprehensive sense, though the Persian use of their equivalent at the time seems to have been more limited. It is probable, however, that later the Persian use became further extended; and through the Arabians, who also adopted it from them, it became the Muhammedan designation of the whole country. When they, in 713, conquered the country watered by the lower course of the Indus, namely, Sinde, they confirmed the use of this more extended application of the Persian word *Hind*, reserving *Sind*, the local form of the same word—apparently without perceiving it was the same—to this particular province.

The later Persian designation is *Hindustan*—the country of the Hindu—and this is generally adopted in

---

* The following paragraphs are chiefly gathered and translated from Lassen's work on the Geography of Ancient India, vol. i.

India itself to denote the whole country, though many Europeans have restricted it to the Northern half, in contradistinction from the Dekhan, or country south of the Vindha-range ('), often excluding even Bengal.

The original native names are different. In the epic mythology occur, Gambudvîpa, the island of the gambu-tree (Eugenia Jambolana), for the central or known world of which India was part, and *Sudarsana*, "of beautiful appearance," to denote both the tree and the "island" named from it. The Buddhist cosmography uses Gampudvîpa for India Proper. Within this the Brahmanical portion, lying to the south of the Himâlajas, is designated as Bhârata or Bhâratavarsha. In the great epic poem called the Mahâ Bhârata, the name is derived from Bhârata, son of Dusjanta, the first known ruler of the country, and several dynasties are called after him Bhâratides, though it is more probable his name rather accrued to him from that of the country, the word being derived from *bhri*, "to bring forth" or "nourish," hence, "the fruitful," "life-nourishing" land. Bhârata is also called (Rig-Ved. i. 96, 3) "the nourisher," *sustentator*.

The native historical name is undoubtedly "Ârjâvata," the district of the Ârja—"the venerable men"—or more literally, "worthy to be sought after," keepers of the sacred laws, the people of honourable ancestry; calling themselves so in contradistinction to the Mlêk'ha, barbarous despisers of the sacred laws (Manu,

i. 22; x. 45), also Ârja-bhûmi, land of the Ârja. The
Manu defines rigidly the original boundaries of this
sacred country; it lies between the Himâlaja and
Vindhja mountains, and stretches from the eastern to
the western seas. Though Ptolemy (Geog. vii. 1) calls
the people of the west coast, south of the Vindhja, Âriaka,
this was a later extension of the original term.

. What gives the word a great historical importance
is the circumstance which must not be passed over here,
that the original native name of the inhabitants of Iran
was either the same or similarly derived. *Airja* in
Zend stood both for " honourable " and for the name of
the Iranian people. Concerning the Medes we have
the testimony of Herodotus that they originally called
themselves Άριοι, and we owe him the information
also that the original Persian name was Άρταιοὶ, a
word which has the same root as Ârja, or at least can
have no very different meaning. They do not seem
ever to have actually called themselves Ârja, although
the word existed in their ancient tongue with the sense
of " noble," " honourable."

The earliest Indian *Sagas* speak of the Arja as already established in Central India, and give no help to
the discovery of when or how they settled there. Like
most other peoples of the old world, they believed themselves aborigines, and they placed the Creation and the
origin of species in the very land where they found themselves living, nor do their myths bear a trace of allusion

to any earlier dwelling-place or country outside their
Bhâratavarsha (*). It is true, that the sanctity they
ascribe to the north country, and the mysterious allusions
to the sacred mountain-country of Meerû, the dwelling of the gods in the far, far north, over the Himâlajas,
is calculated to mislead for a moment with the sugges-
tion that they point to a possible immigration from that
north, but a closer observation shows that that very
sacred regard more probably arose from the very fact
of its being an unknown country; while the effect of
the majestic and inaccessible heights, with their glorious colouring and their peculiar natural productions,
was enough to suggest them the seat of a superior and
divine race of beings.

The fact that Sanskrit, the ancient tongue of the
Aryan Indians, is so closely allied to the languages of
so many western nations, establishes with certainty the
identity of origin of these people, and lays on us the
burden of deciding whether the Aryan Indians migrated to India as the allied peoples migrated to their
countries from a common aboriginal home, or whether
that aboriginal home was India, and all the allied peoples
migrated from it, the Indians alone remaining at
home.

Reason points to the adoption of the former of these
two solutions. In the first place, it is altogether unlikely that in the case of a great migration all should
have migrated rigidly in one direction. It is only

natural to expect they should have poured themselves
out every way, and to look for the original home in a
locality which should have formed a central base of
operations. The very feuds which would in many
cases lead to such outpourings would necessitate the
striking out in ever new directions. Then, there is
nothing in the manners, ideas, speech—in the names
of articles of primary importance to support life, in
which at least we might expect to find such a trace—
of the other peoples to connect them in any way with
India. Had they ever been at home there, some
remnants of local influence would have been retained;
but we find none. Besides this, we have, on the other
hand, very satisfactory evidence of at least the later
journeyings of the Indian family. Their warlike and
conquering entrance into the Dekhan and crossing of
the Vindhja range is matter of positive history. Some
help for ascertaining their earlier route may be found
in the necessity established by the laws and limits of
possibility. Encumbered with flocks and herds, and
unassisted by appliances of transport, we cannot believe them to have traversed the steep peaks of the
Himâlajas. The road through eastern Caboolistan and
the valley of the Pangkora, or that leading from the
Gilgit by way of Attok, or over the table-land of
Deotsu through Cashmere, are all known to us as most
difficult of access, and do not appear at any period to
have been willingly adopted. But the western passes

of Hindukutsch, skirting round the steep Himâlajas—
the way trod by the armies of Alexander and other
warlike hosts, no less than by the more peaceful trains
of merchants, with whom it was doubtless traditional—
affords a highly probable line of march for the first
great immigration.

We are reminded here of the fact already alluded to,
of the common origin of the earliest name of both
Indians and Persians, leading us to suppose they
long inhabited one country in common.   For this supposition we find further support in other similarities :
e. g. between the older Sanskrit of the Vêda and the
oldest poems of the Iranian tongue; also between the
teaching, mythology, the *sagas*, and the spoken language of the two peoples.   On the other hand, we find
also the most diverse uses given to similar expressions,
pointing to a period of absolute separation between
them, and at a remote date : e.g. the Indian word for
the Supreme Being is *déva;* in Zend, *daéva,* as also *dév*
in modern Persian, stands for the Evil Principle.
Again, in Zend *dagju* means a province (and its use
implies orderly division of government and the tranquil
exercise of authority); but in the Brahmanical code
dasju is used for a turbulent horde, who set law and
authority at defiance.

Such transpositions seem the result of some fierce
variance, leading to division and hatred between
peoples long united.

Proceeding now to trace the original wandering farther on, we find some help from Iranian traditions. The *Zendavesta* distinctly tells of a so-called Aîrjanem Vaêgo as a sacred country, the seat of creation, and place it in the farthest east of the highest Iranian table-land, the district of the source of the Oxus and Jaxartes; by the death-bringing Ahriman it was stricken with cold and barrenness(³), and only saw the sun thenceforth for two months of the year. The particularity with which it is described would point to the fact that the locality treated of was a distant one, with which the race had a traditional acquaintance; while at the same time it cannot be adopted too precisely in every detail, because details may be altered by a poetical imagination—merits may be exaggerated by regret for absence, and defects magnified by vexation, or invented in proof of the effects of a predicated curse.

If we may conclude that we have rightly traced up the Indians and Persians to a common home between the easternmost Iranian highlands and the Caspian Sea, it follows from the linguistic analogies of the so-called Indo-European peoples that this same home was also theirs at a time when they were not yet broken up into distinct families. This common local origin gives at once the reason for the analogies in the grammatical structure of their languages, and no less of their mythical traditions, which are far too widely spread, and have entered too radically into the universal

teaching of both, to be supposed for a moment to have
been borrowed by either from the other within the historical period, or at all since their separation.

It remains only to say a few words on the scope and
object of the work, and the profit that may be derived
from its perusal. I know there are many who think
that mere amusement is profit enough to expect from a
tale, and that to look for the extraction of any more
serious result is tedious. But I will give my young
readers—or at least a large proportion of them—credit
for possessing sufficient love of improvement to prefer
that class of amusement which furthers their desire for
information and edification.

The collections of myths with which I have heretofore
presented them have all had either a Christian origin,
or at least have passed through a Christian mould, and
have thus almost unconsciously subserved the purpose
of illustrating some phase of Christian teaching, which
is specially distinguished by keeping in view, not
spasmodically and arbitrarily, as in the best of other
systems, but uniformly, in its sublimest reach and in
its humblest detail, the belief that an eternal purpose
and consequence pervades the whole length and breadth
of human existence.

Whether the story of " Juanita the Bald " was
originally drawn by a Christian desirous of inculcating
the sacred principles of the new covenant, or adapted

to the purpose by such an one from the myth of Œdipus and Antigone; whether that of "St. Peter's Three Loaves" was really a traditional incident of our Lord's wanderings on earth too insignificant to find place in the pages of Holy Writ, or adapted from the myth of Baucis and Philemon; or whether all were adaptations according to the special convictions of various narrators of great primeval traditions, mattered very little, as each had an intrinsic purpose and an interest of its own quite distinct from that accruing to it through ascertaining its place in the history of the world's beliefs. In telling them, it needed not to point a moral, for the moral—i.e. some more or less remote application of the sacred and civilizing teaching of the Gospel —was of the very essence of each.

With the Tales given in the following pages, however, it is quite different. They come direct from the far East, and in most of them nothing further has been aimed at than the amusement of the weary hours of disoccupation, whether forced or voluntary, of a people indisposed by climate, natural temperament, or want of cultivation from finding recreation in the healthy exercise of mental effort.

To me it seems that before we can take pleasure in giving our time to the perusal of such stories, we must invest them with, or discover in them some sort of purpose. Nor is this so far to seek, perhaps, as might appear at first sight.

Some, it must be observed, belong to the class
which deals with the deeds of heroes—fabling forth the
grand all-time lesson of the vigorous struggle of
good with evil; the nobility of unflinching self-sacrifice
and of devotion to an exalted cause, setting the model
for the lowly sister of charity as much as for the victorious leader of armies, and each all the while typical
of Him who gave Himself to be the servant of all, and
the ransom of all. A German writer rises so inspired
from their study that he bursts forth into this pæan :—
*" Eine Fülle der Göttergeschichte thut sich hier auf, und
nirgends lässt sich der eigenthümliche Naturcharacter in
Fortbildung des Mythus vollständiger erkennen, als an
diesen Alterthümern. Götter und vergötterte Menschen
ragen hier, wie an den Wänden der Tempel von Thebe
hoch über das gewöhnliche Menschengestalt. Alles hat
einen riesenhaften Aufschwung zur himmlischen Welt*."*
Subsidiarily to these conceptions of them, stories of
this class have the further merit of being one chief
means of conveying the scanty data we possess concerning the early history of the people of whose literature they form part ([5]).

Others again may be placed in a useful light by
endeavouring to trace in them the journeyings they
have made in their transmigration. Benfey, a modern
German writer who has employed much time and study
" in tracing the *Mährchen* in their ever-varying forms,"

---

* Heeren, *Indische Literatur.*

while pointing out as many others have also done (⁶),
that the great bulk of our household tales have come to
us from the East, and have been spread over Europe in
various ways, points out that this was done for the South
in great measure through the agency of the Turks; but
for the North it was by the Mongolians during their
two centuries of ascendancy in Eastern Europe; the
Slaves received them from them, and communicated
them to the German peoples (⁷).

If therefore you find some tales in one collection
bearing a close resemblance with those you have read in
another, you should make it a matter of interest to
observe what is individual in the character of each, and
to trace the points both of diversity and analogy in the
mode of expression in which they are clothed, and
which will be found just as marked as the difference in
costume of the respective peoples who have told them
each after their own fashion.

All of them have at least the merit of being, in the
main, pictures of life, however overwrought with the
fantastic or supernatural element, not ideal embodiments of the perfect motives by which people ought to
be actuated, but *genre* pictures of the modes in which
they commonly do act. As such they cannot fail to
contain the means of edification, though we are left to
look for and discover and apply it for ourselves. To
take one instance. The Christian hagiographer could
never have written of a hero he was celebrating, as we

find it said of Vikramâditja, that as part of his preparation for the battle of life "while learning wisdom with
the wise, and the use of arms from men of valour," "of
the robber bands he acquired the art of stealing, and of
fraudulent dealers, to lie." If he had been illustrating
the actual biography of a Christian hero, it is a detail
which could not have entered, and if drawing an ideal
picture, it would have been entirely at variance with
the system he was illustrating. Circumstances like
this which fail to serve as subject for imitation, must be
turned to account in exercising the powers of judgment,
as well in distinguishing what to avoid from what to
admire, as in taking note of these very variances between Christian and the best non-christian morality.

*** The author feels bound to apologize for any
inaccuracies which may have crept into these pages
owing to being abroad while preparing them for the
press.

CONTENTS.

THE SAGA OF THE WELL-AND-WISE-WALKING KHAN.

THE SAGA OF ARDSCHI-BORDSCHI AND VIKRAMÂDITJA'S THRONE.

THE SAGA OF THE
WELL-AND-WISE-WALKING KHAN.

DEDICATION.

O THOU most perfect Master and Teacher of Wisdom
and Goodness! Teacher, second only to the incom-
parable Shâkjamuni (¹)! Thou accomplished Nâgâr-
g'una (²)! Thou who wast intimately acquainted with
the Most-pure *Tripítaka* (³), and didst evolve from it
thy wise *madhjamika* (⁴), containing the excellent *paramârtha* (⁵)! Before thee I prostrate myself! Hail!
Nâgârg'una O!

It is even the wonderful and astounding history of
the deeds of the Well-and-wise-walking Khan, which he
performed under the help and direction of this same
Master and Teacher, Nâgârg'una, that I propose to re-
late in the form of the following series of narratives.

B

In the kingdom of Magadha ([6]) there once lived seven brothers who were magicians. At the distance of a mile from their abode lived two brothers, sons of a Khan. The elder of these went to the seven magicians, saying, " Teach me to understand your art," and abode with them seven years. But though they were always setting him to learn difficult tasks, yet they never taught him the true key to their mystic knowledge. His brother, however, coming to visit him one day, by merely looking through a crack in the door of the apartment where the seven brothers were at work acquired perfectly the whole *krijâvidja* ([7]).

After this they both went home together, the elder because he perceived he would never learn any thing of the magicians, and the younger because he had learnt every thing they had to impart.

As they went along the younger brother said, " Now that we know all their art the seven magicians will probably seek to do us some mischief. Go thou, therefore, to our stable, which we left empty, and thou shalt find there a splendid steed. Put a rein on him and lead him forth to sell him, only take care thou go not in the direction of the dwelling of the seven magicians ; and, having sold him, bring back the price thou shalt have received."

When he had made an end of speaking he transformed himself into a horse, and went and placed himself in the stable against his brother arrived.

But the elder brother, knowing the magicians had taught him nothing, stood in no fear of them. Therefore he did not according to the words of his brother; but saying within himself, " As my brother is so clever that he could conjure this fine horse into the stable, let him conjure thither another if he wants it sold. This one I will ride myself." Accordingly he saddled and mounted the horse. All his efforts to guide him were vain, however, and in spite of his best endeavours the horse, impelled by the power of the magic of them from whom the art had been learnt, carried him straight to the door of the magicians' dwelling. Once there he was equally unable to induce him to stir away; the horse persistently stood still before the magicians' door. When he found he could not in any way command the horse, he determined to sell it to these same magicians, and he offered it to them, asking a great price for it.

The magicians at once recognized that it was a magic horse, and they said, among themselves, " If our art is to become thus common, and every body can produce a magic horse, no one will come to our market for wonders. We had best buy the horse up and destroy it." Accordingly they paid the high price required and took possession of the horse and shut it up in a dark stall. When the time came to slaughter it, one held it down by the tail, another by the head, other four by the four legs, so that it should in nowise break away, while the seventh bared his arm ready to strike it with death.

When the Khan's son, who was transformed into the horse, had learnt what was the intention of the magicians, he said, "Would that any sort of a living being would appear into which I might transform myself."

Hardly had he formed the wish when a little fish was seen swimming down the stream: into this the Khan transformed himself. The seven magicians knew what had occurred, and immediately transformed themselves into seven larger fish and pursued it. When they were very close to the little fish, with their gullets wide open, the Khan said, within himself, "Would that any sort of living being would appear into which I might transform myself." Immediately a dove was seen flying in the heavens, and the Khan transformed himself into the dove. The seven magicians, seeing what was done, transformed themselves into seven hawks, pursuing the dove over hill and dale. Once again they were near overtaking him, when the dove took refuge in the Land Bede (*). Southward in Bede was a shining mountain and a cave within it called "Giver of Rest." Hither the dove took refuge, even in the very bosom of the Great Master and Teacher, Nâgârg'una.

The seven hawks came thither also, fast flying behind the dove; but, arrived at the entrance of Nâgârg'una's cave, they showed themselves once more as men, clothed in cotton garments.

Then spoke the great Master and Teacher, Nâgâr-g'una, "Wherefore, O dove, flutterest thou so full of terror, and what are these seven hawks to thee?"

So the Khan's son told the Master all that had happened between himself, his brother, and the seven magicians; and he added these words, "Even now there stand before the entrance of this cave seven men clothed in cotton garments. These men will come in unto the Master and pray for the boon of the *árámela* he holds in his hand. Meantime, I will transform myself into the large bead of the *árámela,* and when the Master would reach the chaplet to the seven men, I pray him that, putting one end of it in his mouth, he bite in twain the string. of the same, whereby all the beads shall be set free."

The Master benevolently did even as he had been prayed. Moreover, when all the beads fell showering on the ground, behold they were all turned into little worms, and the seven men clothed in cotton garments transformed themselves into seven fowls, who pecked up the worms. But when the Master dropped the large bead out of his mouth on to the ground it was transformed into the form of a man having a staff in his hand. With this staff the Khan's son killed the seven fowls, but the moment they were dead they bore the forms of men's corpses.

Then spoke the Master. "This is evil of thee. Behold, while I gave thee protection for thy one life, thou hast taken the lives of these men, even of these seven. In this hast thou done evil."

But the Khan's son answered, "To protect my life there was no other means save to take the life of these seven, who had vowed to kill me. Nevertheless, to testify my thanks to the Master for his protection, and to take this sin from off my head, behold I am ready to devote myself to whatever painful and difficult enterprise the Master will be pleased to lay upon me."

"Then," said the Master, "if this is so, betake thyself to the cool grove, even to the *cîtavana* ([9]), where is the Siddhî-kür ([10]). From his waist upwards he is of gold, from his waist downwards of emerald; his head is of mother-of-pearl, decked with a shining crown. Thus is he made. Him if thou bring unto me from his Mango-tree ([11]), thou shalt have testified thy gratitude for my protection and shalt have taken this sin that thou hast committed from off thy head; for so shall I be able, when I have the Siddhî-kür in subjection under me, to bring forth gold in abundance, to give lives of a thousand years' duration to the men of Gambudvîpa ([12]), and to perform all manner of wonderful works."

"Behold, I am ready to do even as according to thy word," answered the Khan's son. "Tell me only the way I have to take and the manner and device whereby I must proceed."

Then spoke the great Master and Teacher, Nâgâr-g'una, again, saying,—

"When thou shalt have wandered forth hence for the distance of about an hundred miles, thou shalt come to a dark and fearsome ravine where lie the bodies of the giant-dead. At thy approach they shall all rise up and surround thee. But thou call out to them, ' Ye giant-dead, *hala hala sváhá* ([13])!' scattering abroad at the same time these barley-corns, consecrated by the power of magic art, and pass on thy way without fear.

About another hundred miles' space farther hence thou shalt come to a smooth mead by the side of a river where lie the bodies of the pigmy-dead. At thy approach they shall all rise up and surround thee. But thou cry out to them, ' Ye pigmy-dead, *hulu hulu sváhá!*' and, strewing thine offering of barley-corns, again pass on thy way without fear.

At a hundred miles' space farther along thou shalt come to a garden of flowers having a grove of trees and a fountain in the midst; here lie the bodies of the child-dead. At thy approach they shall rise up and running together surround thee. But thou cry out to them, ' Ye child-dead, *rira phad !*' and, strewing thine offering of barley-corns, again pass on thy way without fear.

Out of the midst of these the Siddhî-kür will rise and will run away from before thee till he reaches his mango-

tree, climbing up to the summit thereof. Then thou
swing on high the axe which I will give thee, even the
axe White Moon (¹⁴), and make as though thou wouldst
hew down the tree in very truth. Rather than let thee
hew the mango-tree he will come down. Then seize him
and bind him in this sack of many colours, in which is place
for to stow away an hundred, enclose the mouth thereof
tight with this cord, twisted of an hundred threads of
different colours, make thy meal off this cake which
never grows less, place the sack upon thy shoulder, and
bring him hither to me. ONLY BEWARE THAT BY THE
WAY THOU OPEN NOT THY LIPS TO SPEAK !

"And now, hitherto hast thou been called the Khan's
son, but now, since thou hast found thy way even to
the cave ' Giver of Rest,' thou shalt be called no more
the Khan's son, but ' the Well-and-wise-walking Khan.'
Go now thy way."

When the Master, Nâgârg'una, had given him this
new name, he further provided him with all the provisions for the undertaking which he had promised him,
and, pointing out the way, dismissed him in peace.

When the Well-and-wise-walking Khan had overcome all the alarms and difficulties of the way, and
come in sight of the Siddhî-kür, he set out swiftly to
pursue him; but the Siddhî-kür was swifter than he,
and, reaching the mango-tree, clambered up to the
summit. Then said the Well-and-wise-walking Khan,
" Behold, I come in the name of the great Master and

Teacher, Nâgârg'una. My axe is the axe 'White Moon,' my provision for the journey is the cake which never diminishes, my prison is the sack of many colours, in which is place to stow away an hundred, my cord is the cord twisted of an hundred threads of different colours, I myself am called the Well-and-wise-walking Khan; I command thee, therefore, Siddhî-kür, that thou come down hither to me, otherwise with my axe 'White Moon' will I fell the mango-tree."

At these words the Siddhî-kür cried, in answer, "Fell not the mango-tree. Rather will I come down to thee." With that he came down, and the Khan, taking him, put him in his sack of many colours, in which was place to stow away an hundred, then he made the mouth fast with the cord twisted of an hundred threads of various colours, made his meal off his cake which never diminished, and proceeded on his way to take him to the great Master and Teacher, Nâgârg'una.

As they journeyed on thus day after day, and had grown weary, thus spoke the Siddhî-kür, " Long is the journey, and both of us are weary, tell thou now a story to enliven it."

But, remembering the words of Nâgârg'una, "Beware thou open not thy lips to speak," he answered him never a word.

Then said the Siddhî-kür again, "If thou wilt not tell a story to lighten the journey, at least listen to one from me, and to this thou canst give assent without opening thy lips, if only thou nod thy head backwards towards me. At this sign I will tell a tale." So the Well-and-wise-walking Khan nodded his head backwards towards the Siddhî-kür, and the Siddhî-kür told this tale :—

TALE I.

THE WOMAN WHO SOUGHT HER HUSBAND IN THE PALACE OF ERLIK KHAN.

LONG ages ago there reigned a young Khan whose father had died early and left him in possession of the kingdom. He was a youth comely to look upon, and dazzling in the glory of his might. To him had been given for his chief wife the daughter of a Khan of the South. But the young Khan loved not this wife. At a mile's distance from his palace there lived in her father's house a well-grown, beautiful maiden, of whom he had made his second wife; as she was not a Khan's daughter he feared to take her home to his palace, lest he should displease his mother, but he came often to visit her, and as they loved each other very much, she asked no more.

One night, when the moon was brightly shining, some one knocked at the window, the maiden knew it was the Khan's manner of knocking, so she opened to him,—but with trembling, for he had never been wont to come at that hour; yet by the light of the moon-

beam she saw that it was indeed himself, only instead
of his usual garments, he was habited in shining
apparel, which she could hardly look upon for its
brightness, and he, himself, too, looked more exceeding beautiful than usual. When he had partaken of
her rice-brandy and cakes, he rose and stood upon
the doorstep, saying, "Come, sweet wife, come out
together with me;" and when she had gone a little
way with him, he said, "Come, sweet wife, come a
little farther with me." And when she had gone a
little farther with him, he said again, "Come, sweet
wife, come yet a little farther." So she went yet a
little farther till they had reached nearly to the gates
of the palace, and from within the courts of the palace
there came a noise of shouting and playing on instruments. Then inquired she, "To what end is this
shouting and this music?" And he replied, "It is the
noise of the sacrifice for the rites of the burial of the
Khan(¹)." "And why do they celebrate the rites of the
burial of the Khan?" she asked, now beginning to
fear in earnest. "Because I am dead, sweet wife,
and am even now on my way to the *deva's* kingdom.
But thou listen to me, and do according to my word,
and all shall be well for thee and for our son. Behold,
even now, within the palace, my mother and my chief
wife strive together concerning a jewel which is lost.
But I have purposely hid the jewel under a god's
image in the apartment. Thou, therefore, pass the

night in this elephant-stable of the palace hard by, and
there shall our son be born ; and in the morning, the
elephant-tamers finding thee shall bring thee to my
mother and my chief wife. But thou, take the jewel
and give it to the chief wife and send her away to her
own people. Then shall my mother have joy in thee
alone and in the child, and you two together shall
direct the Government till he be come to man's estate."
Thus spoke the Khan.

While he spoke these words, the wife was so stricken
with fear and grief that she fell to the ground senseless, nor knew that he bore her into the elephant-
stable, and went up to the *deva's* kingdom.

In the night their son was born ; and in the morning, the elephant-tamers coming in, said, " Here is a
woman and a babe lying in the elephant-stable ; this
must not be, who knows but that it might bring evil to
the elephants(²) ?" so they raised her up, with her infant, and took her to the Khan's mother. Then she told
the Khan's mother all that had befallen her, and as
the jewel was found in the place the Khan had told
her, it was taken for proof of her truth. Accordingly,
the jewel was given to the chief wife, and she was
dismissed to her own people ; and as the Khan had
left no other child, the boy born in the elephant-
stable was declared heir, and his mother and the
Khan's mother directed the Government together till
he should come to man's estate.

Thus the lowly maiden was established in the palace as the Khan had promised. Moreover, every month, on the fifteenth of the month, the Khan came in the night to visit her, disappearing again with the morning light. When she told this to the Khan's mother, she would not believe her, because he was invisible to all eyes but hers. And when she protested that she spoke only words of truth, the Khan's mother said, "If it be very truth, then obtain of him that his mother may see him also."

On the fifteenth of the month, when he came again, she said therefore to him, "That thou shouldst come thus to see me every month, on the fifteenth of the month, is good; but that thou shouldst go away and leave me all alone again, this is sad, very sad. Why canst thou not come back and stay with us altogether, without going away any more?"

And he made answer: "Of a truth there would be one way, but it is difficult and terrible, and it is not given to woman to endure so much fear and pain."

But she replied, "If there were but any means to have thee back, always by my side, I would find strength to endure any terror or pain, even to the tearing out of the bones from the midst of my flesh."

"This is the means that must be taken then," said the Khan : "Next month, on the fifteenth of the month, thou must rise when the moon's light is at the full, and

go forth abroad a mile's distance towards the regions
of the South.   There shalt thou meet with an ancient
man of iron, standing on the watch, who, when he
shall have drank much molten metal, shall yet cry,
'Yet am I thirsty.'   To him give rice-brandy and
pass on.   Farther on thou shalt find two he-goats
fighting together mightily, to them give barm-cakes
to eat and pass on.   Farther along thou shalt find a
band of armed men who shall bar thy way; to them
distribute meat and pass on.   Farther on thou shalt
come to a frightful massive black building round which
runs a moat filled with human blood, and from its
portal waves a man's skin for a banner.   At its door
stand on guard two terrible *erliks* (³), servants of
Erlik Khan (⁴); to each, offer an offering of blood
and pass within the building.

"In the very midst of the building thou shalt find a
Mandala (⁵) formed by eight awful sorcerers, and at
the feet of each will lie a heart which will cry to thee,
'Take me! take me!'   In the midst of all will be a
ninth heart which must cry ' Take me *not !*'

"If thou fortified by thy love shall be neither rendered afraid by the aspect of the place, nor terrified by
the might of the sorcerers, nor confounded by the
wailing of the voices, but shalt take up and bear
away that ninth heart, neither looking backwards nor
tarrying by the way, then shall it be granted us to
live for evermore on earth together."

Thus he spoke; and the morning light breaking, she saw him no more. The wife, however, laid up all his words in her heart; and on the fifteenth of the next month, when the moon shone, she went forth all alone without seeking help or counsel from any one, content to rely on her husband's words. Nor letting her heart be cast down by fear or pain, she distributed to each of those she met by the way the portion he had appointed. At last she reached the *Mandala* of sorcerers, and, regardless of the conflicting cries by which she was assailed, boldly carried off the ninth heart, though it said, " Take me not!" No sooner had she turned back with her prize than the eight sorcerers ran calling after her, " A thief has been in here, and has stolen the heart! Guards! Up, and seize her!" But the *Erliks* before the door answered, " Us she propitiated with a blood-offering ; we arrest her not. See you to it." So the word was passed on to the company of armed men who had barred her passage ; but they answered, "Us hath she propitiated with a meat-offering; we arrest her not. See you to it." Then the word was passed on to the two he-goats. But the he-goats answered, "Us hath she propitiated with a barm-cake-offering; we arrest her not. See you to it." Finally, the word was passed on to the ancient man of iron ; but he answered, "Me hath she propitiated with a brandy-offering ; I arrest her not."

Thus with fearless tread she continued all the way

to the palace.   On opening the door of his apartment,
the Khan himself came forward to meet her in his
beauty and might, and .in tenfold glory, never to go
away from her again any more, and they fell into each
other's arms in a loving embrace.

"Scarcely could a man have held out as bravely as
did this woman!" exclaimed the Khan.

And as he uttered these words, the Siddhî-kür replied, "Forgetting his health, the Well-and-wise-walking Khan hath opened his lips."   And with the cry
"To escape out of this world is good!" he sped him
through the air, swift, out of sight.

Of the Adventures of the Well-and-wise-walking Khan
the first chapter, concerning the Woman who brought
back her Husband from the palace of Erlik-Khan.

TALE II.

WHEN the Well-and-wise-walking Khan found that he had missed the end and object of his journey, he forthwith set out again, without loss of time, or so much as returning to his Master and Teacher, Nâgârg'una, but taking only a meal of his cake which never diminished; thus, with similar toils and fears as the first time, he came again at last to the cool grove where lay the child-dead, and among them the Siddhî-kür. And the Siddhî-kür rose up before him, and clambered up the mango-tree. And when the Well-and-wise-walking Khan had summoned him with proud sounding words to come down, threatening that otherwise he would hew down the tree with his axe "White Moon," the Siddhî-kür came down, rather than that he should destroy the mango-tree. Then he bound him again in his bag of many colours, in which was place to stow away an hundred, and bound the mouth thereof with the cord woven of an hundred threads of different tints, and bore him along to offer to his Master and Teacher, Nâgârg'una.

But at the end of many days' journey, the Siddhî-kür said,—

"Now, in truth, is the length of this journey like to weary us even to death, as we go along thus without speaking. Wherefore, O Prince! let me entreat thee beguile the way by telling a tale."

But the Well-and-wise-walking Khan, remembering the words of his Master and Teacher Nâgârg'una, which he spoke, saying, "See thou open not thy lips to speak by the way," remained silent, and answered him never a word. Then the Siddhî-kür, when he found that he could not be brought to answer him, spake again in this wise: "If thou wilt not tell a tale, then, at least, give some token by which I may know if thou willest that I should tell one, and if thou speak not, at least nod thine head backwards towards me; then will I tell a tale."

So the Well-and-wise-walking Khan nodded his head backwards towards the Siddhî-kür, and the Siddhî-kür told this tale, saying,—

THE GOLD-SPITTING PRINCE.

Long ages ago there was a far-off country where a mighty Khan ruled. Neai the source of the chief river of this country was a pool, where lived two Serpent-gods ('), who had command of the water; and as they could shut off the water of the river when they pleased, and prevent it from overflowing and fertilizing the country, the people were obliged to obey their behest, be it what it might. Now, the tribute they exacted of the country was that of a full grown man, to be chosen by lot, every year; and on whoso the lot fell, he had to go, without redemption, whatever his condition in life. Thus it happened one year that the lot fell on the Khan himself. In all the kingdom there was no one of equal rank who could be received instead of him, unless it had been his only son. When his son would have gone in his stead, he answered him, "What is it to me if the Serpents devour me, so that thou, my son, reignest in peace?" But the son said, "Never shall it be that thou, my Khan and father, shouldst suffer this cruel death, while I remain at home. The thought be far from me. Neither will the land receive harm by my death; is not my mother yet alive? and other sons may be born to thee, who shall reign over the land." So he went to offer himself as food to the Serpent-gods.

As he went along, the people followed him for a long stretch of the way, bewailing him; and then they turned them back. But one there was who turned not back: it was a poor man's son whom the Prince had all his life had for his friend; he continued following him. Then the Prince turned and said to him, "Walk thou according to the counsels of thy father and thy mother, and be prosperous and happy on the earth. To defend this noble, princely country, and to fulfil

c 2

the royal word of the Khan, my father, I go forth to be food to the Serpent-gods."

But the poor man's son refused to forsake him. "Thou hast loaded me with goodness and favours," he said, as he wept; "if I may not go instead of thee, at least I will go with thee." And he continued following the Prince.

When they got near the pool, they heard a low, rumbling, horrible sound : it was the two Serpent-gods talking together, and talking about them, for they were on the look-out to see who would be sent to them this year for the tribute. The old gold-yellow Serpent was telling the young emerald-green Serpent how the Prince had come instead of his father, and how the poor man, who had no need to come at all, had insisted on accompanying him.

"And these people are so devoted in giving their lives for one another," said the young emerald-green Serpent, "and have not the courage to come out and fight us, and make an end of paying this tribute at all."

"They don't know the one only way to fight us," answered the gold-yellow old Serpent; "and as all the modes they have tried have always failed, they imagine it cannot be done, and they try no more."

"And what is the one only way by which they could prevail against us?" inquired the young emerald-green Serpent.

"They have only to cut off our heads with a blow of a stout staff," replied the old gold-yellow Serpent, "for so has Shêsa, the Serpent-dæmon, appointed."

"But these men carry shining swords that look sharp and fearful," urged the young emerald-green Serpent.

"That is it!" rejoined the other: "their swords avail nothing against us, and so they never think that a mere staff should kill us. Also, if after cutting off our heads they were to eat them, they would be able to spit as much gold and precious stones as ever they liked. But they know nothing of all this," chuckled the old gold-yellow Serpent.

Meantime, the Prince had not lost a word of all that the two Serpents had said to each other, for his mother had taught him the speech of all manner of creatures. So when he first heard the noise of the Serpents talking together, he had stood still, and listened to their words. Now, therefore, he told it all again to his follower, and they cut two stout staves in the wood, and then drew near, and cut off the heads of the Serpents with the staves—each of them one; and when they had cut them off, the Prince ate the head of the gold-yellow Serpent, and, see! he could spit out as much gold money as ever he liked; and his follower ate the head of the emerald-green Serpent, and he could spit out emeralds as many as ever he pleased.

Then spoke the poor man's son: "Now that we have

killed the Serpents, and restored the due course of the water to our native country, let us return home and live at peace."

But the Khan's son answered, "Not so, for if we went back to our own land, the people would only mock us, saying, 'The dead return not to the living!' and we should find no place among them. It is better we betake ourselves to another country afar off, which knows us not."

So they journeyed on through a mountain pass.

At the foot of the mountains they came to the habitation of a beautiful woman and her daughter, selling strong drink to travellers. Here they stopped, and would have refreshed themselves, but the women asked them what means they had to pay them withal, for they saw they looked soiled with travel. "We will pay whatever you desire," replied the Prince; and he began to spit out gold coin upon the table. When the women saw that he spat out as much gold coin as ever he would, they took them inside, and gave them as much drink as they could take, making them pay in gold, and at many times the worth of the drink, for they no longer knew what they did; only when they had made them quite intoxicated, and they could not get any thing more from them, in despite of all sense of gratitude or hospitality, they turned them out to pass the night on the road.

When they woke in the morning, they journeyed

farther till they came to a broad river; on its banks
was a palm-grove, and a band of boys were gathered
together under it quarrelling.

"Boys! what are you disputing about?" inquired
the Prince.

"We found a cap on this palm-tree," answered one
of the boys, "and we are disputing whose it shall be,
because we all want it."

"And what use would the cap be to you? What
is it good for?" asked the Prince.

"Why, that whichever of us gets it has only to put
it on," replied the boy, "and he immediately becomes
invisible to gods, men, and dæmons."

"I will settle the dispute for you," rejoined the
Prince. "You all of you get you to the far end
of this palm-grove, and start back running, all fair,
together. Whichever wins the race shall be reckoned
to have won the cap. ·Give it to me to hold the
while."

The boys said, "It is well spoken;" and giving the
cap to the Prince, they set off tó go to the other end of
the grove. But they were no sooner well on their way,
than the Prince put on the cap, and then joining hands
with his companion, both became invisible to gods,
men, and dæmons; so that when the boys came back
at full speed, though they were both yet standing in
the same place, none of them could see them. After
wandering about to look for them in vain, they at last

gave it up in despair, and went away crying with disappointment.

The Prince and his follower continued their journey
by the side of the stream till they came to a broad road,
and here at the cross-way was a crowd of dæmons
assembled, who were all chattering aloud, and disputing vehemently.

"Dæmons! What are you quarrelling about?"
asked the Prince.

"We found this pair of boots here," answered the
dæmons, "and whoever puts these boots on has only
to wish that he might be in a particular place, and
immediately arrives there; and we cannot agree which
of us is to have the boots."

"I will settle the dispute for you," replied the
Prince. "You all go up to the end of this road, and
run back hither all of you together, and whichever of
you wins the race, he shall be reckoned to have won
the boots. Give them to me to hold the while."

So the dæmons answered, "It is well spoken;"
and giving the boots to the Prince, they set off to go
to the far end of the road. But by the time they got
back the Prince had put on the invisible cap, and
joining hands with his companion had become invisible
to gods, men, and dæmons, so that for all their looking there was no trace of them to be found. Thus they
had to give up the lucky boots, and went their way
howling for disappointment.

As soon as they were gone the Prince and his follower began to examine the boots, and to ponder what they should do with their treasure.

"A great gift and a valuable," said the latter, "hath been given thee, O Prince, by the favour of fortune, and thy wisdom in acquiring it. Wish now to reach a prosperous place to be happy; but for me I shall not know where thou art gone, and I shall see thy face no more."

But the Prince said, "Nay, but wheresoever I go, thou shalt go too. Here is one boot for me, and the other for thee, and when we have both put them on we will wish to be in the place where at this moment there is no Khan, and we will then see what is further to be done."

So the Prince put on the right boot, and his follower the left boot, and they laid them down to sleep, and both wished that they might come to a land where there was no Khan.

When they woke in the morning they found themselves lying in the hollow of an ancient tree, in the outskirts of a great city, overshadowing the place where the election of the Khan was wont to be made. As soon as day broke the people began to assemble, and many ceremonies were performed. At last the people said, " Let us take one of the *Baling*-cakes out of the straw sacrifice, and throw it up into the air, and on to whosoever's head it falls he shall be our Khan.

So they took the *Baling*-cake out of the straw sacrifice, and it fell into the hollow tree. And the people said, "We must choose some other mode of divination, for the *Baling*-cake has failed. Shall a hollow tree reign over us?"

But others said, "Let us see what there may be inside the hollow tree."

Thus when they came to look into the tree they found the Prince and his follower. So they drew them out and said, "These shall rule over us." But others said, "How shall we know which of these two is the Khan?" While others again cried, "These men are but strangers and vagabonds. How then shall they reign over us?"

But to the Prince and his follower they said, "Whence are ye? and how came ye in the hollow tree?"

Then the Prince began spitting gold coin, and his follower precious emeralds. And while the people were busied in gathering the gold and the emeralds they installed themselves in the palace, and made themselves Khan and Chief Minister, and all the people paid them homage.

When they had learned the ways of the kingdom and established themselves well in it, the new Khan said to his Minister that he must employ himself to find a wife worthy of the Khan. To whom the Minister made answer,—

"Behold, beautiful among women is the daughter of the last Khan. Shall not she be the Khan's wife?"

The Khan found his word good, and desired that she should be brought to him; when he found she was fair to see, he took her into the palace, and she became his wife. But she was with him as one whose thoughts were fixed on another.

Now on the outskirts of the city was a noble palace, well kept and furnished, and surrounded with delicious gardens; but no one lodged there. Only the Minister took note that every third day the Khan's wife went out softly and unattended, and betook herself to this palace.

"Now," thought the Minister to himself, "wherefore goes the Khan's wife every third day to this palace, softly and unattended? I must see this thing."

So he put on the cap which they had of the boys in the palm-grove, and followed the Khan's wife as he saw her go the palace, and having found a ladder he entered by a window as she came up the stairs. Then he followed her into a sumptuous apartment all fitted with carpets and soft cushions, and a table spread with delicious viands and cooling drinks. The Khan's wife, however, reclined her on none of these cushions, but went out by a private door for a little space, and when she returned she was decked as never she had been when she went before the Khan. The room was filled with perfume as she approached, her hair was powdered with glittering jewels, and her attire was all of broidered silk, while her throat, and arms, and ankles were wreathed with pearls. The Minister hardly knew her again; and with his cap, which made him invisible to gods, men, and dæmons, he approached quite near to look at her, while she, having no suspicion of his presence, continued busy with preparations as for some coming event. On a vast circle of porphyry she lighted a fire of sandal wood, over which she scattered a quantity of odoriferous powders, uttering words the while which it was beyond the power of the Minister to understand. While she was thus occupied, there came a most beautiful bird with many-coloured wings swiftly flying through the open window, and when he had soared round three times in the soft vapour of the sweet-scented gums the Princess had been burning, there appeared a bird no longer, but Cuklaketu, the beautiful son of the gods, surpassing all words in his beauty. The transformation was no sooner effected, than they embraced each other, and reclining together on the silken couches, feasted on the banquet that was laid out.

After a time, Cuklaketu rose to take leave, but before he went, he said, " Now you are married to the husband heaven has appointed you, tell me how it is with him."

At these words the Minister, jealous for his master, grew very attentive that he might learn what opinion the Khan's wife had of his master and what love she had for him. But she answered prudently, "How it will be with him I know not yet, for he is still young; I cannot as yet know any thing of either his merits or defects."

And with that they parted; Cuklaketu flying away in the form of a beautiful bird with many-coloured wings as he had come, and the Khan's wife exchanging her glittering apparel for the mantle in which she came from the Khan's palace.

The next time that she went out to this palace, the Minister put on his cap and followed her again and witnessed the same scene, only when Cuklaketu was about to take leave this time, he said, "To-morrow, I shall come and see what your husband is like." And when she asked him, "By what token shall I know you?" he answered, "I will come under the form of a swallow, and will perch upon his throne." With that they parted; but the Minister went and stood before the Khan and told him all that he had seen.

"But thou, O Khan," proceeded the Minister, "Cause thou a great fire to be kept burning before the throne; and I, standing there with the cap rendering me invisible to gods, men, and dæmons, on my head, will be on the look out for the swallow, and when he appears, I will seize him by the feathers of his tail and dash him into the fire; then must thou, O Khan, slay him, and hew him in pieces with thy sword."

And so it was, for the next morning early, while the Khan and his Consort were seated with all their Court in due order of rank, there came a swallow, all smirk and sprightly, fluttering around them, and at last it perched on the Khan's throne. The Princess watched his every movement with delighted eyes, but the Minister, who waited there wearing his cap which made him invisible to gods, men, and dæmons, no sooner saw him perch on the throne, than he seized him by the feathers of his tail and flung him on the fire. The swallow succeeded in fluttering out of the fire, but as the Khan had drawn his sword to slay him and hew him in pieces, the Princess caught his arm and held it tight, so that the swallow just managed to fly away with his singed wings through the open window. Meantime, the Princess was so overcome with fear and excitement that she fainted away into the arms of the attendants, who were struck with wonder that she should care so much about an injury done to a little bird.

As soon as the day came round for her to go to the palace in the outskirts of the city, again the Minister did not fail to follow closely on her steps. He observed that she prepared every thing with greater attention than before and decked herself out with more costly robes and more glittering gems. But when the minutes passed by and the beautiful bird still appeared not, her fear waxed stronger and stronger, and she

stood gazing, without taking her eyes off the sky.   At
last, and only when it was already late, Cuklaketu came
flying painfully and feebly, and when he had exchanged
his bird disguise for the human form, the traces of the
treatment the Minister had given him were plainly
visible in many frightful blisters and scars.

When the Princess saw him in this evil plight, she
lifted up her voice, and wept aloud.   But the Prince
comforted her with his great steadfastness under the
infliction, only he was obliged to tell her that both his
human body and his bird feathers being thus marred,
it would be impossible for him to come and visit
her more.   " But," he said, " the Khan, thy husband,
has proved himself to exceed me in his might, therefore he has won thee from me."   So after much leave-
taking, they parted ; and Cuklaketu flew away as well
as his damaged wings would carry him.

It was observed that after this the Princess grew
much more attached to her husband, and the Khan
rejoiced in the sagacity and faithfulness of his Minister.

Nor was this the only use the Minister made of
his cap, which made him invisible to gods, men, and
dæmons.   He was enabled by its means to see many
things that were not rightly conducted, to correct many
evils, punish many offenders who thought to escape
justice, and learn many useful arts.

One day as he was walking with this cap upon his
head, he came to a temple where, the door being closed,

a servant of the temple, thinking himself alone, began
disporting himself after the following manner : First, he
took out from under a statue of Buddha a large roll of
paper, on which was painted a donkey. Having spread
it out flat on the floor of the temple, he danced round
it five times ; and immediately on completing the fifth
turn, he became transformed into a donkey like the
one that was painted on the paper. In this form he
pranced about for some time, and brayed till he was
tired, then he got on to the paper again, on his hind
legs, and danced round five times as before, and immediately he appeared again in his natural form.
When at last he grew tired of the amusement he rolled
up his paper, and replaced it under the image of
Buddha, whence he had taken it. He had no sooner
done so than the Minister, under cover of his cap, which
made him invisible to gods, men, and dæmons, possessed himself of the paper which had such mysterious
properties, and betook himself with it to the dwelling
of the beautiful woman and her daughter who sold
strong drink to travellers, who had treated his master
and him so shamefully at the outset of their travels.

When they saw him approach, for he now no longer
wore the invisible cap, they began to fear he had come
to bring them retribution, and they asked him with
the best grace they could assume what was his pleasure. But he, to win their confidence, that he might
the better carry out his scheme, replied,—

" To reward you for your handsome treatment of me and my companion, therefore am I come." And at the same time he gave them a handful of gold coin.

And they, recollecting what profit they had derived from his companion before, and deeming it likely there might be means for turning the present visit to similar good account, asked him what were his means for being able to be so lavish of the precious metal.

" Oh, that is easily told," replied the Minister. " It is true I have not the faculty of spitting gold coin out of my mouth like my companion, as you doubtless remember, but I have another way, equally efficacious, of coming into possession of all the money I can possibly desire."

" And what may that way be ?" inquired mother and daughter together in their eagerness.

" I have only to spread out this roll of paper on the ground," and he showed them the roll that he had taken from under the image of Buddha in the temple, " and dance five times round it, and immediately I find myself in possession of as much gold as I can carry."

" What a treasure to possess is that same roll of paper," cried the women, and they exchanged looks expressing the determination each had immediately conceived, of possessing themselves of it.

" But now," proceeded the Minister, not appearing to heed their mutual signs, though inwardly rejoicing that they had shown themselves so ready to fall into

his snare, "but now pour me out to drink, for I am
weary with the journey, and thirsty, and your drink I
remember is excellent."

The women, on their part, were equally rejoiced
that he had given them the opportunity of plying him,
and did not wait to be asked twice. The Minister continued to drink, and the women to pour out drink to
him, till he was in a state of complete unconsciousness.

They no sooner found him arrived at this helpless
condition than they took possession of the mysterious
roll, and forthwith spreading it out on the ground, proceeded to dance round it five times after the manner
prescribed.

When the Minister came to himself, therefore, he
found his scheme had fully taken effect, and the woman
and her daughter were standing heavy and chapfallen
in the form of two asses. The Minister put a bridle
in their mouth, and led them off to the Khan, saying,—

"These, O Khan, are the women who sell strong
drink to travellers, and who entreated us so shamefully
at the time when having slain the dragons we went
forth on our travels. I have transformed them by my
art into two asses. Now, therefore, shall there not be
given them burdens of wood, and burdens of stone to
carry, heavy burdens, so that they may be punished for
their naughtiness?"

And the Khan gave orders that it should be done as
he had said. But when at the end of five years, they

were well weighed down with the heavy burdens, and
the Khan saw them wearied and trembling, and human
tears running down from their eyes, he called the
Minister to him, and said,—

"Take these women, and do them no more harm, for
their punishment is enough."

So the Minister fetched the paper, and having spread
it out on the ground, placed the women on it, making
them stand on their hind legs, and led them round it
five several times till they resumed their natural form.
But with the treatment they had undergone, both were
now so bowed, and shrunk, and withered, that no one
could know them for the beautiful women they had
been.

"As well might he have left them under the form of
asses, as restore their own shape in such evil plight,"
here exclaimed the Khan.

And as he let these words escape him, the Siddhî-
kür replied,—

"Forgetting his health, the Well-and-wise-walking
Khan hath opened his lips." And with the cry, "To
escape out of this world is good!" he sped him through
the air, swift out of sight.

Thus far of the Adventures of the Well-and-wise-
walking Khan the second chapter, concerning the deeds
of the Gold-spitting Prince and his Minister.

TALE III.

WHEN the Well-and-wise-walking Khan found that once again he had missed the end and object of his labour, he set out anew without loss of time and without hesitation, and journeyed through toil and terror till he came to the cool grove where rested the bodies of the dead. The Siddhî-kür at his approach ran away before his face, and clambered up the mango-tree; but when the Well-and-wise-walking Khan had threatened to fell it, the Siddhî-kür came down to him rather than that he should destroy the precious mango-tree. Then he bound him in his bag and laded him on to his shoulder, and bore him away to offer to the Master and Teacher Nâgârgunâ.

But after they had journeyed many days and spoken nothing, the Siddhî-kür said, " See, we are like to die of weariness if we go on journeying thus day by day without conversing. Tell now thou, therefore, a tale to relieve the weariness of the way."

The Well-and-wise-walking Khan, however, mindful of the word of his Master and Teacher Nâgârguna, saying, "See thou speak never a word by the way," answered him nothing, neither spake at all.

Then said the Siddhî-kür, "If thou wilt not tell a tale, at least give me some token by which I may know that thou willest I should tell one, and without speaking, nod thy head backwards towards me, and I will tell a tale."

So the Well-and-wise-walking Khan nodded his head backwards, and the Siddhî-kür told this tale saying,—

HOW THE SCHIMNU-KHAN WAS SLAIN.

Long ages ago there lived on the banks of a mighty river a man who had no wife, and no family, and no possessions, but only one cow; and when he mourned because he had no children, and his cow had no calf, and that he had no milk and no butter to live upon, his cow one day gave birth, not to a calf, but to a monster, which seemed only to be sent to mock him in his misery and distress; for while it had the head, and horns, and long tail of a bull, it had the body of a man. Never was such an ugly monster seen, and when the poor man considered it he said, "What shall I now do with this monster? It is not good for him to live; I will fetch my bow and arrows, and will make an end of him." But when he had strung his bow and fixed his arrow, Massang of the bull's head, seeing what he was going to do, cried out, "Master, slay me not; and doubt not but that your clemency shall have its reward."

At these words the poor man was moved to clemency, and he put up his arrows again, and let Massang live, but he turned away ·his face from beholding him. When Massang saw that his master could not look upon him, he turned him and fled into the woods, and wandered on till he came to a place where was a black-coloured man sitting at the foot of a tree. Seeing him, Massang said, " Who and whence art thou ?"

And the black-coloured man made answer, " I am a full-grown man of good understanding, born of the dark woods."

And Massang said, " Wither goest thou ? I will go with thee and be thy companion."

And the black-coloured man got up, and they wandered on together till they came to a place in the open meadow, where they saw a green-coloured man sitting on the grass. Seeing him, Massang said, " Who and whence art thou ?"

And the green-coloured man replied, " I am a full-grown man of good understanding, born of the green meadows; take me with you too, and I will be your companion."

And he wandered on with the other two, Massang and the black-coloured man, till they came to a place where was a white-coloured man sitting on a crystal rock. Seeing him, Massang said, " Who and whence art thou ?"

And the white-coloured man replied, " I am a full-

grown man of good understanding, born of the crystal
rock; take me with you, and let me be your companion."

And he wandered on with the other three, Massang,
and the black-coloured man, and the green-coloured man,
till they came to a stream flowing between barren sandy
banks; and farther along was a grass-clad hill with a
little dwelling on the top. Of this dwelling they took
possession, and inside it they found provisions of every
kind; and in the yard cattle and all that was required
to maintain life. Here, therefore, they dwelt; three
of them going out every day to hunt, and one staying
at home to keep guard over the place.

Now the first day, Massang went to the hunt, and took
with him the white-coloured man and the green-coloured
man; the black-coloured man being thus left in charge
of the homestead, set himself to prepare the dinner.
He had made the butter, and sat with the milk simmer-
ing, cooking the meat (¹), when he heard a rustling
sound as of one approaching stealthily. Looking round
to discover who came there, he saw a little old woman
not more than a span high, carrying a bundle no bigger
than an apple on her back, coming up a ladder she had
set ready for herself, without asking leave or making
any sort of ceremony.

"Lackaday!" cried the little old woman, speaking
to herself, "methinks I see a youngster cooking good
food." But to him she said in a commanding tone,

"Listen to me now, and give me some of thy milk and meat to taste."

Though she was so small, she wore such a weird, un-canny air that the black-coloured man, though he had boasted of being a full-grown man of good understand-ing, durst not say her "Nay;" though he contented himself with keeping to the letter of her behest, and only gave her the smallest possible morsel of the food he had prepared, only just enough, as she had said, "to taste." But lo and behold! no sooner had she put the morsel to her lips than the whole portion disappeared, meat, milk, pot and all; and, more marvellous still, the little old wife had disappeared with them.

Ashamed at finding himself thus overmatched by such a little old wench, he reasoned with himself that he must invent something to tell his companions which should have a more imposing sound than the sorry story of what had actually occurred. Turning over all his belongings to help himself to an idea, he found two horse's-hoofs, and with these he made the marks as of many horsemen all round the dwelling, and then shot his own arrow into the middle of the yard.

He had hardly finished these preparations when his companions came home from the hunt.

"Where is our meal?" inquired they. "Where is the butter you were to have made, and the meat you were to have cooked?"

"Scarcely had I made all ready," replied the black-

coloured man, "than a hundred strange men, on a
hundred wild horses, came tearing through the place;
and what could I do to withstand a hundred? Thus
they have taken all the butter, and milk, and meat, and
me they beat and bound, so that I have had enough to
do to set myself free, and scarcely can I move from
the effect of their blows. Go out now and see for
yourselves."

So they went out; and when they saw the marks
of the horses'-hoofs all round the dwelling, and the
arrow shot into the middle of the courtyard, they
said, "He hath spoken true things."

The next day Massang went to the hunt, and took
with him the black-coloured man and the white-
coloured man. The green-coloured man being thus
left in charge of the homestead, set himself to prepare
the dinner; and it was no sooner ready than the little
old wife came in, as she had done the day before, and
played the same game.

"This is doubtless how it fell out with the black-
coloured man," said he to himself, as soon as she was
gone; "but neither can I own that I was matched by
such a little old wife, nor yet can I tell the same story
about the horsemen. I know what I will do: I will
fetch up a yoke of oxen, and make them tramp about
the place, and when the others come home, I will say
some men came by with a herd of cattle, and, over-
powering me, carried off the victuals." All this he

did ; and when his companions came home, and saw
for themselves the marks the oxen had made in tramping up the soil, they said, "He hath spoken true
things."

The day after, Massang went hunting, and took with
him the black-coloured man and the green-coloured
man. The white-coloured man being left in charge
of the homestead, set himself to prepare the dinner.
Nor was it long before the same little old woman who
had visited his companions made her appearance ; and
soon she had made an end of all the provisions. "This
is doubtless how it fell out with the green-coloured
man yesterday, and the black-coloured man the day
before," said the white-coloured man to himself; "but
neither can I own any more than they that I was overmatched by such a little old wife, nor yet can I tell the
same story as they." So he fetched a mule in from the
field, and made it trot all round the dwelling, that
when his companions came in he might tell them that a
party of merchants had been by, with a file of mules
carrying their packs of merchandize, who had held him
bound, and eaten up the provisions.

All this he did ; and when his companions came
home, and saw for themselves the marks of the mule-
hoofs all round the dwelling, they said, "He hath
spoken true things."

The next day it was Massang's turn to stay at home,
nor did he neglect the duty which fell upon him of cook-

ing the food against the return of the rest. As he sat
thus occupied, up came the little old woman, as on all
the other days.

"Lackaday !" she exclaimed, as she set eyes on him.
"Methinks I see a youngster cooking good food !"
And to him she cried, in her imperious tone, "Listen to
me now, and give me some of thy milk and meat to
taste."

When Massang saw her, he said within himself,
"Surely now this is she who hath appeared to the
other three; and when they said that strangers had
broken in, and overpowered them, and stolen the food,
was it not that she is a witch-woman and enchanted it
away. She only asks to taste it; but if I do her bidding, who knows what may follow ?" So he observed
her, that he might discover what way there was of
over-matching her; thus he espied her bundle, and
bethought him it contained the means of her witcheries.
To possess himself of it he had first to devise the means
of getting her to go an errand, and leave it behind
her.

"Belike you could help me to some fresh water,
good wife," he said, in a simple, coaxing tone; and
she, thinking to serve her purpose by keeping on good
terms with him, replied,—

"That can I; but give me wherewithal to fetch it."

To keep her longer absent, he gave her a pail with a
hole in it, with which she went out. Looking after

her, he saw that she made her way straight up to the clouds, and squeezed one into her pail, but no sooner was it poured in, than it ran out again. Meantime, he possessed himself of her bundle, and turned it over; withal it was not so big as an apple, it contained many things : a hank of catgut, which he exchanged for a hank of hempen cord; an iron hammer, which he exchanged for a wooden mallet; and a pair of iron pincers, which he exchanged for wooden ones.

He had hardly tied up the bundle again, when the old woman came back, very angry with the trick that had been played upon her with the leaking pail, and exclaiming, "How shall water be brought in a pail where there is a hole ?" Then she added further, and in a yet angrier key, "If thou wilt not give me to taste of thy food, beware! for then all that thou hast becomes mine." And when she found that he heeded her not, but went on with what he was doing, just as if she had not spoken, she cried out, furiously,—

"If we are not to be on good terms, we must e'en match our strength; if we are not to have peace, we must have war; if I may not eat with you, I will fight you."

"That I am ready for," answered Massang, as one sure of an easy victory.

"Not so confident!" replied the old one. "Though I am small and thou so big, yet have I overcome mightier ones than thou."

"In what shall we match our strength?" said Massang, not heeding her banter.

"We will have three trials," replied the old one; "the cord proof, the hammer proof, and the pincers proof. And first the cord proof. I will first bind thee, and if thou canst burst my bonds, well; then thou shalt also bind me."

Then Massang saw that he had done well to possess himself of her instruments, but he gave assent to her mode of proof, and let her bind him as tight as ever she would; but as she had only the hempen cord to bind him with, which he had put in her bundle in place of the catgut, he broke it easily with his strength, and set himself free again. Then he bound her with the catgut, so that she was not able by any means to unloose herself.

"True, herein thou hast conquered," she owned, as she lay bound and unable to move, "but now we will have the pincers proof." And as he had promised to wage three trials with her, he set her free.

Then with her pincers she took him by the breast; but, as he had changed her iron pincers for the wooden ones, he hardly felt the pinch, and she did him no harm. But when, with her iron pincers, he seized her, she writhed and struggled so that he pulled out a piece of flesh as big as an earthen pot, and she cried out in great pain.—

"Of a truth thou art a formidable fellow, but now

we will have the hammer proof," and she made Massang lie 'down; but when she would have given him a powerful blow on the chest with her iron hammer, the handle of the wooden mallet Massang had given her in its stead broke short off, and she was not able to hurt him. But Massang made her iron hammer glowing hot in the fire, and belaboured her both on the head and body so that she was glad to escape at the top of her speed and howling wildly.

As she flew past, Massang's three companions came in from hunting and said, "Surely now you have had a trial to endure." And Massang answered,—

"Of a truth you are miserable fellows all, and moreover have spoken that which is not true. Was it like men to let yourselves be overmatched by a little old wife? But now I have tamed her, let be. Let us go and seek for her corpse; maybe we shall find treasure in the place where she lays it."

When they heard him speak of treasure they willingly went out after him, and, following the track of blood which had fallen from the witch-woman's wounds as she went along, they came to a place where was an awful cleft in a mighty rock, and peeping through they saw, far below, the bloody body of the old witch-woman, lying on a heap of gold and jewels and shining adamant armour and countless precious things.

Then Massang said, "Shall you three go down and hand me up the spoil by means of a rope of which I

will hold the end, or shall I go down and hand it up
to you?"

But they three all made answer together, "This
woman is manifestly none other but a *Schimnu* (²).
We dare not go near her. Go you down."

So Massang let himself down by the rope, and sent
up the spoil by the same means to his companions,
who when they had possession of it said thus to one
another,—

"If we draw Massang up again, we cannot deny
in verity that the spoil is his, as he has won it in every
way, but if we leave him down below it becomes ours."
So they left him below, and when he looked that they
should have hauled him up they gave never a sign or
sound. When he saw that, he said thus to himself,
"My three companions have left me here that they
may enjoy the spoil alone. For me nothing is left but
to die!"

But as it grieved him so to die in his health and
strength, he cast about him to see whether in all that
cave which had been so full of valuables there was not
something stored that was good for food, yet found he
nothing save three cherry-stones.

So he took the cherry-stones and planted them in
the earth, saying, "If I be truly Massang, may these
be three full-grown cherry-trees by the time I wake;
but if not, then let me die the death." And with that
he laid him down to sleep with the body of the *Schimnu*
for a pillow.

Being thus defiled by contact with the corpse, he slept for many years. When at last he woke, he found that three cherry-trees had sprung up from the seeds he planted and now reached to the top of the rock. Rejoicing greatly therefore, he climbed up by their means and reached the earth.

First he bent his steps to his late dwelling, to look for his companions, but it was deserted, and no one lived therein. So, taking his iron bow and his arrows, he journeyed farther.

Presently he came to a place where there were three fine houses, with gardens and fields and cattle and all that could be desired by the heart of man. These were the houses which his three companions had built for themselves out of the spoil of the cave. And when he would have gone in, their wives said—for they had taken to them wives also—"Thy companions are not here; they are gone out hunting." So he took up his iron bow and his arrows again, and went on to seek them, and as he went by the way he saw them coming towards him with the game they had taken with their bows. Then he strung his iron bow and would have shot at them; but they, falling down before him, cried out, "Slay us not. Only let us live, and behold our houses, and our wives, and our cattle, and all that we have is in thine hand, to do with it as it seemeth good to thee."

Then he put up his arrows again, and said to them only these words, "In truth, friends, ye dealt evilly with me in that ye left me to perish in the cave."

But they, owning their fault, again begged him that he would stay with them and let their house be his house, and they entreated him. But he would not stay with them, saying,—

"A promise is upon me, which I made when my master would have killed me and I entreated him to spare my life, for I said to him that I would repay his clemency to him if he spared me. Now, therefore, let me go that I may seek him out."

Then, when they heard those words, they let him go, and he journeyed on farther to find out his master.

One day of his journey, as he was wearied with walking, he sat down towards evening by the side of a well, and as he sat an enchantingly beautiful maiden came towards the well as if to draw water, and as she came along he saw with astonishment that at every footstep as she lifted up her feet a fragrant flower sprang up out of the ground (³), one after another wherever she touched the ground. Massang stretched out his hand to offer to draw water for her, but she stopped not at the fountain but passed on, and Massang, in awe at her beauty and power, durst not speak to her, but rose up and followed behind her the whole way she went.

On went the maiden, and ever on followed Massang, over burning plain and through fearful forest, past the sources of mighty rivers and over the snow-clad peaks of the everlasting mountains (⁴), till they reached the

E

dwelling of the gods and the footstool of dread *Chur-musta* (⁵).

Then spoke *Churmusta*,—

" That thou art come hither is good. Every day now we have to sustain the fight with the black *Schimnu;* to-morrow thou shalt be spectator of the fray, and the next day thou shall take part in it."

The next day Massang stood at the foot of Chur-musta's throne, and the gods waited around in silence. Massang saw a great herd as of black oxen, as it were early in the morning, driven with terror to the east side by a herd as of white oxen; and again he saw as it were late in the evening, the herd as of white oxen driven to the west side by the herd as of black oxen.

Then spoke the great Churmusta,—

" Behold the white oxen are the gods. The black oxen are the *Schimnus*. To-morrow, when thou seest the herd as of black oxen driving back the white, then string thine iron bow, and search out for thy mark a black ox, bearing a white star on his forehead. Then send thine arrow through the white star, for he is the Schimnu-Khan.

Thus spoke the dread Churmusta.

The next day Massang stood ready with his bow, and did even as Churmusta had commanded. With an arrow from his iron bow he pierced through the white star on the forehead of the black ox, and sent him away roaring and bellowing with pain.

Then spake the dread Churmusta,—

"Bravely hast thou dealt, and well hast thou deserved of me. Therefore thou shalt have thy portion with me, and dwell with me for ever."

But Massang answered,—

"Nay, for though I tarried at thy behest to do thy bidding, a promise is upon me which I made when my master would have taken my life. For I said, 'Spare me now, and be assured I will repay thy clemency.'"

Then Churmusta commended him, and bid him do even as he had said. Furthermore he gave him a talisman to preserve him by the way, and gave him this counsel,—

"Journeying, thou shalt be overcome by sleep, and having through sleeping forgotten the way, thou shalt arrive at the gate of the *Schimnu-Khan*. Then beware that thou think not to save thyself by flight. Knock, rather, boldly at the door, saying, 'I am a physician.' When they hear that they will bring thee to the *Schimnu-Khan* that thou mayest try thine art in drawing out the arrow from his forehead. Then place thyself as though thou wouldst remove it, but rather with a firm grasp drive it farther in, so that it enter his brain, first offering up with thine hand seven barley-corns to heaven; and after this manner thou shalt kill the *Schimnu-Khan*."

Thus commanded the dread Churmusta.

Then Massang came down from the footstool of

Churmusta and the dwelling of the gods, and went forth to seek out his master. But growing weary with the length of the day, and lying down to sleep, when he woke he had forgotten the direction he had to take, so he pursued the path which lay before him, and it led him to the portal of the Schimnu palace.

When he saw it was the Schimnu palace, he would have made good his escape from its precincts, but remembering the words of Churmusta, he knocked boldly at the door. Then the Schimnus flocked round him, and told him he must die unless he could do some service whereby his life might be redeemed; and Massang made answer, "I am a physician." Hearing that, they took him in to the Schimnu-Khan, that he might pluck the arrow out of his forehead.

Massang stood before the Schimnu-Khan; but when he should have pulled out the arrow, he only pulled it out a little way, and the Schimnu-Khan said,—

"Thus far is the pang diminished."

Then, however, first casting seven barley-corns on high towards heaven, he plunged it in again even to the centre of his brain, so that he fell down at his feet dead. And as the seven barley-corns reached the heavens, there came down by their track an iron chain with a thundering clang which the dread Churmusta sent down to Massang, and Massang climbed up by the chain to the dwelling of the gods. But there stood by the throne of the Schimnu-Khan a female Schimnu,

out of whose mouth came forth forked flames of fire,
and when she saw Massang ascending to heaven by
the chain, she raised an iron hammer high in air to
strike it, and cleave it in two. But when she struck
it, there issued seven bright sparks, which floated up
to heaven, and remained fixed in the sky; and men
called them the constellation of the Pleiades.

"Thus, for all his promise, and after all his sacrifices,
Massang never went back to repay his master's
clemency!" exclaimed the Khan.

And as he let these words escape him the Siddhî-
kür replied, "Forgetting his health, the Well-and-
wise-walking Khan hath opened his lips!" And with
the cry, "To escape out of this world is good!" he
sped him through the air, swift, out of sight.

Thus far of the Adventures of the Well-and-wise-
walking Khan the third chapter, showing how the
Schimnu-Khan was slain.

TALE IV.

THEN, when he saw he had again missed the end and object of his journey, the Well-and-wise-walking Khan again set out as at the first, till with toil and terror he reached the cool grove where lay the dead. At his approach the Siddhî-kür clambered up into the mango-tree, but rather than let the tree be destroyed he came down at the word of the Khan threatening to fell it. Then the Khan bound him in his bag and bore him away to offer to the Master and Teacher Nâgârǵuna.

But when they had proceeded many days the Siddhî-kür said, "Tell, now, a tale, seeing the way is long and weary, and we are like to die of weariness if we go on thus speaking never a word between us." But the Khan, mindful of the monition of his Master and Teacher Nâgârǵuna, answered him nothing. Then said the Siddhî-kür, "If thou wilt not tell a tale, at least give me the token by which I may know that thou willest I should tell one."

So the Well-and-wise-walking Khan nodded his head

backwards towards him, and the Siddhî-kür told this
tale, saying,—

THE PIG'S HEAD SOOTHSAYER.

Long ages ago a man and his wife were living on the
borders of a flourishing kingdom. The wife was a good
housewife, who occupied herself with looking after the
land and the herds; but the husband was a dull, idle
man, who did nothing but eat, drink, and sleep from
morning to night and from night to morning. One
day, when his wife could no longer endure to see him
going on thus indolently, she cried out to him, "Leave
off thus idling thyself; get up and gird thyself like a
man, and seek employment. Behold, thy father's inheritance is well nigh spent; the time is come that thou
find the means to eke it out."

And when he weakly asked her in return, "Wherein
shall I seek to eke it out?" she answered him, "How
should I be able to tell this thing, but at least get thee
up and make some endeavour; get thee up and look
round the place and see what thou canst find," and
with that she went out to her work in the field.

When she had repeated these words many days, he
at last went out one day, and, not taking the trouble
to bethink him what he should do, he did just what his
wife had said, and went to look round the place to see
what he could find. As he wandered about, he came
to a spot on which a tribe of cattle-herds had lately

been encamped (¹), and a fox, a dog, and a bird were there fighting about something. Approaching to see for what they contended, they all escaped in fear, and he was left in possession of their booty, which was a sheep's paunch full of butter (²). This he brought home and laid up in store. When his wife came home and asked him whence it was, he told her he had found it left on the camping-place of a family of herdsmen who had passed that way seeking pasturage.

"Well it is to be a man!" exclaimed his wife. "I may toil all day without making so much; but you go but out one day of your whole life for one moment of time, and straightway you find all this wealth."

When the man heard these words, he took courage and thought he should be fit to find better fortune still; so he said to his wife, "Give me now only a good horse and clothes meet, and a dog, and a bow and arrows, and you shall see what I can do."

The woman was glad to hear him show so much resolution, so she made haste and gave him all the things that he required, and added a thick felt cloak to keep out the rain, and a cap for his head, and helped him to get on his horse, and slung his bow over his shoulder.

Thus he rode out over many a broad plain, but without purpose or knowledge of whither he went, nor did he fall in with any living creature whatever for many days. At last, riding over a vast steppe, he espied at some distance a fox.

"Ha!" he exclaimed, "there is one of my friends of last time. To be sure, there is no sheep's paunch of butter this time, but if I could only kill him his skin would make a nice warm cap."

As he had never learnt to draw a bow, his arrows were of no service, so he set his horse trotting after the fox; but the fox got away faster than he could follow, and took refuge in the hole of a marmot (³).

"Now I have you!" he cried, and, dismounting from his horse, he took off all his clothes to have freer use of his limbs and bound them on his saddle; the dog he tied to the bridle of the horse, and stopped the mouth of the hole with his cap; then he took a great stone and endeavoured with heavy blows on the earth to crush the fox.

But the fox, taking fright at the noise, rushed out with such impetus that it carried off the cap on its head. The dog, seeing it run, gave chase, and the horse was forced to follow the dog, as they were both tied together; so off he galloped, carrying on his saddle every thing the man had in the world, and leaving him stretched on the ground without a thread of covering.

Getting up, he wandered on to the banks of a river which formed the boundary of the kingdom of a rich and powerful Khan. Going into this Khan's stable, he laid himself down under the straw and covered himself completely, so that no one could see him. Here he was warmed and well rested.

As he lay there the Khan's beautiful daughter came out to take the air, and before she went in again she dropped the Khan's talisman and passed on without perceiving her loss. Though the bauble was precious in itself for the jewels which adorned it, and precious also to the Khan for its powers in preserving his life (⁴), and worthy therefore to claim a reward, the man was too indolent to get up out of the straw to pick it up, so he let it lie.

After sunset the Khan's herds came in from grazing, and the cow-wench, when she had shut them into the stable, swept up the yard without heeding the talisman, which thus got thrown on to a dung-heap. This the man saw, but still bestirred him not to recover it.

The next day there was great stir and noise in the place; the Khan sent out messengers into every district far and near to say that the Khan's beautiful daughter had lost his talisman, and promising rewards to whoso should restore it.

After this too, he ordered the great trumpet, which was only blown on occasion of promulgating the laws of the kingdom, to be sounded and proclamation to be made, calling on all the wise men and soothsayers of the kingdom to exercise their cunning art, and divine the place where the talisman should lay concealed.

All this the man heard as he lay under the straw, but yet he bestirred him not. Early in the morning, however, men came to litter the place for the kine

with fresh straw; and these men, finding him, bid him
turn out. Now that it became a necessity to stir himself, he bethought him of the talisman; and when the
men asked him whence he was, he answered "I am a
soothsayer come to .divine the place where lies the
Khan's talisman."

Hearing that, they told him to come along to the
Khan. "But I have no clothes," replied the man.
So they went and told the Khan, saying, "Here is a
soothsayer lying in· the straw of the stable, who is
come to divine where the Khan's talisman lies hid, but
he cannot appear before the Khan because he has no
clothes."

"Take this apparel to him," said the Khan, "and
bring him hither to me."

When he came before the Khan, the Khan asked
him what he required to perform his divination.

"Let there be given me," answered the man, "a
pig's head, a piece of silk stuff woven of five colours,
(⁵), and a large *Baling* (⁶); these are the things which
I require for the divination."

All these things being given him, he set up the
pig's head on a pedestal of wood, and adorned it with
the silk stuff woven of five colours, and put the *Baling*-
cake in its mouth. Then he sat down over against it,
as if sunk in earnest contemplation. Then on the day
which had been named in the Khan's proclamation for
the day of divination, which was the third day, all the

people being assembled, assuming the air of a diviner
of dreams, he wrapped himself in a long mantle, and
made as though he was questioning the pig's head.
As all the people passed, he seemed to gain the answer
from the pig's head,—

"The talisman is not with this one," and "The
talisman is not with that one," so that he had many
people on his side glad to be thus pronounced free from
all charge of harbouring the Khan's talisman.

At last he made a sign that this kind of divination
was ended; and pronounced that the Khan's talisman
was not in possession of any man.

"And now," said he, "let us try the divination of
the earth." With that, he set out to make a circuit
of the Khan's dwelling. Stepping on and on from
place to place, he continued to seem consulting the pig's
head, till he came to the place in the yard where the
dung-heap was; and here, assuming an imposing attitude, he turned round, and said mysteriously, "Here
somewhere must be found the Khan's talisman." But
when he had turned the heap over, and brought the
talisman itself to light, the people knew not how to
contain themselves for wonderment, and went about
crying,—

"The Pig's head diviner hath divined wonderful
things! The Pig's head diviner hath divined wonderful things!"

But the Khan called to him, and said,—

"Tell me how I shall reward thee for that thou hast restored my talisman to me."

But he, who did not exert himself to think of any thing but just of what was most present to his mind, answered,—

"Let there be given me, O Khan, the raiment, and the horse, the fox, the dog, and the bow and arrows which I have lost."

When the Khan heard him ask for nothing save his horse and dog, and raiment, and a fox, and bows and arrows, he said,—

"Of a truth this is a singular soothsayer. Nevertheless, let there be given him over and above the things that he hath required of us two elephants laden with meal and butter."

So they gave him all the things he had required and two elephants laden with meal and butter to boot. Thus they brought him back unto his own home.

Seeing him yet afar, his wife came out to meet him, carrying brandy. She opened her eyes when she saw the two elephants laden with butter and meal; but knowing that he loved to be left at ease, forbore to question him that night. The next morning she made him tell her the whole story before they got up; but when she heard what little demands he had made after rendering the Khan so great a service as restoring his talisman, she exclaimed,—

"If a man would be called a man, he ought to know better how to use his opportunities."

And with that she sat to work to write a letter in her husband's name to the Khan.

The letter was conceived in these words:—

"During the brief moment that thy life-talisman was in my hands, I well recognized that thou hast a bodily infirmity. It was in order that I might conjure it from thee that I required at thy hands the dog and the fox. What reward the Khan is pleased to bestow, this shall be according to the mind of the Khan."

This letter she took with her own hands to the Khan.

When the Khan had read the letter, he was pleased to think the soothsayer had undertaken to free him of a malady against which he could never have made provision himself, as he had no knowledge of its existence; so he ordered two elephant's-loads of treasure to be given to the woman, who went back to her husband, and they had therewith enough to live in ease and plenty.

Now this Khan had had six brethren, and it happened that once they had gone out to divert themselves, and in a thick wood they saw a most beautiful maiden playing with a he-goat, whom they stood looking at till they were tired of standing, for of looking at one so beautiful they could never be weary.

At last one of them said to her,—

"Whence comest thou, beautiful maiden?"

And she answered him,—

"By following after this he-goat, thus I came hither."

"Will you come with us seven brethren, and be our

wife," rejoined the brother, who had spoken first; and when she willingly agreed they took her home with them.

But they both were evil *Râkshasas* (⁷), who had only come out to find men whose lives to devour; the male *Manggus* (⁸), had taken the form of a he-goat, and the female *Manggus* that of a beautiful maiden, the better to deceive.

When therefore the seven took her home and the goat with her, the two Manggus had ample scope to carry out their design, and every year they devoured the life of one of the brothers, till now there was only the Khan left, and they began to consume the life of him also.

When the ministers saw that all the brothers were dead, and only the Khan left, they held a council, and they said, "Behold, all the other Khans are dead, notwithstanding all the means we have at our command, and despite the arts of all the physicians of this country." Now there remains no other means for us but to send for the Pig's head soothsayer who found the Khan's talisman, and get him to restore the Khan to health." This counsel was found good, and they all said, "Let us send for the Pig's head soothsayer."

Four men were sent off on horseback to call the Pig's head soothsayer, who laid all the case before him.

When he heard it he was greatly embarrassed, and

knew not what to answer, but his vacancy passed, with them, for his being immersed in deep contemplation, and they reverenced him the more. Meantime his wife bid them put up their horses and stay the night.

In the night-time she asked of him what the men had come about, and he told her all his embarrassment.

"True, last time you exerted yourself a little and had good luck," she replied, "but now that you have been sitting here doing nothing, and looking so stupid all this time, whether you will cut as good a figure, who shall say? But go you must, seeing the Khan has sent for you."

The next morning he said to the messengers, "In the visions of the night I have learned even how I may help the Khan, and presently I will come with you."

Then he enveloped himself in a mantle, laid his hair over the crown of his head, took a large string of beads in his left hand, bound the silk stuff woven of five colours round his right arm, and carrying the pigs' head set out with them.

When he arrived with this strange aspect at the Khan's dwelling both the *Manggus* were much alarmed. They thought he must be some cunning soothsayer who knew all about them; they had heard, too, of his success in finding the Khan's talisman.

But the man continuing to support his character of

soothsayer, ordered a *Baling* as big as a man to be
brought to the head of the Khan's bed, and placed the
pig's head on top of it, and then sat himself down over
against it, murmuring words of incantation ([9]).

The *Manggus*, thinking all these preparations showed
that he was a cunning soothsayer, went away to take
counsel together, and the Khan being thus delivered
for the time from their evil arts, his pains began to
yield and he fell into a tranquil sleep. Seeing this his
.attendants thought favourably of the cure, and trusting
therefore the more in the soothsayer's powers they
left him in entire charge of the patient. Being thus
freed from observation he ventured to leave his position of apparent absorption in contemplation, and to
take a stolen glance at the Khan. When he saw him
in such a deep sleep a great fear took him, thinking he
must be very bad indeed, and he did all he could to,
wake him, crying aloud,—

"O great Khan! O mighty Khan!"

Finding that the Khan remained speechless he
thought he must be dead, and resolved that his best part
was to run away. This was not so easy, for the first
open door he found to take refuge in was that of the
Treasury, and the guard called out "Stop thief!" and
when from thence he tried to bestow himself in the
store-chamber, the guard sang out "Stop thief!" At
last he went into the stable, to hide himself there, but
close by the door-way stood the he-goat, whom he

F

feared to pass, lest he should goad him with his horns. However, summoning up all his courage, he got behind him, and sprang on his back , and gave him three blows on his head ; but instantly , even as the blue smoke column is carried in a straight direction by the wind, so sped the he-goat straight off to the Khanin leaving his rider stretched upon the ground. As soon as he had got up again he ran after the he-goat, to see whither he went so fast; following him, he came to the door of the Khanin's apartment, and heard the he-goat talking to her within. The two Manggus spoke thus :—

"The Pig's head soothsayer is a soothsayer indeed," said the he-goat ; " he divined that I was in the stable, and he came there after me, and sprang upon my back, giving me three mighty blows, by which I know the weight of his arm. The best thing we can do is to make good our escape."

The Khanin made answer, " I, also, am of the same mind. I saw when he first came in that he recognized us for what we are. We have had good fortune hitherto, but it has forsaken us now ; it were better we got away. I know what he will do ; in a day or two, when he has cured the Khan by not letting us approach him to devour his life, he will assemble together all the men of the place with their arms, and all the women, telling them to' bring each a faggot of wood for burning. When all are assembled he will say, ' Let that he-goat be brought to me,' so they will bind thee and take

thee before him. Then will he say to thee, ' Lay aside
thine assumed form,' and it will be impossible for thee
not to obey. When he has shown thee thus in thine
own shape they will all fall upon thee, and put thee
to death with swords and arrows, and burn thee in the
fire. And afterwards with me will he deal after the
same manner. Now, therefore, to-morrow or the next
day we will be beforehand with him, and will go where
we shall be safe from his designs."

When the man heard all this, he left off from following the goat, and went back with good courage, to take
up his place again over against the pig's head by the
side of the Khan's couch.

In the morning the Khan woke, refreshed with his
slumber ; and when they inquired how he felt, the
Khan replied that the soothsayer's power had diminished the force of the malady.

" If this be even so," here interposed the soothsayer,
"and if the Khan has confidence in the word of his
servant, command now thy ministers that they call
together all thy subjects—the men with their arms,
and the women each with a faggot of wood for burning." Then the Khan ordered that it should be done
according to his word. When they were all assembled,
the pretended soothsayer, having set up his pig's head,
commanded further that they should bring the he-goat
out of the stable before him ; and when they had bound
him and brought him, that they should put his saddle

on him.   Then he sprang on to his back, and gave him
three blows with all his strength, and dismounted.
Then with all the power of voice he could command,
he cried out to him, "Lay aside thine assumed
form!"

At these words the he-goat was changed before the
eyes of all present into a horrible Manggus, deformed
and hideous to behold.   With swords and sticks,
lances and stones, the whole people fell upon him, and
disabled him, and then burnt him with fire till he was
dead.

Then said the soothsayer, "Now, bring hither the
Khanin." So they went and dragged down the Khanin
to the place where he stood, with yelling and cries of
contempt.

With one hand on the pig's head, as if taking his
authority from it, the soothsayer cried· out to her, in a
commanding voice,—

"Resume thine own form!"

Then she too became a frightful Manggus, and they
put her to death like the other.

The soothsayer now rode back to the Khan's palace,
all the people making obeisance to him as he went
along—some crying, "Hail!" some strewing the way
with barley, and some bringing him rich offerings.
It took him nearly the space of a day to make his
way through such a throng.

When at last he arrived, the Khan received him with

a grateful welcome, and asked him what present he desired of him.   The soothsayer answered, with his usual
simplicity, " In our part of the country we have none
of those pieces of wood which I see you put here into the
noses of the oxen : let there be given me a quantity of
them to take back with me."   The Khan then ordered
there should be given him three sacks of the pieces of
wood for the oxen, and seven elephants laden with
meal and butter to boot.

When he arrived home, his wife came out to meet
him with brandy, and when she saw the seven elephants
with their loads, she extolled him highly ; but when
she came to learn how great was the deliverance he
had rendered to the Khan, she was indignant that he
had not asked for higher reward, and determined to go
the next day herself to the Khan.

The next day she went accordingly, disguised, and
sent in a letter of the following purport to the
Khan :—

" Although I, the Pig's head soothsayer, brought
the Khan round from his malady, yet some remains of
it still hang about him.   It was in order to remove
these that I asked for the pieces of wood for the oxen ;
what guerdon has been earned by this further service it
is for the Khan to decide."

Such a letter she sent in to the Khan.

" The man has spoken the truth," said the Khan, on
reading the letter.   " For his reward, let him and his

wife, his parents and friends, all come over hither and dwell with me."

When they arrived, the Khan said, " When one has to show his gratitude, and dismisses him to whom he is indebted with presents, that does not make an end of the matter. That I was not put to death by the Mang-gus is thy doing; that the kingdom was not given over to destruction was thy doing; that the ministers were not eaten up by the Manggus was thy doing: it is meet, therefore, that we share between us the in-heritance, even between us two, and reign in perfect equality." With such words he gave him half his authority over the kingdom, and to all his family he gave rich fortunes and appointments of state. And thus his wife became Khanin; so that while he could indulge himself in the same idle life as before, she also enjoyed rest from her household and pastoral cares ([10]).

" Though the woman despised her husband's under-standing," exclaimed the Khan, " yet was it always his doings which brought them wealth after all !"

And as he let these words escape him, the Siddhî-kür replied, "Forgetting his health, the Well-and-wise-walking Khan hath opened his lips." And with the cry, " To escape out of this world is good !" he sped him through the air, swift out of sight.

TALE V.

WHEN the Well-and-wise-walking Khan found that he had again missed the end and object of his journey, without hesitation or loss of time he once more betook himself to the cool grove, and summoned the Siddhî-kür to come with him, threatening to hew down the mango-tree.

But as he bore him along, bound in his bag of many colours, in which was place to stow away an hundred, the Siddhî-kür spoke thus, saying, " Tell thou now a tale to beguile the weariness of the way." But the Well-and-wise-walking Khan answered him nothing. Then said the Siddhî-kür again, " If thou wilt not tell a tale, at least give the token that I may know thou willest I should tell one."

So the Khan nodded his head backwards and the Siddhî-kür told this tale, saying,—

HOW THE SERPENT-GODS WERE PROPITIATED.

Long ages ago there reigned over a flourishing province, a Khan named Kun-snang (¹). He had a son

named "Sunshine" by his first wife who afterwards
died.   He also had a second son named "Moonshine,"
by his second wife.   Now the second wife thought
within herself, "If Sunshine is allowed to live, there
is no chance of Moonshine ever coming to the throne.
Some means must be found of putting Sunshine out of
the way."

With this object in view she threw herself down
upon her couch and tossed to and fro as though in an
agony of pain.   All the night through also instead of
sleeping, she tossed about and writhed with pain.
Then the Khan spake to her, saying, "My beautiful
one! what is it that pains thee, and with what manner
of ailment art thou stricken?"   And she made
answer,—

"Even when I was at home I suffered oftwhiles after
the same manner, but now is it much more violent; all
remedies have I exhausted previous times, there remains only one when the pain is of this degree, and
that means is not available."

"Say not that it is not available," answered the
Khan, "for all means are available to me.   Speak but
what it is that is required, and whatever it be shall be
done, even to the renouncing of my kingdom.   For
there is nothing that I would not give in exchange
for thy life."

But for a long time she made as though she would
not tell him, then finally yielding to his repeated in-

quiries, she said, " If there were given me the heart of
a Prince, stewed in sesame-oil (^{2}), I should recover : it
matters not whether the heart of Sunshine or of
Moonshine, but that Moonshine being my own son,
his heart would not pass through my throat. This
means, O Khan, is manifestly not available, for
how should it be done to take the life of Prince
Sunshine? Therefore say no more, and let me
die."

But the Khan answered, " Of a truth it would grieve
me to take the life of Prince Sunshine. Nevertheless,
if there be no other means of saving thy life, the thing
must be done. I have not to consider ' Shall the life
of the Prince be spared or not?' but, ' Which shall be
spared, the life of the Prince, or the life of the
Khanin?' And in this strait who could doubt, but
that it is the life of the Khanin that must be spared by
me? Therefore, be of good cheer, beautiful one, for
that the heart of Prince Sunshine shall be given thee
cooked in sesame-oil."

This, he said, intending in his own mind to have the
heart of a kid of the goats prepared for her in sesame-
oil, saying, " Behold, here is the heart of Prince Sunshine," but to send away the Prince into a far country
that she might not know he was not dead. Only when she
was restored to health again, then he purposed to fetch
back his son. But Moonshine being in his mother's
apartments overheard this promise which the Khan had

given, and he ran and told his brother all that the
Khan, his father, had said, saying, "When the Khan
rises he will give the order to put thee to death; how
shall this thing be averted?" and he wept sore, for he
loved his brother Sunshine even as his own life.

Then Sunshine answered, saying, "Seeing this is so,
remain thou with our parents, loving and honouring
them, and being loved by them. For me, it is clear
the time is come that I must get me away to a far
country. Farewell, my brother!"

But Moonshine answered, "Nay, brother, for if thou
goest, I also go with thee. How should I live alone
here, without thee, my brother?" Therefore they
rose quickly before the Khan could get up, and going
privately to a priest in a temple hard by, that no one
else might hear of their design and betray it to the
Khan, they begged of him a good provision of baling-
cakes (³), to support life by the way; and he gave them
a good provision, even a bag-full, and they set out on
their journey while it was yet night. It was the fifteenth
of the month, while the moon shed abroad her light,
and they journeyed towards the East, not knowing
whither they went. But after they had journeyed
many days over mountain and plain, and come to a
land where was no water, but a muddy river the water
whereof could not be drunk, and where was no habitation of man, Moonshine fell down fainting by the way.
Sunshine therefore ran to the top of a high hill to see

if he could discern any stream of water, but found none.
When he came back Moonshine was dead! Then he
fell down on the ground, and wept a long space upon
his body, and at nightfall he buried it with solicitude
under a heap of stones, crying, "Ah! my brother, how
shall I live without thee, my brother?" And he prayed
that at Moonshine's next re-birth (¹) they might again
live together.

Journeying farther on, he came to a pass between
two steep rocks, and in one of them was a red door.
Going up to the door, he found an ancient Hermit living
in a cave within, who addressed him, saying, "Whence
art thou, O youth, who seemest oppressed with recent
grief?" And Sunshine told him all that had befallen
him. Without again speaking the Hermit put into the
folds of his girdle a bottle containing a life-restoring
cordial, and going to the spot where Moonshine lay
buried, restored him to life. Then said he to the two
princes, "Live now with me, and be as my two sons."
So they lived with him, and were unto him as his two
sons.

The desert where this Hermit lived belonged to the
kingdom of a Khan dazzling in his glory and resistless
in might. Now it was about the season when the
Khan and his subjects went every year to direct the
flowing of water over the country for fructifying the
grain-seeds; but it was the custom every year at this
season first, in order to make the Serpent-gods (⁵) who

lived at the water-head propitious, to sacrifice to them a youth of a certain age; and on this occasion it fell to the lot of a youth born in the Tiger-year (⁶). When the Khan had caused search to be made through all the people no youth was found among them all born in the Tiger-year. At last certain herdsmen came before him, saying, "While we were out tending our cattle, behold we saw in a cave nigh to a pass between two steep rocks a Hermit who has with him two sons, and one of them born in the Tiger-year."

When the Khan had listened to their word he immediately sent three envoys to fetch the Hermit's son for the sacrifice (⁷).

When the three envoys of the Khan had come and stood knocking before the red door of the Hermit's cave, the Hermit cried out to them, asking what they wanted of him. Then answered the chief of them, "Because thou hast a son living with thee born in the Tiger-year, and the Khan hath need of him for the sacrifice; therefore are we come, even that we may bring him to the Khan."

When the Hermit had heard their embassage, he answered them, "How should a Hermit have a son with him out here in the desert?" But he took Sunshine, who was the youth born in the Tiger-year, and motioned him into a farther hole of the cave where was a great vessel of pottery; into this vessel he made him creep, then fastening the mouth of the vessel with earth, he made it to appear like to a jar of rice-brandy (⁸). Meantime, however, the Khan's envoys had broken down the door, and began searching through every recess of the cave. Finding nothing, they were filled with fury, and in their anger beat the Hermit on whose account they had come a bootless errand. But when Sunshine heard the men ill-treating the Hermit who had been to him as a father, he could not refrain himself, and called out from within the brandy-jar, "Unhand my father!" Then the envoys immediately left off beating his father, but they turned and seized him and carried him off to the Khan, while the Hermit was left weeping with great grief at the loss of his adopted son, even as one like to die.

As the envoys dragged Sunshine along before the palace, the Khan's daughter was looking out of window, and when she heard that the handsome youth was destined for the Serpent-sacrifice, she was filled with compassion. She went therefore to the men who had the charge to throw him into the water, saying, "See how comely he is! He is worthy to be saved, throw him not into the water. Or else if you will throw him in, throw me in also with him." Then the men went and showed the Khan her words; whereupon the king was wroth, and said, "She is not worthy to be called the Khan's daughter; let them therefore be both sewn up into one bullock's skin, and so cast into the water." The men therefore did according to the Khan's bidding, and sewing them both up in one bullock-hide together, cast them into the water to the Serpent-gods.

Then began Sunshine to say, "That they should throw me to the Serpent-gods, because I was the only youth to be found who was born in the Tiger-year, was not so bad; but that this beautiful maiden, who hath deigned to lift her eyes on me, and to love me, should be so sacrificed also, this is unbearable!"

And the Khan's daughter in like manner cried, "That I who am only a woman should be thrown to the Serpent-gods, is not so bad; but that this noble and beautiful youth should be so sacrificed also, this is unbearable!"

When the Serpent-gods heard these laments, and saw how the prince and the maiden vied with each other in generosity, they sent and fetched them both out of the water, and gave them freedom. Also as soon as they were set free, they let the water gently flow over the whole country, just as the people desired for their rice irrigation.

Meantime, Sunshine said to the Khan's daughter, "Princess, let us each now return home. Go thou to thy father's palace, while I go back to the Hermitage, and visit my adopted father, who is like to die of grief for the loss of me. After I have fulfilled this filial duty, I will return to thee, and we will live for ever after for each other alone."

The princess then praised his filial love, and bid him

go console his father, only begging him to come to her right soon, for she should have no joy till he came back.

Sunshine went therefore to the Hermit, whom he found so worn with grief, that he was but just in time to save him from dying; so having first washed him with milk and water, he consoled him with many words of kindness.

The princess, too, went home to the palace, where all were so astonished at her deliverance that at first she could hardly obtain admission. When they had made sure it was herself in very truth, the people all came round her, and congratulated her with joy, for never had any one before been delivered from the sacrifice to the Serpent-gods.

Then said the Khan, "That the Khan's daughter should be spared by the Serpent-gods was to be expected. They have the youth born in the Tiger-year for their sacrifice."

But the princess answered, "Neither has he fallen sacrifice. Him also they let free; and indeed was it in great part out of regard for his abnegation and distress over my suffering that we were both let free."

Then answered the Khan, "In that case is our debt great unto this youth. Let him be sought after, and besought that he come to visit us in our palace."

So they went again to the cave in the rocky pass, and fetched Sunshine; and when he came near, the Khan went out to meet him, and caused costly seats to be brought, and made him sit down thereon beside him.

Then he said to him, "That thou hast delivered this country from the fear of drought, is matter for which we owe thee our highest gratitude; but that thou and this my daughter also have escaped from death is a marvellous wonder. Tell me now, art thou in very truth the son of the Hermit?"

"No," replied Sunshine, "I am the son of a mighty Khan; but my step-mother, seeking to make a difference between me and this my brother standing beside me, who was her own born son, and to put me to death, we fled away both together; and thus fleeing we came to the Hermit, and were taken in by his hospitality."

When the Khan had heard his words, he promised him his daughter in marriage, and her sister, to be wife to Moonshine. Moreover, he endowed them with immeasurable riches, and gave them an escort of four detachments of fighting-men to accompany them home. When they had arrived near the capital of the kingdom, they sent an embassage before them to the Khan, saying,—

"We, thy two sons, Sunshine and Moonshine, are returned to thee."

The Khan and the Khanin, who had for many years past quite lost their reason out of grief for the loss of their children, and held no more converse with men, were at once restored to sense and animation at this news, and sent out a large troop of horsemen to meet them, and conduct them to their palace. Thus the two princes returned in honour to their home.

When they came in, the Khan was full of joy and glory, sitting on his throne; but the Khanin, full of remorse and shame at the thought of the crime she had meditated, fell down dead before their face.

"That wretched woman got the end. that she deserved!" exclaimed the Khan.

"Forgetting his health, the Well-and-wise-walking Khan hath opened his lips," said the Siddhî-kür. And with the cry, "To escape out of this world is good!" he sped him through the air, swift out of sight.

Thus far of the Adventures of the Well-and-wise-walking Khan the fifth chapter, showing how the Serpent-gods were appeased.

G

TALE VI.

WHEN the Well-and-wise-walking Khan found that he had again missed the end and object of his journey, he proceeded · once more by the same manner and means to the cool grove. And, having bound the Siddhî-kür in his bag, bore him on his shoulder to present to his Master and Teacher Nâgârg'una.

But by the way the Siddhî-kür asked him to tell a tale, and when he would not answer begged for the token of his assent that he should tell one, which when the Khan had given he told this tale, saying,—

THE TURBULENT SUBJECT.

Long ages ago there lived in a district called Brschiss(¹) a haughty, turbulent man. As he feared no man and obeyed no laws, the Khan of that country sent to him, saying, " Since thou wilt obey no laws, thou canst not remain in my country. Get thee gone hence, or else submit to the laws!"

But the turbulent man chose rather to go forth in

exile than submit to the laws. So he went wandering forth till he came to a vast plain covered with feather-grass, and a palm-tree standing in the midst, with a dead horse lying beneath it. Under the shade of the palm-tree([2]) he sat down, saying, " The head of this horse will be useful for food when my provisions are exhausted." So he bound it into his waist-scarf and climbed up into the palm-tree to pass the night.

He had scarcely composed himself to sleep when there was a great noise of shouting and yelling, which woke him up; and behold there came thither towards the palm-tree, from the southern side of the steppe, a herd of dæmons, having ox-hide caps on their heads, and riding on horses covered with ox-hides. Nor had they long settled themselves before another herd of dæmons came trooping towards the palm-tree from the northern side of the steppe, and these wore paper caps and rode on horses wearing paper coverings.

All these dæmons now danced and feasted together with great howling and shouting. The man looked down upon them from the tree-top full of terror, but also full of envy at their enjoyment. As he leant over to watch them, the horse's head tumbled out of his girdle right into their midst and scattered them in dire alarm in every direction, not one of them daring to look up to see whence it came. It was not till the morning light broke, however, that the man ventured to come down. When he did so, he said, " Last night there was much feasting and drinking going on here, surely there must be something left from such a banquet." Searching through the long feather-grass all about, he discovered a gold goblet full of brandy(³), from which he drank long draughts, but it continued always full. At last he turned it down upon the ground, and immediately all manner of meats and cakes appeared. "This goblet is indeed larder and cellar!" said the man, and taking it with him he went on his way.

Farther on he met a man brandishing a thick stick as he walked.

"What is your stick good for that you brandish it so proudly?" asked the turbulent man.

"My stick is so much good that when I say to it, 'Fly, that man has stolen somewhat of me, fly after him and kill him and bring me back my goods,' it instantly flies at the man and brings my things back."

"Yours is a good stick, but see my goblet; whatsoever you desire of meat or drink this same goblet provides for the wishing. Will you exchange your stick against my goblet?"

"That will I gladly," rejoined the traveller.

But the turbulent man, having once effected the exchange, cried to the stick, "Fly, that man has stolen my goblet, fly after him and kill him and bring me back my goblet!" Before the words had left his lips the stick flew through the air, killed the man, and brought back the goblet. Thus he had both the stick and the goblet.

Farther on he saw a man coming who carried an iron hammer.

"What is your hammer good for?" inquired he as they met.

"My hammer is so good," replied the traveller, "that when I strike it nine times on the ground immediately there rises up an iron tower nine storeys high."

"Yours is a good hammer," replied the turbulent man, "but look at my goblet; whatever you desire of meat or drink this same goblet provides for the wishing. Will you change your hammer against my goblet?"

"That will I gladly," replied the wayfarer.

But the turbulent man, having once effected the exchange, cried to the stick, "Fly, that man has stolen my goblet, fly after him and kill him and bring me back the goblet." The command was executed as soon as spoken, and the turbulent man thus became possessed of the hammer as well as the stick and the goblet.

Farther on he saw a man carrying a goat's leather bag.

"What is your bag good for?" inquired he as they met.

"My bag is so good that I have but to shake it and

there comes a shower of rain, but if I shake it hard then it rains in torrents."

"Yours is a good bag," replied the turbulent man, "but see my goblet; whatsoever you desire of meat or drink it provides you for the wishing. Will you exchange your bag against my goblet?"

"That will I gladly," answered the traveller.

But no sooner had the turbulent man possession of the bag than he sent his stick as before to recover the goblet also.

Provided with all these magic articles, he had no fear in returning to his own country in spite of the prohibition of the Khan. Arrived there about midnight, he established himself behind the Khan's palace, and, striking the earth nine times with his iron hammer, there immediately appeared an iron fortress nine storeys high, towering far above the palace.

In the morning the Khan said, "Last night I heard 'knock, knock, knock,' several times. What will it have been?" So the Khanin rose and looked out and answered him, saying, "Behold, a great iron fortress, nine storeys high, stands right over against the palace."

"This is some work of that turbulent rebel, I would wager!" replied the Khan, full of wrath. "And he has brought it to that pass that we must now measure our strength to the uttermost." Then he rose and called together all his subjects, and bid them each bring their share of fuel to a great fire which he kindled all round the iron fortress; all the smiths, too, he summoned to bring their bellows and blow it, and thus it was turned into a fearful furnace.

Meantime the turbulent man sat quite unconcerned in the ninth storey with his mother and his son, occupied with discussing the viands which the golden goblet provided. When the fire began to reach the eighth storey, the man's mother caught a little alarm, saying, "Evil will befall us if this fire which the Khan has kindled round us be left unchecked." But he answered, "Mother! fear nothing; I have the means of settling that." Then he drew out his goat's-leather bag, went with it up to the highest turret of the fortress, and shook it till the rain flowed and pretty well extinguished the fire; but he also went on shaking it till the rain fell in such torrents that presently the whole neighbourhood was inundated, and not only the embers of the fire but the smiths' bellows were washed away, and the people and the Khan himself had much ado to escape with their lives. At last the gushing waters had worked a deep moat round the fortress, in which the turbulent man dwelt henceforth secure, and the Khan durst admonish him no more.

"Thus the power of magic prevailed over sovereign might and majesty," exclaimed the Khan; and as he uttered these words the Siddhî-kür said, "Forgetting his health, the Well-and-wise-walking Khan hath opened his lips." And with the cry, "To escape out of this world is good!" he sped him through the air, swift out of sight.

Of the Adventures of the Well-and-wise-walking Khan the sixth chapter, of how it fell out with the Turbulent Subject.

TALE VII.

WHEN the Well-and-wise-walking Khan found that he had again missed the end and object of his labour, he proceeded again by the same manner and means to the cool grove, and having bound the Siddhî-kür in his bag, bore him on his shoulder to present to his Master and Teacher Nâgârg'una.

But by the way the Siddhî-kür asked him to tell a tale; and when he would not answer, craved the token of his assent that he should tell one, which when the Khan had given, he told this tale, saying,—

THE WHITE BIRD AND HIS WIFE.

Long ages ago, there lived in a land called Fair-flower-garden, a man, who had three daughters, who minded his herds of goats(¹), the three alternately.

One day, when it was the turn of the eldest sister to go with them, she fell asleep during the mid-day heat, and when she awoke, she found that one of the goats was missing. While she wandered about seeking it,

she came to a place where was a great red door. When
she had opened this, she found behind it, a little farther
on, a great gold door. And when she had opened this,
she found farther on another door all of shining
mother-o'-pearl. She opened this, and beyond it again
there was an emerald door, which gave entrance to a
splendid palace full of gold and precious stones,
dazzling to behold. Yet in all the whole palace there
was no living thing save one white bird perched upon a
costly table in a cage.

The bird espying the maiden, said to her, "Maiden,
how camest thou hither?" And she replied, "One of
my father's goats has escaped from the flock, and as I
dare not go home without it, I have been seeking it
every where; thus came I hither." Then the White
Bird said, "If thou wilt consent to be my wife (²), I
will not only tell thee where the goat is, but restore it
to thee. If, however, thou refuse to render me this
service, the goat is lost to thy father's flock for ever."
But the maiden answered, "How can I be thy wife,
seeing thou art a bird? Therefore is my father's goat
lost to his flock for ever." And she went away weeping for sorrow.

The next day, when the second daughter took her
turn with the herds, another goat escaped from the
flock; and when she went to seek it, she also came to
the strange palace and the white bird; but neither
could she enter into his idea of her becoming his wife;

and she therefore came home, sorrowing over the loss to the herd under her care.

The day following, the youngest daughter went forth with the goats, and a goat also strayed from her. But she, when she had come to the palace, and the white bird asked her to become his wife, with the promise of restoring her goat in case of her consent, answered him, "As a rule, creatures of the male gender keep their promises; therefore, O bird! I accept thy conditions." Thus she agreed to become his wife.

One day there was to be a great gathering, lasting thirteen days, in a temple in the neighbourhood. And when all the people were assembled together, it was found that it was just this woman, the wife of the white bird, who was more comely than all the other women. And among the men there was a mighty rider, mounted on a dappled grey horse, who was so far superior to all the rest, that when he had trotted thrice round the assembly and ridden away again, they could not cease talking of his grace and comeliness, and his mastery of his steed.

When the wife came back home again to the palace in the rock, the white bird said to her, "Among all the men and women at the festival, who was regarded to have given the proofs of superiority?" And she answered, "Among the men, it was one riding on a dappled grey horse; and among the women, it was I." Thus it happened every day of the festival, neither

was there any, of men or women, that could compete
with these two.

On the twelfth day, when the woman that was
married to the white bird went again to the festival,
she had for her next neighbour an ancient woman, who
asked her how it had befallen the other days of the
feast; and she told her, saying, "Among all the women
none has overmatched me; but among the men, there
is none to compare with the mighty rider on the dappled
grey horse. If I could but have such a man for my
husband, there would be nothing left to wish for all the
days of my life!" Then said the ancient woman,
"And why shouldst thou not have such a man for thy
husband?" But she began to weep, and said, "Because
I have already promised to be the wife of a white bird."
"That is just right!" answered the ancient woman.
"Behold, to-morrow is the thirteenth day of the assembly; but come not thou to the feast, only make as
though thou wert going: hide thyself behind the
emerald door. When thou seemest to be gone, the
white bird will leave his perch, and assuming his man's
form, will go into the stable, and saddle his dappled
grey steed, and ride to the festival as usual. Then
come thou out of thy hiding-place, and burn his perch,
and cage, and feathers; so will he have henceforth to
wear his natural form." Thus the ancient woman
instructed the wife of the white bird.

The next day the woman did all that she had been

told, even according to the words of the ancient woman.
But as she longed exceedingly to see her husband return, she placed herself behind a pillar where she could
see him coming a long way.   At last, as the sun began
to sink quite red towards the horizon, she saw him
coming on his dapple-grey horse.   "How is this?"
he exclaimed, as he espied her.   "You got back sooner
than I, then?"   And she answered, "Yes, I got home
the first."   Then inquired he further, "Where is my
perch and cage?"   And she made answer, "Those
have I burned in the fire, in order that thou mightest
henceforth appear only in thy natural form."   Then he
exclaimed, "Knowest thou what thou hast done?   In
that cage had I left not my feathers only, but also my
soul (³)!"   And when she heard that, she wept sore,
and besought him, saying, "Is there no means of
restoration?   Behold! there is nothing that I could
not endure to recover thy soul."   And the man answered, "There is one only remedy.   The gods and
dæmons will come to-night to fetch me, because my soul
is gone from me; but I can keep them in perpetual con-
test for seven days and seven nights.   Thou, meantime, take this stick, and with it hew and hew on at the
mother-o'-pearl door without stopping or resting day
or night.   By the close of the seventh night thou
shalt have hewn through the door, and I shall be free
from the gods and dæmons; but, bear in mind, that if
thou cease from hewing for one single instant, or if

weariness overtake thee for one moment, then the gods
and dæmons will carry me away with them—away from
thee." Thus he spoke. Then the woman went and
fetched little motes of the feather-grass, and fixed her
eyelids open with them, that she might not be overtaken
by slumber; and with the stick that her husband had
given her she set to work, when night fell, to hew and
hew on at the mother-o'-pearl door. Thus she hewed
on and on, nor wearied, seven days and seven nights:
only the seventh night, the motes of grass having
fallen out of one of her eyes so that she could not keep
the lid from closing once, in that instant the gods and
dæmons prevailed against her husband, and carried
him off.

Inconsolable, she set forth to wander after him,
crying, "Ah! my beloved husband. My husband of
the bird form!" Notwithstanding that she had
not slept or left off toiling for seven days and
seven nights, she set out, without stopping to take
rest, searching for him every where in earth and
heaven (⁴).

At last, as she continued walking and crying out,
she heard his voice answering her from the top of a
mountain. And when she had toiled up to the top of
the mountain, crying aloud after him, she heard him
answer her from the bottom of a stream. When she
came down again to the banks of the stream, still
calling loudly upon him, there she found him by a

sacred *Obö*, raised to the gods by the wayside (⁵). He sat there with a great bundle of old boots upon his back, as many as he could carry.

When they had met, he said to her, "This meeting with thee once more rejoices my heart. The gods and dæmons have made me their water-carrier; and in toiling up and down from the river to their mountain (⁶) so many times, I have worn out all these pairs of boots."

But she answered, "Tell me, O beloved, what can I do to deliver thee from this bondage?"

And he answered, "There is only this remedy, O faithful one. Even that thou return now home, and build another cage like to the one that was burned, and that having built it, thou woo my soul back into it. Which when thou hast done, I myself must come back thither, nor can gods or dæmons withhold me."

So she went back home, and built a cage like to the one that was burned, and wooed the soul of her husband back into it; and thus was her husband delivered from the power of the gods and dæmons, and came back to her to live with her always.

———

"In truth that was a glorious woman for a wife!" exclaimed the Khan.

"Forgetting his health, the Well-and-wise-walking Khan hath opened his lips," replied the Siddhî-Kür.

And with the cry, "To escape out of this world is good!" he sped him through the air, swift out of sight.

Thus far of the Adventures of the Well-and-wise-walking Khan the seventh chapter, of how it befell the White Bird and his Wife.

TALE VIII.

When the Well-and-wise-walking Khan found that he had again missed the end and object of his labour, he proceeded yet again as heretofore to the cool grove, and having taken captive the Siddhî-kür bore him along to present to the Master and Teacher Nâgârg'una.

But by the way the Siddhî-kür asked him to tell a tale, and when he would not speak, craved of him the token that he willed he should tell one ; which, when he had given, he told this tale, saying,—

HOW ÂNANDA THE WOOD-CARVER AND ÂNANDA THE PAINTER STROVE AGAINST EACH OTHER.

Long ages ago there lived in a kingdom which was called Kun-*s*mon (¹), a Khan named Kun-*s*nang (²). When this Khan departed this life his son named Chamut Ssakiktschi (³) succeeded to the throne.

In the same kingdom lived a painter named Ânanda(⁴), and a wood-carver also named Ânanda. These men were friends of each other apparently, but jealousy reigned in their hearts.

H

One day, now, it befell that Ânanda the painter, whom
to distinguish from the other, we will call by his Tibetian name of Kun-*d*gah instead of by his Sanskrit
name of Ânanda, appeared before the Khan, and spoke
in this wise : " O Khan, thy father, born anew into the
kingdom of the gods, called me thither unto him, and
straightway hearing his behest, I obeyed it." As he
spoke he handed to " All-protecting" the Khan,
a forged strip of writing which was conceived after this
manner :—

" To my son Chotolo (⁵) Ssakiktschi !

" When I last parted from thee, I took my flight
out of the lower life, and was born again into the kingdom of the gods (⁶). Here I have my abode in pleni-
tude, yea, superabundance of all that I require. Only
one thing is wanting. In order to complete a temple
I am building, I find not one to adorn it cunning in
his art like unto Ânanda our wood-carver. Wherefore,
I charge thee, son Chotolo-Ssakiktschi, call unto thee
Ânanda the wood-carver, and send him up hither to
me. The way and means of his coming shall be explained unto thee by Kun-*d*gah the painter."

Such was the letter that Kun-*d*gah the painter, with
crafty art, delivered to Kun-tschong (⁷), the Khan.
Which when the Khan had read he said to him—
" That the Khan, my father, is in truth born anew
into the gods' kingdom is very good."

And forthwith he sent for Ânanda the wood-carver,

and spoke thus to him : "My father, the Khan, is new
born into the gods' kingdom, and is there building a
temple. For this purpose he has need of a wood-
carver ; but can find none cunning in his art like unto
thee. Now, therefore, he has written unto me to send
thee straightway above unto him." With these words
he handed the strip of writing into his hands.

But the Wood-carver when he had read it thought
within himself, "This is indeed contrary to all rule
and precedent. Do I not scent here some craft of
Kun-*d*gah the painter ? Nevertheless, shall I not find
a means to provide against his mischievous intent ?"
Then he raised his voice, and spoke thus aloud to the
Khan :—

"Tell me, O Khan, how shall I a poor Wood-carver
attain to the gods' kingdom ?"

"In this," replied the Khan, "shall the Painter
instruct thee."

And while the Wood-carver said within himself,
"Have I not smelt thee out, thou crafty one ?" the
Khan sent and fetched the Painter into his presence.
Then having commanded him to declare the way and
manner of the journey into the gods' kingdom, the
Painter answered in this wise,—

"When thou hast collected all the materials and
instruments appertaining to thy calling, and hast
gathered them at thy feet, thou shalt order a pile of
beams of wood well steeped in spirit distilled from

sesame grain to be heaped around thee. Then to the accompaniment of every solemn-sounding instrument kindle the pile, and rise to the gods' kingdom borne on obedient clouds of smoke as on a swift charger."

The Wood-carver durst not refuse the behest of the Khan; but obtained an interval of seven days in order to collect the materials and instruments of his calling, but also to consider and find out a means of avenging the astuteness of the Painter. Then he went home, and told his wife all that had befallen him.

His wife, without hesitating, proposed to him a means of evading while seeming to fulfil the decree. In a field belonging to him at a short distance from his house, she caused a large flat stone to be placed, on which the sacrifice was to be consummated. But under it by night she had an underground passage made, communicating with the house.

When the eighth day had arrived the Khan rose and said, "This is the day that the Wood-carver is to go up to my father into the gods' kingdom."

And all the people were assembled round the pile of wood steeped in spirit distilled from sesame grain, in the Wood-carver's field. It was a pile of the height of a man, well heaped up, and in its midst stood the Wood-carver calm and impassible, while all kinds of musical instruments sent up their solemn-sounding tones.

When the smoke of the spirit-steeped wood began to

rise in concealing density, the Wood-carver pushed aside the stone with his feet, and returned to his home by the underground way his wife had had made for him.

But the Painter, never doubting but that he must have fallen a prey to the flames, rubbed his hands and pointing with his finger in joy and triumph to the curling smoke, cried out to the people,—

"Behold the spirit of our brother Ânanda the wood-carver, ascending on the obedient clouds as on a swift charger to the kingdom of the gods!"

And all the people followed the point of his finger with their eyes and believing his words, they cried out,—

"Behold the spirit of Ânanda the wood-carver, ascending to adorn the temple of the gods' kingdom."

And now for the space of a whole month the Wood-carver remained closely at home letting himself be seen by no one save his wife only. Daily he washed himself over with milk, and sat in the shade out of the coloured light of the sun. At the end of the month his wife brought him a garment of white gauze, with which he covered himself; and he wrote, he also, a feigned letter, and went up with it to "All-protecting" the Khan.

As soon as the Khan saw him he cried out,—

"How art thou returned from the gods' kingdom? And how didst thou leave my father 'All-knowing' the Khan?"

Then Ânanda the wood-carver handed to him the forged letter which he had prepared, and he caused it to be read aloud before the people in these words :—

"To my son, Chotolo-Ssakiktschi.

"That thou occupiest thyself without wearying in leading thy people in the way of prosperity and happiness is well. As regards the erection of the temple up here, concerning which I wrote thee in my former letter, Ânanda the wood-carver hath well executed the part we committed to him, and we charge thee that thou recompense him richly for his labour. But in order to the entire completion of the same, we stand in need of a painter to adorn with cunning art the sculpture he hath executed. When this cometh into thy hands, therefore, send straightway for Kun-*d*gah the painter, for there is none other like to him, and let him come up to us forthwith; according to the same way and manner that thou heretofore sendedst unto us Ânanda the wood-carver, shall he come."

When the Khan had heard the letter, he rejoiced greatly, and said, "These are in truth the words of my father, 'All-knowing' the Khan." And he loaded Ânanda the wood-carver with rich rewards, but sent and called unto him Kun-*d*gah the painter.

Kun-*d*gah the painter came with all haste into the presence of the Khan, who caused the letter of his father to be read out to him; and he as he heard it was seized with great fear and trembling; but when he saw Ânanda the wood-carver standing whole before him, all white from the milk-washing and clad in the costly garment of gauze as if the light of the gods' kingdom yet clove to him, he said within himself,—

"Surely the fire hath not burnt him, as I see him before mine eyes, so neither shall it burn me; and if I refuse to go a worse death will be allotted me, while if I accept the charge I shall receive rich rewards like unto Ânanda." So he consented to have his painter's gear in readiness in seven days, and to go up to the gods' kingdom by means of the pile burnt with fire.

When the seven days were passed, all the people assembled in the field of Kun-dgah the painter, and the Khan came in his robes of state surrounded by the officers of his palace, and the ministers of the kingdom. The pile was well heaped up of beams of wood steeped in spirit distilled from sesame grain; in the midst they placed Kun-dgah the painter, and with the melody of every solemn-sounding instrument they set fire to the pile. Kun-dgah fortified himself for the torture by the expectation that soon he would begin to rise on the clouds of smoke; but when he found that, instead of this, his body sank to the ground with unendurable pain, he shouted out to the people to come and release him. But the device whereby he had intended to drown the cries of the Wood-carver prevailed against him. No one could hear his voice for the noise of the resounding instruments; and thus he perished miserably in the flames.

"Truly that bad man was rewarded according to his deserts!" exclaimed the Prince.

And as he let these words escape him thoughtlessly, the Siddhî-kür replied, "Forgetting his health, the Well-and-wise-walking Prince hath opened his lips." And with the cry, "To escape out of this world is good!" he sped him through the air, swift out of sight.

TALE IX.

WHEN the Well-and-wise-walking Khan found that he had again missed the end and object of his labour, he proceeded yet again to the cool grove, and having in the same manner as heretofore taken captive the Siddhî-kür, bore him along to present to his Master and Teacher Nâgârg'una.

But by the way the Siddhî-kür asked him to tell a tale, and when he would not speak craved the token that he willed he should tell one, which when the Prince had given he told this tale, saying,—

FIVE TO ONE.

Long ages ago there lived among the subjects of a great kingdom six youths who were all boon companions. One was a smith's son, and one was a woodcarver's son; one was a painter's son, and one was a doctor's son; one was an accountant's son, and one was a rich man's son, who had no trade or profession, but plenty of money.

These six determined on taking a journey to find the

opportunity of establishing themselves in life; so they all six set out together, having taken leave of their friends, and the rich man's son providing the cost.

When they had journeyed on a long way together without any thing particular befalling them, as they were beginning to weary of carrying on the same sort of life day by day, they came to a place where the waters of six streams met, flowing thither from various directions, and they said, "All these days we have journeyed together, and none of us have met with the opportunity of settling or making a living. Let us now each go forth alone, each one following back the course of one of these rivers to its source, and see what befalls us then." So each planted a tree at the head of the stream he chose, and they agreed that all should meet again at the same spot, and if any failed to appear, and his tree had withered away, it should be taken as a token that evil had befallen him, and that then his companions should follow his river, and search for him and deliver him.

Having come to this agreement, each one went his way.

The rich man's son followed the wanderings of his stream without falling in with any one till he had reached the very source of the river-head; here was a meadow skirting a forest, and on the border of the forest a dwelling. Towards this dwelling the youth directed his steps. There lived here an ancient man along with his ancient wife, who when they saw the youth opening the gate cried out to him,—

"Young man! wherefore comest thou hither, and whence comest thou?"

"I come from a far country," answered the youth, "and I am journeying to find the occasion of settling myself in life; and thus journeying, my steps have brought me hither."

When the ancient man and his wife saw that he was a comely youth and well-spoken, they said, "If this is indeed so, it is well that thy steps have brought thee hither, for we have here a beautiful daughter, charming in form and delightful in conversation; take her and become our son."

As they said these words the daughter appeared on the threshold of the dwelling, and when the youth saw her he said within himself, "This is no common child of earth, but one of the daughters of the heavenly gods ([1]). What better can befall me than that I should marry her and live here the rest of my days in her company?"

The maiden, too, said to him, "It is well, O youth, that thy steps have brought thee hither." Thus they began conversing together, and the youth established himself on the spot and lived with his wife in peace and happiness.

This dwelling, however, was within the dominions of a mighty Khan. One day, as his minions were disporting themselves in the river, they found a ring all set with curious jewels, in cunning workmanship, which the rich youth's wife had dropped while bathing, and the stream had carried it along to where the Khan's minions were. As the ring was wonderful to behold, they brought it to the Khan.

The eyes of the Khan, who was a man of understanding, no sooner lighted on the ring than he turned and said to his attendants,—

"Somewhere on the borders of this stream, and higher up its course, lives a most beautiful woman, more beautiful than all the wives of the Khan; go fetch her and bring her to me."

The Khan's attendants set out on their mission, and visited all the dwellers on the banks of the stream, but they found no woman exceeding in beauty all the wives of the Khan till they came to the wife of the rich youth. When they saw her, they had no doubt it must be she that the Khan had meant. Saying, therefore, ".The Khan hath sent for thee," they carried her off to the palace; but the rich youth followed mourning, as near as he could approach.

When the Khan saw her, he said, "This is of a truth no child of earth; she must be the daughter of the heavenly gods. Beside of her all my other wives are but as dogs and swine," and he took her and placed her far above them all. But she only wept, and could think of nothing but the rich youth. When the Khan saw how she wept and thought only of the rich youth, he said to his courtiers, " Rid me of this fellow." And so, to please the Khan, they treacherously invited him to a lone place on the bank of the river, as if to join in some game; but when they had got him there they thrust him into a hole in the ground, and then rolled a piece of rock on the top of it, and so put him to death.

In the meantime, the day came round on which the six companions had agreed to come together at the spot where the six streams met;. and there the five others arrived in due course, but the rich youth came not; and when they looked at the tree he had planted by the side of his stream, behold, it had withered away. In accordance with their promise, therefore, they all set out to follow the course of his stream and to search him out. But when they had wandered on a long way and found no trace of him, the accountant's son sat down to reckon, and by his reckoning he discovered that he must have gone so far into such a kingdom, and that he must lie buried under a rock. Following the course of his reckoning, the five soon came upon the spot where the rich youth lay buried under the rock. But when they saw how big the rock was, they said, " Who shall suffice to remove the rock and uncover the body of our companion ?"

" That will I !" cried the smith's son, and, taking his hammer, he broke the rock in pieces and brought to light the body of the rich youth. When his com-

panions saw him they were filled with compassion and
cried aloud, " Who shall give back to us our friend, the
companion of our youth ? "

" That will I ! " cried the doctor's son, and he mixed
a potion which, when he had given it to the corpse to
drink, gave him power to rise up as if no harm had
ever befallen him.

When they saw him all well again, and free to speak,
they every one came round him, assailing him with
manifold questions upon how he had fallen into this
evil plight, and upon all that had happened to him since
they parted.   But when he had told them all his story
from beginning to end, they all agreed his wife must
have been a wonderful maiden indeed, and they cried
out, " Who shall be able to restore his wife to our
brother ? "

" That will I ! " cried the wood-carver's son.   " And
I ! " cried the painter's son.

So the wood-carver's son set to work, and of the log
of a tree he hewed out a *Garuda*-bird(²), and fashioned
it with springs, so that when a man sat in it he could
direct it this way or that whithersoever he listed to go ;
and the painter's son adorned it with every pleasant
colour. Thus together they perfected a most beautiful
bird.

The rich youth lost no time in placing himself inside
the beautiful garuda-bird, and, touching the spring,
flew straight away right over the royal palace.

The king was in the royal gardens, with all his court about him, and quickly espied the garuda-bird, and esteemed himself fortunate that the beautiful garuda-bird, the king of birds, the bearer of Vishnu, should have deigned to visit his residence; and because he reckoned no one else was worthy of the office, he appointed the most beautiful of his wives to go up and offer it food.

Accordingly, the wife of the rich youth herself went up on to the roof of the palace with food to the royal bird. But the rich youth, when he saw her approach, opened the door of the wooden garuda and showed himself to her. Nor did she know how to contain herself for delight when she found he was therein.

"Never had I dared hope that these eyes should light on thee again, joy of my heart!" she exclaimed. "How madest thou then the garuda-bird obedient to thy word to bring thee hither?"

But he, full only of the joy of finding her again, and that she still loved him as before, could only reply,—

"Though thou reignest now in a palace as the Khan's wife in splendour and wealth, if thine heart yet belongeth to me thine husband, come up into the garuda-bird, and we will fly away out of the power of the Khan for ever."

To which she made answer, "Truly, though I reign· now in the palace as the Khan's wife in splendour and wealth, yet is my heart and my joy with thee alone, my husband. Of what have my thoughts been filled all through these days of absence, but of thee only, and for whom else do I live?"

With that she mounted into the wooden garuda-bird into the arms of her husband, and full of joy they flew away together.

But the Khan and his court, when they saw what had happened, were dismayed.

"Because I sent my most beautiful wife to carry food to the garuda-bird, behold she is taken from me," cried the Khan, and he threw himself on the ground as if he would have died of grief.

But the rich youth directed the flight of the wooden garuda-bird, so that it regained the place where his five companions awaited him.

"Have your affairs succeeded?" inquired they, as he descended.

"That they have abundantly," answered the rich youth.

While he spoke, his wife had also descended out of the wooden garuda-bird, whom when his five companions saw, they were all as madly smitten in love with her as the Khan himself had been, and they all began to reason with one another about it.

But the rich youth said, "True it is to you, my dear and faithful companions, I owe it that by means of what you have done for me, I have been delivered from the power of cruel death, and still more that there has been restored to me my wife, who is yet dearer far to me. For this, my gratitude will not be withheld; but what shall all this be to me if you now talk of tearing her from mine arms again?"

Upon which the accountant's son stood forward and said, "It is to me thou owest all. What could these have done for thee without the aid of my reckoning,? They wandered hither and thither and found not the place of thy burial, until I had reckoned the thing, and told them whither to go. To me thou owest thy salvation, so give me thy wife for my guerdon."

But the smith's son stood forward and said, "It is to me thou owest all. What could all these have done for thee without the aid of mine arm? It was very well that they should come and find the spot where thou wert held bound by the rock; but all they could do was to stand gazing at it. Only the might of my arm shattered it. It is to me thou owest all, so give me thy wife for my guerdon."

Then the doctor's son stood forward and said, "It is to me thou owest all. What could all these have done without the aid of my knowledge? It was well that they should find thee, and deliver thee from under the rock; but what would it have availed had not my potion restored thee to life? It is to me thou owest all, so give me thy wife for my guerdon."

"Nay!" interposed the wood-carver's son, "nay, but it is to my craft thou owest all. The woman had never been rescued from the power of the Khan but by

I

means of my wooden garuda-bird. Behold, are we six unarmed men able to have laid siege to the Khan's palace ? And as no man is suffered to pass within its portal, never had she been reached, but by means of my bird. So it is I clearly who have most claim to her."

"Not so !" cried the painter's son. "It is to my art the whole is due. What would the garuda-bird have availed had I not painted it divinely ? Unless adorned by my art never had the Khan sent his most beautiful wife to offer it food. To me is due the deliverance, and to me the prize, therefore."

Thus they all strove together ; and as they could not agree which should have her, and she would go with none of them but only the rich youth, her husband, they all seized her to gain possession of her, till in the end she was torn in pieces.

"Then if each one had given her up to the other he would have been no worse off," cried the Prince. And as he let these words escape him, the Siddhî-kür replied, "Forgetting his health, the Well-and-wise-walking Khan hath opened his lips." And with the cry, "To escape out of this world is good !" he sped him through the air, swift out of sight.

Of the Adventures of the Well-and-wise-walking Khan the ninth chapter, of the story of Five to One.

TALE X.

WHEN the Well-and-wise-walking Khan found that the Siddhî-kür had once more escaped, he went forth yet another time to the cool grove, and sought him out as before ; and having been solicited by him to give the sign of consent to his telling a tale, the Siddhî-kür commenced after the following manner :—

THE BITING CORPSE.

Long ages ago, there lived two brothers who had married two sisters. Nevertheless, from some cause, the hearts of the two brothers were estranged from each other. Moreover, the elder brother was exceeding miserly and morose of disposition. The elder brother also had amassed great riches; but he gave no portion of them unto his younger brother. One day the elder brother made preparations for a great feast, and invited to it all the inhabitants of the neighbourhood. The younger brother said privately to his wife on this occasion, "Although my brother has never behaved as a brother unto us, yet surely now that he is going to have such a great gathering of neighbours and acquaintances, it beseemeth not that he should fail to invite also his own flesh and blood."

Nevertheless he invited him not.   The next day, however, he said again to his wife, " Though he invited us not yesterday, yet surely this second day of the feast he will not fail to send and call us."

Nevertheless he invited him not.   Yet the third day likewise he expected that he should have sent and called him; but he invited him not the third day either.   When he saw that he invited him not the third day either, he grew angry, and said within himself, " Since he has not invited me, I will even go and steal my portion of the feast."

As soon as it was dark, therefore—when all the people of his brother's house, having well drunk of the brandy he had provided, were deeply sunk in slumber, —the younger brother glided stealthily into his brother's house, and hid himself in the store-chamber. But it was so, that the elder brother, having himself well drank of the brandy, and being overcome with sound slumbers (¹), his wife supported him along, and then put herself to sleep with him in the store-chamber. After a while, however, she rose up again, chose of the best meat and dainties, cooked them with great care, and went out, taking with her what she had prepared. When the brother saw this, he was astonished, and, abandoning for the moment his intention of possessing

himself of a share of the good things, went out, that he
might follow his brother's wife.   Behind the house was
a steep rock, and on the other side of the rock a dismal,
dreary burying-place.   Hither it was that she betook
herself.   In the midst of a patch of grass in this burying-place was a piece of paved floor; on this lay the
body of a man, withered and dried—it was the body of
her former husband (²); to him, therefore, she brought
all these good dishes.   After kissing and hugging him,
and calling upon him by name, she opened his mouth,
and tried to put the food into it.   Then, see! suddenly
the dead man's mouth was jerked to again, breaking
the copper spoon in two.   And when she had opened
it again, trying once more to feed him, it closed again
as violently as before, this time snapping off the tip of
the woman's nose.   After this, she gathered her dishes
together, and went home, and went to bed again.
Presently she made as though she had woke up, with
a lamentable cry, and accused her husband of having
bitten off her nose in his sleep.   The man declared he
had never done any such thing; but as the woman had
to account for the damage to her nose, she felt bound
to go on asseverating that he had done it.   The dispute grew more and more violent between them, and
the woman in the morning took the case before the
Khan, accusing her husband of having bitten off the tip
of her nose.   As all the neighbours bore witness that
the nose was quite right on the previous night, and the

tip was now certainly bitten off, the Khan had no alter-
native but to decide in favour of the woman; and the
husband was accordingly condemned to the stake for
the wilful and malicious injury.

Before many hours it reached the ears of the younger.
brother that his elder brother had been condemned to
the stake; and when he had heard the whole matter,
in spite of his former ill-treatment of him, he ran forthwith before the Khan, and gave information of how the
woman had really come by the injury, and how that his
brother had no fault in the matter.

Then said the Khan, "That thou shouldst seek to
save the life of thy brother is well; but this story that
thou hast brought before us, who shall believe? Do
dead men gnash their teeth and bite the living? Therefore in that thou hast brought false testimony against
the woman, behold, thou also hast fallen into the
jaws of punishment." And he gave sentence that all
that he possessed should be confiscated, and that he
should be a beggar at the gate of his enemies (³), with
his head shorn (⁴). "Let it be permitted to me to
speak again," said the younger brother, "and I will
prove to the Khan the truth of what I have advanced."
And the Khan having given him permission to speak,
he said, "Let the Khan now send to the burying-place
on the other side of the rock, and there in the mouth
of the corpse shall be found the tip of this woman's
nose." Then the Khan sent, and found it was even as

he had said.   So he ordered both brothers to be set at liberty, and the woman to be tied to the stake.

" It were well if a Khan had always such good proof to guide his judgments," exclaimed the Well-and-wise-walking Khan.

And as he let these words escape him, the Siddhî-kür replied, "Forgetting his health, the Well-and-wise-walking Khan hath opened his lips."   And with the cry, " To escape out of this world is good," he sped him through the air, swift out of sight.

TALE XI.

WHEREFORE the Well-and-wise-walking Khan went forth yet again, and fetched the Siddhî-kür. And as he brought him along, the Siddhî-kür told this tale :—

THE PRAYER MAKING SUDDENLY RICH.

Long ages ago, there was situated in the midst of a mighty kingdom a god's temple, exactly one day's journey distant from every part of the kingdom. Here was a statue of the Chongschim Bodhisattva (') wrought in clay. Hard by this temple was the lowly dwelling of an ancient couple with their only daughter. At the mouth of a stream which watered the place, was a village where lived a poor man. One day this man went up as far as the source of the stream to sell his fruit, which he carried in a basket. On his way home he passed the night under shelter of the temple. As he lay there on the ground, he overheard, through the open door of the lowly dwelling, the aged couple reasoning thus with one another: "Now that we are both old and well-stricken in years, it were well that we married our only daughter to some good man," said the father. "Thy words are words of truth," replied the mother. "Behold, all that we have in this world is our daughter and our store of jewels. Have we not all our lives through offered sacrifice at the shrine of the Chongschim Bodhisattva? have we not promoted his worship, and spread his renown? shall he not therefore direct us aright in our doings? To-morrow, which is the eighth day of the new moon, therefore, we will offer him sacrifice, and inquire of him what we shall do with our daughter *Suvarnadharî* (²): whether we shall devote her to the secular or religious condition of life."

When the man had heard this, he determined what to do. Having found a way into the temple, he made a hole in the Buddha-image, and placed himself inside it. Early in the morning, the old man and his wife came, with their daughter, and offered their sacrifice. Then said the father, "Divine Chongschim Bodhisattva! let it now be made known to us, whether is better, that we choose for our daughter the secular or religious condition of life? And if it be the secular, then show us to whom we shall give her for a husband."

When he had spoken these words the poor man inside the Buddha-image crept up near the mouth of the same, and spoke thus in solemn tones :—

" For your daughter the secular state is preferable. Give her for wife to the man who shall knock at your gate early in the morning."

At these words both the man and his wife fell into great joy, exclaiming, "*Chutuktu* (³) hath spoken! Chutuktu hath spoken!"

Having watched well from the earliest dawn that no one should call before him, the man now knocked at the gate of the old couple. When the father saw a stranger standing before the door, he cried, "Here in very truth is he whom Buddha hath sent!" So they entreated him to come in with great joy; prepared a great feast to entertain him, and, having given him their daughter in marriage, sent them away with all their store of gold and precious stones.

As the man drew near his home he said within himself, "I have got all these things out of the old people, through craft and treachery. Now I must hide the maiden and the treasure, and invent a new story." Then he shut up the maiden and the treasure in a wooden box, and buried it in the sand of the steppe (⁴).

When he came home he said to all his friends and neighbours, "With all the labour of my life riches have not been my portion. I must now undertake certain practices of devotion to appease the dæmons of hunger; give me alms to enable me to fulfil them." So the people gave him alms. Then said he the next day, "Now go I to offer up 'the Prayer which makes suddenly rich.'" And again they gave him alms.

While he was thus engaged it befell that a Khan's son went out hunting with two companions, with their bows and arrows, having with them a tiger as a pastime to amuse them while journeying. They rode across the steppe, just over the track which the poor man had followed; and seeing there the sand heaped up the Prince's attention fell on it, and he shot an arrow right into the midst of the heap. But the arrow, instead of striking into the sand, fell down, because it had glanced against the top of the box.

Then said the Khan's son, "Let us draw near and see how this befell."

So they drew near; and when the servants had dug away the sand they found the wooden box which the man had buried. The Khan's son then ordered the servants to open the box; and when they had opened it they found the maiden and the jewels.

Then said the Khan's son, "Who art thou, beautiful maiden?"

And the maiden answered, "I am the daughter of a serpent-god."

Then said the Khan's son, "Come out of the box, and I will take thee to be my wife.

But the maiden answered, "I come not out of the box except some other be put into the same."

To which the Prince replied, "That shall be done," and he commanded that they put the tiger into the box; but the maiden and the jewels he took with him.

Meantime the poor man had completed the prayers and the ceremonies 'to make suddenly rich,' and he said, "Now will I go and fetch the maiden and the treasure." With that he traced his way back over the steppe to the place where he had buried the box, and dug it out of the sand, not perceiving that the Prince's servants had taken it up and buried it again. Then, lading it on to his shoulder, he brought the same into his inner apartment. But to his wife he said, "To-night is the last of the ceremony 'for making suddenly rich.' I must shut myself up in my inner apartment to perform it, and go through it all alone. What noise soever thou mayst hear, therefore, beware, on thy peril, that thou open not the door, neither approach it."

This he said, being minded to rid himself of the maiden, who might have betrayed the real means by which he became possessed of the treasure, by killing her and hiding her body under the earth.

Then having taken off all his clothes, that they might not be soiled with the blood he was about to spill, and prepared himself thus to put the woman to death, he lifted up the lid of the box, saying, "Maiden, fear nothing!" But on the instant the tiger sprang out upon him and threw him to the ground. In vain he cried aloud with piteous cries. All the time that his bare flesh was delivered over to the teeth and claws of the unpitying tiger his wife and children were laughing, and saying, "How is our father diligent in offering up 'the Prayer which makes suddenly rich!'"

But when, the next morning, he came not out, all the neighbours came and opened the door of the inner apartment, and they found only his bones which the tiger had well cleaned; but having so well satisfied its appetite, it walked out through their midst without hurting any of them.

In process of time, however, the maiden whom the Khan's son had taken to his palace had lived happily with him, and they had a family of three children; and she was blameless and honoured before all. Nevertheless, envious people spread the gossip that she had come no one knew whence; and when they brought the matter before the king's council it was said, "How shall a Khan's son whose mother was found in a box under the sand reign over us? And what will be thought of a Khan's son who has no uncles?"

These things reached the ears of the Khanin, and, fearing lest they should take her sons from her and put them to death that they might not reign, she resolved to take them with her and go home to her parents.

On the fifteenth of the month, while the light of the moon shone abroad, she took her three sons and set out on her way.

When it was about midday she had arrived nigh to the habitation of her parents; but at a place where formerly all had been waste she found many labourers at work ploughing the land, directing them was a noble youth of comely presence. When the youth saw the Khan's wife coming over the field he asked her whence she came; answering, she told him she had journeyed from afar to see her parents, who lived by the temple of Chongschim Bodhisattva on the other side of the mountain.

"And you are their daughter?" pursued the young man.

"Even so; and out of filial regard am I come to visit them," answered the Khanin.

"Then you are my sister," returned the youth, "for I am their son; and they have always told me I had an elder sister who was gone afar off."

Then he invited her to partake of his midday meal, and after they had dined they set out together to find the lowly dwelling of their parents. But when they had come round to the other side of the mountain in the place where the lowly habitation had stood, behold there was now a whole congeries of palaces, each finer than the residence of the husband of the Khanin! All over they were hung with floating streamers of gay-coloured silks. The temple of the Chongschim Bodhisattva itself had been rebuilt with greater magnificence than before, and was resplendent with gold, and diamonds, and streamers of silk, and furnished with mellow-toned bells whose sound chimed far out into the waste.

"To whom does all this magnificence belong?" inquired the Khanin.

"It all belongs to us," replied the youth. "Our parents, too, are well and happy; come and see them."

As they drew near their parents came out to meet them, looking hale and hearty and riding on horses. Behind them came a train of attendants leading horses for the Khanin and her brother. They all returned to the palace where the parents dwelt, all being furnished with elegance and luxury. When they had talked over all the events that had befallen each since they parted, they went to rest on soft couches.

When the Khanin saw the magnificence in which her parents were living she bethought her that it would be well to invite the Khan to come and visit them. Accordingly she sent a splendid train of attendants to ask him to betake himself thither. Soon after, the Khan arrived, together with his ministers, and they were all of them struck with the condition of pomp and state in which the Khanin was living, far exceeding that of the Khan himself, the ministers owned, saying, "The report we heard, saying that the Khanin had no relations but the poor and unknown, was manifestly false;" and the Khan was all desire that she should return home. To this request she gave her cordial assent, only, as her parents were now well stricken in years, and it was not likely she should have the opportunity of seeing them more, she desired to spend a few days more by their side. It was agreed, therefore, that

the Khan and his ministers should return home, and
that after three days the Khanin also should come and
join him.

Having taken affectionate leave of the Khan and seen
him depart, she betook herself to rest on her soft couch.

When she woke in the morning, behold, all the magnificence of the place was departed! There were no
stately palaces; the temple of the Chongschim Bodhisattva was the same unpretending structure it had
always been of old, only a little more worn down by time
and weather; the lowly habitation of her parents was a
shapeless ruin, and she was lying on the bare ground
in one corner of it, with a heap of broken stones for a
pillow. Her parents were dead long ago, and as for a
brother there was no trace of one.

Then she understood that the *devas* had sent the
transformation to satisfy the Khan and his ministers,
and, that done, every thing had returned to its natural
condition.

Grateful for the result, she now returned home, where
the Khan received her with greater fondness than before.
The ministers were satisfied as to the honour of the
throne, all the gossips were put to silence from that
day forward, and her three sons were brought up and
trained that they might reign in state after the Khan
their father.

———————

"Truly, that was a woman favoured by fortune beyond expectation!" exclaimed the Khan.

And as he let these words escape him the Siddhî-kür replied, "Forgetting his health, the Well-and-wise-walking Khan hath opened his lips." And with the cry, " To escape out of this world is good!" he sped him through the air, swift out of sight.

———

Thus far of the adventures of the Well-and-wise-walking Khan the eleventh chapter, concerning " The Prayer making suddenly Rich."

TALE XII.

WHEREFORE the Well-and-wise-walking Khan went forth yet again and fetched the Siddhî-kür; and as he brought him along the Siddhî-kür told this tale :—

"CHILD-INTELLECT" AND "BRIGHT-INTELLECT."

Long ages ago there lived a Khan who was called Küwôn-ojôtu (¹). He reigned over a country so fruitful that it was surnamed "Flower-clad." All round its borders grew mango-trees and groves of sandal-wood (²), and vines and fruit-trees, and within there was of corn of every kind no lack, and copious streams of water, and a mighty river called "The Golden," with flourishing cities all along its banks.

Among the subjects of this Khan was one named Gegên-uchâtu (³), renowned for his wit and understanding. For him the Khan sent one day, and spoke to him, saying, "Men call thee ' him of bright understanding.' Now let us see whether the name becomes thee. To this end let us see if thou hast the wit to steal the Khan's talisman, defying the jealous care of the Khan and all his guards. If thou succeedest I will recompense thee with presents making glad the heart; but if not, then I will pronounce thee unworthily named, and in consequence will lay waste thy dwelling and put out both thine eyes." Although the man ventured to prefer the remark, "Stealing have I never learned," yet the Khan maintained the sentence that he had set forth.

In the night of the fifteenth of the month, therefore, the man made himself ready to try the venture.

But the king, to make more sure, bound the talisman fast to a marble pillar of his bed-chamber, against which he lay, and leaving the door open the better to hear the approach of the thief, surrounded the same with a strong watch of guards.

Gegên-uchâtu now took good provision of rice-brandy, and going in to talk as if for pastime with the Khan's guards and servants, gave to every one of them abundantly to drink thereof, and then went his way.

At the end of an hour he returned, when the rice-brandy had done its work. The guards before the gate were fast asleep on their horses; these he carried off their horses and set them astride on a ruined wall. In the kitchen were the cooks waiting to strike a light to light the fire: over the head of the one nearest the fire he drew a cap woven of grass (⁴), and in the sleeve of the other he put three stones. Then going softly on into the Khan's apartment, without waking him, he

put over his head and face a dried bladder as hard as
a stone; and the guards that slept around him he tied
their hair together. Then he took down the talisman
from the marble pillar to which it was bound and made
off with it. Instantly, the Khan rose and raised the
cry, "A thief has been in here!" But the guards could
not move because their hair was tied together, and
cries of "Don't pull my hair!" drowned the Khan's
cries of "Stop thief!" As it was yet dark the Khan
cried, yet more loudly, "Kindle me a light!" And
he cried, further, "Not only is my talisman stolen, but
my head is enclosed in a wall of stone! Bring me
light that I may see what it is made of." When the
cook, in his hurry to obey the Khan, began to blow the
fire, the flame caught the cap woven of grass and
blazed up and burnt his head off; and when his fellow
raised his arm to help him put out the fire the three
stones, falling from his sleeve, hit his head and made
the blood flow, giving him too much to attend to for
him to be able to pursue the thief. Then the Khan
called through the window to the outer guards, who
ought to have been on horseback before the gate, to
stop the thief; and they, waking up at his voice, began
vainly spurring at the ruined wall on which Gegên-
uchâtu had set them astride, and which, of course,
brought them no nearer the subject of their pursuit,
who thus made good his escape with the talisman, no
man hindering him, all the way to his own dwelling.

The next day he came and stood before the Khan. The Khan sat on his throne full of wrath and moody thoughts.

"Let not the Khan be angry," spoke the man of bright understanding, "here is the talisman, which I sought not to retain for myself, but only to take possession of according to the word of the Khan."

The Khan, however, answered him, saying, "The talisman is at thy disposition, nor do I wish to have it back from thee. Nevertheless, thy dealings this night, in that thou didst draw a stone-like bladder over the head of the Khan, were evil, for the fear came therefrom upon me lest thou hadst even pulled off my head; therefore my sentence upon thee is that thou be taken hence to the place of execution and be beheaded by the headsman."

Hearing this sentence, Gegên-uchâtu said, within himself, "In this sentence that he hath passed the Khan hath not acted according to the dictates of justice." Therefore he took the Khan's talisman in his hand and dashed it against a stone, and, behold, doing so, the blood poured out of the nose of the Khan until he died!

"That was a Khan not fit to reign!" exclaimed the Well-and-wise-walking Khan.

And as he let these words escape him the Siddhî-kür replied, "Forgetting his health the Well-and-wise-walking Khan hath opened his lips." And with the cry, " To escape out of this world is good !" he sped him through the air, swift out of sight.

TALE XIII.

WHEREFORE the Well-and-wise-walking Khan went forth yet again and fetched the Siddhî-kür, and as he brought him along the Siddhî-kür told him, according to the former manner, this tale, saying,—

THE FORTUNES OF SHRIKANTHA.

Long ages ago there was a Brahman's son whose name was *Shrikantha*(¹). This man sold all his inheritance for three pieces of cloth-stuff. Lading the three pieces of cloth-stuff on to the back of an ass, he went his way into a far country to trade with the same(²).

As he went along he met a party of boys who had caught a mouse and were tormenting it. Having tied a string about its neck, they were dragging it through the water. The Brahman's son could not bear to see this proceeding and chid the boys, but they refused to listen to his words. When he found that they would pay no heed to his words, he bought the mouse of them for one of his pieces of stuff, and delivered it thus out of their hands.

When he had gone a little farther he met another party of boys who had caught a young ape(³) and were tormenting it. Because it did not understand the game they were playing, they hit it with their fists, and when it implored them to play in a rational manner and not be so hasty and revengeful, they but hit it again. At the sight the Brahman was moved with compassion and chid the boys, and when they would not listen to him he bought it of them for another of his pieces of stuff, and set it at liberty.

Farther along, in the neighbourhood of a city, he met another party of boys who had caught a young bear and were tormenting it, riding upon it like a horse and otherwise teazing it; and when by his chiding he could not induce them to desist, he bought it of them for his last piece of stuff, and set it at liberty.

By this means he was left entirely without merchandize to trade with, and he thought within himself, as he drove his donkey along, what he should do; and he found in his mind no better remedy than to steal something out of the palace of the Khan wherewith to commence trading. Having thus resolved, he tied his donkey fast in the thick jungle and made his way with precaution into the store-chambers of the Khan's palace. Here he possessed himself of a good provision of pieces of silk-stuff, and was well nigh to have escaped with the same when the Khan's wife, espying him, raised the cry, "This fellow hath stolen somewhat from the Khan's store-chamber!"

At the cry the people all ran out and stopped Shrikantha and brought him to the Khan. As he was found with the stuffs he had stolen still upon him, there was no doubt concerning his guilt, so the Khan ordered a great coffer to be brought, and that he should be put inside it, and, with the lid nailed down, be cast into the water.

The force of the current, however, carried the coffer into the midst of the branches of an overhanging tree on an island, where it remained fixed; nevertheless, as the lid was tightly nailed down, it soon became difficult to breathe inside the box. Just as Shrikantha was near to die for want of air, suddenly a little chink appeared, through which plenty of air could enter. It was the mouse he had delivered from its tormentors who had brought him this timely aid ([4]). "Wait a bit," said the mouse, as soon as he could get his mouth through the aperture, "I will go fetch the ape to bring better help."

The ape came immediately on being summoned, and tore away at the box with all his strength till he had made a hole big enough for the man to have crept out; but as the box was surrounded by the water he was still a prisoner. "Stop a bit!" cried the ape, when he saw this dilemma; "I will go and call the bear."

The bear came immediately on being summoned, and dragged the coffer on to the bank of the island, where Shrikantha alighted, and all three animals waited on him, bringing him fruits and roots to eat.

While he was living here water-bound, but abundantly supplied by the mouse, the ape, and the bear with fruits to sustain life, he one day saw shining in a shallow part of the water a brilliant jewel as big as a pigeon's egg. The ape soon fetched it at his command, and when he saw how big and lustrous it was he resolved that it must be a talisman. To put its powers to the test, he wished himself removed to *terra firma*. Nor had he sooner uttered the wish than he found himself in the midst of a fertile plain. Having thus succeeded so well, he next wished that he might find on waking in the morning a flourishing city in the plain, and a shining palace in its midst for his residence, with plenty of horses in the stable, and provisions of all kinds in abundance in the store-chamber; shady groves were to surround it, with streams of water meandering through them.

When he woke in the morning he found all prepared even as he had wished. Here, therefore, he lived in peace and prosperity, free from care.

Before many months had passed there came by that way a caravan of merchants travelling home who had passed over the spot on their outward-bound journey.

"How is this!" exclaimed the leader of the caravan,

"Here, where a few months ago grew nothing but grass; here is there now sprung up a city in all this magnificence!" So they came and inquired concerning it of the Brahman's son.

Then Shrikantha told them the whole story of how it had come to pass, and moreover showed them the talisman. Then said the leader of the caravan, "Behold! we will give thee all our camels and horses and mules, together with all our merchandize and our stores, only give us thou the talisman in exchange." So he gave them the talisman in exchange, and they went on their way. But the Brahman's son went to sleep in his palace, on his soft couch with silken pillows.

In the morning, when he woke, behold the couch with the silken pillows was no more there, and he was lying on the ground in the island in the midst of the water!

Then came the mouse, the ape, and the bear to him, saying—

"What misfortune is this that hath happened to thee this second time?" So he told them the whole story of how it had come to pass. And they, answering, said to him, "Surely now it was foolish thus to part with the talisman; nevertheless, maybe we three may find it." And they set out to follow the track of the travelling merchants. They were not long before they came to a flourishing city with a shining palace in its midst, surrounded by shady groves, and streams meandering through them. Here the merchants had established themselves.

When night fell, the ape and the bear took up their post in a grove near the palace, while the mouse crept within the same, till she came to the apartment where the leader of the caravan slept—here she crept in through the keyhole. The leader of the caravan lay asleep on a soft couch with silken pillows. In a corner of the apartment was a heap of rice, in which was an arrow stuck upright, to which the talisman was bound, but two stout cats were chained to the spot to guard it. This report the mouse brought to the ape and the bear. "If it is as thou hast said," answered the bear, "there is nothing to be done. Let us return to our master." "Not so!" interposed the ape. "There is yet one means to be tried. When it is dark to-night, thou mouse, go again to the caravan leader's apartment, and, having crept in through the keyhole, gnaw at the man's hair. Then the next night, to save his hair, he will have the cats chained to his pillow, when the talisman being unguarded, thou canst go in and fetch it away." Thus he instructed the mouse.

The next night, therefore, the mouse crept in again through the keyhole, and gnawed at the man's hair. When the man got up in the morning, and saw that his hair fell off by handfuls, he said within himself, "A mouse hath done this. To-night, to save what hair remains, the two cats must be chained to my pillow."

And so it was done. When the mouse came again, therefore, the cats being chained to the caravan leader's pillow, she could work away at the heap of rice till the arrow fell; then she gnawed off the string which bound the talisman to it, and rolled it before her all the way to the door. Arrived here, she was obliged to leave it, for by no manner of means could she get it up to the keyhole. Full of sorrow, she came and showed this strait to her companions. "If it is as thou hast said," answered the bear, "there is nothing to be done. Let us return to our master."

"Not so!" interposed the ape; "there is yet one means to be tried. I will first tie a string to the tail of the mouse, then let her go down through the keyhole, and hold the talisman tightly with all her four feet, and I will draw her up through the keyhole." This they did; and thus obtained possession of the talisman.

They now set out on the return journey, the ape sitting on the back of the bear, carrying the mouse in his ear and the talisman in his mouth. Travelling thus, they came to a place where there was a stream to cross. The bear, who all along had been fearing the other two animals would tell the master how little part he had had in recovering the talisman, now determined to vaunt his services. Stopping therefore in the midst of the stream, he said, "Is it not my back which has carried ye all—ape, mouse, and talisman—over all this ground? Is not my strength great? and are not my

services more than all of yours?" But the mouse
was asleep snugly in the ear of the ape, and the ape
feared to open his mouth lest he should drop the talisman; so there was no answer given. Then the bear
was angry when he found there was no answer given,
and, having growled, he said, "Since it pleases you
not, either of you, to answer, I will even cast you both
into the water." At that the ape could not forbear
exclaiming, "Oh! cast us not into the water!" And
as he opened his mouth to speak, the talisman dropped
into the water. When he saw the talisman was lost,
he was full dismayed; but for fear lest the bear should
drop him in the water, he durst not reproach him till
they were once more on land.

Arrived at the bank, he cried out, "Of a surety thou
art a cross-grained, ungainly sort of a beast; for in
that thou madest me to answer while I had the talisman
in my mouth, it has fallen into the water, and is more
surely lost to the master than before." "If it is even as
thou hast said," answered the bear, "there is nothing to
be done. Let us return to the master." But the mouse
waking up at the noise of the strife of words, inquired
what it all meant. When therefore the ape had told
her how it had fallen out, and how that they were now
without hope of recovering the talisman, the mouse replied, "Nay, but I know one means yet. Sit you here
in the distance and wait, and let me go to work."

So they sat down and waited, and the mouse went

back to the edge of the stream. At the edge of the
stream she paced up and down, crying out as if in great
fear. At the noise of her pacing and her cries, the
inhabitants of the water all came up, and asked her the
cause of her distress. "The cause of my distress," replied the mouse, "is my care for you. Behold there is
even now, at scarcely a night's distance, an army on
the march which comes to destroy you all; neither can
you escape from it, for though it marches over dry
land, in a moment it can plunge in the water and live
there equally well." "If that is so," answered the inhabitants of the water, "then there is no help for us."
"The means of help there is," replied the mouse. "If
we could between us construct a pier along the edge of
the water, on which you could take refuge, you would
be safe, for half in and half out of the water this army
lives not, and could not pursue you thither." So the
inhabitants of the water replied, "Let us construct a
pier." "Hand me up then all the biggest pebbles you
can find," said the mouse, "and I will build the pier."
So the inhabitants of the water handed up the pebbles,
and the mouse built of the pebbles a pier. When the
pier was about a span long, there came a frog bringing
the talisman, saying, "Bigger than this one is there no
pebble here!" So the mouse took the talisman with
great joy, and calling out, "Here it is!" brought the
same to the ape. The ape put the talisman once
more in his mouth, and the mouse in his ear; and

having mounted on to the back of the bear, they brought the talisman safely to Shrikantha (ᵇ).

Shrikantha not having had his three attendants to provide him with fruits for so many days was as one like to die; nevertheless, when he saw the talisman again, he revived, and said, "Truly the services are great that I have to thank you three for." No sooner, however, had he the talisman in his hand, than all the former magnificence came back at a word—a more flourishing city, a more shining palace, trees bending under the weight of luscious fruits, and birds of beautiful plumage singing melodiously in the branches.

Then said Shrikantha again to his talisman, "If thou art really a good and clever talisman, make that to me, who have no wife, a daughter of the *devas* should come down and live with me, and be a wife to me." And, even as he spoke, a *deva* maiden came down to him, surrounded with a hundred maidens, her companions, and was his wife, and they lived a life of delights together, and a hundred sons were born to him."

"Of a truth that was a Brahman's son whom fortune delighted to honour," exclaimed the Well-and-wise-walking Khan. And as he had marched fast, and they were already far on their journey when the Siddhî-kür began his tale, they had reached even close to the precincts of the dwelling of the great Master and Teacher Nâgârg'una, when he spoke these words. Nevertheless, the Siddhî-kür had time to exclaim, "Excellent! Excellent!" and to escape swift out of sight.

But the Well-and-wise-walking Khan stood before Nâgârg'una.

Then spoke the great Master and Teacher Nâgârg'una, unto him, saying,—

"Seeing thou hast not succeeded in thine enterprise, thou hast not procured the happiness of all the inhabitants of Gambudvîpa, nor promoted the well-being of the six classes of living beings (⁵). Nevertheless, seeing thou hast exercised unexampled courage and perseverance, and through much terror and travail hast fetched the Siddhî-kür these thirteen times, behold, the stain of blood is removed from off thee, though thou fetch him not again. Moreover, this that thou hast done shall turn to thy profit, for henceforth thou shalt not only be called the Well-and-wise-walking Khan, but thou shalt exceed in good fortune and in happiness all the Khans of the earth."

TALE XIV.

NOTWITHSTANDING this generous promise and bountiful remission of his master Nâgârg'una, the Khan set out on his journey once again, even as before, determined this time to command his utterance and fulfil his task to the end. Treading his path with patience and earnestness he arrived at the cool grove, even to the foot of the mango-tree. There he raised his axe "White Moon," as though he would have felled it.

Then spoke the Siddhî-kür, saying, "Spare the leafy mango-tree, and I will come down to thee."

So the Khan put up his axe again and bound the Siddhî-kür on his back, to carry him off to Nâgârg'una.

Now as the day was long, and the air oppressive, so that they were well weary, the Siddhî-kür began to tempt the Khan to speak, saying,—

"Lighten now the journey by telling a tale of interest."

But how weary soever the Khan was, he pressed his lips together and answered him never a word.

Then the Siddhî-kür finding he could not make him

speak, continued, "If thou wilt not lighten the journey by telling a tale of interest, tell me whether I shall tell one to thee."

And when he found that he still answered him not, he said, "If thou wilt that I tell the tale, make me a sign of consent by nodding thine head backwards."

Then the Well-and-wise-walking Khan nodded his head backwards, and the Siddhî-kür proceeded to tell the tale in these words :—

THE AVARICIOUS BROTHER.

Long ages ago there dwelt in a city of Western India two brothers.

As the elder brother had no inheritance, and made a poor living by selling herbs and wood, he suffered the common fate of those in needy circumstances, and received no great consideration from his fellow-men.

The younger brother on the other hand was wealthy, yet gave he no portion of his riches to his brother.

One day he gave a great entertainment, to which he invited all his rich neighbours and acquaintances, but to his brother he sent no invitation.

Then spoke the brother's wife to her husband, saying,—

"It were better that thou shouldst die than live thus dishonoured by all. Behold, now, thou art not even invited to thy brother's entertainment."

"Thy words which thou hast spoken are true," replied the husband. "I will even go forth and die."

Thus saying, he took up his hatchet and cord, and
went out into the forest, passing over many mountains
by the way. On the banks of a stream, running through
the forest, he saw a number of lions and tigers (¹),
and other savage beasts, so he forbore to go near that
water, but continued his way till he came to the head
of the stream, and here in the sheltering shade of a
huge rock were a number of *Dakinis* (²), dancing and
disporting themselves to tones of dulcet music. Presently one of the *Dakinis* flew up on high out of the
midst of those dancing, and took out of a cleft in the
rock a large sack, which she brought down to the
grassy bank where the dancing was going on. Having
spread it out on the ground in the presence of them
all, she took a hammer out of it, and began hammering
lustily into the bag. As she did so, all kinds of articles of food and drink that could be desired presented
themselves at the mouth of the sack. The *Dakinis* now
left off dancing, and began laying out the meal; but
ever as they removed one dish from the mouth of the
bag, another and another took its place.

When they had well eaten and drank, the first
Dakini hammered away again upon the bag, and forthwith there came thereout gold and silver trinkets, dia-
dems, arm-bands, *nûpuras* (³), and ornaments for all
parts of the body. With these the *Dakinis* decked

themselves, till they were covered from head to foot with pearls and precious stones, and their hair sparkling with a powdering of gems ('). Then they flew away, the first Dakini taking care to lay up the bag and hammer in the cleft of the rock before taking her flight.

When they were far, far on their way, and only showed as specks in the distant sky, then the man came forth from his hiding-place, and having felled several trees with his axe, bound them together one on to the end of the other with his cord, and by this means climbed up to the cleft in the rock, where the *Dakini* had laid up the hammer and bag, and brought them away.

He had no sooner got down to the ground again, than to make proof of his treasure even more than to satisfy his ravenous appetite, he took the hammer out of the bag, and banged away with it on to the bag, wishing the while that it might bring him all manner of good things to eat. All sorts of delicious viands came for him as quickly as for the *Dakinis*, of which he made the best meal he had ever had in his life, and then hasted off home with his treasure.

When he came back he found his wife bemoaning his supposed death.

" Weep not for me !" he exclaimed, as soon as he was near enough for her to hear him ; " I have that with me which will help us to live with ease to the end of our days." And without keeping her in suspense, he hammered away on his bag, wishing for clothes, and household furniture, and food, and every thing that could be desired.

After this they gave up their miserable trade in wood and herbs, and led an easy and pleasant life.

The neighbours, however, laid their heads together and said,—

"How comes it that this fellow has thus suddenly come into such easy circumstances?"

But his brother's wife said to her husband,—

"How can thine elder brother have come by all this wealth unless he hath stolen of our riches?" As she continued saying this often, the man believed it, and called his elder brother to him and asked him, "Whence hast thou all this wealth; who hath given it to thee?" And when he found he hesitated to answer, he added, "Now know I that thou must have stolen of my treasure; therefore, if thou tell me not how otherwise thou hast come by it, I will even drag thee before the Khan, who shall put out both thine eyes."

When the elder brother had heard this threat, he answered, "Going afar off to a place unknown to thee, having purposed in my mind to die, I found in a cleft of a rock this sack and this hammer (ʰ)."

"And how shall this rusty iron hammer and this dirty sack give thee wealth?" again inquired his brother; and thus he pursued his inquiries until by degrees he made him tell the whole story. Nor would he be satisfied till he had explained to him exactly the situation of the place and the way to it. No sooner had he acquainted himself well of this than, taking with him a cord and an axe, he set out to go there.

When he arrived, he saw an immense number of deformed, ugly spirits, standing against the rock in eight rows, howling piteously. As he crept along to observe if there was any thing he could take of them to make his fortune as his brother had done, one of them happened to look that way and espied him, after which it was no more possible to escape.

"Of a surety this must be the fellow who stole our bag and hammer!" exclaimed the ugly spirit. "Let us at him and put him to death."

The Dakinis were thoroughly out of temper, and did not want any urging. The words were no soon uttered than, like a flock of birds, they all flew round him and seized him.

"How shall we kill him?" asked one, as she held him tight by the hair of his head till every single hair seemed as if forced out by the roots.

"Fly with him up to the top of the rock, and then dash him down!" cried some. "Drop him in the middle of the sea!" cried others. "Cut him in pieces, and give him to the dogs!" cried others again. But the sharp one who had first espied him said, "His punishment is too soon over with killing him; shall we not rather set a hideous mark upon him, so that he shall be afraid to venture near the habitations of his kind for ever?"   "Well spoken!" cried the Dakinis in chorus, something like good-humour returning at the thought of such retribution.   "What mark shall we set upon him?"

"Let us draw his nose out five ells long, and then make nine knots upon it," answered the sharp-witted Dakini.

This they did, and then the whole number of them flew away without leaving a trace of their flight.

Fully crestfallen and ashamed, the avaricious brother determined to wait till nightfall before he ventured home, meantime hiding himself in a cave lest any should chance to pass that way and see him with his knotted nose.   When darkness had well closed in only he ventured to slink home, trembling in every limb both from remaining fright at the life-peril he had passed through, and from fear of some inopportune accident having kept any neighbour abroad who might come across his path.

Before he came in sight of his wife he began calling out most piteously,—

"Flee not from before me!   I·am indeed thine own, very own husband.   Changed as I am, I am yet indeed the very self-same.   Yet a few days I will endeavour to endure my misery, and then I will lay me down and die."

When his neighbours and friends found that he came out of his house no more, nor invited them to him, nor gave entertainments more, they began to inquire what ailed him; but he, without letting any of them enter, only answered them from within, "Woe is me! woe is me!"

Now there was in that neighbourhood a Lama(⁶), living in contemplation in a *tirtha*(⁷) on the river bank. "I will call in the same," thought the man, "and take his blessing ere I die." So he sent to the *tirtha* and called the Lama.

When the Lama came, the man bowed himself and asked his blessing, but would by no means look up, lest he should see his knotted nose. Then said the Lama, "Let me see what hath befallen thee; show it me." But he answered, "It is impossible to show it!"

Then the Lama said again, "Let me see it; showing it will not harm thee." But when he looked up and let him see his knotted nose, the sight was so frightful that a shudder seized the Lama, and he ran away for very horror." However, the man called after him and entreated him to come back, offering him rich presents; and when he had prevailed on him to sit down again, he told him the whole story of what had befallen him.

To his question, whether he could find any remedy, the Lama made answer that he knew none; but, remembering his rich presents, he thought better to turn the matter over in case any useful thought should present itself to his mind, and said he would consult his books.

"Till to-morrow I will wait, then, to hear if thy books have any remedy; and if not, then will I die."

The next morning the Lama came again. "I have found one remedy," he said, "but there is only *one*. The hammer and bag of which your brother is possessed could loose the knots; there is nothing else."

How elated so ever he had been to hear that a remedy had been found, by so much cast down was he when he learnt that he would have to send and ask the assistance of his brother.

"After all that I have said to him, I could never do this thing," he said mournfully, "nor would he hear me." But his wife would not leave any chance of remedying the evil untried; so she went herself to the elder brother and asked for the loan of the sack and hammer.

Knowing how anxious his brother had been to be possessed of such a treasure, however, the brother thought the alleged misfortune was an excuse to rob him of it; therefore he would not give it into her hand. Nevertheless, he went to his brother's house with it, and asked him what was the service he required of his sack. Then he was obliged to tell him all that had befallen, and to show him his knotted nose. "But," said he, "if with thy hammer thou will but loose the knots, behold the half of all I have shall be thine."

His brother accepted the terms; but not trusting to the promise of one so avaricious, he stipulated to have the terms put in order under hand and seal. When this was done he set to work immediately to swing his hammer, and let it touch one by one the knots in his brother's nose, saying as he did so,—

"May the knots which the eight rows of evil *Dakinis* made so strong be loosed."

And with each touch and invocation the knots began to disappear one after the other.

. But his wife began to regret the loss of half their wealth, and she determined on a scheme to save it, and yet that her husband should be cured. "If," said she, "I stop him before he has undone the last knot he cannot claim the reward, because he will not have removed *all* the knots, and it will be a strange matter if I find not the means of obtaining the hammer long enough to remedy *one* knot myself." As she reasoned thus he had loosed the eighth knot.

"Stop!" she cried. "That will do now. For *one* knot we will not make much ado. He can bear as much disfigurement as that."

Then the elder brother was grieved because they had broken the contract, and went his way carrying the sack, and with the hammer stuck in his girdle. As he went, the younger brother's wife went stealthily behind him, and when he had just reached his own door, she sprang upon him, and snatched the hammer from out his girdle. He turned to follow her, but she had already reached her own house before he came up with her, and entering closed the door against him : then in triumph over her success, she proceeded to attempt loosing the ninth knot. Only swinging it as she had seen her brother-in-law do, and not knowing how to temper the force so that it should only just have touched the nose, the blow carried with it so much moment that the hammer went through the man's skull, even to his brain, so that he fell down and died.

By this means, not the half, but the whole of his possessions passed to his elder brother.

"If the man was avaricious, the woman was doubly avaricious," here exclaimed the Khan, "and by straining to grasp too much, she lost all."

"Forgetting his health, the Well-and-wise-walking Khan hath opened his lips," cried the Siddhî-kür. And with the cry, "To escape out of this world is good," he sped him through the air once again, swift out of sight.

TALE XV.

WHEN therefore the Well-and-wise-walking Khan found that he had once more failed in the end and object of his mission, he once more took the way of the shady grove, and once more in the same fashion as before he took the Siddhî-kür captive in his sack. As he bore him along weary with the journey through the desert country, the Siddhî-kür asked if he would not tell a tale to enliven the way, and when he steadfastly held his tongue, the Siddhî-kür bid him, if he would that he should tell one, but give a token of nodding his head backwards, without opening his lips.

Then he nodded his head backwards, and the Siddhî-kür told this tale, saying,—

THE USE OF MAGIC LANGUAGE.

Long ages ago there lived in Western India a King who had a very clever son. In order to make the best advantage of his understanding, and to fit him in every way to become an accomplished sovereign, the

King sent him into the Diamond-kingdom (¹), that he
might be thoroughly instructed in all kinds of knowledge.   He was accompanied in his journey by the son
of the king's chief minister, who was also to share his
studies, but who was as dull as he was intelligent.   On
their arrival in the Diamond-kingdom, they gave each
of them the sum with which they had been provided
by their parents to two Lamas to conduct their educa-
tion, and spent twelve years with them.

At the end of the twelve years the minister's son
proposed to the king's son that they should now return
home, and as the Lamas allowed that the king's son
had made such progress in the five kinds of knowledge
that there was nothing more he could learn, he agreed
to the proposal, and they set out on their homeward
way.

All went well at first; but one day passed, and then
another, and yet another, that they came to no source
of water, and being parched nigh unto death with
thirst, the minister's son would have laid him down to
die.   As he stood hesitating about going on, a crow
passed and made his cry of "*ikerek.*"   The prince now
encouraged his companion, saying, " Come but a little
way farther, and we shall find water."

" Nay, you deceive me not like an infant of days,"
answered the minister's son.   "How shall we find
water ?   Have we not laboured over the journey these
three days, and found none; neither shall we find it

now? Why should we add to this death of thirst the pangs of useless fatigue also?"

But the king's son said again, "Nay, but of a certainty. we shall now find it."

And when he asked, "How knowest thou this of a certainty?" he replied, "I heard yon crow cry as he passed, 'Go forward five hundred paces in a southerly direction, and you will come to a source of pure, bright fresh water.'"

The king's son spoke with so much certainty that he had not strength to resist him; and so they went on five hundred paces farther in a southerly direction, and then they indeed came upon a pure, bright spring of water, where they sat down, and drank, and refreshed themselves.

As they sat there, the minister's son was moved with jealousy, for, thought he within himself, in every art this prince has exceeded me, and when we return to our own country, all shall see how superior he is to me in every kind of attainment. Then he said aloud to the king's son,—

"If we keep along this road, which leads over the level plain, where we can be seen ever so far off, may be robbers will see us, and, coming upon us, will slay us. Shall we not rather take the path which leads over the mountain, where the trees will hide us, and pass the night under cover of the wood?" And this he said in order to lead the prince into the forest, that he might

slay him there unperceived. But the prince, who had
no evil suspicion, willingly agreed to his words, and
they took the path of the mountain. When they had
well entered the thick wood, the minister's son fell
upon the prince from behind, and slew him. The
prince in dying said nothing but the one word,
" ABARASCHIKA (²)."

As soon as he had well hidden the body, the minister's
son continued on his way.

As he came near the city, the King went out to.greet
him, accompanied by all his ministers, and followed by
much people; but when he found that his son was not
there, he fell into great anxiety, and eagerly inquired
after him. "Thy son," answered the minister's son,
" died on the journey."

At these words, the King burst into an agony of
grief, crying, " Alas, my son! mine only son! Without thee, what shall all my royal power and state, what
shall all my hundred cities, profit me?" Amid these
bitter cries he made his way back to the palace. As
he dwelt on his grief, the thought came to him, " Shall
not my son when dying at least have left some word
expressive of his last thoughts and wishes?" Then he
sent and inquired this thing of his companion, to which
the minister's son made answer, " Thy son was overtaken with a quick and sudden malady, and as he
breathed out his life, he had only time to utter the
single word, ABARASCHIKA."

Hearing this the King was fully persuaded the word must have some deep and hidden meaning; but as he was unable to think it out, he summoned all the seers, soothsayers, magicians, and astrologers (ᵃ) of his king-dom, and inquired of them what this same word ABA-RASCHIKA could mean. There was not, however, one of them all that could help him to the meaning. Then said the King, "The last word that my son uttered, even mine only son, this is dear to me. There is no doubt that it is a word in which by all the arts that he had studied and acquired he knew how to express much, though he had not time to utter many words. Ye, therefore, who are also learned in cunning arts ought to be able to tell the interpretation of the same, but if not, then of what use are ye? It were better that ye were dead from off the face of the earth. Wherefore, I give you the space of seven days to search in all your writings and to exercise all your arts, and if at the end of seven days ye are none of you able to tell me the in-terpretation, then shall I deliver you over to death."

With that he commanded that they should be all secured in an exceeding high fortress for the space of seven days, and well watched that they might not escape.

The seven days passed away, and not one of them was at all nearer telling the interpretation of ABARASCHIKA than on the first day. "Of a certainty we shall all be put to death to-morrow," was repeated all through the place,

M

and some cried to the *devas* and some sat still and wept, speaking only of the relations and friends they would leave behind.

Meantime, a student of an inferior sort, who waited on the others and learned between whiles, had contrived to escape, not being under such strict guard as his more important brethren. At night-time he took shelter under a leafy tree. As he lay there a bird and its young ones came to roost on the boughs above him. One of the young ones instead of going to sleep went on complaining through the night, "I'm so hungry! I'm so hungry!" At last the old bird began to console it, saying, " Cry not, my son ; for to-morrow there will be plenty of food."

" And why should there be more food to-morrow than to-day ?" asked the young bird.

" Because to-morrow," answered the mother, " the Khan has made preparations to put a thousand men to death. That will be a feast indeed !"

" And why should he put so many men to death ? " persisted the young bird.

" Because," interposed the father, " though they are all wise men, not one of them can tell him such a simple thing as the meaning of the word ABARASCHIKA."

" What does it mean, then ?" inquired the young bird.

" The meaning of the word is this : ' This, my bosom friend, hath enticed me into a thick grove, and there,

wounding me with a sharp knife, hath taken away my
life, and is even now preparing to cut off my head.' "
This the old bird told to his young.

The young student, however, hearing these words
waited to hear no more, but set off at his best speed
towards the tower where all his companions were con-
fined. About daybreak he reached the gates, and
made his way in all haste in to them. In the midst of
their weeping and lamenting over the morning which
they reckoned that of their day of death, he cried out,—

"Weep no more! I have discovered the meaning of
the word."

Just then the Khan's guard came to conduct them to
the Khan for examination preparatory to their being
given over to execution. Here the young student declared to the Khan the meaning of the word ABARAS-
CHIKA. Having heard which the Khan dismissed them
all with rich presents, but privately bid them declare to
no man the meaning of the word. Then he sent for the
minister's son, and without giving him any hint of his
intention, bid him go before him and show him where
lay the bones of his son, which when he had seen and
built a tomb over them, he ordered the minister and
his son both to be put to death.

"That Khan's son, so well versed in the five kinds
of knowledge, would have been an honour and orna-

ment to his kingdom, had he not been thus untimely cut off," exclaimed the Khan.

And as he let these words escape him, the Siddhî-kür replied, "Forgetting his health, the Well-and-wise-walking Khan hath opened his lips." And with the cry, "To escape out of this world is good!" he sped him through the air, swift out of sight.

TALE XVI.

When therefore the Well-and-wise-walking Khan saw that he had again failed in the end and object of his journey, he once more took the way of the cool grove; and having taken the Siddhî-kür captive as before in his bag, in which there was place for a hundred, and made fast the mouth of the same with his cord woven of a hundred threads of different colours, he bore him along to present to his Master and Teacher Nâgârg'una.

And as they went the Siddhî-kür asked him to beguile the way with a tale, or else give the signal that he should tell one. And when the Well-and-wise-walking Khan had given the signal that the Siddhî-kür should tell one, he began after this wise, saying,—

THE WIFE WHO LOVED BUTTER.

Long ages ago there dwelt in the neighbourhood of a city in the north part of India called Taban-*Minggan* (¹) a man and his wife who had no children, and nine cows (²) for all possessions. As the man was very fond of meat he used to kill all the calves as soon as they were born that he might eat them, but the wife cared only for butter. One day when there were no more calves the man took it into his head to slaughter one of the cows; "What does it signify," said he to himself, "whether there are nine or eight?" So he killed one of the cows and ate it. When the meat of this cow was all at an end, he said to himself, "What does it matter whether there are eight cows or seven?" And with that he slaughtered another cow and ate it. When the meat of this cow had come to an end, he said within himself again, "What does it matter whether there are seven cows or six?" and with that he slaughtered another cow and ate it. This he continued doing till there was one only cow left. At last, when the wife saw that there was but one only cow left, she could refrain herself no longer. Determined to save this only cow from being slaughtered, she never let it out of her sight, but wherever she went led it after her by a string.

One day, however, when the man had been drinking well of rice-brandy, and was sound asleep, the wife having to go out to fetch water, she thought it would be safe to leave the cow behind this once; but scarcely was she gone out when the man woke up, and, seeing the cow left alone behind, slaughtered it to eat.

When the woman came back and found the last remaining cow was killed, she lifted up her voice and wept, saying, "What is there now left to me where-

withal to support life, seeing that the last and only
cow that remained to us is killed." As she said these
words, she turned her in anger and went away, and as
she went the man cut off one of the teats of the cow
and threw it after her. The woman picked up the teat
and took it along with her; but she went along still
crying till she came to a cave in a mountain side, where
she took shelter. There she cast herself down on the
ground, addressing herself in earnest prayer to the
Three Precious Treasures(³) and the Ruler of Heaven
and Earth, saying, "Now that my old man has brought
me to the last extremity, depriving me of all that I had
to support life, grant now, ye Three Precious Treasures,
and thou Ruler of Heaven and Earth, that I may have
in some way that which is needful to support life!"
Thus she prayed. Also, she flung from her the teat of
the cow which she had in her hand, and behold! it
clove to the side of the cave, and when she would have
removed it, it would no more be removed, but milk ran
therefrom as from the living cow. And the milk
thereof was good for making butter, which her soul
loved.

Thus she lived in the cave, and was provided with
all she desired to support life. One day it befell that
the memory of her husband coming over her, she said
within herself, "Perhaps, now that the last cow is
slaughtered and eaten, my old man may be suffering
hunger; who knows!" Thus musing, she filled a

sheep's paunch(⁴) with butter, and went her way to the
place where her husband lived, and having climbed on
to the roof, she looked down upon him through the
smoke-hole(⁵).

He sat there in his usual place, but nothing was set
before him to eat saving only a pan of ashes, which he
was dividing with a spoon, saying the while, "This is
my portion for to-day;" and "That much I reserve for
the portion of to-morrow." Seeing this, the wife
threw her paunch of butter hastily through the roof,
and then went back to her cave.

Then thought the husband within himself, "Who is
there in heaven or earth who would have brought me
this butter-paunch but my very wife? who surely has
said within herself, 'Perhaps, now that the last cow is
slaughtered, my old man is suffering hunger.'" And
as every night she thus supplied him with a butter-
paunch, he got up at last and followed her by the track
of her feet on the snow till he came to the cave where
she dwelt. Nevertheless, seeing the teat cleaving to
the side of the cave, he could not resist cutting it off to
eat the meat thereof. Then he took to him all the
store of butter the woman had laid up and returned
home; but the wife, finding her place of refuge was
known to him, and that he had taken all her store, left
the cave and wandered on farther.

Presently she came to a vast meadow well watered
by streams, and herds of hinds grazing amid the grass;

nor did they flee at her approach, so that she could milk them at will, and once more she could make butter as much as ever she would.

One day it befell that, the memory of her husband coming over her, she said within herself, "Perhaps, now that he will have exhausted all the store of cow-milk-butter, my old man may be suffering hunger; who knows!" So she took a sheep's paunch of the butter made of hind's milk and went to the place where her husband lived. As she looked down upon him through the smoke-hole in the roof, she found him once more engaged sparingly dividing his portions of ashes. So she threw the butter-paunch to him through the smoke-hole and went her way. When she had done this several days, her husband rose and followed her by her track on the snow till he came to where the herd of hinds were grazing. But when he saw so many hinds, he could not resist satisfying his love of meat; only when he had slaughtered many of the hinds, these said one to another, "If we remain here, of a surety we shall all be put to death;" therefore they arose in the night and betook them afar, far off, whither neither the man nor his wife could follow them.

When the wife found her place of refuge was known to her husband, and that he had dispersed her herd of hinds, she left the grassy meadow and wandered on farther.

Presently, a storm coming on, she took shelter in a

hole in a rock where straw was littered down; so she laid herself to sleep amid the straw. But the hole was the den of a company of lions, tigers, and bears, and all manner of wild beasts; but they had a hare for watchman at the opening of the hole. At night, therefore, they all came home and laid down, but they perceived not the woman in the straw; only in the night, the woman happening to move, a straw tickled the nose of the hare. Then said the hare to a tiger who lay near him, "What was that?" But the tiger said, "We will examine into the matter when the morning light breaks." When the morning light broke, therefore, they turned up all the straw and found the woman lying. When the tiger and the other beasts saw the woman lying in their straw, they were exceeding wroth, and would have torn her in pieces. But the hare said, "What good will it do you to tear the woman in pieces? Women are faithful and vigilant animals; give her now to me, and I will make her help me watch the cave." So they gave her to the hare, and the hare bade her keep strict watch over the cave, and by no means let any one of any sort enter it; and he treated her well and gave her plenty of game to eat, which the wild beasts brought home to their lair.

Thus she lived in the den of the wild beasts and did the bidding of the hare. One day, however, it befell that, the memory of her husband coming over her, she said within herself, "Perhaps, now that the hinds are all dispersed, my old man may be suffering hunger; who knows!" So she took with her a good provision of game, of which the wild beasts brought in abundance, and went to the place where her husband lived. He sat as before, dividing his portions of ashes; so she threw the game she had brought down through the smoke-hole.

When she had thus provisioned him many days, he said within himself, "Who is there in heaven or earth who should thus provide for me, but only my loving wife?" So the next night he rose up and tracked her by the snow till he came to the den of the wild beasts.

When the wife saw him, she cried, "Wherefore camest thou hither? This is even a wild beasts' lair. Behold, seeing thee they will tear thee in pieces!" But the man would not listen to her word, answering, "If they have not torn thee in pieces, neither will they tear me." Then, when she found that he would not escape, she took him and hid him in the straw. At night, when the wild beasts came home, the hare said to the tiger, "Of a certainty I perceive the scent of some creature which was not here before;" and the tiger answered, "When morning breaks we will examine into the matter." Accordingly, when morning broke they looked over the place, and there in the straw they found the woman's husband. When they saw the man they were all exceedingly wroth, nor could the hare by any means restrain them that they should not tear them both in pieces. "For," said they, "if of one comes two, of two will come four, and of four will come sixteen, and in the end we shall be outnumbered and destroyed, and our place taken from us." So they tore them both in pieces, both the wife and her husband.

"That woman fell a sacrifice to her devotion to her husband, who deserved it not at her hand!" exclaimed the Khan.

And as he let these words escape him, the Siddhî-kür replied, "Forgetting his health, the Well-and-wise-walking Khan hath opened his lips." And with the cry, "To escape out of this world is good!" he sped him through the air, swift out of sight.

TALE XVII.

WHEREFORE the Well-and-wise-walking Khan once more took the way of the cool grove, and brought thence bound the Siddhî-kür, who by the way told him this story, saying—,

THE SIMPLE HUSBAND AND THE PRUDENT WIFE.

In the southern part of India lived a man who had a very large fortune and a very notable wife, but possessing little sense or capacity himself, nor sufficient understanding to think of trading with his fortune. One day a caravan of merchants came by, with whom the wife made some exchanges of merchandize while the husband stood by and looked on. When they were gone, the wife said to him, "Why should not you also go forth and trade even as these merchants trade?" And he willing to do her a pleasure made answer, "Give me wherewithal to trade, and I will see what I can do."

"This is but reasonable," thought the wife. "For

how shall he trade except he have some sort of merchandize to trade withal." So she made ready for
him an ass to ride, and a camel's burden of rice to
trade with, and arms to defend him from robbers, and
provisions to sustain him by the way. Thus she sent
him forth.

On he rode till he came to the sea-shore, and as he
could go no farther he laid him down here at the foot of
a high cliff to sleep. Just where he lay was the entrance
to a cave which he failed to discover. Towards evening a caravan of merchants travelling by, took shelter
in this cave, leaving a bugle lying on the ground near
the· entrance, that in case of an attack of robbers
the first who heard their approach might warn the
others.

The man's face being turned, as he lay also towards
the entrance of the cave, came very near the mouthpiece of the bugle. About the middle of the night
when he was sleeping very heavily he began also to
snore, and his breath accidentally entering the bugle
gave forth so powerful a note ('), that it woke all the
merchants together. "Who sounded the bugle?"
asked each. "Not I," "Nor I," "Nor I," answered
one and all. "Then it must be the thieves themselves
who did it in defiance," said one. "They must be in
strong force thus to defy us!" answered another.
"We had better therefore make good our escape before
they really attack us," cried all. And without wait-

ing to look after their goods, they all ran off for the
dear life without so much as looking behind them.

In the morning, finding the merchants did not return,
the simple man put together all the merchandize they
had left behind them and returned home with it.   All
the neighbours ran out to see him pass with his train
of mules and cried aloud, " Only see what a clever
trader ! Only see how fortune has prospered him ! "

Quite proud of his success and not considering how
little merit he had had in the matter, he said, " To-
morrow I will go out hunting ! " But his wife knowing
he had not capacity to have come by all the merchandize except through some lucky chance, and thinking
some equally strange adventure might befall him when
out hunting, determined to be even with him and to
know all that might come to pass.

Accordingly the next day she provided him with a
horse and dog, and bow and arrows, and provisions for
the way.   Only as he went forth, she said, " Beware,
a stronger than thou fall not upon thee ! " But he, puffed
up by his yesterday's success, answered her, " Never
fear ! There is none can stand against me."   And she,
smiling to see him thus highminded, made reply,
" Nevertheless, the horseman *Surja-Bagatur* (²) is terrible to deal with.   Shouldst thou meet him, stand
aside and engage him not, for surely he would slay
thee."   Thus she warned him. But he mounted his
horse and rode away, crying, " Him I fear no more
than the rest ! "

As soon as she had seen him start the wife dressed herself in man's clothes, and mounting a swift horse (³) she rode round till she came by a different path to the same place as her husband. Séeing him trot across a vast open plain she bore down right upon him at full gallop. The man, too much afraid of so bold a rider to recognize that it was his wife, turned him and fled from before her. Soon overtaking him, however, she challenged him to fight, at the same time drawing her sword. "Slay me not!" exclaimed the simple man, slipping off his horse, "Slay me not, most mighty rider, *Surja-Bagatur!* Take now my horse and mine arms, and all that I have. Leave me only my life, most mighty Surja-Bagatur!" So his wife took the horse and the arms, and all that he had and rode home.

At night the simple man came limping home foot-sore and in sorry plight. "Where is the horse and the arms?" inquired his wife as she saw him arrive on foot.

"To day I encountered the mighty rider, Surja-Bagatur, and having challenged him to fight," answered he, "I overcame him and humbled him utterly. Only that the wrath of the hero at what I had done might not be visited on us, I propitiated him by making him an offering of the horse and the arms and all that I had."

So the woman prepared roasted corn and set it before him; and when he had well eaten she said to him,

"Tell me now, what manner of man is the hero Surja-Bagatur, and to what is he like (¹) ?"

And the simple man made answer, "But that he wore never a beard, even such a man would he have been as thy father."

And the wife laughed to herself, but told him nothing of all she had done.

"That was a prudent woman, who humbled not her husband by triumphing over him !" exclaimed the Khan.

And as he let these words escape him, the Siddhî-kür replied, "Forgetting his health, the Well-and-wise-walking Khan hath opened his lips." And with the cry, "To escape out of this world is good !" he sped him through the air, swift out of sight.

Of the adventures of the Well-and-wise-walking Khan the seventeenth chapter, of the Simple Husband and the Prudent Wife.

TALE XVIII.

WHEN therefore the Well-and-wise-walking Khan saw that the Siddhî-kür had again made good his escape, he set out and came to the cool grove, and took him captive and brought him, bound in his bag. And by the way the Siddhî-kür told this tale, saying,—

HOW SHANGGASBA BURIED HIS FATHER.

Long ages ago, there lived in a city of Northern India a father and son. Both bore the same name, and a strangely inappropriate name it was. Though they were the poorest of men without any thing in the world to call their own, and without even possessing the knowledge of any trade or handicraft whereby to make a livelihood to support them at ease, they were yet called by the name of Shanggasba, that is " Renowned possessor of treasure (¹)."

As I have already said, they knew no trade or handicraft ; but to earn a scanty means of subsistence to keep body and soul together, they used to lead a wandering sort of life, gathering and hawking wood.

One day as they were coming down the steep side of a mountain forest, worn and footsore, bending under the heavy burden of wood on their backs, Shanggasba, the father, suddenly hastened his tired, tottering steps, and, leading the way through the thickly-meeting branches to a little clear space of level ground, where the grass grew green and bright, called to his son to come after him with more of animation in his voice than he had shown for many a weary day.

Shanggasba, the son, curious enough to know what stirred his father's mind, and glad indeed at the least indication of any glimpse of a new interest in life, increased his pace too, and soon both were sitting on the green grass with their bundles of wood laid beside them.

"Listen, my son!" said Shanggasba, the father, "to what I have here to impart to thee, and forget not my instructions."

"Just as this spot of sward, on which we are now seated, is bared of the rich growth of trees covering the thicket all around it, so are my fortunes now barren compared with the opulence and power our ancestor Shanggasba, 'Renowned possessor of treasure,' enjoyed. Know, moreover, that it was just on this very spot that he lived in the midst of his power and glory. Therefore now that our wanderings have brought us hither, I lay this charge upon thee that when I die thou bring hither my bones, and lay them under the ground in this place. And so doing, thou too shalt enjoy fulness of might and magnificence like to the portion of a king's son. For it was because my father's bones were laid to rest in a poor, mean, and shameful place, that I have been brought to this state of destitution in which we now exist. But thou, if thou keep this my word, doubt not but that thou also shalt become a renowned possessor of treasure."

Thus spoke Shanggasba, the father; and then, lifting their faggots on to their shoulder, they journeyed on again as before.

Not long after the day that they had held this discourse, Shanggasba, the father, was taken grievously ill, so that the son had to go out alone to gather wood, and it so befell that when he returned home again the father was already dead. So remembering his father's admonition, he laded his bones upon his back, and carried them out to burial in the cleared spot in the forest, as his father had said.

But when he looked that the great wealth and honour of which his father had spoken should have fallen to his lot, he was disappointed to find that he remained as poor as before. Then, because he was weary of the life of a woodman, he went into the city, and bought a hand-loom and yarn, and set himself to weave linen cloths which he hawked about from place to place.

Now, one day, as he was journeying back from a town where he had been selling his cloths, his way brought him through the forest where his father lay buried. So he tarried a while at the place and sat down to his weaving, and as he sat a lark came and perched on the loom. With his weaving-stick he gave the lark a blow • and killed it, and then roasted and ate it.

But as he ate it he mused, "Of a certainty the words of my father have failed, which he spoke, saying, ' If thou bury my bones in this place thou shalt enjoy fulness of might and magnificence.' And because this weaving brings me a more miserable profit even than hawking wood, I will arise now and go and sue for the hand of the daughter of the King of India, and become his son-in-law."

Having taken this resolution, he burnt his hand-loom, and set out on his journey.

Now it so happened that just at this time the Princess, daughter of the King of India, having been absent for a long time from the capital, great festivities of thanks-giving were being celebrated in gratitude for her return in safety, as Shanggasba arrived there; and notably, on a high hill, before the image of a Garuda-bird (²), the king of birds, Vishnu's bearer, all decked with choice silk rich in colour.

Shanggasba arrived, fainting from hunger, for the journey had been long, and he had nothing to eat by the way, having no money to buy food, but now he saw things were beginning to go well with him, for when he saw the festival he knew there would be an offering of *baling* cakes of rice-flour before the garuda-bird, and he already saw them in imagination surrounded with the yellow flames of the sacrifice.

As soon as he approached the place therefore he climbed up the high hill, and satisfied his hunger with the *baling ;* and then, as a provision for the future, he took down the costly silk stuffs with which the garuda-bird was adorned and hid them in his boots.

His hunger thus appeased, he made his way to the King's palace, where he called out lustily to the porter in a tone of authority, " Open the gate for me ! "

But the porter, when he saw what manner of man it was summoned him, would pay no heed to his words, but rather chid him and bid him be silent.

Then Shanggasba, when he found the porter would pay no heed to his words, but rather bid him be silent, blew a note on the great princely trumpet, which was only sounded for promulgating the King's decrees.

This the King heard, who immediately sent for the porter, and inquired of him who had dared to sound the great princely trumpet. To whom the porter made answer,—

" Behold now, O King, there stands without at the gate a vagabond calling on me to admit him because he has a communication to make to the King."

" The fellow is bold ; let him be brought in," replied the King. So they brought Shanggasba before the King's majesty.

"What seekest thou of me?" inquired the King.
And Shanggasba, nothing abashed, answered plainly—

"To sue for the hand of the Princess am I come,
and to be the King's son-in-law."

The ministers of state, who stood round about the
King, when they heard these words, were filled with
indignation, and counselled the King that he should
put him to death. But the King, tickled in his fancy
with the man's daring, answered,—

"Nay, let us not put him to death. He can do us
no harm. A beggar may sue for a king's daughter,
and a king may choose a beggar's daughter, out of
that no harm can come," and he ordered that he should
be taken care of in the palace, and not let to go forth.

Now all this was told to the Queen, who took a very
different view of the thing from the King's. And
coming to him in fury and indignation, she cried out,—

"It is not good for such a man to live. He must be
already deprived of his senses; let him die the death!"

But the King gave for all answer, "The thing is not
of that import that he should die for it."

The Princess also heard of it; and she too came to
complain to the King that he should cause such a man
to be kept in the palace; but before she could open
her complaint, the King, joking, said to her,—

"Such and such a man is come to sue for thy hand;
and I am about to give thee to him."

But she answered, "This shall never be; surely the

King hath spoken this thing in jest. Shall a princess now marry a beggar?"

"If thou wilt not have him, what manner of man wouldst thou marry?" asked the King.

"A man who has gold and precious things enough that he should carry silk stuff (³) in his boots, such a one would I marry, and not a wayfarer and a beggar," answered the Princess.

When the people heard that, they went and pulled off Shanggasba's boots, and when they found in them the pieces of silk he had taken from the image of the garuda-bird, they all marvelled, and said never a word more.

But the King thought thereupon, and said, "This one is not after the manner of common men." And he gave orders that he should be lodged in the palace.

The Queen, however, was more and more dismayed when she saw the token, and thus she reasoned, "If the man is here entertained after this manner, and if he has means thus to gain over to him the mind of the King, who shall say but that he may yet contrive to carry his point, and to marry my daughter?" And as she found she prevailed nothing with the King by argument, she said, "I must devise some means of subtlety to be rid of him." Then she had the man called into her, and inquired of him thus,—

"Upon what terms comest thou hither to sue for the hand of my daughter? Tell me, now, hast thou great treasures to endow her with as thy name would import, or wilt thou win thy right to pay court to her by thy valour and bravery?" And this she said, for she thought within herself, of a surety now the man is so poor he can offer no dowry, and so he needs must elect to win her by the might of his bravery, which if he do I shall know how to over-match his strength, and show he is but a mean-spirited wretch.

But Shanggasba made answer, "Of a truth, though I be called 'Renowned possessor of treasure,' no treasure have I to endow her with; but let some task be appointed me by the King and Queen, and I will win her hand by my valour."

The Queen was glad when she heard this answer, for she said, "Now I have in my hands the means to be rid of him." At this time, while they were yet speaking, it happened that a Prince of the Unbelievers advanced to the borders of the kingdom to make war upon the King. Therefore the Queen said to Shanggasba,—

"Behold thine affair! Go out now against the enemy, and if thou canst drive back his hordes thou shalt marry our daughter, and become the King's son-in-law.

"Even so let it be!" answered Shanggasba. "Only let there be given to me a good horse and armour, and a bow and arrows."

All this the Queen gave him, and good wine to boot, and appointed an army in brave array to serve under him. With these he rode out to encounter the enemy.

They had hardly got out of sight of the city, however, when the captain of the army rode up to him and said, "We are not soldiers to fight under command of a beggar: ride thou forth alone."

So they went their way, and he rode on alone. He had no sooner come to the borders of the forest, however, where the ground was rough and uneven, than he found he could in no wise govern his charger, and after pulling at the reins for a long time in vain, the beast dashed with him furiously into the thicket. "What can I do now?" mourned Shanggasba to himself as, encumbered by the unwonted weight of his armour, he made fruitless efforts to extricate himself from the interlacing branches; "surely death hath overtaken me!" And even as he spoke the enemy's army appeared riding down towards him. Nevertheless, catching hold of the overhanging bows of a tree, by which to save himself from the plungings of the horse, and as the soil was loose and the movement of the steed impetuous, as he clung to the tree the roots were set free by his struggles, and rebounding in the face of the advancing enemy, laid many of his riders low in the dust.

The prince who commanded them when he saw this, exclaimed, "This one cannot be after the manner of common men. Is he not rather one of the heroes making trial of his prowess who has assumed this outward form?"

And a great panic seized them all, so that they turned

and fled from before him, riding each other down in the confusion, and casting away their weapons and their armour.

As soon as they were well out of sight, and only the clouds of dust whirling round behind them, Shanggasba rose from the ground where he had fallen in his fear, and catching by the bridle one of the horses whose rider had been thrown, laded on to him all that he could carry of the spoil with which the way was strewn, and brought it up to the King as the proof and trophy of his victory.

The King was well pleased to have so valiant a son-in-law, and commended him and promised him the hand of the Princess in marriage. But the Queen, though her first scheme for delivering her daughter had failed, was not slow to devise another, and she said, "It is not enough that he should be valiant in the field, but a mighty hunter must he also be." And thus she said to Shanggasba, "Wilt thou also give proof of thy might in hunting?"

• And Shanggasba made answer, "Wherein shall I show my might in hunting?"

And the Queen said, "Behold now, there is in our mountains a great fox, nine spans in length, the fur of whose back is striped with stripes; him shalt thou kill and bring his skin hither to me, if thou wouldst have the hand of the Princess and become the King's son-in-law."

"Even so let it be," replied Shanggasba; "only let there be given me a bow and arrow, and provisions for many days."

All·this the Queen commanded should be given to him; and he went out to seek for the great fox measuring nine spans in length, and the fur of his back striped with stripes.

Many days he wandered over the mountains till his provisions were all used and his clothes torn, and, what was a worse evil, he had lost his bow by the way.

"Without a bow I can do nothing," reasoned Shanggasba to himself, "even though I fall in with the fox. It is of no use that I wait for death here. I had better return to the palace and see what fortune does for me."

But as he had wandered about up and down without knowing his way, it so happened that as he now directed his steps back to the road, he came upon the spot where he had laid down to sleep the night before, and there it was he had left the bow lying. But in the meantime the great fox nine spans long, with the fur of his back striped with stripes, had come by that way, and finding the bow lying had striven to gnaw it through. In so doing he had passed his neck through the string, and the string had strangled him. So in this way Shanggasba obtained possession of his skin, which he forthwith carried in triumph to the King and Queen. The King when he saw it exclaimed, "Of a truth now is Shanggasba a mighty hunter, for he has killed the great fox nine spans long, and with the fur of his back striped with stripes. Therefore shall the hand of the Princess be given to him in marriage."

But the Queen would not yet give up the cause of her daughter, and she said, "Not only in fighting and hunting must he give proof of might, but also over the spirits he must show his power." Then Shanggasba made answer, "Wherein shall I show my power over the spirits?"

And the Queen said, "In the regions of the North, among the Mongols, are seven dæmons who ride on horses : these shalt thou slay and bring hither, if thou wouldst ask for the hand of the Princess and become the King's son-in-law."

"Even so let it be," replied Shanggasba; "only point me out the way, and give me provisions for the journey."

So the Queen commanded that the way should be shown him, and appointed him provisions for the journey, which she prepared with her own hand, namely, seven pieces of black rye-bread that he was to eat on his way out, and seven pieces of white wheaten-bread that he was to eat on his way home. Thus provided, he went forth towards the region of the North, among the Mongols, to seek for the seven dæmons who rode on horses.

Before night he reached the land of the Mongols, and finding a hillock, he halted and sat down on it,

and took out his provisions: and it well-nigh befell
that he had eaten the white wheaten-bread first ; but
he said, "Nay, I had best get through the black bread
first." So he left the white wheaten-bread lying
beside him, and began to eat a piece of the black rye-
bread. But as he was hungry and eat fast, the hiccups
took him; and then, before he had time to put the
bread up again into his wallet, suddenly the seven
dæmons of the country of the Mongols came upon him,
riding on their horses. So he rose and ran away in
great fear, leaving the bread upon the ground. But
they, after they had chased him a good space, stopped
and took counsel of each other what they should do
with him, and though for a while they could not agree,
finally they all exclaimed together, "Let us be satisfied
with taking away his victuals." So they turned back
and took his victuals ; and the black rye-bread they
threw away, but the white wheaten-bread they ate,
every one of them a piece.

The Queen, however, had put poison in the white
wheaten-bread, which was to serve Shanggasba on his
homeward journey; and now that the seven dæmons
ate thereof, they were all killed with the poison that was
prepared for him, and they all laid them down on the hillock and died, while their horses grazed beside them (⁴).

But in the morning, Shanggasba hearing nothing more
of the trampling of the dæmons chasing him, left off
running, and plucked up courage to turn round and

look after them; and when he saw them not, he turned stealthily back, looking warily on this side and on that, lest they should be lying in wait for him. And when he had satisfied himself the way was clear of them, he bethought him to go back and look after his provisions. When he got back to the hillock, however, he found the seven dæmons lying dead, and their horses grazing beside them. The sight gave him great joy; and having packed each one on the back of his horse, he led them all up to the King and Queen.

The King was so pleased that the seven dæmons were slain, that he would not let him be put on his trial any more. So he delivered the Princess to him, and he became the King's son-in-law. Moreover, he gave him a portion like to the portion of a King's son, and erected a throne for him as high as his own throne, and appointed to him half his kingdom, and made all his subjects pay him homage as to himself.

———

"This man thought that his father's words had failed, and owned not that it was because he buried his bones in a prosperous place that good fortune happened unto him," exclaimed the Prince.

And as he let these words escape him, the Siddhî-kür replied, "Forgetting his health, the Well-and-wise-walking Khan hath opened his lips." And with the cry, "To escape out of this world is good!" he sped him through the air, fleet out of sight.

TALE XIX.

WHEREFORE the Well-and-wise-walking Khan once more took the way of the cool grove, and having brought thence the Siddhî-kür bound in his bag, and having eaten of his cake that never diminished to strengthen him for the journey, as they went along the Siddhî-kür told him this tale, saying,—

THE PERFIDIOUS FRIEND.

Long ages ago there lived in a northern country of India a lioness who had her den in the side of a snow-capped mountain. One day she had been so long without food that she was near to have devoured her cub; determining, however, to make one effort first to spare it, she went out on a long journey till she came to a fair plain where there were a number of cows grazing. When she saw the herd of cows she could not refrain a terrible roar; but the cows, hearing the roar of the lioness, said one to another, " Let us make haste to

escape from the lioness," and they all went their way.
But there was one of the cows which had a calf, and
because she could neither make the calf go fast enough
to escape the lioness, nor could bring herself to forsake
it, she remained behind and fell a prey to the wild
beast. The lioness accordingly made a great feast,
chiefly on the blood of the cow, and carried the flesh
and the bones to her den.

The calf followed the traces of its mother's flesh, and
when the lioness lay down to sleep the calf came along
with her own cub to suck, and the lioness being overcome, and as it were drunken with the blood she had
taken, failed to perceive what the calf did. In the
morning, as the calf had drunk her milk, she forbore to
slay it, and the calf and the cub were suckled together.
After two or three days, when there was nothing left
for the lioness to eat but a few bones of the cow, she
devoured them so greedily in her hunger that one big
knuckle-bone stuck in her throat, and as she could by
no means get it out again, she was throttled by it till
she died. Before dying she spoke thus to the calf and
the cub, " You two, who have been suckled with the
same milk, must live at peace with each other. If some
day an enemy comes to you and tries to set you one
against the other, pay no heed to his words, but remain
at one as before." Thus she charged them.

When the lioness was dead the cub betook himself
into the forest, and the calf found its way to the sunny

● O

slope of a mountain side; but at the hour of evening
they went down to the stream together to drink, and
after that they disported themselves together.

There was a fox, however, who had been used to feed
on the remnants of the lion's meals, and continued now
to profit by those of the cub; he saw with a jealous eye
this growing intimacy with the calf, and determined to
set them at variance(²).

One day, therefore, when the cub had just killed a
beast and lay sucking its blood, the fox came to him
with his tail no longer cockily curled up on his back,
but low, sweeping the ground, and his ears drooping.
When the cub saw him in this plight, he exclaimed,
"Fox! what hath befallen thee? Tell me thy grief,
and console thyself the while with a bite of this hind."
But the fox, putting on a doleful tone, answered him,
"How should I, thine uncle, take pleasure in eating
flesh when thou hast an enemy? hence is all pleasure
gone from me." But the cub answered carelessly, "It
is not likely any one should be my enemy, fox; therefore set to and eat this hind's flesh." "If thou
refusest in this lighthearted way to listen to the words
of thine uncle," answered the fox, "so shall the day
come when thou wilt berue it." "Who then, pray, is
this mine enemy?" at last inquired the cub. "Who
should it be but this calf? Saith he not always, 'The
lioness killed my mother; therefore when I am strong
enough I will kill the cub.'" "Nay, but we two are

brothers," replied the cub; "the calf has no bad
thoughts towards me." "Knowest thou then really
not that thy mother killed his mother?" exclaimed the
fox. And the cub thought within himself, "What the
fox says is nevertheless true; and, further, is he not
mine uncle, and what gain should he have to deceive
me?" Then said he aloud, "By what manner of
means does the calf purpose to kill me? tell me, I
pray." And the fox made answer, "When he wakes
to-morrow morning, observe thou him, and if he
stretches himself and then digs his horns into the
earth, and shakes his tail and bellows, know that it is
a sure token he is minded to kill thee." The cub, his
suspicions beginning to be excited, promised to be
upon his guard and to observe the calf.

Having succeeded thus far the fox went his way,
directing his steps to the sunny side of the mountain
slope where the calf was grazing. With his tail
trailing on the ground, and his ears drooping, he stood
before the calf. "Fox! what aileth thee?" inquired
the calf cheerily; "come and tell me thy grief." But
the fox answered, "Not for myself do I grieve. It is
because thou, O calf! hast an enemy; therefore do I
grieve." But the calf answered, "Be comforted, fox,
for it is not likely any should be an enemy to me."
Then replied the fox, "Beware thou disregard not my
words, for if thou do, of a certainty a day shall come
when thou shalt berue it." But the calf inquired,

saying, "Who then could this enemy possibly be?"
And the fox told him, saying, "Who should it be other
than the lion-cub in the forest on the other side the
mountain? Behold! doth he not use to say, 'Even as
my mother killed and devoured his mother, so also will
I kill and devour him.'" "Let not this disturb thee,
fox," interposed the calf, "for we two are brothers; he
hath no bad thoughts against me." But the fox warned
him again, saying, "Of a surety, if thou disregard my
words thou shalt berue it. Behold! I have warned
thee." Then the calf began to think within himself,
"Is it not true what he says that the cub's mother
killed my mother; and, further, what gain should he,
mine uncle, have in deceiving me?" Then said he
aloud, "If thy warning be so true, tell me further, I
pray thee, by what manner of means doth he design to
put me to death?" And the fox told him, saying,
"When he wakes to-morrow morning observe thou
him, and if he stretch himself and shake his mane, if
he draws his claws out and in, and scratches up the
earth with them, then know that it is a sure token he
is minded to slay thee." The calf, his suspicions beginning to be awakened, promised to be upon his
guard and to observe the cub.

The next morning, when they woke, each observed
the other as he had promised the fox, and each by
natural habit, which the fox had observed of old, but
they not, gave the signs he had set before them for a

token. At this each was filled with wrath and suspicion against the other, and when at sunrise they both
went down to the stream to drink, the cub growled at
the calf, and the calf bellowed at the cub. Hence
further convinced of each other's bad intentions, they
each determined at the same instant to be beforehand
with the other. The calf dug his horns into the breast
of the cub and gored it open, and the cub sprang upon
the calf's throat and made a formidable wound, from
whence the blood poured out. Thus they contended
together till all the blood of both was poured out, and
they died there before the face of the fox.

Then came a voice out of *svarga* (³), saying, " Put
never thy trust in a false friend, for so doing he shall
put thee at enmity with him who is thy friend in truth."

***

" Nevertheless, as the cub was killed as well as the
calf, the perfidy of the fox profited him nothing as soon
as he had made an end of eating their flesh !" exclaimed the Khan.

And as he let these words escape him, the Siddhî-kür
replied, " Forgetting his health, the Well-and-wise-
walking Khan hath opened his lips." And with the cry,
"To escape out of this world is good !" he sped him
through the air, swift out of sight.

TALE XX.

WHEREFORE the Well-and-wise-walking Khan once more took the way of the cool grove; and having brought thence the Siddhî-kür bound in his bag, and having eaten of his cake that never diminished, to strengthen him for the journey, as they went along the Siddhî-kür told him this tale, saying,—

BHIXU LIFE.

Long ages ago there lived in a country in the north of India, namely Nepaul, on the banks of a river named the Hiranjâvati (¹), an old man and his old wife, who had no sons, but only one daughter. But this one daughter was all in all to them; and they had only one care in life, and that care was, how to establish her safely and well, that she might not be left alone in the world when they were on it no more. Nevertheless, though the maiden was fair to see, and wise and prudent in her ways, and though her parents had laid by a rich dowry for her portion, it so chanced that no one

offered to marry her. Yet the years went by, and the
man and his wife were both growing old, and they said,
"If we marry her not now, soon will she be left all
alone in the world."

In a hut at some distance lived another aged couple,
who were very poor; but they had one only son. Then
said the father of the maiden to her mother, "We
must give our daughter to the son of this poor couple
for a wife, otherwise she will be left alone in the
world."

So they married the maiden to the son of this poor
old couple, and they took him into their house, and he
lived together with them.

After a time, the husband felt a desire to return and
see his parents; so he took his wife with him, and they
went to seek his parents. At home, however, they
were not, for they led a Bhixu life, and were gone on a
begging expedition through all the tribes; therefore
they went on, seeking them. About this time, a
mighty Khan had given orders for a great distribution
of alms (²). All that any one asked for, it was given
him, whatsoever it might be. Only concerning the
measure of rice-brandy distributed to any one person
was there any restriction; but of all the rest there was
no stint.

The man and his wife therefore came with the rest
of the people, and obtained their portion, according
to their desire. When all had been well served, and

had returned every one to his home, the man said to his wife, " If we would really be rich, and enjoy life, the way to do it is to go round through all the tribes, living on alms. So living, we have all we need desire. Moreover we need stand in no fear of thieves and robbers; our strength will not be brought down by labour by day, nor our sleep disturbed with anxiety by night; in drought and murrain we shall have no loss to suffer, for the herds of which we shall live will not be our own. To travel about ever among new people is itself no small pleasure. Moreover we shall never be vexed with paying tribute of that we have earned with the toil of our arms. If even we go back and take to us the inheritance thy parents promised to us, in how many days would it be all spent, and we become again even as now! But by going from tribe to tribe, living on alms, our store is never diminished, and there is nothing we shall lack (³)."

Thus they lived many months, begging alms and lacking nothing, even as the man had said. Nevertheless, in the midst of their wanderings, a son was born to them. Then said the woman, " These wild tribes among whom we now are, give us nothing but rice-brandy, which is no food for me; neither have I strength to carry the child as he gets older." And as she knew her husband loved a vagabond life, and could not hear of going to live at home with her parents, she added, " Let us now go see my parents, and beg of

them that they give us of their herds an ass, on which
the infant may ride withal when we go round among
the tribes seeking alms." To this proposition the man
did not say "Nay," and they journeyed towards the
house of the woman's parents, along the bank of the
river Hiranjâvati.

When they arrived at home, they found that the
woman's parents were dead, nor was there the least
remnant left of all their possessions : the herds were
dispersed, and the flocks had fallen a prey to the
wolves and the jackals ; nothing remained but a few
tufts of wool, which had got caught on the ant-
heaps (⁴). The wife picked up the tufts, saying, " We
will collect all these, and weave a piece of stuff out of
them." But her husband pointed out that, at no great
distance, was a plain with many tents, where, by asking alms, they could have plenty of barley and rice,
without the trouble of weaving. They continued their
way therefore towards the tents ; but the woman continued saying, " When we have woven our piece of
stuff, we will sell it, and buy a bigger piece, and then
we will sell that and buy a bigger ; and so on, till
we have enough to buy an ass, then we will set our
little one on it instead of carrying him. Then perhaps
our ass will have a foal, and then we shall have two
asses." " Certainly," answered her husband, "if our
ass has a foal we shall have two asses." But the child
said, "If our ass has a foal, I will take the foal, and

will ride him, going about among the tribes, I also, asking alms even as you (⁵)." When his mother heard him
speak thus, she was angry, and bid him hold his peace;
she also went to correct him by hitting him with a
stick, but the boy tried to escape from her, and the
blow fell upon his head and killed him. Thus their
child died.

At the time that the woman's parents died, and the
herds were dispersed, and the flocks devoured by
wolves and jackals, one only lamb had escaped from
the destruction, and had taken refuge in a hole in the
ground, where it remained hid all day, and only came
out at night to graze (⁶). One day a hare came by, and
as the lamb was not afraid of the hare, she did not hide
herself from him ; therefore the hare said to her, "O lamb,
who art thou ? " And the lamb answered, " I belong
to a flock whose master died of grief because his children went away and forsook him; and when he died,
the wolves and the jackals came and devoured all his
flock, and I, even I only, escaped of them all, and I
have hid myself in this hole. Thou, O hare, then, be
my protector." Thus spoke the lamb.

But the hare answered, " Must not a lamb live in a
flock ? How shall a lamb live in a hole all alone ?
Behold, I will even bring thee to a place where are
flocks of sheep, with whom thou mayest live as becometh
a lamb."

"It were better we stayed here," replied the lamb

trembling; "for if we meet the wolf in the open country, how shall we escape him?" "For that will I provide," answered the hare; "only come thou with me." So they set out, the lamb and the hare together, for to seek a place where grazed flocks in goodly company,

As they went along, they saw on the ground a hand-loom, which some one sitting out there to weave had left behind. The hare bid the lamb put it on her back, and bring it along with her. The lamb did as she was bid. A little farther they saw a piece of yellow stuff lying on the ground: this also the hare bid the lamb pick up and bring with her. The lamb did as she was bid. And a little farther on they saw a piece of paper, with something written on it, blown along by the wind; this likewise the hare bid the lamb bring with her. And the lamb did as she was bid.

A little farther on they saw a wolf coming. As he drew near them, the hare said to the lamb, "Bring me now my throne." Then the lamb understood that he meant the hand-loom, and she set it in the way. Then the hare continued, "Spread abroad over me my gold-coloured royal mantle." Then the lamb understood that he meant the piece of yellow stuff he had bid her pick up, and she spread it over him as he sat on the hand-loom for a throne. Then said the hare again "Reach me the document which the moon sent down to me on the fifteenth of the month (⁷)." So the lamb understood that he meant the piece of written paper he had bid her pick up, and she gave it into his hand.

By this time the wolf had come up with them, and when he saw the hare seated so majestically on the hand-loom for a throne, and with the royal mantle of yellow stuff about him, and the written document in his hand, the lamb moreover standing quietly by his side, he said within himself, " These must be very extraordinary beasts, who do not run away at my approach, after the manner of common beasts." Therefore he stood still, and said to the hare, "Who and whence art thou?" But the hare, still holding the piece of written paper in his hand, made as though he were reading from it as follows :—" This is the all high command of the god Churmusta (⁸) unto the most noble and honourable hare, delivered unto him by the hands of the moon, on the fifteenth of the month. On the same most noble and honourable hare I lay this charge, that he do bring me, before the fifteenth of the next moon, the skins of a thousand rapacious, flock-scattering wolves." And as the hare read these words, he erected his ears with great importance and determination of manner, and made as though he would have come down from his throne to attack the wolf.

The wolf, still more alarmed at this proceeding, took flight, nor so much as looked back to see whether the hare was really pursuing him.

As soon as he was well on his way, the hare and the lamb set out once more on their journey, taking another direction from the wolf, and arrived happily at one of the most fertile pastures in the kingdom of Nepaul.

"The prudence of that hare was equal to his good feeling," exclaimed the Khan.

And as he let these words escape him, the Siddhî-kür replied, " Forgetting his health, the Well-and-wise-walking Khan hath opened his lips." And with the cry, "To escape out of this world is good !" he sped him through the air, swift out of sight.

TALE XXI.

Wherefore the Well-and-wise-walking Khan once more took the way of the cool grove; and having brought thence the Siddhî-kür bound in his bag, the Siddhî-kür as they went along told him this tale, saying,—

HOW THE WIDOW SAVED HER SON'S LIFE (¹).

Long ages ago there lived in *Chara Kitad* (²), which lieth to the east of India, a king named *Daibang* (³), who had one only son. But this son never showed himself to the people. No one in the whole empire had once set his eyes on him. Every day he sent and fetched a handsome youth of the people to come and comb his hair for him, and immediately that he had made an end of combing him he had him put to death. Every day one. This went on for many years, and no one dared to withhold their son from the king's command. At last it came to the turn of a youth who was a widow's son. The widow, therefore, full of anguish at the thought of her son, her eldest stay and consolation, being taken from her and slain, made cakes of dough kneaded with her own milk, and gave them to her son, saying, "Manage so that while thou art combing the hair of the Khan, he shall eat one of these cakes."

The widow's son, therefore, came and stood before the Khan; and as he combed the Khan's hair with the Khan's golden comb, he saw that the ears of the Khan were formed like to the ears of an ass, and that it was that his subjects might not know he had ears like to the ears of an ass, that he put to death every day the young men, who, combing his hair, had seen them. Nevertheless, the widow's son went on combing the Khan's hair, and eating the cakes his mother had given him the while.

At last the Khan said, "What eatest thou?"

And he answered, "Cakes kneaded of rice-flour and milk; such cakes do I eat."

And when the Khan asked for some to taste, he gave him one, and the Khan ate it. When the Khan had eaten the cake, he said, "The scent and the flavour of these cakes is good. How are they composed? tell me."

The widow's son answered, "My mother made them for me with milk of her own breast, and kneaded them with rice-flour."

When the Khan heard that, he said within himself, "How shall I put this youth to death, seeing he and I have both partaken of one mother's milk? That were unnatural and unheard of." Then said he aloud, "If that be so, I will not put thee to death this day; but only take an oath of thee that thou tell no man that I have ears like to asses' ears. Shouldst thou, however, break thine oath, then, know that thou shalt surely be put to death."

"Unto no man, O Khan," swore the youth, "will I declare this thing. Neither unto my mother herself." And having thanked the Khan for sparing his life he went his way.

Day after day, however, all the youths who went in to comb the Khan's hair were put to death as before, and all the people wondered greatly why the widow's son had been spared. Nevertheless, remembering the oath which he had given the Khan, he told no man how it had befallen for all their wondering and inquiring, nor even his own mother.

But as he continued thus keeping his own counsel, and telling no man the reason why the Khan killed all the other youths who combed his hair and spared him, the secret vexed his heart, nor could he stand against the oppression of his desire to speak it, so that he fell ill, and like to die. Nor were medicaments nor yet offerings in sacrifice (*) of any avail to heal him of that sickness, though many Lamas were called to see him. At last a Lama came, who having felt his pulse said, " In this kind of sickness medicaments avail nothing;

only tell what it is thou hast on thine heart, and as soon as thou shalt have told it, to whomsoever it may be, thou shalt be relieved, and be well again. Other remedy is there none." Thus spoke the Lama.

Then all they that stood by the bed spoke to him, saying, "If it be that thou hast any thing on thy mind, as the Lama has said, even though it be the least matter, speak it now and recover. Of what good shall it be to thee to keep the secret if, after all, thou diest?"

But neither so would he break his oath to the Khan. But at night when they were all gone, and his mother only was with him, and she urged him much, he told her, saying, "Of a truth have I a secret; but I have sworn to the Khan that I will tell it to no man, nor yet even to thee, my mother."

Then spoke his mother again, saying, "If this be so, then go out far from the habitations of men, and hiding thy face in a crack of the earth where the soil is parched for want of moisture; or else, in the hollow of an ancient tree, or in a narrow cleft of the everlasting rock, and speak it there."

And the youth listened to her word; and he went out far from the habitations of men till he came where there was a hole of a marmot in the ground. Putting his mouth into the hole he cried, "Our Khan, Daibang, has ears even like to the ears of an ass!" and he repeated the same four times, and was well again.

P

But the marmot living in the hole, had heard the words, and she repeated them to the echo, and the echo told them to the wind, and the wind brought them to the Khan.

So the Khan sent, and called the youth, even the widow's son, before him, saying, "Charged I thee not that thou told no man this thing, and swarest thou not unto me that thou wouldst declare it to no man, nor even to thine own mother? How then hast thou gone and spoken it abroad?"

But the youth answered, saying, "To no man either at home or abroad have I spoken the thing, O Khan!"

"How then came the words back to me unless it be that thou hast spoken them, seeing that none other knows the thing save thee?" again asked the Khan.

"I know not," replied the youth, "unless it be that through refraining of myself that I might keep the secret I fell ill, and when all medicaments and offerings of sacrifice failed, there came a Lama who said there was no remedy save that I should unburden that which oppressed my mind. Then to save my life, and yet not betray the Khan's confidence, I spoke it in the hole of a marmot in the waste, far from the habitations of men."

Then when the Khan found he was so faithful and discreet he believed his word, and forbore to put him to death. Further he said to him, "Tell me, now, canst thou devise any means by which these asses' ears may be concealed, so that I may go forth among my subjects like other Khans?"

"If the Khan would listen to the word of one so humble, even now a means of concealment is plain to my mind," replied the youth.

And the Khan answered him, "Speak, and I will listen to what thou hast to advise."

The youth therefore spoke, saying, "O mighty Khan! Let now a high-fashioned cap be made to cover thine head, and let there be on either side lappets to the cap, covering the ears. Then shall all men when they see the Khan wearing such a cap deem it beseeming to wear such a cap likewise." Thus the youth counselled the Khan.

And the Khan found the counsel good, and he made him a high-fashioned cap with lappets covering the ears; and when the ministers of state and the counsellors and nobles saw the Khan wearing such a cap, they made to themselves caps like unto it, and all men wore it, and it was known by the name of "the lappet cap." But no man knew that the king's ears were like to asses' ears.

Furthermore, the Khan no longer had need to put to death the youths who combed his hair, and all the people rejoiced greatly. But for the youth, even the widow's son, he made him steward over all his household, and whatsoever he did, he did with prudence and judgment, his mother advising him.

" The Khan who put so many youths to death to save his own reputation did not deserve so good a counsel!" exclaimed the Khan.

And as he let these words escape him, the Siddhî-kür replied, "Forgetting his health, the Well-and-wise-walking Khan hath opened his lips." And with the cry, "To escape out of this world is good!" he sped him through the air, swift out of sight.

TALE XXII.

Wherefore the Well-and-wise-walking Khan once more took the way of the cool grove, and, having brought thence the Siddhî-kür as on the other times, bound in his bag with the cord woven of a hundred threads, as they went along the Siddhî-kür told him this tale, saying,—

THE WHITE SERPENT-KING.

Long ages ago there lived in the east part of India a Khan whose possessions were so large that he had ten thousand cities, and for the administration of the affairs of the same he had not less than thirty ministers. He had also a gold frog that could dance, and a parrot that spoke wisely. A tamer was also appointed to have care of them, and every day this keeper brought them before the Khan to divert him. The frog danced every day a new dance, and the parrot now gave wise answers to the questions he proposed, now sang melodious songs with accomplished art.

One day there came to the court of this King a

minstrel from a strange land, in whose playing and singing the Khan took so great pleasure that he gave him many rich presents, and the man went about saying, "In all his dominions the King has no favourite in whom he takes so great delight as in me who am a stranger; neither is there any other who knows how to please him as I." When the keeper of the gold frog and the parrot heard him make this boast, he answered him saying, "Nay, much greater pleasure hath the Khan in his gold frog and his parrot, of whom I am keeper." And they strove together. In the end the minstrel said, "To-morrow we will both go up to the Khan together, and while your gold frog dances his most elaborate dance, and your parrot sings his most melodious songs, I also will play and sing my *sagas* to the Khan; and behold! to whichever the Khan gives ear while he regards not the other, he shall be accounted to have most pleased the Khan."

The next day they did even as the minstrel had said, and when the minstrel began to sing the Khan paid no more heed at all to the frog or the parrot, but listened only to the strange minstrel's words.

Then the tamer who had charge of the frog and the parrot, when he saw that the strange minstrel was preferred, lost heart and came no more before the Khan, but went and let fly the parrot, and threw the gold frog out of a window of the palace. As he threw the gold frog out of the window of the palace a crow was flying by, and seeing the frog thrown out, and that it knew not which way to turn, he caught it in his beak and flew away to a ledge of a rock. As he was about to devour her, the frog said,—

"O crow! if thou art minded to devour me, first wash me in water, and then come and devour me."

And the remark pleased the crow, and he said to the frog,—

"Well spoken, O frog! What is thy name?"

And the frog made answer,—

"*Bagatur-Ssedkiltu* ('). That is my name."

So the crow took her down to wash her in the streamlet which flowed ceaselessly out of a hole in the rock. But the frog had no sooner gained the water than she crept into the hole. The crow called after her,—

"*Bagatur-Ssedkiltu!* Bagatur-Ssedkiltu, come thou here!"

But the frog answered him,—

"I should be foolish indeed if I came of my own account to give up my sweet life to your voracity. The Three Precious Treasures (²) may decide whether I have so little courage and pride as that!"

So saying, she leapt into a cleft of the rock out of reach of the crow.

Meantime her former tamer had come up, and began searching about, trying to recover her, having bethought him he might incur the King's anger in having

let her go. And when he saw her not he began
digging up the earth and hewing the rock all round
the streamlet.

When the frog saw him digging up the earth and
breaking the rock all round the streamlet, she cried
out to him,—

"Dig not up the source of this spring. The King
of the same hath given me charge over it, and I will
not that thou lay it bare by digging round it." She
said further, "Though now thou art in sorrow and distress, I will presently render thee a gift that shall be a
gift of wonder. Listen and I will tell thee. I am the
daughter of the Serpent-king, reigning over the white
mother-o'-pearl shells([3]). One day I went out to see
the King's daughter bathe, and she, seeing me, sent
and had me fished out of the stream with a mother-
o'-pearl pail, and took me with her."

Meantime, the King began to notice that the parrot
and the frog came no more to entertain him, so he sent
for the tamer, and inquired what had become of his
charges.

"The frog is gone her way in the stream," answered
the man, "and the parrot must have been taken by a
hawk."

The Khan was wroth at this answer, and ordered
that the man should be taken and put to death.

Then came the first of the thirty ministers to the
Khan, saying,—

"If we put this man to death, no more dancers or singers will come any more to this court."

And the Khan answered,—

"It is well spoken; let him not be put to death." He sent him into banishment, however, with three men to see him over the border of his dominions, and a goat to carry his provisions. But he also had him shod with a pair of shoes made out of stone, forbidding him to return until the stone shoes should be worn through.

As soon as his guards had left him, the tamer sat down by the side of the stream, and after soaking the stone shoes with water, rubbed them with a piece of rough stone till they were all in holes. Then he came back to his own country, with the goat that had carried his provisions, and made him dig roots out of the earth for him to eat. And he lived upon the roots.

One day he saw an owl flying by, which held in its mouth a white serpent. The tamer knew him to be a serpent-prince, and to make the owl release him, took off his girdle and held it in his mouth, after the manner in which the owl held the serpent, and, standing over against the owl, he cried out, "The thing held in the mouth burns with fire!" at the same time dropping the girdle from his mouth suddenly, as if it scorched him.

When the owl had heard his words, she also let the serpent fall out of her beak.

Then the tamer took up the serpent, and put it on a piece of grass near, and covered it with his cap. He had hardly done so, when there came up out of the water a whole train of princes of the serpent-dæmons, riding on horses, on to the bank of the stream, where they dispersed themselves, searching about every where for the white serpent, which was a serpent-prince.

After they had searched long and found nothing, there came up out of the water, riding on a white horse, a white serpent, having on a white mantle and a white crown (¹).

He, seeing the tamer, said to him,—

"I am the Serpent-king, reigning over the white mother-o'-pearl shells. I have lost my son. O man! say if thine eyes have lighted on him."

The tamer asked of him, "What was thy son like?"

And the Serpent-king answered,—

"Even a white serpent was my son."

"If that is so," answered the tamer, "thy son is with me. Even now a mighty Garuda-bird had him in his beak and prepared to devour him. But I, who am a tamer of all living creatures, knew how to entreat him so that he should give the white serpent up to me."

Then he lifted his cap from off the grass and delivered the White Serpent-prince unto the Serpent-king, his father.

The Serpent-king was full of delight at getting back his son, and called a great feast of all his friends and acquaintance among the serpent-princes to celebrate his joy. And the tamer he took into his palace, and he dwelt with him.

After a time, however, the man desired to return to his own country, and spoke to the Serpent-king to let him go. Then said the White Serpent-king, who reigned over the white mother-o'-pearl shells—

"Behold, as thou hast dealt well with me, I will not let thee go without bestowing somewhat on thee, and telling thee what good fortune shall befall thee. Behold these two times hast thou served me well; and long time have I sought thee to reward thee, for first thou didst release my daughter, the Princess Gold-frog, from servitude, putting her out of the window of the palace, and now thou hast restored my son, even mine only son, to me. Know, therefore, that of thee shall be born four sons, every one of whom shall be a king in Gambudvîpa. Nevertheless, seeing it will befall that, ere that time come, thou shalt pass through a season of trial, and be in need, I give unto thee this *Mirjalaktschi* (⁵) and this wand. Whensoever thou wantest for food, touch but this *Mirjalaktschi* with the wand, and immediately every kind of viand shall be spread out before thee." .

Then he brought him up to the edge of the water to let him depart, giving him a brightly painted *Mirja-*

laktschi and a mother-o'-pearl wand; moreover, he gave him a red-coloured dog also.

Then the White Serpent-king went his way down under the water again to his palace, and the tamer turned him towards his own country, the red-coloured dog following behind him.

"Thus was the promise of Princess Goldfrog fulfilled," exclaimed the Khan.

And as he let these words escape him, the Siddhî-kür replied, "Forgetting his health, the Well-and-wise-walking Khan hath opened his lips." And with the cry, "To escape out of this world is good!" he sped him through the air, swift out of sight.

TALE XXIII.

Wherefore the Well-and-wise-walking Khan once more took the way of the cool grove ; and having taken the Siddhî-kür, and bound him in his bag, as at other times, he brought him along to the great Master and Teacher Nâgârg'una. As they went along by the way, the Siddhî-kür told him this tale, of how it fell out with the red-coloured dog, saying,—

WHAT BECAME OF THE RED-COLOURED DOG.

When it was evening they went, the tamer and the red-coloured dog together, into a grove to sleep, and by day they journeyed on. One day, when they made their evening halt, the red-coloured dog laid aside her dog's form, and appeared as a beautiful maiden, clothed in shining robes of white, and with a crown of white flowers on her head; and, when the tamer saw her, he loved her.

Moreover, she said to him, "Me hath the Serpent-king given to thee to be thy wife." And he married her, and she was his wife. Every morning she put on the form of the red-coloured dog again, and they journeyed on. One morning, however, before she put on the dog form, she went down to bathe in the river, and while she was gone, the man burnt the dog form, saying, "Now must she always remain as a beautiful woman."

But when she came up from bathing, and found what he had done, she said, with many other moving and sorrowful words, "Now can I no more walk with thee, and share thy wanderings."

So they remained in that place.

Again, another day she went down to bathe in the river, and as she bathed some of her hairs falling off, were carried down the stream.

At a place near the mouth of the stream, a maid belonging to the service of the Khan had gone down to fetch water, and these hairs came out of the water clinging to her water-jar. And as the hairs were wonderful to behold, being adorned with the five colours and the seven precious things (¹), she wondered at them, and brought them to the Khan for him to see.

The Khan had no sooner examined them than he came to this conclusion, saying,—

"Somewhere along the course of this stream it is evident there must be living a surpassingly beautiful woman. Only to such an one could these hairs belong."

Then he called the captain of his guard, and bid him

take of armed men as many as ever he would, and by all means to bring unto him the woman to whom these hairs belonged. Thus he instructed him.

But the woman had knowledge of what was going forward, and she came weeping to her husband, and showed the thing to him, "And now," she said, "the Khan's soldiers will surround the place, neither is there any way of escape, nor any that can withstand the orders of the Khan. Hadst thou not burnt the red dog form, then had I had a means of refuge."

Then the man wept too, and would have persuaded her to escape, but she said,—

"It skills not, for they would pursue us and overtake us, and put you to death out of revenge. By going at their command without resistance, at least they will save you alive."

While they were speaking the captain of the Khan's guard came with his men-at-arms, and posted them about the place. Then, while they were taking their measures to completely surround the inclosure that the woman might by no means break through, she said to her husband,—

"The only remedy that remains is that thou wait quietly for the space of a year, and in the meantime I will arrange a stratagem. Then on the fifteenth day of the month *Pushja* ('), I will go up on to the edge of a mountain with the Khan. But thou, meantime, make to thyself a garment of magpie's feathers, then come

and dance before us, in it; and I will invent some
plan for escaping with thee."

Thus she advised him. And the soldiers came and
took her to the Khan; the husband making no resistance, even as she had counselled him.

Also, he let a year pass according to her word; but
being alone, and in distress for the loss of his wife, he
neglected his work and his business, and came to
poverty. Then bethought he him of the word of the
White Serpent-king, saying, " There shall come a season
when thou shalt be in poverty." So he took out his
Mirjalaktschi, and touched it with the mother-o'pearl-
wand, and it gave him all manner of food, and he lived
in abundance. Then he set snares, and caught mag-
pies, exceeding many, and made to himself a covering
out of their feathers, and practised himself in dancing
grotesque dances.

On the fifteenth day of the month *Pushja*, the
Khanin arranged to go with the Khan to visit the
mountain. On the same day the husband came there
also, dressed even as she had directed him, in a costume
made of magpie's feathers. Having first attracted the
attention of the Khan by his extraordinary appearance,
he began dancing and performing ludicrous antics.

The Khan, who was by this time tired of the songs
of the foreign minstrel, nor had found any to replace
the gold frog and the parrot, observed him with great
attention. But the Khanin seeing how exact and ex-

pert her husband was in following out her advice for recovering her, felt quite happy as she had never done before since she was taken from him; and to encourage him to go on dancing she laughed loud and merrily.

The Khan was astonished, when he saw her laugh thus, and he said, "Although for a whole year past I have devised every variety of means to endeavour to make thee at least bear some appearance of cheerfulness, it has profited nothing; for thou hast sat and mourned all the day long, nor has any thing had power to divert thee. Yet now that this man, who is more like a monster than a man, has come and made all these ridiculous contortions, at this thou hast laughed!"

And she, having fixed in her own mind the part she had to play, continued laughing, as she answered him,—

"All this year, even as thou sayest, thou hast laboured to make me laugh; and now that I have laughed, it would seem almost that it pleaseth thee not."

And the Khan hasted to make answer, "Nay, foɪ in that thou hast laughed thou hast given me pleasure; but in that it was at a diversion which another prepared for thee, and not I, this is what pleased me not. I would that thou hadst laughed at a sport devised for thee by me."

Then answered the Khanin, "Wouldst thou in very

Q

truth prepare for me a sport at which I would surely
laugh?"

And the Khan hasted to make answer, "That
would I in very truth; thou knowest that there is
nothing I would not do to fulfil thy bidding and
desire."

"If that be so," replied the Khanin. "Know that
there is one thing at which I would laugh in right
good earnest; and that is, if it were thou who worest
this monstrous costume. That this fellow weareth it is
well enough, but we know not how monstrous he may
be by nature. But if thou, O Khan, who art so comely
of form and stature, didst put it on, then would it be a
sight to make one laugh indeed."

And her words pleased the Khan. So he called the
man aside into a solitary place that the courtiers and
people might not see what he did, and so become a
laughing-stock to them. Then he made the man exchange his costume of magpie's feathers against his
royal attire and mantle, and went to dance before the
Khanin, bidding the man take his place by her side.

No sooner, however, did the Khanin see him thus
caught in her snare than she returned with her own
husband, habited in the Khan's royal habiliments, to
the palace. She also gave strict charge to her guard,
saying,—

"That juggler who was dancing just now upon the
hill, dressed in a fantastic costume of magpie's feathers,

has the design of giving himself out for being the Khan. Should he make the attempt, set dogs([3]) on him and drive him forth out of the country. Of all things, on peril of your lives, suffer him not to enter the palace."

Scarcely had she made an end of speaking and conducted her husband into the palace, when the Khan appeared, still wearing the magpie costume, because the Khanin's husband had gone off with her, wearing his royal habiliments, and would have made his way to his own apartments; but the guards seeing him, and recognizing the man in the magpie disguise the Khanin had designated, ordered him out.

The Khan asserted his khanship, and paid no heed to the guards; but the more he strove to prove himself the Khan, the more were the guards convinced he was the man the Khanin had ordered them to eject, and they continued barring the way against him and preventing his ingress. Then he grew angry and began to strive against them till they, wearied with his resistance, called out the dogs and set them on him.

The dogs, taking him for a monstrous wild bird, eagerly ran towards him, so that he was forced to turn and flee that he might by any means save his life. But the dogs were swifter than he and overtook him, and, springing upon him, tore him in pieces and devoured him.

Thus the husband of the Khanin became installed in all his governments and possessions.

Moreover, that night there were born to the Khan

four sons, who were every one exceeding great rulers
in Gambudvîpa, even as the White Serpent-king, reigning over the white mother-o'-pearl shells, had foretold.

The eldest of these four was renowned as the spiritual ruler of all India (⁴). In one night he translated
all the sacred books into a thousand different languages
for the use of *devas* and men, and in one other night he
erected a hundred thousand sacred temples all over
his dominions.

The brother next to him was endowed with all kinds
of power and strength in his earliest youth, and with
every capacity. This Prince was renowned as ruler of
the Mongols by the name of *Barin Tochedaktschi
Erdektu* (⁵), for so expert and mighty was he in the
use of the bow that if he shot his arrow at four men
standing side by side together, every one of them was
certain to fall to the earth, transfixed through the
centre of the heart.

The next brother raised up to himself a mighty host of
a hundred thousand men by pulling out a single hair of
his head, and he led them forth to battle, and was known
to the whole earth by the name of Gesser-Khan (⁶).

The fourth brother fitted out four caravans of mer-
chandise all in one day, and sent them forth to the
four quarters of heaven. By these means he obtained
possession of the All-desire-supplying talisman, Tschin-
tâmani, and was Ruler of the Treasures of the earth,
with the title of *Barss-Irbiss* (⁷), Shah of Persia.

Conclusion of the Adventures of the Well-and-wise-walking Khan.

The Well-and-wise-walking Khan listened till the Siddhî-kür had made an end of speaking, but opened never his lips. Though he heaped up wonders upon wonders as a man heaps up faggots on a funeral pile, yet spake he never a word.

Therefore the sack remained fast bound with the cord of a hundred threads of different colours, nor could the Siddhî-kür find means to escape out of the same; but the Well-and-wise-walking Khan bore him along to his journey's end, even to the feet of his great Master and Teacher Nâgârg'una.

And Nâgârg'una took the mighty dead, even him endowed with perfection of capacity and fulness of power, and laid him up in the cool grove on the shining mountain of Southern India, venerated by all men as the Siddhitu-Altan even unto this day.

By this means also great prosperity crowned the whole land of Gambudvîpa. To all the men thereof were given knowledge and length of days. The laws were obeyed and religion honoured, and happiness had her abode among them.

THE SAGA OF ARDSCHI-BORDSCHI AND VIKRAMÂDITJA'S THRONE.

HISTORICAL NOTICE OF VIKRAMÂDITJA.

The name of Vikramâditja is a household word in the epic mythology of India; and freely it seems to have been adopted by or conferred upon those who emulated the heroic acts of some first great bearer. But as the legendary chroniclers are more occupied with extolling the merits of their favourites, than with establishing their place in the page of history, it becomes a well-nigh impossible task for the modern investigator to trace out and fix the times and seasons of all those who, either in fact or in fiction, have borne the name, or even to distinguish with certainty how many there have been, still less, what are the peculiar deeds and attributes of each.

A writer ([1]), who has examined painstakingly into the matter, tells us that the popular mind is only conscious of *one* Vikramâditja, so that without troubling itself to consider the insufficiency of one life to embrace all the aggregate of wonderful works it has to tell of him, it supposes him rather to have had a prolonged or recurring existence as marvellous in itself as the events of which it is composed. On the other hand, he found that native writers made out the number variously from four to nine, though he could not find that they determined with precision the existence of more than two. An additional difficulty arises from this, that the very distinctive super-appellations derived from their deeds by heroes bearing the name seem to have passed over to others along with the name itself; as, for instance, *Gardabharápa* = " donkey-form," given to one of them on account of his being temporarily transformed into a donkey by his father; the name of *Sakjaditja* is similarly given indiscriminately to others who lived at different periods, though the origin of the word can only be found in an exploit of one of them, who with the aid of Shêsa, the serpent-god, destroyed an oppressor named Sâkja ([2]). While the name Vikramâditja itself seems rather a descriptive appellation than a name, being composed of the two Sanskrit words, *vikrama* and *áditja*—the sun, or bright exposition of heroic virtue.

You may form some idea of the uncertainty thus created if you imagine the Roman historians to have been silent, and suppose, that nothing remained to us of the lives of the Emperors, for instance, but certain panegyrics of bards and traditions of the people, eked out by a little scanty assistance from inscriptions and coins, and unsystematic and untrustworthy chronicles.

You may then conceive, how with no fixed dates marked out for determining the period of the reign of each, and no literary criterion to distinguish incongruities, a fertile imagination, aiming rather at exciting admiration than conveying information, could run riot with the mass of the acts and adventures, the victories and achievements of the whole number, because the names or titles of " Augustus " and " Cæsar " could be applied to many or all.

There is also the further difficulty that the heroic myths of India have travelled on from tribe to tribe, and from province to province (³), the character of the hero and his exploits incurring many transformations and fresh identifications under the process (⁴).

Not to go into the elaborate discussion which the intricate study of the Indian dynasties has called forth, it may suffice in this place to observe that, in the absence of more regular records, the greatest aid we have in arriving at some fixed knowledge of the events of a remote age in India is derived from inscriptions and coins (⁵). And, as a specimen of the thought and care that has been brought to bear on the matter, to specify the interesting circumstance connected with this particular instance, that the nearest approach to a satisfactory determination of the date of the chief bearer of the name of Vikramâditja that is likely to be attained has been arrived at from the observation of the influence of Greek art on the execution of certain of the coins ([6]) which have been preserved and collected, connecting them with the period succeeding Alexander's invasion. A careful collation of these specimens with the most authentic list of the kings has given tolerable authority for asserting that the date of 57 B.C. may be assumed for the date of the first historic ([7]) Vikramâditja, whose chief honour lies in having overcome and superseded the descendants of the foreign race of rulers who had been in possession of his native country before his time. In pursuing the history of his dynasty, however, the help so far afforded by the coins ceases, and the only written records of him are the collections of popular fables of his deeds. Only one of these collections, and of that the date is unknown, has any pretension to rank as history; and even this is full of wonders and manifest exaggerations. Its author, Ravipati Gurumûrti by name, informs the reader, however, that he had brought together and compared many Sanskrit manuscripts, and sifted much oral tradition in its compilation.

According to this account, Vikramâditja was the son of a Brahman named Kandrasarman, the fourth son of Vishnusarman, inhabiting a city called Vedanârâjanapura, a name not found in any other writer. Dissatisfied with the ordinary occupations on which he was kept employed by his parents, he ran away from home and after many adventures came to Uggajini, where he married the daughter of Dhvagakîrti, the reigning sovereign of Malâva ([8]). His son Vikramâditja was the more celebrated hero, and according to another MS. (quoted in W. Taylor's Examination of the Mackenzie MSS.) the former of these two was not called Vikramâditja at all, but Govinda.

Feeling an interior conviction of his great destiny, Vikramâditja (the son) determined on obtaining supernatural aid in fulfilling it; and, with this view, he devoted himself to prayer and retirement, until he had obtained an apparition of the goddess Kali, the chosen wife of Shiva, who gave him the solemn promise that he should be invulnerable to all enemies with the exception of one who should be supernaturally born; and that he should rejoice in a happy reign of a thousand years ([9]). By the shrewd advice of his half-brother Bhatti, whom he made his minister, he contrived to obtain out of this promise double the length of years actually named, for he arranged to reign for only six months at a time, spending six months in contemplation in the jungle, so that it took two thousand years to make up a thousand years' reign ([10]). In another account, he is made to reign 949 years; and, on the other hand, in another ([11]) only a hundred and six years.

It might have been expected that a people who raised themselves at so remote a period to a comparatively high degree of civilization, and in other departments of mental exertion distinguished themselves in so marked a manner, should of all things

have possessed a copious historical literature, but there
are other things to take into account which explain
why the contrary is the case ([12]). A German writer ([13])
has put the case very summarily. "Their religion," he
says, "has destroyed all history for the Hindus. They
are taught to look on life as a mere passing condition
of probation and sorrow, and its incidents, consequently, as unworthy to be recorded." But this is
a hardly fair statement, and only true to a certain
extent. Benfey ([14]) perhaps reaches nearer the mark
when he says,—"The life of man was for them but a
small portion of the immense divine life pervading the
whole universe. It lay, so to speak, rolled up in a
fold of the mantle of the godhead. Viewed thus, history became a theme so vast that the infinitesimal
human element of it was lost to view. Theosophies,
idealisms, allegories, myths, filled up the place of the
record of the doings of mortals." Troyer([15]) takes nearly
the same view, but further calls attention to the influence exercised by the religious teaching concerning
re-births and transmigration of souls in working
against history becoming a science. Historical cha-
racters lost their positive identity, and the effect a
man's acts under a previous existence were taught to
exercise on his fate diminished the responsibility and
merit of, and consequently the interest in, his actions.

To arrive at a more exact view, however, it is necessary to distinguish between the parts which Brahman

and Buddhist teaching have respectively to bear in the matter. The Brahmanical castes became subdivided into groups composed of many families, with no common founder, the preservation of whose name and deeds would have afforded an instigation to building up the materials of a national history. Only at a comparatively late period some traditions were kept up of the heads of these groups, but this in such a way as to serve rather to throw back attention on to the past and restrain it from the contemplation and record of contemporary events. Caste took the place of country, and the interest of the individual was drawn away from national to local interest.

Next, the history of the gods possessed a much higher importance in their eyes than that of the kings of the earth, while at the same time the humanistic conception of their character rendered the myths concerning them of a nature to clash with and supersede the records of earthly notabilities. Their wars and their loves and their undertakings were indeed often superhuman in scale, but they were yet for the most part no more exalted in nature, than the occupations of men. But from this habit of making their divinities actors in gigantic human incidents, their mind grew used to regard the marvellous and unreal as possible and true, and was at no pains to fix any data with exactness.

Then their contemplative mode of life kept them

out of actual contact with what was going on in the world around them. Most Brahmans lived engrossed by the service of the temple, or else occupied with their families or their disciples. Very few are the examples of their acting as ministers or judges, or taking any part in public life.

Further, many elements of history may be said to have scarcely existed at all. All changes of manners and customs, all growth of arts and sciences, were impeded by the appointment of fixed laws, and remained pretty much the same for long periods.

Again, the subdivision of the country into multitudinous governments, and the comparatively short duration of any large union of them under one dynasty —as, for instance, the Maurja or the Gupta—further weakened any tendency to the formation of a national spirit. The best preserved attempts at history are those of Lankâ (Ceylon), Orissa, Cashmere, the Dekhan, and other kingdoms or provinces which have all along preserved their identity. Where one country fell under the empire of another its history naturally lapsed in that of the conquering state, or became altogether lost; and as such annexations were mostly effected by violence, it is only to be expected that the conqueror should discourage any thing that would keep up the memory of the rulers he had superseded. The Chronicle of Cashmere, called the Râga Taraginî, or "Stream of Kings," is perhaps the best written. It was compiled by Kalhana Pandita, who lived, however, as late as 1150 of our era, and is carried down to the year 1125. He appears to have laboured to make it as complete and reliable as the vague and scattered materials at his disposal admitted; yet so little was even he capable of appreciating the value of accuracy, that he ascribes to a reign (removed from his own date by no more remote period than 600 years) a length of 300 years. And this is but a small fable by comparison with others of his statements. This Chronicle possesses the peculiarity of being almost the only work of an historical nature compiled under Brahman influence.

The only work which has any pretension to universality in its scope is the *Karnâtaka Râgakula*. But though it begins with an account of the creation of the world and the incarnations of Vishnu, and narrates the deeds of typical heroes like Pandarva and Vikramâditja, it yet only contains the history of the Dekhan, and is, after all, a modern work edited at the bidding of English rulers. The only earlier work of the same character is one professing to give the general history of India from Ashokja to Pratîtasena, written in the fourteenth century. This, however, is believed not to have been compiled by a native Indian, and is, at any rate, not the work of a Brahman, though possibly of a Buddhist.

In the matter of historical compilation we have in general more to thank Buddhism than Brahmanism for.

The simple *Sûtra*, or colloquies of Shâkjamuni with his
disciples, written in *masajja*, a poetical prose pleasingly
broken into a sort of cadence, themselves form a kind
of history of the country contained in this sort of
memoir of its great religionist. The simple *Sûtra*
are of two classes. The first class consists of an
account of Buddha's own wanderings and personal
dealings both with his disciples and others, and were
probably compiled([16]) by the first great *Sangha*, or
Synod, within 100 years after his death([17]), though
bearing marks in many places of having been recon-
structed at a later period. The other class takes notice
of events and persons belonging to a subsequent
period. Besides these there are the *Máhajána-Sûtra*,
a more detailed and developed continuation of the
same species of chronicle, but bearing marks of having
been compiled at a much more advanced date still, for
they introduce ideas which do not belong to the early
teaching of Buddhism, but to a very late development.

These writings possess great historical importance,
but yet are by no means free from the faults of inac-
curacy of date and arrangement; of idealizations of the
persons treated of; the introduction of fabulous incidents, transmigrations, and such like. The very desire
of the Buddhists to make their records more complete
and useful than the Brahmans', often led to additional
complications, because it induced all· manner of inter-
polations—as for instance, whole series of kingly

personages, the account of whose lives is not even to
be set down to the exaggerations of ill-preserved
tradition, but to pure fabrication of the imagination.

More reliance on the whole is to be placed on the
great epic poems, and, chiefly, the *Purâna* and *Mahâ
Bhârata*.

The works which we now find extant, with the title
of *Purâna* (ancient)—eighteen in number,—are, however, at best but·the reproduction of six older compilations, either collected from the recitations of *Sûtas*
(bards), or themselves reproductions of · still older
compilations, which have probably perished for ever.
They contain pretty well all that is known concerning
the origin, mode of life, heroic deeds, and ways of
theological thought, of those Indian nations who
acknowledged either Vishnu or Shiva for their highest
god; and traces are to be distinguished by which the
statement of earlier and purer belief has been distorted or biassed according to the tenets of the later
compiler.

The *Mahâ Bhârata* concerns itself more exclusively
with the deeds of the gods and heroes, and is itself
often referred to in the *Purânas*. Both of them bear
witness that it was the frequent custom, on occasions
of great gatherings of the people for public sacrifices
and popular festivals, and also in the places of retirement of religious teachers round whom disciples
gathered, that the stories of gods and heroes should

be sung or told, and eagerly listened to. Such stories were collected into the *Mahá Bhárata* by *Vjása* = "the Arranger" (who also occupied himself with the recompilation of the Véda), son of *Satjavati* = "the truthful one," daughter to Vasu, king of Magadha. Vasu had conferred great benefits on his subjects, and was held in proportionate honour. His great work was the construction of a canal, of which mythology has thus preserved the memory. The mountain-god, Kôlâhola, fell in love with the stream-goddess, Shirktimatî. As she sported past the tower of Kêdi, he barred her further progress by here damming her course with a mountain. Vasu saw her distress, and came to rescue her by striking the mountain with his foot, and thus delivering her from her imprisonment. The goddess in gratitude devoted her twin children to his service. He made her son the leader of his armies, and married her daughter Girikâ, by whom he also had twins—a son, whom he made king of Matsja; and a daughter, Satjavati, who, as we have seen, married the father of Vjâsa. This was the Rishi Parâsara who obtained for her the name of *Gandha,* and the corresponding character of "sweet-scented," as heretofore, from the occupation to which she had been devoted by her father of ferrying people across the Jamuna, she had acquired a smell of fish. She is also called, *Gandha-kali* = "the sweet-scented dark one," which latter appellation is explained by the story that she made

R

Parâsara observe that the other Rishis were in the
habit of watching her from the other side of the river,
on which he constructed a mist to conceal her, or make
her "dark" to them. Why "the Arranger" of legends
should have "the truthful one" ascribed to him for his
mother, is easy enough to see. Parâsara was reckoned
his father because he was the inventor of chronology,
which ought to precede any attempt to make chronicles
out of traditions. The legend further says that Para-
sâra made acquaintance with *Satjavati* while on a
pilgrimage, which may be taken as an embodiment of
the fact that it was such gatherings which afforded
opportunity for collecting *Sagas*.

Of somewhat similar nature is the *Râmâjana*—a
collection of *Sagas* concerning Rama, sometimes called
the brother, and sometimes an incarnation of Vishnu,
but also containing stories of other gods, as well as a
variety of quasi-religious episodes. While displaying
the usual exaggerations common to the Sagas of all
nations, these Indian Sagas have one leading peculiarity
in the frequent *Avatára*, or incorporation of Vishnu or
Rama in the persons of their heroes ([18]).

Lassen ([19]) reckons both the Mahâ Bhârata and the
Râmâjana to have been compiled about 300—50 B.C;
but it is impossible to fix the dates of any of them with
absolute certainty. One theory for arriving at it is,
that they possess strong inherent evidence of being
Brahmanical productions; and as they contain no

allusion to so great an event as the establishment of Buddhism, while they yet make allusions to certain predictions of the wane of Brahmanism (seemingly suggested by details of the mode of the sudden spread of. the teaching of Shâkjamuni), it may be inferred that the latest date for their compilation (which in any case must have extended over a prolonged period) would be coeval with the period of the greatest development in Central India of the latter school.

It is evident, however, that none of these poems are of a nature to supply any sound basis for the historiographer. The very lists of the kings that they supply, carry with them inherent evidence of untrustworthiness in the readiness with which recourse is had to the introduction of supernatural means for supplying missing links in the fabulous periods of their chronology.

In the tenth century and later, several Muhammedan writers undertook the history of India; but they are very untrustworthy. For this place, it may suffice to mention that, by the most important of them, Vikramâditja is made out to be a grandson of Porus, and his name transformed into that of Barkamaris ([20]).

I will now give you a specimen of what are considered the purely legendary accounts of Vikramâditja's origin, and you will see that they are barely more extravagant than the historical one I have introduced above ([21]).

In a jungle ([22]) situated between the rivers Subhra-
matî and Mahi, in Gurgâramandala, lived the Rishi
Tâmralipta, who gave his daughter Tamrasena for a
wife to King Sadasvasena. They lived happily, and
had a family of six sons, but only one daughter, Madanrekhâ. One day, when a servant of theirs named
Devasarman was working in the forest, he heard the
voice of some invisible being speaking to him, and
bidding him go and demand for it the hand of Madanrekhâ in marriage. When he hesitated, not daring to
ask so great a matter of his master, the voice threatened
him with fearful penalties if he failed to obey its behest.
As the voice continued day after day to admonish him,
he at last begged his master to come and listen to it
for himself; who, recognizing it for that of King Gandharva, whom Indra had transformed into an ass, he felt
constrained to comply, and he accordingly bestowed
his daughter on him. Though proud of the alliance of
so great a king as Gandhârva, Tâmrasena was nevertheless distressed that her daughter's husband should
wear so ungainly an appearance. What was her joy
when she one day discovered that, whenever he went
to visit her, he left his donkey's form outside the door,
and appeared like other men. She was not slow to
take advantage of the circumstance by burning the
donkey's form : the spell was thus destroyed, and
Gandharva delivered from the operation of the curse.
After a time they had a son, whom Gandharva desired

his wife to call Vikramâditja, telling her at the same time that her handmaid would also have a son, who was to be called Bhartrihari, and who should devote himself to his service. Having uttered these counsels, he went up to the deva's paradise. Meantime, Madanrekhâ, having heard that her father designed to kill the infant, delivered it to the care of a gardener's wife, with the charge to conceal it, and then put an end to her own life. The gardener's wife fled with the young prince to Uggajini, where he passed his youth. The incidents of the burning of. a form temporarily laid aside, of danger threatening the life of the infant, of a flight from his birthplace, and of a half-brother, in some way inferior to himself, yet devoted to him, pervade, not only both these accounts, but also the more detailed legend which is to follow in the text.

While all this uncertainty surrounds the circumstances of Vikramâditja's birth, his mode of attaining the throne, and the extent and even the locality of his dominions, are narrated with equal diversity; while, though an important era still in use is dated from him, extending from 57 B.C. to 319 A.C. when commences the Ballabhi-Gupta dynasty, the particular event by which he deserved so distinguished a commemoration has been by no means determined with certainty([23]).

In a version of his story called Vikramakaritra, it is said simply, that King Prasena of Uggajinî dying without heirs, Vikramâditja was chosen king ([24]). Ac-

cording to another, the last king of the Greco-Indian
dynasty abdicated in his favour out of disgust with life
after the death of his wife. According to the legends
a *Vetála*([25]) obtained possession of the throne and
every night strangled the king, who had been raised
to it in the course of the day by the ministers, untïl
Vikramâditja undertook to maintain himself in power,
and succeeded in propitiating the *Vetála*. It is easy
to read under cover of this imagery the original fact
of a hero delivering his people from an oppressor.

What people or country it was that Vikramâditja
delivered is difficult to decide, as he is named in the
sagas of many nations as belonging to each([26]). We
have already seen him seated king in the capital of
Malwa. The more legendary accounts ascribe to him
the widest range of dominion. In the Ganamegaja-
Râgavansâvali([27]) we find him in possession of Bengal,
Hindostan, the Dehkan, and Western India; and in
the *Bhogaprabandha*([28]) he is reckoned conqueror of the
whole of India; while in the Bhavishja-Purâna([29]) it is
told that he had 800 kings tributaries under him,
though whether the list could be authentically made
out is more than questionable. What can be proved
with some certainty is, that he reigned over Malwa,
Cashmere, and Orissa, from which it may perhaps be
inferred that he was also master of the intervening
country—namely, the Punjaub and the eastern portion
of Rajputana([30]).

Besides his glories as a warrior and deliverer of his country, the honour is also ascribed to him of being the patron of science and art. There is reason to think he promoted the study of architecture, though no monuments actually remain which can with certainty be ascribed to his reign. He attracted to his court the most distinguished poets and learned men of his epoch, and an obscure poem concerning nine jewels said to have adorned his throne is generally understood to represent the votaries of a certain cycle of the arts and sciences whom he had under his protection. It is true some of those he is said to have protected are found to have actually lived at a subsequent period; but this is only one of the chronological inaccuracies to which I have already adverted as so common—the fact remains that he did actually promote the pursuit of letters, not only on the testimony of these exaggerated accounts, but also in the improvement which may be observed from his time forward in the condition of public muniments. One of the most fantastic stories about him, in which ([31]) Indra defers to him to decide between the respective claims to perfection in dancing of two *apsarasas*, or nymphs, shows at least that he was considered an authority in matters of taste. The oldest Sanskrit dictionary extant is reckoned the work of Amarasinha, or Amaradeva, his minister, and one of the six of the above-named nine jewels who are believed to have had an historical existence ([32]); in this dictionary the Ram and the Bull of the Zodiac are mentioned in such a way that it may be inferred he was familiar with the present nomenclature of the twelve signs, giving support to the theory that the Greeks received that terminology from the Chaldees, and did not originate it, as was long supposed([33]). An inscription found at Buddha-Gaja, and copied by Wilmot in the year 1783, is preserved in As. Res. i. 284, though the original stone has since been lost, in which a curious legend is told of him, showing that as early as A.D. 948 (fixed by experts for the date of the inscription) an undisputed tradition taught that the oldest Sanskrit dictionary was written by one of the nine jewels of Vikramâditja's throne. This legend says, "This Amaradeva, one of the nine jewels of Vikramâditja's throne, and his first minister, was a man of great talent and learning. Once, when on a journey, this famous man found in the uninhabited forest the place where Vishnu was incarnate in the person of Buddha. Here, therefore, he determined to remain in prayer till Buddha should show himself to him. At the end of twelve years of austerities he heard a voice calling to him and asking what he desired. On his reply that he desired the god should appear to him, he was told that in the then degenerate condition of the world such a favour was impossible; but that he might set up an image of him, which would answer the same purpose as an apparition. In consequence of this communication he erected a

stately temple, which he furnished with images of
Vishnu and his *avatars*, or incarnations, Pândava,
Brahma, Buddha, and the rest.

One of the earliest dramatists of India, Kâlidâsa,
many of whose plays possess great literary merit,—
though some ascribed to him are manifestly by
inferior hands,—may have been, it is thought, one of
those who wrote under Vikramâditja's protection.
In a play called *Maghadúta*, he describes his capital
of Uggajini with an enthusiasm which suggests it was
his own favourite place of residence. His plays contain valuable pictures of the manners of the times. And
from these, among other details, it appears it was not
only considered an indispensable qualification of a well-
bred man, that he should be conversant with the great
heroic poems, but that they were commonly in the
mouth of the people also. Other details imply the
attainment of a degree of civilization and refinement,
which it would probably surprise most of us to find
existing at this date. His two most meritorious pieces
are entitled *Abhignana-Shukuntalá* (" The finding of
Shukuntalâ"), and *Vikramorvashi-Urvashi* ("Urvashi
won by Heroism." We have also three hundred short
poems by Vikramâditja's brother or by some courtier
poet who gave him the honour of the composition ;
these poems display unusual powers of description and
delicacy of sentiment. The first *shataka*, or hundred
poems, is entitled *shringára*, containing love-songs ;

the second, *niti*, on the government of the world; and
the third, *vairágja*, the suppression of human passions.
It is probable that the writer of a justly celebrated
drama named *Mrikkhakatika*, whose name has been
merged in that of King Shûdraka, King of Bidisha
(now Bhilsa), his patron to whose pen he modestly
ascribed his work, lived also not long after this time.

The length of Vikramâditja's reign is as difficult to
fix as any other circumstance of his history, and it is
not clear whether the æra which dates from him was
originally reckoned from the commencement or the end
of his reign; we have already seen the duration which
fable ascribes to it; to this may be added the further
fabled promise which, it is told, the great gods Vishnu
and Shiva made concerning him, that he should come
back to earth in the latter times to deliver his people
from the oppression of the Mussulman invaders, just as
the Mongols expect Ghengis Khan and Timour ([34]), and
just as in Europe similar promises of a future return as
a deliverer linger round the memories of King Arthur,
Charlemagne, and Frederick Barbarossa.

The legend of the Wisdom of Vikramâditja being so
mysteriously connected with his throne, that whosoever
sat on it was endowed with some measure of his excel-
lences; and that the figures with which it was adorned
guarded it from the approach of the unworthy, is
brought forward in the story of more than one Indian
sovereign.　Travelling in the wake of Buddhist litera-

ture, the myth came to the far East, where **Mongolian** bards have worked out of it a *saga* connected with one of their own rulers ([35]), with such variations in the treatment as might be expected at their hands.

THE SAGA OF ARDSCHI-BORDSCHI AND VIKRAMÂDITJA'S THRONE.

THE BOY-KING.

LONG ages ago there lived a mighty king called Ardschi-Bordschi ([1]).

In the neighbourhood of his residence was a hill where the boys who were tending the calves were wont to pass away the time by racing up and down. But they had also another custom, and it was, that whichever of them won the race was king for the day—an ordinary game enough, only that when it was played in this place the Boy-king thus constituted was at once endowed with such extraordinary importance and majesty that every one was constrained to treat him as a real king. He had not only ministers and dignitaries among his playfellows, who prostrated themselves before him and fulfilled all his behests, but whoever passed that way could not choose but pay him homage also.

At last the report of the matter filled all the land, and came also to the ears of the King himself.

Ardschi-Bordschi had the whole matter exposed before him, and he inquired into all the manners and ways of the boys; then he said,—

"If this thing happened every day to one and the same boy, then would I acknowledge in him a *Bodhisattva* (²); but as every day a different boy may win the race, and it would seem that whichever of them is called king is clothed with equal majesty, it appears manifestly to me that the virtue is not in the boy, but in the hill of which he makes his throne."

Nevertheless the matter troubled the King, and he desired above all things to obtain some certain knowledge concerning it, not seeing how to search it out.

<hr />

THE FALSE FRIEND([1])

IN the meantime, it had come to pass that one of Ardschi-Bordschi's subjects had gone out over the sea to search for precious stones. Being detained on his journey beyond the allotted time, he was desirous of making provision for his wife and children whom he had left behind, and, finding that a friend of his company purposed to return home, he trusted to him one of the jewels of which he had become possessed, saying, "When thou comest to the place, deliver this jewel into the hands of my wife, that she may be provided withal until the time of my return. The man, however, sold the jewel and spent the proceeds on his own purposes. When, therefore, the jewel-merchant came home, he inquired of his wife, saying, "By a man named Dsük I sent unto you a jewel so-and-so;" and when he learnt of his wife that the man had brought no jewel, he took the matter before the King. The King commanded the man called Dsük to be brought before him. But the man having got wind that he would have to appear before the King to be judged for the matter, he gave presents to two chief men of the court, and agreed with them, saying, "You will stand witness for me that in presence of you two I delivered the jewel to the man's wife ([2])."

When, therefore, they were all before the King, the King spoke to the man named Dsük, saying, "Did you, or did you not, give the jewel to the man's wife?" And he boldly made answer, "In presence of these two witnesses I delivered the jewel to her;" while the two great men of the court stood forward and deposed, they also, "Yea, O King! even in our presence he delivered over the jewel."

As the King could not gainsay the word of the witnesses, he decided the case according to their testimony, and the man named Dsük was released and went away to his home rejoicing at having been so successful in his stratagem to deceive the King, and the two great men of the court and the jewel-merchant went down every one to his home.

It so happened, however, that their way home lay

past the hill where the Boy-king sat enthroned. Now as they passed by, the four together, the Boy-king sent and called them into his presence, nor could they fail of compliance with his word.

When they had paid him their obeisance, bowing themselves many times before him, the Boy-king, rising in his majesty, thus spoke,—

"The decision of your King is hasty, and can never stand. I will judge your cause. Do you promise to abide by my decision?"

But the majesty of the Boy-king was upon him, and they could not choose but accept.

The Boy-king therefore set the four men apart in four several places, and to each one of them he gave a lump of clay, saying, "Fashion this lump of clay like to the form of the jewel which was sent."

When they had all finished the task, it was found that the model of the man who sent the jewel and that of the man who was the bearer of it were alike; but the two great men of the court, who had never seen the jewel, were thrown into great embarrassment by this means, and their models were neither like those of the sender and bearer, nor were they like each other's.

When the Boy-king saw this he thus pronounced judgment :—

"Because both these men saw and knew the jewel, they could make its image in clay; but it is manifest the two witnesses have never seen the jewel, but have

made up their minds to deceive the King by false testimony.   Such conduct is most unworthy of all in
great men of the King's court."

Then he ordered the two false witnesses and the
man named Dsük to be secured and taken to the King,
all three confessing their crime; and he sent with them
this declaration, written in due form of law :—

"According to the principles of earthly might and
the sacred maxims of religion hast thou not decided.
O Ardschi-Bordschi! thus should not an upright and
noble ruler deal.   Unless it is given thee to discern
good from evil, truth from falsehood, it were better
thou shouldst lay aside thy kingly dignity.   But
if thou desirest to remain king, then judge nothing
without duly investigating the matter, even as I."

With such a letter the Boy-king sent the prisoners
to Ardschi-Bordschi.

When the King read the letter, he exclaimed, "What
manner of boy is this who writes thus to the King?
He must be a being highly endowed with wisdom.   If
it was the same boy who appeared every day so gifted,
I should hold him to be a *Bodhisattva,* or indeed a very
Buddha; but as on different days different boys attain
to the same sagacity, the source must remain one and
the same for all.   Shall it not be that in the foundations of their hill or mound is some *stupa*(³), where
Buddhas or *Bodhisattvas* have propounded sacred
teaching to men?   Or shall it be that there lies hidden

therein some jewel('), gifted to impart wisdom to mortals? In some such way, of a certainty, the spot is endowed with singular gifts."

Thus he spoke, and concluded the affair of the jewel in accordance with the Boy-king's judgment, delivering the two witnesses over to punishment, and condemning the man named Dsük to pay double the value of the jewel to the merchant whom he had defrauded.

THE PRETENDED SON.

KING Ardschi-Bordschi's minister had one only son. This son went out to the wars, and returned home again after two years' absence. Just while the minister was engaged with preparations for a festival of joy to celebrate the return of his son, there appeared before him suddenly another son in all respects exactly like his own. In form, colour, and gait there was no sort of difference to be discerned between them. Moreover, the horses they rode, their clothing, their quivers, their mode of speech, were so perfectly similar that none of the minister's friends, nor the very mother of the young man, nor yet his wife herself, could take upon them to decide which of the two was his very son.

It was not very long before there was open feud in the house between the two; both youths declaring with equal energy and determination, " These are *my* parents,

S

my wife, *my* children. . . ." Finding the case quite
beyond his own capacity to decide the minister brought
the whole before the King.   As the King found himself similarly embarrassed he sent and called all the
relations; and to the mother he said, "Which of these
two is your son?" and to the wife, "Which of these
two is your husband?" and to the children, "Which
of these two is your father?"   But they all answered
with one consent, "We are not in a condition to decide,
for no man can tell which is which."

   Then King Ardschi-Bordschi thought within himself,
"How shall I do to bring this matter to an end?   It
is clear not even the man's nearest relations can tell
which of these two is the right man; how then can I,
who never saw either of them before?   Yet if I let
them go without deciding the matter, the Boy-king
will send and tell me I am not gifted to discern the
true from the false, and counsel me before all the people
to lay aside my kingly dignity.   Now then, therefore,
let us prove the matter even as the Boy-king would have
it proved.   We will call the men hither before us, and
will examine them concerning their family and ancestors; he that is really the man's son will know the
names of his generations, but he that merely pretendeth,
shall he not be a stranger to these things?"   So he
sent and called the men before him again separately
and inquired of them, saying, "Tell me now the names
of thy father, and grandfather, and great-grandfather

up to the earliest times, so shall I distinguish which of you is really this man's son." But the one of them who had come the last from the wars, was no man but a *Schimnu* [1], who had taken the son's form to deceive his parents, he by his demoniacal knowledge could answer all these things so that the very father was astonished to hear him, while the real son could go no farther back than to give the name of his grandfather.

When Ardschi-Bordschi therefore found how much the *Schimnu* exceeded the real son in knowledge of his family, he pronounced that he was the rightful son, and the wife and parents and friends and all the people praised the sagacity of the king in settling the matter.

Thus the *Schimnu* was taken home with joy in the midst of the gathering of the family, and the real son not knowing whither to betake himself, followed afar off, mourning as he went.

It so happened that their homeward way lay past the mound, where the Boy-king sat enthroned, who, hearing the feet of many people, and the voice of the minister's son wailing behind, called them all unto him, nor could they fail of compliance with the word of the Boy-king in his majesty.

When they had paid him their obeisance, bowing themselves many times before him, the Boy-king, rising in his majesty, thus spoke :—

" The decision of your King is hasty, and can never

s 2

stand. I will judge your cause. Do you promise to abide by my decision?"

Then they could not choose but accept; and he made them state their whole case before him, and explain how Ardschi-Bordschi had decided, which when he had heard, he said,—

"I will set you the proof of whether of you two is the rightful son; let there be brought me hither a water-jug." And one of the boys who stood in waiting that day upon the Boy-king's throne, ran and fetched a water-jug, holding in measure about a pint.

When he had brought it, the Boy-king ordered him to place it before the throne; then said he, "Let me see now whether of you two can enter into this water-jug; then shall we know which is the rightful son."

Then the rightful son turned away sorrowful and mourned more than before, "For," said he, "how should I ever find place for so much as my foot in this water-jug?"

But the *Schimnu*, by his demoniacal power easily transformed himself, and entered the jug.

The Boy-king, therefore, no sooner saw him enclosed in the water-jug, than he bound him fast within it by sealing the mouth with the diamond-seal, which he might not pass (²), undismayed by the appalling howling with which the *Schimnu* rent the air, at finding himself thus taken captive.

Thus bound he sent him back to Ardschi-Bordschi, together with all the family concerned in the case, and with them this declaration written in due form of law :—

" According to the principles of earthly might, and the sacred maxims of religion hast thou not decided, O Ardschi-Bordschi ! Thus should not an upright and noble ruler deal. The wife and children of thine own subject hast thou given over to the power of a wicked *Schimnu;* and sent the rightful and innocent away lamenting. Unless it is given thee to discern good from evil, truth from falsehood, it were better thou shouldst lay aside thy kingly dignity. But if thou desirest to remain king, then judge nothing without duly investigating the matter even as I."

With such a letter the Boy-king sent the men back to Ardschi-Bordschi.

When the King read the letter, he exclaimed, " What manner of boy is this, who writes thus to the King ? He must be a being highly endowed with wisdom. If it was the same boy who appeared every day so gifted, I should hold him to be a *Bodhisattva* or indeed a very Buddha; but as on different days different boys attain to the same sagacity, the source must remain one and the same for all. Shall it not be that on the foundations of this hill or mound is a *stupa*, where Buddhas or *Bodhisattvas* have propounded sacred teaching to men. Or shall it be that there lies hidden therein some treasure gifted to impart wisdom to mortals? In some way of a certainty the spot is endowed with singular gifts."

Thus he spoke; and concluded the affair of the two sons in accordance with the Boy-king's judgment, giving over the rightful one to his family, and delivering the *Schimnu* to be burned.

ARDSCHI-BORDSCHI DISCOVERS VIKRAMÂDITJA'S THRONE.

ARDSCHI-BORDSCHI could not rest, because of this matter of the Boy-king. "For," said he, "if there is in my dominions a *stupa* where so great wisdom is to be acquired, is it not to the King that it should belong, that he may rule the people with sagacity? Let Us at least see this thing, and perhaps We may discover what is the source of the prodigy."

Very early in the morning, therefore, he arose, and calling all his ministers, and counsellors, and all the great men of his court to him, he went forth to the mound, and there he found all even as it had been told him. There were the boys tending the calves; and when they had leisure to play, they all ran a race over the hill, and he who won the race was installed king on top of the mound, the other boys paying him homage, and making obeisance to him as to a real king.

Then the most mighty king, even Ardschi-Bordschi

himself, propounded the question to the Boy-king, saying, "Tell us whence is it that thou, who art only a
boy and a herd of the calves, hast this wisdom, surpassing the wisdom of the King. The wisdom by which it
is given thee to discern between right and wrong, truth
and falsehood, shall it not also tell thee what is the
source of this prodigy ?"

Then the Boy-king, rising in his majesty, made
answer,—

"Let the King cause labourers to be fetched, and let
them dig under this mound, from the time of the rising
of the sun even until the setting thereof again ; thus
shall it be found whence ariseth the prodigy."

With these words the Boy-king came down from the
mound, and Ardschi-Bordschi caused labourers to be
fetched, and they began digging at the mound as the
sun rose above the mountains, and ceased not till the
setting thereof again ; but then they came upon a
throne of gold, all dazzling with brightness, and by its
light (¹) they went on working through the night, till
the whole was delivered from its covering of earth. So
great was its splendour when the morning sun rose
upon it again, that all beholders were struck with awe,
and the people prostrated themselves before it.

Ardschi-Bordschi was filled with surpassing joy when
he saw it, for now he saw he had attained the desired
seat of wisdom, by means of which he should rule his
people aright (²).

Heading a procession of all that was great and noble in his realm, he had the throne brought, amid many ceremonies, to his own residence. Then having called the wise men of the kingdom, and inquired of them a lucky day, he summoned a great gathering of all his subjects, to attend his mounting of this throne of prodigy, amid singing, and offering of incense, and sounding of trumpet-shells (³).

The throne, which had been set up in his dwelling, meantime, was all of pure and shining gold. The foundation of it rested on four terrible lions of gold; and it was reached by sixteen steps of precious stones, on every one of which were two figures of cunning workmanship—the one a warrior, the other a *Sûta* (¹)—sculptured in wood, standing to guard the approach thereof. No such beautiful work had ever before been seen in all the dominions of Ardschi-Bordschi.

When therefore the ministers and people were all arranged in order of rank, and a great silence had been proclaimed on the shell-trumpets, the King, habited in raiment of state, proceeded to mount the throne.

Ere he had set foot on the lowest step, however, the two figures of sculptured wood that stood upon it, abandoning their guardant attitude, suddenly came forward, and placed themselves before him, as in defiance—the warrior striking him in the breast, while the *Sûta* addressed him thus :—

"Surely, O Ardschi-Bordschi! it is not in earnest that thou art minded to ascend the steps of this sacred throne?" And all the thirty-two sculptured figures answered together,—

"Halt! O Ardschi-Bordschi!"

But the *Sûta* proceeded,—

"Knowest thou not, O Ardschi-Bordschi, that this throne in the days of old was the seat of the god Churmusta, and that after him it was given to none to set upon it, till Vikramâditja rose. Wherefore, O Ardschi-Bordschi, approach not to occupy it. Unless thou also art prepared to devote thy days, not to thine own pleasure, but to the service of the six classes of living beings ('), renounce the attempt to set foot on it." And all the thirty-two sculptured figures answered together,—

"Halt! O Ardschi-Bordschi!"

But the *Sûta* proceeded,—

"Art thou such a king as the great Vikramâditja? then come and sit upon his throne; but if not, then desist from the attempt." And all the thirty-two sculptured figures answered together,—

"Halt! O Ardschi-Bordschi!"

When they cried the third time, "Halt! O Ardschi-Bordschi!" the King himself, and all who stood there with him, fell on their faces before the throne, and worshipped it.

Then spoke another *Sûta*,—

"Listen, O Ardschi-Bordschi, and all ye people give ear, and I will tell you out of the days of old what manner of king was the hero Vikramâditja."

THE SÛTA TELLS ARDSCHI-BORDSCHI CONCERNING VIKRAMÂDITJA'S BIRTH.

LONG ages ago there lived a King named Gandharva. To him was wedded Udsesskülengtu-Gôa-Chatun (¹), the all-charming daughter of the mighty king Galindari.

Gandharva was a noble King, and ruled the world with justice and piety. Nevertheless Gandharva had no heir, though he prayed continually to Buddha that he might have a son. And as he thus prayed and mourned continually, Udsesskülengtu-Gôa came to him one day, and said, "My lord, since thou art thus grieved at heart because no heir is given to us, take now unto thee another wife, even a wife from among thy people, and perhaps so shalt thou be blessed with succession to the throne." And her words pleased the King, and he chose a wife of low degree, and married her, and in due time she bore him a son.

But when Udsesskülengtu-Gôa, the all-charming one, saw that the heart of the King was taken from her, and given to the wife of low degree, because she had borne him a son, while she was less favoured by heaven, she was grieved in spirit, and said within herself, "What shall I do now that the heart of my lord is taken from me? Was it not by my father's aid that he attained the throne? And was it not even by my advice that he took this wife who has borne him a son? And yet his heart is taken from me." Nevertheless she complained not to him, but mourned by herself apart.

Then one of her maidens, when she saw her thus mourning apart, came to her, and said, "Is there not living by the *kaitja* (²), on the other side of the mountain, a lama, possessed of prodigious powers? Who shall say but that he might find a remedy for the grief of the Khan's wife." And Udsesskülengtu-Gôa listened to the maiden's words, and leaving off from mourning, she rose, and called to her four of the maidens, and prepared her to make the journey to visit the holy man at the *kaitja*, on the other side the mountain, taking with her good provision of tea (³) and other things needful for the journey. .

Arrived at the *kaitja*, she made the usual obeisance, and would have opened her suit; but the hermit was at that moment sunk in his meditations, and paid her no heed until she had three times changed (⁴) her place of kneeling. Then he said, "Exalted Queen! what grief or what necessity brings thee hither to this *kaitja* thus devoutly?" And when she had told him all her story, he replied,—

" Mayst thou be blessed with succession to the throne

and with many children to gladden thee." At the same time he gave her a handful of earth, bidding her boil it in oil—sesame oil(⁵)—in a porcelain vessel, and eat it all up.

The Queen returned home, and, believing in the promise of the hermit, she boiled the earth in sesame oil in a new porcelain vessel, when behold it was changed into barley porridge; but she neglected to eat up the whole of it. Some time after the maiden who had counselled the visit to the hermit, seeing that some of the porridge still remained in the porcelain vessel, she also ate of it, saying, "Who knows what blessing it may bring to me also?"

Many months had not passed when all manner of propitious tokens appeared upon the land. Showers of brilliant blossoms fell in place of rain from heaven, the melodious voice of the *kalavinka*(⁶) made itself heard, and delicious perfumes filled the air. In the midst of this rejoicing of nature the Queen bore the King a son.

The gladness of the King knew no bounds that now he had an heir to the throne who was born of a princess and not of a wife of low degree, and he ordered public rejoicings throughout the whole kingdom. Further, in his joy he sent an expedition, with the younger wife at its head, and many great men of state, to go to the lama of the *kaitja*, on the other side of the mountain, and learn what should be the fate of the child.

When they came to him he was again sunk in his meditations; but when they had opened their matter to him, almost without looking up, he replied,—

"Tell the King your master that there be got ready for the child against he grow up fifteen thousand waggon-loads of salt, for that will be but small compared with what will be required for the use of his kitchen."

With such a message the expedition returned to the King.

When Gandharva heard the prognostics of the hermit, he was struck with astonishment, and with indignation against the child, not understanding the intention of the words. Then he called together the people and announced the thing to them, adding these words, "Of a truth the child must be a hundredfold a *schimnu;* how could a man use fifteen thousand waggon-loads of salt for the seasoning of his food? It is not good for such an one to live. Let him be taken forth and slain!"

But his ministers interceded with him and said, "Nay, shall the son of the King and the heir to his royal throne be slain? Shall we not rather take him to some solitary place and leave him to his fate in a thick wood?"

And the King found their words good; so two of his ministers took the child a long way off to a solitary place, and left him exposed in a thick wood. But as they turned to go away, and one of them yet lingered, the child called after him, saying,—

"Wait a little space, sir minister; I have a word to say to you!"

And the minister stood still in great astonishment. But the child said, "Bear these words faithfully unto the King :—

"It is said that when the young of the peacock are first fledged their feathers are all of one blue colour, but afterwards, as they increase in proportions, their plumage assumes the splendid hues admired by men. Even so when a King's son is born. For a while he remains under the tutelage of his parents; but if, when he has come to man's estate, he would be a great king, worthy to be called king of the four parts of the universe([7]), it will behove him to call together the princes of the four parts of the universe to a great assemblage and prepare for them a sacred festival([8]), at which such may be their number who may come together to honour it, that fifteen thousand waggon-loads of salt may even fall short of what is required!

"So the parrots, when they first break through their egg-shell, appear very much like any other birds, but when they are full grown they learn the speech of man and grow in sagacity and wisdom([9]). Even so when a King's son is born. For a while he remains under the tutelage of his parents; but when he comes to man's estate, if he would be a mighty king, worthy of being

called king of the four parts of the universe, it will
behove him to call together all kings and devas
and princes of the earth, with all the countless Bodhisattvas, and all the priests of religion, and prepare
for them a great religious banquet. At such a banquet ·
it is well if fifteen thousand waggon-loads of salt suffice
for the seasoning. This for your King."

The minister took the message of the child word for
word to the Gandharva, who when he heard it clasped
his hands in agony and rose up, saying,—

"What is this that I have done! Of a certainty the
child was a *Bodhisattva* ([10]). But it is the truth that
what I did to him I did in ignorance. Run now swiftly
and fetch me back my son." The minister therefore
set out on his way without stopping to take breath;
but what haste soever he made the King's eagerness
was greater, and at the head of a great body of the
people Gandarva himself took his way in all speed to
the place in the thick grove where they had laid the
child. And since he did not find him at the first, he
broke out into loud lamentations, saying,—

"O thou, mine own Bodhisattva! who so young yet
speakest words of wisdom, even young as thou art
exercise also mercy and forgiveness. O how was I
mistaken in thee! Set it not down to me that I knew
thee not!"

While he wandered about searching and thus lamenting, the cry of a child made itself heard from the depths

of a grotto there was in the grove, which when the King had entered he found eight princes of the serpent-gods ([11]) busy tending the child. Some had woven for him a covering of lotus-blossoms; others were dropping honey into his mouth; others were on their knees, bowing their foreheads to the ground before him. Thus he saw them engaged, only when he entered the cave they all at once disappeared without leaving a trace behind ([12]).

Then the King laid the child on a litter borne by eight principal men, and amid continual lamenting of his fault, saying, "O my son, Bodhisattva, be merciful; I indeed am thy father," he brought him to his dwelling, where he proclaimed him before all the people the most high and mighty Prince Vikramâditja.

When the *Sûta* had concluded this narrative, he turned to Ardschi-Bordschi and said,—

"Thus was Vikramâditja wise in his earliest youth; thus even in infancy he earned the homage of his own father; thus was he innately great and lofty and full of majesty. If thou, O Ardschi-Bordschi! art thus nobly born, thus indwelt with power and might, then come and mount this throne; but, if otherwise, then on thy peril desist from the attempt."

Then Ardschi-Bordschi once more approached to ascend the throne; but as he did so two other of the sculptured figures, relinquishing their guardant attitude, stood forward to bar the way, the warrior-figure

striking him on the breast, and the *Sûta* thus addressing him,—

"Halt! O Ardschi-Bordschi! as yet hast thou but
heard the manner of the wonderful birth of Vikramâditja; as yet knowest thou not what was the manner
of his youth."

And all the thirty-two sculptured figures answered
and said,—

"Halt! O Ardschi-Bordschi!"

But the *Sûta* continued, saying, "Hearken, O Ardschi-Bordschi! and ye, O people, give ear, and I will tell
you out of the days of old concerning the youth of
Vikramâditja.

THE SÛTA TELLS ARDSCHI-BORDSCHI CONCERNING VIKRAM-
ÂDITJA'S YOUTH.

GANDHARVA, the hero's father, was himself also a mighty
man of valour, and a prince devoting himself to the
well-being of his people. He not only carried on wars
against the enemies of his country, but exerted himself
to the utmost to deliver his subjects from the onslaught
of the wicked *Schimnus*.

One day, therefore, he went forth alone to do
battle with a prince of the *Schimnus;* and in order
that he might be in a condition the better adapted to
match him, he left his body behind him, under shadow

T

of an image of Buddha. His younger wife, even the wife of low degree, happening by chance to see him leaving the temple without his body, was so delighted with the wonderfully beauteous appearance he thus presented that she went to Udsessküleng-Gôa-Chatun, saying, " Our master, so long as he went in and out among us, always was clothed in human form like other men ; but to-day, when he started on his expedition against the *Schimnus*, he wore such a brilliant and beautiful appearance that it would be a joy if he looked the same when he is with us." But Udsessküleng-Chatun replied, " Because you are young you understand not these things. It is only to preserve his body from the fine piercing swords of the *Schimnus* that he left it behind him."

The younger wife, however, was not satisfied with the explanation, and said within herself, " If I go and burn the body which the King has left behind him, *then* must he wear his beautiful spirit-appearance when he comes back to us."

She called together, therefore, all the other maidens, and having kindled a great fire of sandal-wood, went back to the temple, and fetched Gandharva's body from beneath the image of Buddha, and burned it.

While this was going on the King appeared in his radiant form in the heavens, and spoke thus to Udsessküleng-Gôa-Chatun, saying,—

" From my beloved subjects, for whom I have

laboured so untiringly, and from my dear wives and children and friends, and from my body which has served me so faithfully that I cannot but love it also—I am called to part. As my body is burnt, I cannot more visit the earth. My only concern, however, is this, that I know within seven days the host of the *Schimnus* will come down upon you, and I shall not be there to defend you. Take, therefore, this counsel, giving which is all I can do for you more, for I go to *Nirvâna* ('). Get you up then, and escape with the young prince, even with the *Bodhisattva* Vikramâditja, within these seven days, so that the *Schimnus'* host coming may not find you."

After these words they saw him no more, for he entered then upon Nirvâna.

The officers and ministers and household and subjects gave themselves to distressful grief when they knew that they should see their good master Gandharva no more, but Udsessküleng-Chatun said, " If I give myself over thus to grief it will not bring back my lord the Khan ; it were better that I stir myself to fulfil his all-wise counsel, and bear his son to a place of safety." Having thus spoken, she called all her maidens together and the child, and went to seek safety from the *Schimnus* in her own country. As they journeyed, the young maiden who had given her the counsel to visit the hermit of the *kaitja*, and who had eaten what was left of the porridge made of earth

T 2

boiled in sesame oil in the porcelain vessel, she also
had a child, and when the Khanin was astonished at
the thing, the maid confessed that she had eaten of the
porridge which the hermit gave her that was left behind
in the porcelain vessel, and the Khanin remembered
that she had neglected to fulfil the counsel of the
hermit, saying to her, "Eat it all up."

The other maidens now objected to the burden of
having another infant to take care of on a perilous
journey, and would have put it to death. But the
Khanin said, "Nay, but shall a child that came of the
hermit's blessing be slain?" And when she found she
could not prevail with them to take it she bid them
not slay it, but leave it in shelter of a cave which there
was by the way.

Then they journeyed farther amid many dangers and
privations till they came to the capital of the mighty
King *Kütschin-Tschidaktschi* (²) in the outskirts of which
they encamped. All the people gathered, however,
on the other side of the way, struck with admiration
by the wondrous beauty of Udsessküleng-Chatun, all
inquiring whence she could be, and flocking to gain a
sight of her (³).

The Khan, seeing this gathering of people from the
terrace of his palace, sent to inquire what it was, and a
man of the train of the Khanin sent answer, "It is the
wife of a mighty King who is escaping from the fear
of the *Schimnus,* her lord having entered *Nirvâna.*"
The King, therefore, went down, and spoke with the

Khanin, and having learnt from her that such was really the case, the younger wife having burnt his body, and he having appeared in the sky to bid her escape with their son from before the fury of the *Schimnus*, ordered his ministers to appoint her a dwelling for her and her son, and her train of followers, and to provide them richly with all things befitting their rank.

All this the ministers did, and the Khanin and her son were hospitably entertained.

Thus Vikramâditja was brought up in a strange land, but was exercised in all kinds of arts; and increased in strength, well-favoured in mind and body. He learned wisdom of the wise, and the use of arms from men of valour; from the soothsayer learned he cunning arts, and trading from sagacious traders; from robber bands learned he the art of robbery; and from fraudulent dealers to lie.

It happened that while they were yet dwelling in this place, a caravan of five hundred merchants came by, and encamped on the banks of a stream near at hand.

As these men had journeyed along they had found a boy at play in a wolf's den.

"How can a child live thus in a wolf's den?" said one of the merchants; and with that they set themselves to lure the child to them.

"How canst thou, a child of men, live thus in common with a wolf's cubs?" inquired they. "It were better thou camest with us."

But the child answered, "I am in truth a wolf-child, and had rather remain with my wolf-parents."

But Galbischa, the chief of the merchants, said, "It must not be. A child of men must be brought up with men, and not with wolves." So the merchants took the boy with them, and gave him the name of Schalû (⁴).

Thus it came to pass that the child was with them, when they encamped the night after they had taken him, in the neighbourhood of the city where Vikramâditja and his mother lived. In the night the wolves came near, and began to howl (⁵). Therefore, the merchants asked Schalû in sport, "What are the wolves saying?"

But Schalû answered in all seriousness, "These wolves that you hear are my parents; and they are saying to me, 'Years ago a party of women passed by this way, and left thee with us as soon as thou wert born; and we have nurtured thee, and made thee strong and brave; and thou, without regard to our affection to thee, hast gone away with strangers. Nevertheless, because we love thee, we will give thee yet this piece of advice. To-night, there will be heavy torrents of rain, and the river by which your caravan is encamped, will overflow its banks. While the merchants, therefore, are engaged in hurry and confusion seeking shelter, then break thou away from them, darling, and come back to us. This further warning give we thee, that in the neighbourhood prowls a robber.'"

Now it was so that Prince Vikramâditja, having seen

the encampment of the merchants, was lurking in the thicket, to exercise his prowess in robbing them. Thus when he overheard how Schalû expounded all that the wolves said, he thought within himself, "This is no ordinary youth. That torrents of rain are about to fall might be a guess, even though the sky presents no indication of a coming storm; but how could he guess that I was prowling about to rob the caravan? this, at least, shows he has command of some sort of supernatural knowledge." Determining therefore to discover some means of possessing himself of the boy, he went away for that night, because the merchants having been warned by the wolves of his designs, they would be on the watch to take him had he attempted an attack.

The merchants, meantime, believing the words of the wolves expounded to them by Schalû, removed their encampment to a high hill, out of the way of chances of damage by inundation. When night had fallen thick around, the rain began to fall in heavy torrents, and the river overflowed its banks, making particular havock of the very spot on which their tent had been pitched. When the merchants in the morning saw this part of the plain all under water, and the floods pouring over it, they said one to another, "Without Schalû's aid we had certainly all been washed away ("')," and out of gratitude they loaded him with rich presents.

At the end of the next day's journey they selected

the dry bank of a small tributary of the river for their camping-place. Prince Vikramâditja, who, in pursuance of his determination of overnight, had watched their movements from afar, drew near, under cover of the shades of evening, and set himself once more to overhear what Schalû might have to say. By-and-by two wolves approached, and began howling. Then the merchants asked Schalû, saying, "What do the wolves say?" And Schalû answered, "These are the wolves who have been to me from my birth up in the place of parents, and they say, 'Behold, we have watched over thee ever since thou wast born, and made thee brave and strong, nevertheless, unmindful of our aid, thou hast forsaken us, and betaken thyself to men, who are our enemies. This is the last time that we can come after thee (⁷); but of our affection we give thee this counsel: sleep not this night, for there is a robber again lurking about the camp. Early in the morning also, if thou goest out to the banks of the stream, thou shalt find a dead body brought down by the waters; fish it out, and cut it open, for in the right thigh is enclosed the jewel Tschin-tâmani (⁸), and whoso is in possession of this talisman, has only to desire it, and he will become a mighty King, ruler of the four parts of the earth.'"

When Vikramâditja had heard these words, he gave up his marauding intention for that night also, his victims having been set upon their guard. But he was satisfied with the prospect of having the talisman for his booty. Going higher up the stream, therefore, he fished out the dead body as it floated down before it came to the merchants' encampment, opened the thigh, and took out the jewel, and then committed it to the waters again, so that when the merchants and Schalû took it, they found the treasure was gone. But he thought within himself the while, "This Schalû is no common boy; some pretext I must find to possess myself of him before the caravan leaves the neighbourhood."

The next morning, therefore, before they struck their tents, he came to them in the disguise of a travelling merchant, he also bringing with him stuffs and other objects of barter, on which he had set a private mark. While pretending to trade, he contrived to pick a quarrel, as also to leave some of his wares unperceived hidden in one of the tents. Then he went to King Kütschün-Tschidaktschi, and laid this complaint before him :—

"Behold, O King, I was engaged in trading with a company of five hundred merchants who are encamped outside this city, but a dispute arising, they fell upon me, and used me contumeliously, and drove me forth from among them, and, what is worst of all, they have retained among them the half of my stuffs."

In answer to this complaint, the King sent two officers of the court, and an escort of two hundred fighting-

men, with instructions to investigate the matter, and if
they found that the five hundred merchants had really
stolen the stuffs, to put them all to the edge of the
sword ; but if they found this was not the case, then to
bring Vikramâditja to him for judgment.

Then Vikramâditja once more prostrated himself before the King, and said, " Upon all my things have I
set a mark (so and so), whereby they may be recognized, so that clearly may it be established whether
they have my stuffs in possession or not."

When the King's envoys came to the encampment of
the five hundred merchants, they arraigned them, saying,—

" Young Vikramâditja lays this complaint against ye
before the King, namely, that you have used him shamefully, driving him away from you contumeliously, and
laying violent hands on his stuffs, wherewith he sought
to trade with you. Know therefore that the command
of our all-powerful King is, that if the stuffs of Vikramâditja are found in your tents, you be all put to the
edge of the sword." And the merchants answered
cheerfully, " Come in and search our tents, for we have
no man's goods with us, saving only our own."

Then the King's envoys searched through all the
tents, no man hindering them, so persuaded were the
good merchants that none of their company had defrauded any man. As they searched, behold, they
found hidden in one of the tents, where Vikramâditja

had concealed them, the stuffs bearing his marks, so and so, even as he had testified before the King.

When the merchants saw this they cried, saying, "Surely some evil demon hath done this thing, for in our company is none who ever took any man's goods;" and they all began to weep with one accord.

The King's envoys, however, said, "Weeping will bring you no help; we must do according to the words of our all-powerful king." And they called on the two hundred fighting-men to put the whole company of merchants to the edge of the sword.

When the commotion was at the highest—the merchants entreating mercy and protesting their innocence, and the envoys declaring the urgency of the King's decree, and the fighting-men sharpening their swords —there stood forward young Vikramâditja, and spoke, saying, "Nay, let not so many men be put to death. Leave them their lives if they give me in exchange the boy Schalû, whom they have in their company."

Then the merchants said to Schalû, "Already hast thou once saved our lives; go now with this man, and save them for us even this second time."

And Schalû made answer, "To have saved the lives of five hundred men twice over, shall it not bring me good fortune?" So he went with Vikramâditja, and the merchants loaded him with rich merchandize out of gratitude, for his reward.

When Vikramâditja came home, bringing the boy

with him, his mother inquired of him, saying, " Vikram-âditja, beloved son, where hast thou been, and whence hast thou the child which thou hast brought ?"

And Vikramâditja answered, " Beloved mother, when thou wast on thy way hither fleeing from before the face of the *Schimnus*, did not one of thy maidens leave a new-born infant in a wolves' den ?"

And his mother answered, " Even so did one of my maidens, and the child would now be about this age." So they took Schalû to them, and he was unto Udsess-küleng-Chatun as a son, but unto Vikramâditja as a bro-ther ; and he went with him whithersoever he went.

One day Vikramâditja came to his mother, and said to her, " Beloved mother ! Live on here in tranquillity, while I, in company with Schalû, will go to the capital where my father, the immortal Gandharva, reigned, and see what is the fate of our people, and how I may recover the inheritance."

But Udsessküleng-Chatun made answer, " Vikram-âditjâ, beloved son ! Is not the way long, and beset with evil men, who are so many and so bold ? How then wilt thou ever arrive, or escape their wiles ?"

Vikramâditja said to her, " How great soever the distance may be, by hard walking I will set it behind me ; and how many soever the enemy may be, I shall overcome them, defying the violent with strength, and the crafty with craftiness."

Thus he and Schalû set out to go to the immortal

Gandharva's capital. Inquiring by the way what fate had befallen the kingdom, he found that Gandharva had no sooner entered *Nirvána,* than his neighbour King Galischa, had made the design to obtain possession of his throne ; but that the *Schimnus'* host had been beforehand with him, and had already commenced to take possession. They made a compact, however, by which the government was left to King Galischa, on condition of his sending to the *Schimnus* in Gandharva's palace, a tribute of a hundred men daily with a nobleman at their head.

Then Vikramâditja was grieved when he learned that it was thus the usurping prince dealt with his subjects, and he proceeded farther on his way. When he had come nigh the capital, he heard sounds of wailing, proceeding from a hut on the outskirts ; going in to discover the cause, Vikramâditja found lying, with her face upon the floor, a woman all disconsolate, and weeping piteously.

"Mother ! What is thy grief wherewith thou art so terribly oppressed ?" inquired Vikramâditja of her.

" Ah !" replied the woman, " there is no cure for my grief. This King Galischa, who has seized the kingdom of the immortal Gandharva, has entered into a compact with the *Schimnus* to pay them a tribute of a hundred men every day with a nobleman at their head. I had two sons, one of them is gone I know not whither, and now to-day they have come and taken the other to send in the tribute to the *Schimnus,* nor can I by any means resist the will of the King. That is why I wail, and that is why I am inconsolable." And she went on with her loud lament (⁹).

But Vikramâditja bid her arise and be of good cheer, saying, " I will bring back thy son to thee alive this day, for I will go forth to the *Schimnus* in his stead."

Then the woman said, "Nay, neither must this be. Thou art brave with the valour of youth, even as a young horse snorting to get him away to the battle. But when thou art devoured by the *Schimnus,* then shall thy mother grieve even as I; and belike she is young and has many years before her, whereas my life is well-nigh spent, and what matter if I go down to the grave in sorrow? Who am I that I should bring grief to the mother of thee, noble youth !"

But Vikramâditja said, " Leave that to me, and if I send not back to thee thine own son as I have promised, then will I send back to thee this youth, Schalû, who is my younger brother, and he shall be thy son."

When he drew near the dwelling of King Galischa, the King was just marshalling one hundred subjects, with a nobleman at their head, who were to be sent that day to the *Schimnus* in tribute in Gandharva's palace. But the King, espying him, inquired who and whence he was.

Then Vikramâditja answered him, " I am Vikramâditja, son of Gandharva. When he died, my mother carried me, being an infant of days, far away for fear of the *Schimnus*. But now that I have grown to man's estate, I am come together with my younger brother to see after the state of my father's kingdom."

Galischa then said, " It is well for thee that Heaven preserved thee from coming before, otherwise thou mightest have had all the travail which has fallen upon me; nevertheless, as I came first, I am in possession. But I have every day in sorrow and agony to send a tribute of one hundred subjects, with a nobleman at their head, to be devoured by the *Schimnus*."

" This have I learnt," replied Vikramâditja, " and it is even on that account that I am here. For have I not seen the grief of a mother mourning over her son, and it is to take his place, and to go in his stead, that I came hither to thee."

And Galischa said, " How canst thou, youth that thou art, defy all the might of the *Schimnus*, doubt not now but that they will devour thee before thou art aware."

" Then," replied the magnanimous prince, " if I do not prevail against the *Schimnus*, this I shall gain, that because I have given my life for another, I shall in my next birth rise to a higher place ([10]) than at present."

" If that is thy mind," replied the King, " then do even as thou hast said."

So Vikramâditja went out with the tribute of blood, and sent back the youth whom he had come to replace, to his mother.

When the King saw him go forth with firm step,

and as it were dancing with joy over his undertaking, he said, "There is one case in which he might turn out to be our deliverer; but if that case does not befall, then will he but have come to swell the number of victims of the *Schimnus.* Let us, however, all wait here together through the day, to see what may befall."

Vikramâditja and his companions meantime arrived at Gandharva's palace; and Vikramâditja, as if he had known the place all his life, went straight up to the throne-room, where was the great and dazzling *Sinhâsana* ([11]). Ascending it, therefore, he sat himself in it, and, while his tears flowed down, he cried, "Oh for the days of my father, the immortal Gandharva; for he reigned gloriously! But since he hath entered *Nirvâna* we have had nothing but weariness. What would my father have said had he seen his subjects made by hundreds at a time food for the *Schimnus?* *Schimnus,* beware! lest I destroy your whole race from off the face of the earth."

Thus spoke Vikramâditja, till, inspired by his royal courage, he had sent all the hundred victims of this tribute back to their homes, defying the anger of the *Schimnus.* But to the King he sent word, "The *Schimnus* of whom thou standest in mortal dread will I curb and tame. Meantime, let there be four hundred vessels of brandy prepared." And the King did as he said, and sent and put out four hundred vessels filled with strong brandy in the way.

When, therefore, the *Schimnus* came that they might devour their victims as usual, they first came upon the four hundred vessels of brandy, and seeing them, they set upon them greedily, and drank up their contents. Overcome by the strong spirit, they lay about on the ground half-senseless, and Vikramâditja came upon them and slew them, and hewed them in pieces.

He had hardly despatched the last of them when their Schimnu-king, informed of what had been done, came down in wrath and fury, flourishing his drawn sword. But Vikramâditja said to him, "Halt! King of the *Schimnus;* taste first of my brandy, and if it overcome thee, then shalt thou be my slave; but if not, then will I serve thee. Then the King of the *Schimnus* drank up all the brandy, and, overpowered by the strong spirit, fell down senseless on the earth.

As he was about to slay him like the others, Vikramâditja thought within himself, "After all, it will bring greater fame to overcome him in fair fight than to slay him by stratagem." So he sat down and waited till he came to himself; then he defied him to combat; and when he stood up to fight, he raised his sword and cut him in two.

Then see! of the two halves there arose two men; and when he cut each of these in two, there were four men; and when he cut these in two, there were eight men, who all rushed upon him. Then the Prince transformed himself into eight lions, which roared terribly, and tore the eight men in pieces, and destroyed them utterly.

While this terrible combat was going on, there were frightful convulsions of nature ([12]): mountains fell in, and in the place where they had stood were level plains; and plains were raised up, and appeared as mountains, water gushed out of them and overran the land, and all the subjects of Gandharva fell senseless on the earth. But when Vikramâditja had made an end of the *Schimnus*, and resumed his own form again, he made a great offering of incense, and the earth resumed her stability; the people were called back to life, and all was gladness and thanksgiving. All the people, and King Galischa at their head, acknowledged Vikramâditja as their lawful sovereign, and he ascended the throne of his father Gandharva. Then he sent for the Queen-mother, and made the joy of all his people.

When the *Sûta* had made an end of the narrative of Vikramâditja's youth, he addressed himself to Ardschi-Bordschi, saying,—

"If thou canst boast of being such a King as Vikramâditja, then come and ascend this throne; but if not, then beware, at thy peril, that thou approach it not."

Ardschi-Bordschi then drew near once more to ascend the throne, but two other of the sculptured figures, forsaking their guardant attitude, came forward and warned him back.

Then another *Sûta* addressed him, saying, " Halt ! O Ardschi-Bordschi ! As yet thou hast only heard concerning the birth and the youth of Vikramâditja ; now hearken, and I will tell thee some of his mighty deeds."

And all the sculptured figures answered together,— " Halt ! O Ardschi-Bordschi !"

THE SÛTA TELLS ARDSCHI-BORDSCHI CONCERNING VIKRAM-
ÂDITJA'S DEEDS.

VIKRAMÂDITJA ACQUIRES ANOTHER KINGDOM.

WHILE Vikramâditja continued to rule over his subjects in justice, and to make them prosperous and happy, another mighty king entered *Nirvâna*. As he left no son, and as there was no one of his family left, nor any one with any title to be his heir, a youth of the people was elected to fill the throne. The same night that he had been installed on the throne, however, he came to die. The next day another youth was elected, and he also died the same night. And so it was the next night, and the next, and yet no one could divine of what malady all these kings died.

At last the thing reached the ears of Vikramâditja.

Then Vikramâditja arose, and Schalû with him, and disguising themselves as two beggars, they took the

way to the capital of this sorely-tried kingdom, to bring
it deliverance.

When they came near the entrance of the city, they
turned in to rest at a small house by the wayside.
Within they found an aged couple, who were preparing
splendid raiment for a handsome youth, who was their
son; but they cried the while with bitter tears.   Then
said Vikramâditja,—

"Why do you mourn so bitterly, good people?"

"Our King is dead," replied they, "and as he has
left no succession, one of the people was chosen by lot
to fill the office of King, but he died the same night;
and when another was similarly chosen, he likewise
died.   Thus it happens every night.   Now, to-day the
lot has fallen on our son; he will therefore of a certainty die to-night: therefore do we mourn."

Then answered Vikramâditja, "To me and my companion, who are but two miserable beggars, it matters
little whether we live or die.   Keep your son with you,
therefore, and we two will ascend the throne this
morning in his place and die to-night in his stead."

But the parents replied, "It is not for us to decide
the thing.   Behold, the matter stands in the hands of
three prudent and experienced ministers, but we will
go and bring the proposal before them."

The parents went, therefore, and laid the proposal of
the beggars before the three prudent and experienced
ministers, who answered them, saying, "If these men

are willing to die after reigning but twenty-four hours
why should we say them nay? Let them be brought
hither to us."

Then the beggars were brought in, and the ministers
installed them on the throne, saying to the people,
" Hitherto we have been accustomed to meet together
early in the morning to bury our King. But this time,
as we shall have two kings to bury instead of one, see
that you come together right early."

Vikramâditja meantime set himself to examine all
the affairs of the kingdom, that he might discover to
what was to be ascribed the death of the King every
night. And when he had well inquired into every
matter, he found that it had formerly been the custom
of the King to make every night a secret offering (^{1})
to the *devas*, and to the genii of earth and water, and
to the eight kinds of spirits, but that the succeeding
kings had neglected the sacrifice, and therefore the
spirits had slain them. Then the most high and magnanimous king Vikramâditja appointed out of the
royal treasury what was necessary to pay for the
accustomed offering; then he called upon the spirits
and offered the sacrifice. The spirits, delighted to see
their honour return, made the king a present of a handsome Mongolian tent and went up again.

The people, too, who had come together early in the
morning, with much wood to make the funeral obse-
quies of the Kings, were filled with delight to find the

spell broken, and in return they gave him the jewel Dsching, filling the air with their cries of gladness and gratitude, calling him the King decreed by fate to rule over them. Thus Vikramâditja became their King.

***

VIKRAMÂDITJA MAKES THE SILENT SPEAK.

WHILE now Vikramâditja reigned over all his people in justice and equity complaint was brought before him against one of his ministers, that he oppressed the people and dealt fraudulently with them; and Vikramâditja, having tried his cause, judged him worthy of death. But when he was brought before him to receive sentence he pleaded for life so earnestly that the magnanimous King answered him, "Why should the life of the most abject be taken? Let him but be driven forth from the habitation of men."

So they drove him forth from the habitation of men. Now it had been the minister's custom, in pursuance of a vow, to observe three fast-days every month (¹). And so it happened, that one day after they had driven him forth from the habitations of men, on the day succeeding one of his fasts, he found himself quite without any thing to eat; nor could he discover any fruit or any herb which could serve as a means of subsistence. Recollecting, then, that one day he had made four little offering-tapers out of wax and bread crumbs, he went and searched out the shrine where he had offered them, that he might take them to eat. But see! when he stretched forth his hand to take one of them it glided away from before him and hid itself behind another of the offering-tapers; and when he would have taken that one, they both hid themselves behind the third. And when he stretched forth his hand to have taken the third, the three together, in like manner, glided behind the fourth. And when he stretched forth his hand to have taken the four together, they all glided away together from off the altar and out of the shrine altogether, and so swiftly that it was as much as he could do to follow after them and keep them in sight. Going on steadily behind them he came at last to a cave of a rock, and brushwood growing over it. Herein they disappeared. Then when he would have crept in after them into the cave of the rock, two he-goats, standing over the portal of the cave, sculptured in stone, spoke to him, saying, "Beware, and enter not! for this is a place of bad omen. Within this cave sits the beauteous *Dâkinî* (²) *Tegrijin Nâran* (³) sunk in deep contemplation and speaketh never. Whoso can make her open her lips twice to speak to man, to him is the joy given to bear her home for his own. But let it not occur to thee to make the bold attempt of inducing her to open her lips to speak, for already five hundred sons of kings have tried and failed; and behold they all languish in interminable prison at the feet of the Silent Haughty One, sunk in deep contemplation."

And as they spoke they bent low their heads, and pointed their horns at him, to forbid him the entrance.

The minister, however, had no mind to try the issue, but rather seized with a great panic he turned him and fled without so much as heeding whither his steps led him. Thus running he chanced to come with his head at full butt against the magnanimous King Vikramâditja, just then taking his walk abroad.

"How now, evil man?" exclaimed the magnanimous King. "Whence comest thou, fleeing as from an evil conscience?"

Then the minister prostrated himself before him, and told him all he had learnt from the two he-goats sculptured in stone, concerning Naran-Dâkinî.

When Vikramâditja had heard the story, he commanded that the evil minister should be guarded, to see whether the event proved that he had spoken the truth ; but, taking with him Schalû and three far-sighted and experienced ministers, he went on till he came to the cave and saw the two he-goats sculptured in stone standing over the portal. The he-goats would have made the same discourse to him as to the evil minister, but he commanded them silence. Then he transformed Schalû into an *aramâlâ* (') in his hand, but the three ministers into the altar that stood before the Dâkinî, and the lamp that burned thereon, and the granite

vessel for burning incense placed at the foot of the
same (⁵); laying this charge upon them: "I will come
in," said he, "as though a wayfarer who knew you not,
and sitting down I will tell a *saga* of olden time. Then
all of you four give an interpretation of my *saga* quite
perverse from the real meaning, and if the Dâkinî be
prudent and full of understanding she will open her
lips to speak to vindicate the right meaning of the
story."

Presently, therefore, after he had completed the
transformation of Schalû and the three far-seeing and
experienced ministers, and having himself assumed the
appearance of a king on his travels, he entered the
cave and sat down over against the altar which stood
before the Dâkinî Naran, the Silent Haughty One,
sunk in deep contemplation. Then said he, "In that it
was told me in this place dwells the all-fair Tegrijin
Naran-Dâkinî, I, who am King of Gambudvîpa, am
come hither to visit her;" and as he spoke he looked
furtively up towards the Dâkinî, to see whether he had
moved her to open her lips to speak.

But the all-beauteous Naran-Dâkinî, the Silent
Haughty One, sat still and gave forth no sign.

Then spoke the King again, saying, "On occasion of
this my coming, O Naran-Dâkinî, tell thou me one of
the *sagas* of old; or else, if thou prefer to hold thy
peace, then will I tell one to thee."

Again he looked up, but Naran Dâkinî Tegrijin, the

Silent Haughty One, sat sunk in deep contemplation
and gave forth no sign.

As the King paused, one of the far-seeing and experienced ministers, even the one whom he had transformed into the altar that stood before the Dâkinî,
spoke, saying,—

"While from the lips of the all-beauteous Naran-
Chatun([6]) no word of answer proceeds, how should it
beseem me, the Altar, a non-souled object, to speak.
Nevertheless, seeing that so great and magnanimous a
King has come hither and has propounded a question,
I will yet dare, even I, to answer him. For, seeing
that Naran-Chatun is so immersed in her own contemplations, she cannot give ear to the words of the
King, I who, standing all the day before her in silence,
and hearing no word of wisdom in any of the *sagas* of
old, even I would fain be instructed by the words of
the King."

And as the altar thus spoke, Naran Tegrijin Dâkinî
cast a glance of scorn upon it, but the Silent Haughty
One opened never her lips to speak.

Then the King took up his parable and poured forth
one of the *sagas* of old after this manner, saying,—

WHO INVENTED WOMAN ? ([7])

"Long ages ago there went forth daily into one place
four youths out of four tribes, to mind their flocks, one
youth out of each tribe, and when their flocks left

them leisure they amused themselves with pastimes together. Now it came to pass that one day one of them rising earlier than the rest, and finding himself at the place all alone, said within himself,—

"'How is the time weary, being here all alone!'

"And he took wood and sculptured it with loving care until he had fashioned a form like to his own, and yet not alike. And when he saw how brave a form he had fashioned, he cared no more to sport with the other shepherd youths, but went his way.

"The next morning the second of the youths rose earlier than the rest, and, coming to the place all alone, said within himself,—

"'How is the time weary, being here all alone!'

"And he cast about him for some pastime,'and thus he found the form which the first youth had fashioned, and, finding it exceeding brave, he painted it over with the five colours, and when he saw how fair a form he had painted he cared no more to sport with the other shepherd youths, but went his way.

"The next morning the third of the youths rose earlier than the rest, and, coming to the place all alone, said within himself,—

"'How is the time weary, being here all alone!'

"And he cast about him for some pastime; thus he discovered the form which the first youth had fashioned and the second youth had painted, and he said,—

"'This figure is beautiful in form and colour, but it

has no wit or understanding.' So he infused into it wit
and understanding.

"And when he saw how clever was the form he had
endowed with wit and understanding, he cared no more
to sport with the shepherd youths, and he went his
way.

"The fourth morning the fourth of the youths rose
up the earliest, and, finding himself all alone at the
trysting-place, said within himself,—

"'How is the time weary, being here all alone!'

"And, casting about to find some pastime, he discovered the form which the first youth had fashioned so
brave, and the second youth had painted so fair, and
the third youth had made so clever in wit and understanding, and he said,—

"'Behold the figure is beautiful in form and fair to
behold in colour, and admirable for wit and understanding, but what skills all this when it hath not
life?' And he put his lips to the lips of the figure and
breathed softly into them, and behold it had a soul(ᵇ)
that could be loved, and was woman.

"And when he saw her he loved her, and he cared
no more to sport with the shepherd youths, but left all
for her, that he might be with her and love her.

"But when the other shepherd youths saw that the
figure had acquired a soul that could be loved, and was
woman, they came back all the three and demanded
possession of her by right of invention.

"The first youth said, 'She is mine by right of invention, because I fashioned her out of a block of wood that had had no form but for me.'

"The second said, 'She is mine by right of invention, because I painted her, and she had worn no tints fair to behold but for me.'

"The third said, 'She is mine by right of invention, because I gave her wit and understanding, and she had had no capacity for companionship but for me.'

"But the fourth said, 'She is mine by right of invention, because I breathed into her a soul that could be loved, nor was there any enjoyment in her but for me.'

"And while they all joyed in the thought of possessing her, they continued to strive on that they might see which should prevail. And when they found that none prevailed against the rest, they brought the matter before the King for him to decide.

"Say now therefore, O Naran-Dâkinî, I charge thee, in favour of which of these four was the King bound to decide that he had invented woman?"

And as the King left off from speaking he looked towards Naran-Dâkinî as challenging her to answer.

But Naran-Dâkinî, the Silent Haughty One, sat immersed in deep contemplation and held her peace, speaking never a word.

Then when the far-sighted and experienced ministers saw that she held her peace, one of them, even the one

whom Vikramâditja had transformed into the lamp
before the altar, spoke, saying,—

"It were meet indeed that an unsouled object such
s I, the Lamp, should not venture to speak in presence
of our mistress, Naran-Chatun. But as so great a King
has come to visit us, and has propounded to us a question to which Naran-Chatun does not see fit to reply,
even I, the Lamp, will attempt to answer him. To me,
then, it seems that the answer is clear, for by whom could
the figure be said to be invented saving by the youth who
first fashioned it? He who gave a mere block of wood
a beautiful form must be allowed to have invented it."

Naran-Dâkinî cast a glance of disgust and scorn upon
the lamp, yet spoke she never a word.

Then spoke the far-seeing and experienced minister
whom Vikramâditja had transformed into the thurible
at the foot of the altar, saying,—

"It were meet indeed that an unsouled object such
as I, the Incense-burner, should not venture to speak in
presence of our mistress, Naran-Chatun. But as so
great a King has come to visit us, and has propounded
a question to us to which Naran-Chatun does not see
fit to reply, even I, the Thurible, will attempt to answer
him. And to me indeed the answer is plain, for to
whom could the figure be said to belong, if not to the
youth who painted it and made a mere stump beautiful
and lifelike with fair tints of colour?"

At these words of the incense-vessel Naran-Dâkinî

cast upon it a look of scorn and contempt, but opened not her lips to speak.

Then spoke Schalû, whom Vikramâditja had transformed into his *aramâlâ*, with impetuosity, saying, "Nay, but surely he alone could have the right of invention who endowed a painted log with wit and understanding. Surely he who made a stump of a tree to think must be allowed to have invented it."

When Naran-Dâkinî saw with what a confident air the *aramâlâ* pronounced this sentence, even as though he had settled the whole matter, she could contain herself no longer, and then burst from her lips these words, while her eyes lighted on the objects that had spoken with exceeding indignation,—

"Of miserable understanding are ye all! How then venture ye, unsouled objects, to expound the matter when I, a reasonable being, scarcely dare pronounce upon the question? What other interpretation of this parable, however, can there be than this :—The youth who first fashioned the figure of a block of wood, did not he stand in place of the father? He who painted it with tints fair to behold, did not he stand in place of the mother? He who gave wit and understanding, is not he the Lama? But he who gave a soul that could be loved, was it not he alone who made woman? To whom, therefore, else should she have belonged by right of invention? And to whom should woman belong if not to her husband?"

Thus Tegrijin Naran Dâkinî had been brought to speak once; but the proposition requiring that the Silent Haughty One should speak twice to man, the magnanimous King proceeded without making allusion to his first success, saying,—

"Now that I have told a *saga* of old, it is the turn that one of you should also tell us a tale to entertain the mind." And as he spoke he addressed himself to Naran-Dâkinî. Nevertheless Naran-Dâkinî had entered again into her deep contemplation, and held her peace, saying never a word.

Then said the far-seeing and experienced minister whom the King had transformed into the altar,—

"As Naran-Chatun continues to sit in her place and to utter no sound in answer to the word of the high King who has come so far to visit us, even I, though I be an unsouled object, will venture to reply, asking him that he will again open to us the treasures of story."

At these words Naran-Dâkinî cast a meaning glance upon her altar, but spoke not.

Then opened the magnanimous King again the treasures of story.

THE VOICE-CHARMER([9]).

"Long ages ago two were travelling through a mountainous country, a man and his wife. And behold as

they journeyed there reached them from the other side
of a rock a voice of such surpassing sweetness that the
two stood still to listen, the man and his wife; and not
they only, but their very beasts pricked up their ears
erect to drink in the sound.

"Then spoke the woman,—

"'A man with a voice so melodious must be a man
goodly to see. Shall we not stop and find him out?'"

"But the saying pleased not her husband, nor was
he minded that she should see who it was that sang so
sweetly; therefore he answered her,—

"'Wherefore should we search him out; is it not
enough that we hear his voice?'

"When the wife had heard his answer, she said no
more about searching out whence the voice proceeded;
only the first time they passed a mountain-rill she said
to her husband,—

"'Behold, I faint for thirst in this heat. Now, as
thou lovest me, fetch me a draught of that cool water
from the mountain-rill.' So the man got down from
his horse, and, taking his wife's cup(¹⁰), went to the rill
to fetch water.

"While he was thus occupied, the wife slid down
from off her horse also, and, going silently behind him,
pushed him over the precipice and killed him. Then
she set out to find out who it was sang so melodiously.
When she had followed up the sound she found herself
in presence, not of a man goodly to behold, but of a

λ

wretched, loathsome object, sunk down against the foot of the rock, deformed in person and covered with sores. Notwithstanding that the undeception was so revolting, she yet took him up on her back and carried him with her; but as the man was heavy and the way steep, the fatigue so wearied her that at the end of a little time she died.

"Was this woman to be counted a good woman or a bad?"

When the King had made an end of telling the tale, he looked towards Naran-Dâkinî as challenging her to answer.

But Naran-Dâkinî held her peace and spoke never a word.

Then, when the far-seeing and experienced minister whom Vikramâditja had transformed into the lamp saw that she yet held her peace, he said,—

"How should an unsouled being such as I, the Lamp, find out the right meaning? nevertheless, not to leave the words of the high King without an answer, I will even venture to suggest that to me it seemeth she must be counted a good woman; because though she killed her husband, yet she made atonement for her fault by raising the sick man and carrying him with her —"

But before he could make an end of speaking Naran-Dâkinî cast at him a glance of contempt and scorn, and she exclaimed,—

"How should there be any good in a woman who

killed her lawful husband, and that only because her ears were tickled with the artful melody of an harmonious voice? Of a truth she must have been a veritable *schimnu*, and if she took the sick man with her, was it not only that she might devour him at leisure?"

Then spoke Vikramâditja,—

"Naran-Chatun! being he who hath induced thee to open thy lips to speak these two times to man, give me my guerdon that thou accompany me home to be my wife."

Very willingly coming down from her altar, Tegrijin Naran Dâkinî at these words gave herself to Vikramâditja to accompany him home to be his wife.

Vikramâditja having then given back to Schalû and to his three far-seeing and experienced ministers their natural shapes, and to the five hundred sons of kings who had failed in winning Naran-Dâkinî theirs, with Naran-Dâkinî by his side, and all the rest in a long procession behind him, the King arrived at his capital. Here he called together all his people Tai-tsing (¹¹) to a great assembly, where he promulgated rules of faith and religion. By his good government he made all his people so happy as no other sovereign ever did, sitting upon his throne with his consort Tegrijin Naran as the fate-appointed rulers.

When the *Sûta* had made an end of this narration of Vikramâditja's deeds, he addressed himself to Ardschi-Bordschi, saying,—

"If thou canst boast. of being such a King as Vikramâditja, then come and ascend this throne, but if not, then beware at thy peril that thou approach it not."

Now Ardschi-Bordschi had seventy-one wives; taking by the hand the chief of them therefore, he bid her make obeisance before the throne and ascend it with him. Ere they had set foot on the first step other two of the sculptured figures came forward, forsaking their guardant attitude, and warned him back, the warrior smiting him in the breast, and the *Sûta* thus addressing him,—

"Halt! O Ardschi-Bordschi, and thou his wife! nor touch so much as with thy prostrate heads the sacred steps. But first know what manner of woman was the chief wife of Vikramâditja.

"The chief wife of Vikramâditja was Tsetsen Bud-schiktschi (¹²), and she never had a word, or look, or thought but for her husband. If thy wife be such a princess as she, then draw near to ascend the throne together, but if otherwise, then at your peril draw not near it.

"But," he said furthermore, "hearken, and I will tell you, who have seventy-one wives, the story of what befell seventy-one parrots and the wife of another high King to whom one of them was counsellor."

And all the sculptured figures answered together,—

"Halt! O Ardschi-Bordschi!"

THE SÙTA TELLS ARDSCHI-BORDSCHI CONCERNING THE SEVENTY-ONE PARROTS AND THEIR ADVISER.

LONG ages ago the wife of a high King was ill with a dire illness, nor could the art of any physician suffice to cure her till one came who said, " Let there be given her parrots' brains to eat."

When, therefore, the high King saw that eating parrots' brains brought health it seemed good to him to take a tribute of parrots' brains from his subjects.

He called unto him, therefore, the governor of a tributary province and commanded him, saying, " Let there be delivered to me a tribute of the brains of seventy-one parrots, otherwise thou must die the death."

That governor went out therefore trembling with fear, and he called unto him immediately a birdcatcher and agreed with him for the price of the brains of seventy-one parrots.

Now the birdcatcher knew a certain tree in which there roosted every night seventy-one parrots, and he said within himself, " If I could spread one net over the whole tree, with one haul the whole affair would be finished." So he went and bought a great net ready to spread over the whole tree.

But among these seventy-one parrots was one parrot exceeding wise, who was always on the watch to see what the birdcatcher was about. When, therefore, he

saw him buy so great a net he said to his companions,
"To what end can the man have bought so big a net
if not to spread round the whole tree? let us, therefore, in future roost on yonder rock." After this they
went to roost on the rock. After they had roosted
four or five nights on the rock the wise parrot caught
sight of the birdcatcher prowling about, having followed them thither and being engaged in settling in
his own mind how he should lay his nets. Then the
wise parrot said to his companions, "The man has come
hither after us even to this rock; let us now, therefore,
avoid his snares by roosting in some other place."

But his companions, instead of accepting his counsel
were provoked, and answered him, saying, "How are
we to endure thus changing our place of roosting every
night. We left our tree which sheltered us well and
came to this rock to please thy fancy; and now thou
wouldst have us make another change. But we will
no more listen to thy suspicions."

They roosted, therefore, still upon the rock, and that
night the birdcatcher came with his nets and encom-
passed them all.

When they woke and found themselves imprisoned,
loud were their shrieks of lamentation as they fluttered
and beat their wings fruitlessly against the net; calling
also on the wise parrot, saying, "You who were so
wise in foreseeing the danger, have you no means for
delivering us out of it?"

" Yes," replied the wise parrot, " I have thought of
that. Leave off every one of you from shrieking and
fluttering about, and beating your wings against the
net, which is a new one and not the least likely to give
way. On the contrary, lie all of you on your backs
with your heads hanging as if you were dead. The
birdcatcher being satisfied you are dead will not kill
you over again. Then observe and see that the approach to this one rock is very narrow, and when a
man comes up it there is only just room for one foot-
hold at the ledge whence he can reach us, and it is as
much as he can do to get up and down with the use
of both his hands as well as his feet; he will not,
therefore, go to carry us down or put us in a bag, but
will throw us one by one over the cliff, and sure
enough he will say out the number as he throws each
down. Let, therefore, those who are thrown down first
remain still lying without motion so that he may not
suspect any of the rest are alive, only when he says
out the number, ' Seventy-one !' then up and away, as
at a signal of a race."

The other parrots did not venture to dispute the
word of the wise parrot this time, but all did exactly
as he had said. When the birdcatcher came and
found what a steep rugged path he had to climb he
vowed all sorts of vengeance on the parrots for giving
him so much fatigue, and swore that he would break
all their bones, for the brain was the only part he

cared to keep uninjured. When he had got up to the ledge of rock by which he could reach them, however, and found that they seemed already stone dead, seeing that to wreak any vengeance on creatures that could not feel would be childish, he contented himself with throwing them below one by one, calling out as he did so the number to each. In this way he had thrown over the seventy; last of all there remained the wise parrot, but the net having fallen upon him he was rather longer loosing him than the rest, so that he had called out " Seventy-one!" before he was ready to throw him down, moreover, his whetstone happening at that same instant to tumble out of his girdle, the other parrots took the sound of its fall for that of the wise parrot, and all of them together they spread their wings and flew far away.

The birdcatcher saw this in time before he had let go his hold of the wise parrot.

" Ah! vile, cunning parrots," he exclaimed in great wrath and indignation, "what labour have you given me, and at last I have no benefit for my exertion! One, at least, of you is still in my power, and on him will I be avenged for the mischief of all the rest; I will take him home and torture him at leisure, and then cook him alive. The wise parrot heard all this, but thought to wait till his fury was a little spent. But finding as time wore on the man only got more and more wroth; and the matter beginning to get serious, as they were coming near his dwelling, the wise parrot at last said, "What end will it serve that thou kill me? It will not bring the other parrots back—and, indeed, what grudge hast thou against me? I never killed thee at any former time (¹) that thou shouldst now kill me. Thou hast attacked my life, and I have defended it by fair dealing. Other grudge against me hast thou none; then why shouldst thou seek to maim and injure me? Moreover, if thou do, be sure that the day will come (²) when I should repay thee. But now, if thou sell me who am a wise and understanding parrot, thou shalt receive for my price 100 ounces of silver, and if with seventy-one ounces thou buy seventy-one other parrots for him who hired thee there will still remain twenty-nine ounces with which thou mayest make merry with all thy friends and acquaintance."

When, therefore, the birdcatcher found he was a wise and understanding parrot, he took him and sold him to a rich merchant for 100 ounces of silver.

The merchant also, who bought the parrot, finding him so wise and full of understanding, employed him in all sorts of ways to watch over his belongings. At last, one day he came and said to the parrot, "Hitherto thou hast done me good service in watching over the merchandize, and I have regarded thee as my brother, now, therefore, that I go on a journey of seventy-one days I entreat thee to watch over, as a sister-in-law, my wife, who is very gay and thoughtless.

The wise parrot answered, " Be of good heart, brother, all shall be right in thine absence."

At which the merchant replied, " If thou sayest so, brother Parrot, I can go forth on my journey without anxieties."

He had not been gone long when his young wife rose up, saying, " Now indeed I am for once my own mistress: I will go out and see all my friends, and particularly those I dare not visit when my husband is here." So she arrayed herself in all her gayest attire. But when she would have gone out the parrot stopped her, saying, " Wait, sister-in-law. A wife behoves it rather to set her household affairs in order, than to go abroad paying visits when her husband is absent."

" Bad parrot!" exclaimed the wife, " what hast thou to do to hinder my taking a little pleasure?"

The parrot answered, " Thy husband when he went away gave me strict charge over thee, saying, ' I command thee that thou hinder her from going forth alone.' This, however, it is not in me to do, for thou art greater in might than I; and if I command thee not to go thou wilt not obey by words. Only now, therefore, before thou goest out sit down first and listen to the story that I will tell thee."

When the wife heard him promise to tell a story, she sat down, for she loved to listen to the stories of the wise parrot.

Then the parrot began to tell her a story in this wise.

HOW NARAN GEREL SWORE FALSELY AND YET TOLD THE TRUTH.

"Long ages ago there lived a King named Tsoktu Ilagukssan ('), who had one only daughter, whom he kept as the apple of his eye, and guarded so jealously that she never saw any thing or any body. If any man went near her apartment his legs were immediately broken and his eyes put out. So relentless was the command of the King.

"One day Naran Gerel ('), such was the daughter's name, however, came to her father, saying, "Being shut up here all day seeing nothing and no man, my life is weariness unto me. Let me now go abroad on the fifteenth of the month, that I may see something."

"But the King would not listen to her; only as she continued day by day urging her request, the King at last gave permission that on a certain day she might go abroad; but he gave orders also at the same time that on that day every bazaar should be shut, every window closed, and that all men, women, and beasts should be shut up close out of sight of the Princess; and that whoso walked abroad, or but looked out of window should be punished with death.

"On the fifteenth of the month, therefore, a new chariot was appointed to Naran Gerel, and she went forth surrounded by a train of her maidens, and drove all through the city; every bazaar being shut up, every window closed, and all men, women, and beasts within doors out of sight.

"Nevertheless, the King's minister Ssaran (⁵), overcome by his curiosity to see the Princess, had gone up to the highest window of his house, to obtain a glimpse of her unperceived. But what care soever he took to be seen of none, the Princess, in her anxiety to make the best use of her eyes on this her one opportunity of seeing the world, discerned him.

"Never having seen any man but her father, who was already well stricken in years, the appearance of the Minister, who was still young, so charmed her that she instantly conceived a desire to see more of him, and accordingly made a sign to him by raising the first finger of her right hand and marking a circle round it with the other hand; then clasping both hands tight together and throwing them open again, finally laying one finger of each hand together and pointing with them towards the palace.

"Very much perplexed at finding himself discovered by the Princess, Ssaran came down; and when his wife saw him looking so bewildered, she inquired of him, saying, 'Hast thou seen the Princess?'

"'Not only have I seen the Princess,' replied Ssaran,

'but she hath seen me; and made all manners of signs, of which I understand nothing, but that of course they were to threaten some dreadful chastisement.'

"'And of what nature were the signs, then?' further inquired his wife; and when he had described them to her, she replied,—

"'These signs by no means betoken threatening. Listen, and I will tell thee the interpretation of the same. In that she raised the first finger of the right hand on high, she signified that in the neighbourhood of her dwelling is a shady tree; that with the other hand she described a circle round it, showed that the garden where the tree stands is surrounded by a high wall; that she clasped both hands together and then threw them open again, said, "Come unto me in the garden of flowers;" and the laying of one finger of each hand together, said, "May we be able to meet?"'

"'This were very well,' replied Ssaran, 'were the King's decree not so terrible, and his wrath so unsparing.'

"But his wife answered him, 'When a King's daughter calls, can fear stand in the way? Go now at her bidding, only take this jewel with thee.'

"Ssaran accepted his wife's counsel, and, stowing the jewel away in a safe place in the folds of his robe, betook himself to the shady tree in the garden of the Princess. Here he found the Princess awaiting him, and they spent the day happily together.

" Towards evening, just as Ssaran was about to take leave of the Princess, they suddenly found themselves surrounded by a hundred armed men, whom the captain that the King had set over the garden had sent to take them both prisoners. Into a dark dungeon they were accordingly thrown to await the King's decree saying by what manner of means they should be put to death.

" Naran Gerel, who had been used to see every one obey her and bow before her, desired the men to let her go home to her father; but the captain said, ' How many men have suffered maiming and death for nothing but because they have ventured near the precincts of thine apartment! Now therefore it is thy turn that thou be put to death also. So will there be an end of this peril to the King's subjects.'

"When Naran Gerel found she could prevail nothing with the captain, she turned to Ssaran and entreated him that he should devise some way of escape; but, sunk in fear and apprehension of the King's terrible anger, he could not collect his ideas.

" ' How comes it,' then inquired the Princess, ' that if thou hast so little presence of mind as thou now displayest, thou wert able to distinguish and unravel, and find courage to follow, the tokens that I gave thee with my hands as I drove along the way ?'

" ' That,' said he, ' I discovered by the sharp wit of my wife, who also gave me courage to obey thy call.'

" ' And did she furnish thee with knowledge and

courage, and yet send thee forth with no sort of talis-man?' said Naran Gerel.

"'She gave me nothing but this jewel,' replied the minister; 'and of what use can that be?'

"The Princess, however, took the jewel, and, throwing it out of window, cried to the guard, 'Ye men who are set to guard us, give ear. To persons sentenced to death is a jewel of no further use; take it one of you to whom it is permitted to live, only let whichever of you takes it in possession do us this service, that he go to the house of the minister Ssaran, and knock three times at the door.'

"One of the guard therefore took the jewel, and went and knocked three times at the door of the minister Ssaran. But the wife of the minister, knowing by this token that her husband was thrown into prison together with Naran Gerel, the King's daughter, made haste and attired herself in her finest apparel, and filled a basket with all manner of juice-giving fruits. With these she came to the gate of the prison where her husband was held bound, and spoke thus to the captain of the guard,—

"'My husband being stricken with the fever, the physician hath ordered that I take these fruits to him;' and the captain of the guard made answer, 'If this be so, then take the fruits in to him, but loiter not; return in all speed.' As soon as the wife entered the prison she changed dresses hastily with Naran Gerel, bidding her escape and go hence privately to her own apartment, while she remained beside her husband.

"In the meantime morning had come, and the King and all his court and his judges were astir, and before all other causes the captain of the guard went to give account of the arrest of Naran Gerel and the minister Ssaran. The high King was very wroth when he heard what his daughter had done and the minister, and commanded that they should instantly be brought before him. So the captain of the guard went straight to the prison, and without waiting so much as to look at them brought the two prisoners before the throne of the King.

"When the King saw the minister and his wife standing before him, he asked them in a voice of thunder,—

"'Where is Naran Gerel?'

"And the minister's wife made answer,—

"'How can we tell thee this thing, seeing we have been kept in durance all through the night?"

"'And wherefore have ye been kept in durance all through the night?' pursued the King.

"'Concerning that also we know nothing further than that the captain of the guard told us it was by the King's decree,' replied the woman.

"'Explain this matter,' then said the King, addressing the minister. And he, his wife telling him what to say, made answer, 'Most high King, how shall I explain the matter, seeing that I myself fail to know why we were arrested? My wife desired to see the garden of the King, and I, thinking it was not beyond a minister's privilege, took her yesterday to walk there, and we spent the day together under the shady tree. For this were we put in prison.'

"The King then spoke to the captain of the guard, saying, 'Shall not a man pass the day in a garden with his wife? Wherefore should they be put in prison? Behold, since thou hast done this thing, thy life is in this man's hand.' And he delivered the captain of the guard to the minister to deal with him as he listed.

"But the captain of the guard said, 'For observing the King's decree am I to be put to death? Before I die, however, let this justice be done. Let Naran Gerel be summoned hither, and let her say on the trial of barley-corns whether it was not she whom I arrested in the King's garden.'

"So the King sent and called Naran Gerel and bid her say on the trial of barley-corns whether it were not she whom the captain of the guard had arrested in the King's garden.

"But Naran Gerel answered, 'Am I not then the King's daughter? How should I, then, make the trial of barley-corns like one of the common herd of the people? But call me an assembly, and before the assembly I will swear. Shall not that suffice for the King's daughter?' But this she said because in the trial of barley-corns if one speak falsely the barley-

Y

corns will surely spring into the air and burst with a loud noise; but if truth, then only they remain quiet. Naran Gerel therefore feared to make the trial of barley-corns.

"But the King said, 'The words that Naran Gerel hath spoken are words of justice. Let an assembly be called.' So they called together an assembly, Naran Gerel having exchanged glances with the minister's wife agreeing how they should proceed.

"Meantime the minister and his wife went home. The wife therefore stained her husband all over with a black stain so that he looked quite black, and she said to him, 'When the time comes that the Princess has to take the oath in the assembly, do thou find thyself there doubled up and making unmeaning grimaces and uncouth antics with an empty water-pitcher. Perhaps the Princess will find the means to escape hereby out of the judgment that threatens her.'

"The assembly was now gathered. The King was on his throne, and Naran Gerel stood at its foot; and the minister, under the form of a crippled beggar, black and loathsome to behold, was there also.

"Then the King called upon Naran Gerel to take the oath. And first espying the pretended cripple, he commanded, saying, 'Let that revolting object be removed;' and all the people loathed him. But the minister, who acted the part of a cripple, only mouthed and wriggled the more, and would not be removed, and as he threatened to make a disturbance the King bid them unhand him again.

"But Naran Gerel stood forward, saying, 'Whereon shall I take this oath? On the barley-corns it beseemeth not the King's daughter to swear even as a common wench. And if I swear on any well-looking man in this assembly, I shall run danger of having the former accusation brought against me again. I will therefore swear by this cripple whom all have loathed. Those who would accuse me to the utmost cannot see any offence if I swear by an object so ungainly and revolting.'

"By this means, as she had sworn by a cripple who was no cripple, she counted that it was no oath, while the King and all the people were satisfied she had spoken the truth. The captain of the guard was handed over to the minister's pleasure, who let him go free, and the minister and Naran Gerel were pronounced innocent."

"The wife of the minister Ssaran was a devoted wife, well-being and true to her husband," said the wise parrot when he had finished this tale. "If, therefore, thou art devoted and brave even as the wife of the minister Ssaran, then go abroad and pay visits according to thy desire; but if not, then beware that thou set not foot outside the door."

After these words the merchant's wife gave up her

intention of going out, and remained at home. And thus the wise parrot dealt with her every day of the seventy-one days that the merchant was absent.

Then said the Sûta further to Ardschi-Bordschi, "If thy wife, O Ardschi-Bordschi! is worthy to be compared to the wife of the minister Ssaran, not to mention the comparison with Tsetsen Büdschiktschi, wife of the magnanimous King Vikramâditja, then may she prostrate herself with her forehead upon the foot of this throne; but if not, then on her peril let her not approach it."

NOTES.

1. Kalmuck. "The Khalmoucks or Calmuks, are very far from enjoying in Asia the importance our books of geography assign them. In the Khalmoukia of our imagining, no one knew of the Khalmouks. At last we met with a Lama who had travelled in Eastern Tibet, and he told us that one of the Kolo tribes is called Khalmouk." The Kolos are a nomad people of Eastern Tibet, of predatory habits, living in inaccessible gorges of the Bayen Kharet mountains, guarded by impassable torrents and frightful precipices, towards the sources of the Yellow River; they only leave their abode to scour the steppes on a mission of pillage upon the Mongolians. The Mongolians of the Koukou-Noor (Blue Lake) hold them in such terror, that there is no monstrous practice they do not ascribe to them. They profess Buddhism equally with the Mongolians. See "Missionary Travels in Tartary, Tibet, and China," by Abbé Huc, vol. i. chap. iv.

2. "The various Dekhan dialects, i.e. of the Tuluvas, Malabars, Tamuls, Cingalese, of the Carnatic, &c., though greatly enriched from Sanskrit, would appear to have an entirely independent origin. The same may be said of the popular traditions." Lassen, vol. i. 362—364.

3. The Tirolean legend of the Curse of the Marmolata, which I have given at pp. 278—335 of "Household Stories from the Land of Hofer," may well be thought to be a reproduction and reapplication of this, one of the most ancient of myths.

4. Even the *Mahâ Bhârata*, however, gives no consecutive and reliable account of the original settlement in the country. Franz Bopp, one of the earliest to attempt its translation, thus happily describes it. He likens it to an Egyptian obelisk covered with hieroglyphics, "*an dem die Grundform von der Erde zum Himmel strebe, aber eine Fülle von Gestalten, (von denen eine auf die andre deute, eine ohne die andre räthselhaft bleibe,) neben und durch einander hinziehe und Irdisches und Himmlisches wundersam verbinde.*"—The pervading plan of the work is one straining from earth upwards to heaven, but overlaid with a multiplicity of figures, each one so intimately related with the other, that any would be incomprehensible without the rest; the thread of the life of one interwoven with those of the others, and all of them together creating a wondrous bond between the things of this world and the things which are above.

5. "The only way to gain acquaintance with the early history of India is by making use of its *Sagas.*" Lassen, *Indische Alterthumskunde*, vol. i., pref. p. vii. But I shall have more to say on this head when I come to the story of Vikramâditja.

6. Some, however, seem to go too far, when they labour to prove that this is the case with every individual European legend, many of which are manifestly created by Christianity; and write as if every accidental similarity of incident necessarily implied parentage or connexion.

7. See introduction to his Translation of Pantschatantra. I have thought it worth while to mention this on account of the present collection being Mongolian.

DEDICATION.

1. Shâkjamuni—the family name of Buddha, the originator of Buddhism. It means "Hermit of the tribe of Shâkja," the *Shâkja* being one of the earliest Indian dynasties of which there are any records. His great-grandfather was Gajasena, whose son Sinahânu married Kâkkanâ, also of the Shâkja lineage. Their son Shuddhodana married Mahâpragâpatî (more commonly called by her subsequently received name of Mâja = "the creative power of the godhead") a daughter of Angana, Kâkkanâ's brother, and became the father of Buddha[1].

---

[1] Lassen, *Indische Alterthumskunde*, ii. 67, 68.

According to the Mahavansha, Gajasona was descended from Ixvâku, through the fabulous number of eighty-two thousand ancestors! He was also wont to call himself *Shramana-Gautama*, to mark his alliance with a certain priestly family of Brahmans and thereby disarm any animosity on their part toward his teaching. He was also called Shâkjasinha = "Lion of the tribe of Shâkja," to show that he belonged to the warrior caste.

He was brought up as heir to the crown, and was trained in the use of arms and in all matters appertaining to the duties of a ruler. At the age of sixteen he was married, and we have the names of his three wives— Utpalavarnâ, Jashodharâ, and Bhadrakâkkanâ. Up to the age of twenty-eight he lived a life entirely devoted to the pursuit of pleasure, his time being passed between the respective attractions of three splendid palaces built for him by his father. At about this age he appears to have grown weary of this desultory kind of life, and one day, meeting in his walks with an old man, a sick man, a corpse, and a priest, he was led to turn his thoughts upon the evils and the evanescence of life. Rambling on instead of returning home he sat down to rest under the shade of a gambu-tree, and here he found fresh food for his melancholy reflections in the miserable condition of the country people living around. The legend says the *Devatâ*, or gods, appeared to him in the shape of these suffering people in order further to instruct him in his new views of existence. In all probability his previous mode of life never having brought him in contact with the actual miseries of the needy this sight appeared to him in the light of an apparition.

The result of his deliberations was the resolve to withdraw to a place of solitude, where he might be free to consider by what means human beings could be relieved from their miseries[1].

With this view he forsook his family and his palatial residences, and having laid aside his rich clothing he wandered forth unknown to all, begging his food by the way till he found the retirement he sought in the hermitages of various Brahmans of Gajâsbira, a hill in the neighbourhood of Gaja[2], whence he is sometimes called Gajashiras.

---

[1] Mahavansha, ii. v. 11.

[2] Now called Gaya, still an important town in the province of Behar. *Vihara*, whence Behar (for B and V are allied sounds in Sanskrit), is the Buddhist word for a college of priests, and the substitution of Behar

He first placed himself under the teaching of the Brahman Arâda Kâlâma, afterwards under that of another called Rudraka, who was so struck with the progress he made in the acquisition of every kind of knowledge that he soon associated him with himself in the direction of his disciples. Five of these (four of them belonging to the royal Shâkja family), Âgnâta, Ashvagit, Bhadraka, Vashpa, and Mahârâta, grew so much attached to him and his views that they subsequently became the first followers of his separate school of teaching.

Having after some years exhausted the satisfaction he found in the pursuit of study he set out restlessly on a new search after happiness, followed by the five disciples I have named, and retired with them to a more exclusive solitude still, where for six years he gave himself up to unbroken contemplation amid the most rigid austerities. After this he seems to have somewhat alienated his companions by relaxing his severe mode of life, for they forsook him about this time and took up their abode in the neighbourhood of Vârânasî[1], where they continued to live as he had shown them at the first[2].

This mode of life even he, however, does not appear to have altered except in the matter of abridging his fasts, for his habitual meditations went on as before, and they were believed to have so illumined his understanding that he finally received the appellation of *Buddha* = "the enlightened one," while from his favourite habit of making these meditations under the shade of the *ashvattha*, the "trembling leaf" fig-tree, that tree, which has acquired so prominent a place in Buddhist records, legends, and institutions, came to be called the *bodhiruma*, literally, "tree of knowledge," and it has even been distinguished by naturalists from the *ficus indica*, of which it is a variety, by the title of *ficus religiosa*. It became so inseparable an adjunct of Buddhism that wherever the teaching of Shâkjamuni was spread this tree was transplanted too[3].

---

for Magadha, the more ancient name of the province, points to a time when Buddhism flourished there and had many such colleges (see Wilson in Journal of As. Soc. v. p. 124).

[1] Benares.

[2] Burnouf, *Introd. à l'Hist. du Buddhisme*, i. 157.

[3] In the far east of India and in Ceylon, where it is not indigenous, we have historical evidence that it was introduced by the Buddhists;

The oppression of solitude appears to have overcome Shâkjamunî at last, and he consequently took the resolution of journeying to Vâranasî to

---

also in Java. Lassen, *Indische Alterthumskunde*, i. 257; also p. 260, note 1, where he gives the following comparative descriptions of the two species, though he also points out that in ancient descriptions the characteristics of the two trees are often confused. The *ficus indica* or banian (it received the name of banyan from the Indian merchants, Banjans, by whose means it was propagated), is called in Bengal *Njagrôdha* and *Vata* (the Dutch call it "the devil's tree "). The *ficus religiosa* is called *ash-vattha*, and *pippala*. They plant the one by the side of the other with marriage ceremonies in the belief that otherwise the banian would not complete its peculiar mode of growth. Hence arises a most pleasing contrast between the elegant lightness of the shining foliage of the *ficus religiosa* and the solemn grandeur of the *ficus indica* with its picturesque trunks, its abundant leafage, its spangling of golden fruits, its pendulous roots, enabling it to reproduce itself after the fashion of a temple with countless aisles. It affords cool salubrious shade, a single one forming in time a forest to itself, and sufficing to house thousands of persons. The leaves of both supply excellent food for elephants, and birds and monkeys delight in its fruit, which, however, is not edible by man, nor is its wood of much use as timber. The *pippala* does not grow to nearly so great a size as the other, never attaining so many stems, but nothing can be more graceful than its appearance when, overgrowing from a building or another tree; its leaves tremble like those of the aspen (Lassen, i. 255—261, and notes). Under its overarching shade altars were erected and sacrifice offered up. To injure it wilfully was counted a sin (an instance is mentioned in Bp. Heber's "Journey," i. 621). A most prodigious Boddhi-tree, or rather five such growing together, still exists in Ceylon, which tradition says was transplanted thither with most extraordinary pomp and ceremonies at the time of the introduction of Buddhism into the island. They grow upon the fourth terrace of an edifice built up of successive rows of terraces, forming the most sacred spot in the whole island. Upon the above supposition this Boddhi-grove would be something like 2000 years old. Several very curious legends concerning it are given in a paper called "Remarks on the Ancient City of Anarâja-pura," by Captain Chapman, in Trans. of R. As. of Gr. Br. i. and iii. The Brahmans honoured it as well as the Buddhists, and made it a parable of the universe, its stem typifying the connexion of the visible world

seek out his former companions.   At their first meeting they were so
scandalized to see him look so well and hearty instead of emaciated by
austerities that they refused to pay him any respect.   But when he
showed them that he had attained to the illumination of a Buddha they
accepted his teaching and put themselves entirely under his guidance.
The number of his disciples increased meantime amazingly.   As they
lived by alms they received the name of *Bhixu* as a term of reproach.
Ere long we find him sending out sixty of them, whom he invested with
a certain high dignity he called *Arhat*[1], to spread his teaching wherever
they came.   He himself wandered for nineteen years over the central and
eastern districts of the country, teaching,—his agreeable presence and
benevolence of manner, and, the legends say, the wonderful things he
did, winning him numerous converts wherever he went[2].   Some gave
themselves up to a life of contemplation in the jungle, others associated
themselves with him in his travels.   When the rainy season set in they
had to find shelter for the four months in such colleges of Brahmans or
houses of families as they found well inclined towards them.   This *Varshavasana*, as it was called, afforded them additional opportunity of
making known their ideas.

Shâkjamuni himself seems to have won over several kings to his way
of thinking; one of them, king of Pankâla, he made an *Arhat ;* another,
the king of Koshala, stirred himself very much to awaken Shuddodana
to a sense of the merit of his son, sending to congratulate him because
one of whom he was progenitor had found the means by which mortals
might attain to unending happiness.   For once, making an exception to
the proverb that a prophet meets with little honour in his own country,
fortune favoured him in this matter also, and his father, who violently
opposed his withdrawal from his due mode of life in the first instance,

---

with a divine invisible spirit, and the up and-down growth of the branches
and roots the restless striving of all creatures after an unattainable perfection ; but it was the Buddhists for whom it became in the first instance
actually sacred by reason of the conviction said to have been received by
Shâkjamuni while observing its growth (reminding forcibly of the tradition about Sir I. Newton and the apple), that the perpetual struggles of
this changeful life could only find ultimate satisfaction in that reunion
with the source whence they emanated, which he termed *Nirvâna*.

[1] Burnouf, i. 295.
[2] Burnouf, p. 194.

sent eight messengers one after the other to beg him to come and adorn his court with his wisdom. Each one of these, however, was so won by his teaching that he never returned to the king, but remained at the feet of Shâkjamuni. Last of all the king sent his minister Karka, who, though he also adopted his views, prevailed on him to let him take back the message that he would satisfy his father's requests. The king meantime built a *vihâra* for him under a grove of his favourite *Njagrodha*, or sacred fig-tree. His return home happened in the twelfth year after his departure, but when he had made his teaching known among his kindred he set out on his travels again, only returning at intervals, as to any other vihâra, for the rainy season. A great many of his family joined themselves to him, among them his son Râhula, and his nephew Ânanda, who became one of his most celebrated followers.

In the twentieth year of his Buddhahood and the fifty-sixth of his age, he was seized with a serious illness, during which he announced his conviction that his end, or *nirvâna*, was at hand, that is, his entering on that state which was the ultimate object which he bid his followers strive to attain—the completion of all possible knowledge and the consequent dissolution of personal individuality[1] ; further, that it should take place at Kushinagara, the capital of the Malla people[2]. Soon after, he accomplished his prediction by setting out for this place, visiting by the way many of the spots where he had establishments of disciples, and arriving there in a state of utter exhaustion and prostration. On this journey he made more converts, but after his arrival gave himself up to contemplation which he considered necessary to perfect his fifth or highest degree of knowledge, until his death. This took place under a *Shala*-grove, or grove of sal-trees. His body was by his own desire treated with the

---

[1] *Nirvâna* means literally in Sanskrit "the breathing out," "extinction"—extinction of the flame of life, eternal happiness, united with the Deity. Böhtlingk and Roth's Sanskrit Dictionary, iv. 208. In Buddhist writings, however, it is difficult to make out any idea of it distinct from annihilation. Consult Schmidt's Trans. of *sSanang sSetzen*, pp. 307—331 ; Schott. Buddhaismus, p. 10 and 127 ; Köppen, i. 304—309. " Existence in the eye of Buddhism is nothing but misery. . . . Nothing remained to be devised as deliverance from this evil but the destruction of existence. This is what Buddhists call *Nirwana*." (Alwis' Lectures on Buddhism, p. 29.)

[2] Concerning the locality of the Malla people, see Lassen, *Indische Alterthumskunde*, i. 549.

honours only to be paid to a *Kakravartin*[1], or supreme ruler. After burning his body the ashes were preserved in an urn of gold. His death is reckoned to have taken place in the year 543 B.C.[2], according to the Buddhists of Ceylon and Southern India generally. Those of the northern provinces, the Japanese and Mongolians, have a very different chronology, and place his birth about the year 950 B.C. The Chinese are divided among themselves about it and say variously, 688, 1070, and 1122[3].

A great number of claimants demanded his ashes in memorial of him, and finally, by the advice of a Brahman named Drona, they were partitioned among eight cities, in each of which a *kaitja*, or shrine[4], was erected to receive them. A great gathering of his followers was held at Kushinagara, of which Kâshjapa was *sanghasthavira*, or president, Buddha having himself previously designated him for his successor. He had been a distinguished Brahman. It is said by one of the exaggerations common in all Indian records that there were seven hundred thousand of the new religionists present. Five hundred were selected from among the most trustworthy to draw up the *Sanghiti*, or good laws of Buddha. Then they broke up, determining to travel over Gambudvîpa, consoling the scattered Bhixu for the loss of their master, and to meet again at Râgagriha at the beginning of the month *Ashâdha* (answering to the end of our June) for the *Varshavasana*.

This synod lasted seven months. Its chief work was the compilation of the *Tripitaka*—"the three baskets" or "vessels" supposed to contain all Shâkjamuni's teaching: 1. The *Sutra-pitaka*, containing the conversation of Shâkjamuni (of these I have had occasion to speak in another place[5]); 2. The *Vinaja-pitaka*, containing maxims by which the dis-

---

[1] This word is a favourite with Buddhist writers, and means literally "him of the rolling wheel," primarily used to denote a conqueror riding on his chariot. See Lassen, *Indische Alterthumskunde*, i. 810, n. 2.

[2] Lassen, ii. 52, n. 1, and 74, n. 6; and i. 356, n. 1.

[3] Professor Wilson seems to have been so much perplexed by these divergencies of chronology, that in a paper by him, published in Journ. of R. As. Soc. vol. xvi. art. 13, he endeavours to show on this (and also on other grounds) that it is possible no such person ever existed at all!

[4] See Burnouf, p. 348, n. 3; see also infra, n. 3 to "The False Friend;" also note 2 to "Vikramâditja's Birth."

[5] Supra, Notice of Vikramâditja, pp. 238, 239.

ciple's life was to be guided; and the *Ahidharma-pitaka*, containing an exposition of religious and philosophical teaching. The first was under the revision of Ânauda; the second under that of Upâli; and the third under that of Kâcjapa. The *Tripitaka* also bears the name of *Sthavira*, because only such took part in its compilation; also "of the five hun-dred," because so many were charged with its compilation.

It is important, however, to bear in mind, because of the monstrous exaggerations and extravagant incidents subsequently introduced [1] that these were only compilations preserved by word of mouth; the art of writing was scarcely known in India at this time. "After the *Nirvâna* of Buddha, for the space of 450 years, the text and commentaries and all the words of the Tathâgato were preserved and transmitted by wise priests orally. But having seen the evils attendant upon this mode of transmission, 550 *rahats* of great authority, in the cave called *Alôka* (Alu), in the province of Malaya, in Lankâ, under the guardianship of the chief of that province caused the sacred books to be written [2]." As this "text and commentaries" are reckoned to consist of 6,000,000 words, and the Bible of about 500,000, we may form some idea of the impossi-bility of so vast a body of language being in any way faithfully preserved by so treacherous a medium as memory.

Megasthenes (Fragm. 27, p. 421, b.) and Nearchos (Fragm. 7, p. 60, b.) particularly mention that the Indians had no written laws, but their code was preserved in the memory of their judges; thus testifying to the practice of trusting to memory in the most important matters. Schwanbeck (Megast. *Ind.* p. 51) remarks that the Sanskrit word for a collection of laws—*Smriti*—means also memory. J. Prinsep (in his paper on the Inscriptions of the Rocks of Girnar, in Journ. of As. Soc. of Beng. vii. 271) is inclined to think some of the rock-cut inscriptions are as early as 500 B.C.; which would show they had some knowledge of a written character then; Lassen, however, is of opinion that this is altogether too early; but there seems no doubt that there are some both of and

---

[1] "Only about a hundred years elapsed between the visit of Fa-Hian to India and that of Soung-yun, and in the interval the absurd traditions respecting Sâkya-Muni's life and actions would appear to have been in-finitely multiplied, enlarged, and distorted." (Lieut.-Col. Sykes' Notes on the Religious, Moral, and Political State of Ancient India, in Journ. of R. As. Soc. No. xii. p. 280.)

[2] Turnour, in Journ. of As. Soc. of Bengal, 722.

anterior to the reign of Ashoka, 246 B.C. Megasthenes indeed mentions that he had heard they used a kind of indurated cotton for writing on. But the use, neither of this material nor of a written character, could have been very common or extended, for Nearchos (Strabo, xvi. § 67) wrote, "It is said by some, the Indians write on indurated cotton stuff, but others say they have not even the use of a written alphabet."

Though thus disfigured and overlaid as time went by, the great intention which Shâkjamuni himself seems to have had in view in the preparation of his doctrine was to destroy the exclusiveness of the Brahmanical castes, and that most especially in its influence on the future and final condition of every man, and thus he accepted men of all castes, even the very lowest [1], and the out-caste too, among not only his disciples but among his priesthood. It was thus in its origin a system of morals rather than of faith. It was full of maxims inculcating virtue to be pursued—not indeed out of obedience to the will of a Divine and all perfect Creator—but with the object of escaping the necessity of the number of re-births taught by the Brahmans and of sooner attaining to *nirvâna*. It set up, therefore, no mythology of its own [2], nor put forward any statement of what gods were to be honoured. Nevertheless it was grafted on to the mythology prevailing at the time, and many of the gods then honoured are incidentally mentioned in the *Sutra* as accepted objects of veneration. The Vêda, or sacred teaching of the Brahmans, is quoted in almost every page [3]. The gods who thus come in for mention in the simple *Sutra* are the following [4]:—The three gods of the later mythology bear here the names of (1) Brahmâ and Pelâmaha; (2) Hari, Ganârdana, Nârâjana, and Upêndra (it is important to note that the name of Krishna does not appear at this period at all); (3) Shiva and Shankara. Indra was now placed at the head of gods of the second rank. We have also Shakra, Vâsava, and Shakipati, called the husband of Shaki. Of the other Lôkapâla, Kuvera and Varunna are named. It is doubtless only by accident that more do not find mention. Of the demigods Visvakarman, the Gandharba, Kinnara, Garuda, Jaxa the Serpent-god, Asura, and Danava, along with other evil genii and serpent-gods. The most often named—particularly in the colloquies between Buddha and his disciples

---

[1] Lassen, ii. 440.   [2] Lassen, ii. 453, 454.
[3] Burnouf, *Introd. a l'Hist. du Buddh.* i. 137.
[4] Burnouf, *Introd.* &c. i. 131 et seq.

—is Indra with the adjunctive appellation of *Kaushika*. Indra was at the time of Shâkjamuni himself the favourite god ; the other great gods had not yet received the importance they afterwards acquired, nor had any thing like the idea of a trine unity or equality been broached [1] as we shall presently see ; even these allusions were but scanty [2]. It was long before the whole Brahmanical system of divinities came to form an integral part of the Buddhist theosophy [3].

Hence Shakjâmuni, as well as his contemporary and earliest succeeding disciples, lived for the most part [4] on good terms with the Brahmans, some of whom were among the most zealous in securing the custody of some part of his ashes. But they were not long ere they perceived that as this new teaching developed itself its tendency was to supersede their order. Then, a life and death struggle for the upper-hand ensued which lasted for centuries, for while the Buddhists were on the one side fighting against the attempted extermination, on the other side they were spreading their doctrines over an ever-fresh field by the journeyings of their missionaries, a proceeding the more exclusive Brahmans had never adopted. This went on till by the one means and the other Buddhism had been almost entirely banished from Central India, where it took its rise, but had established itself on an enduring basis as remote from its original centre as Ceylon, Mongolia, China, Japan, the Indian Archipelago, and perhaps even Mexico [5]. This state of things was hardly established before the 14th century [6]. But from information on the condition of religion in India preserved by the Chinese pilgrim Fahien, who traversed a great part of Asia, A.D. 399—414, Buddhism had already at that time suffered great losses, for at Gaja itself the temple of Buddha was a deserted ruin. From the writings of another Chinese pilgrim, Hiuen Thsang, whose travels took place in the 7th century, it would seem that the greatest Brahmanical persecution of the Buddhists did not take place before 670 [7]. That it had cleared them out of Central India by the

---

[1] "There is no reference even in the earlier Vêda to the *Trimurti* : to Donga, Kali, or Rama." (Wilson, *Rig-Vêda Sanhita.*)

[2] Burnouf, i. 90, 108.

[3] Lassen, ii. 426, 454, 455 and other places.

[4] "No hostile feeling against the Brahmans finds utterance in the Buddhist Canon." (Max Müller, Anc. Sanskr. Literature.)

[5] Lassen, iv. 644, 710.

[6] Lassen, ii. 440.

[7] Lassen, iv. 646—709.

date I have named above is further confirmed by Mâdhava, a writer of the 14th century, quoted by Professor Wilson, who "declares that at his date not a follower of Buddha was to be found in all Hindustan, and he had only met some few old men of that faith in Kashmir." "At the present day," adds Wilson, "I never met with a person who had met with natives of India Proper of that faith, and it appears that an utter extirpation of the Buddha religion in India Proper was effected between the 12th and 16th centuries." Nevertheless it is the system of religion which next after the Catholic Church counts the greatest number of followers.

Dr. Gützlaff (in his "Remarks on the Present State of Buddhism," in "Journ. of R. As. Soc." xvi. 73.) tells us two-thirds of the population of China is Buddhist. In Ungewitter's *Neueste Erdebeschreibung*, the whole population is stated from native official statistics at 360,000,000; whence it would follow that there are 270,000,000 Buddhists in China alone; probably, however, the Chinese figures are to some extent an exaggeration.

Before concluding this brief notice of Buddhism it remains to say a few words on the later developments of the system which have too often been identified with its original utterances.

It does not appear to have been before the 10th century that Shâkja-muni was reckoned to be an incarnation of a heavenly being; at least the earliest record of such an idea is found in an inscription at Gaya, ascribed to the year 948[1], while much of his own teaching bears traces of a lingering belief in a great primeval tradition of the unity of the Godhead and the promise of redemption[2], as well as the great primary laws of obedience and sacrifice more perfectly preserved to us in the inspired writings committed to the Hebrews. The history of the deluge, as given by Weber from the Mahâ Bhârata, is almost identical in its leading features with the account in Genesis, bearing of course some additions. A great ship was laden with pairs of beasts, and seeds of every kind of plants, and was steered safely through the floods by Vishnu under the form of a great fish, who ultimately moored it on the mountain Naubandhana, one of the Himâlajas in Eastern Kashmere. The early Vêda hymns, too, had thus spoken of the Creation, "At that time there was neither being nor no being; no world, no air, nor any

---

[1] As. Rec. i. 285.
[2] Genesis iii. 15.

thing beyond it. Death was not, neither immortality; nor distinction of day and night. But It (*tad*) respired alone, and without breathing; alone in Its self-consciousness (*Svadha*, which hence came to be used for 'Heaven'). Besides It was nothing, only darkness. All was wrapt in darkness, and undistinguishable fluid. But the bulk thus enveloped was brought forth by the power of contemplation. Love (*Kama*) was first formed in Its mind, and this was the original creative germ [1]." And the Vêda was, we have seen, adopted in the main by Shâkjamuni; but the development of his views came to imply that there was no Creator at all, existences being only a series of necessary evolutions [2]. And when later a Creator came again to be spoken of, the term was involved in the most inconceivable contradictions [3]. A distinguished Roman Orientalist also writes:—" The Vêda, and principally the Jazur-Vêda and the Isa-Upanishad, contain not only many golden maxims, but distinct traces of the primitive Monotheism. But these books exercise little influence on the religion of the people, which is a mass of idolatry and superstition; moreover, they are themselves filled with the most absurd stories and fables. The Jazur-Vêda, which is the freest from these defects, is a comparatively recent production, and the author has manifestly drawn upon not only both Old and New Testament, but also the Koran [4]."

An infusion of the revealed doctrines taught by Christianity was also received into it from the teaching of the missionaries of the first ages after the birth of Christ, though similarly disfigured and overwrought. To distinguish the influence of the one and the other would be a fascinating study, but one too vast for the limits of the present pages. When we come presently to the history of Vikramâditja we shall find it presents us with a striking idea of the facility with which various ideals can be heaped upon one personality; this will serve as a key to the mode in which an unenlightened admiration for the story of our Divine Redeemer's life on earth may be supposed to have induced the ascribing of His supernatural manifestations to another being, already accepted as Divine. It is true that certain appearances of Vishnu and Shiva on earth would seem to have been believed before the Christian era; and

---

[1] Rig-Vêda, bk. x. ch. xi.

[2] Burnouf, *Introd.* i. 618.

[3] See infra, Note 8 of this " Dedication;" on the word " *Bede*," p. 346.

[4] *Verità della Religione Cristiana-Cattolica sistematicamente dimostrata*, da Monsignor Francesco Nardi U. di S. Rota. Roma, 1868.

apart from the Indian writings, the dates of which are so difficult to fix, the testimony of Megasthenes (the Historian of Seleucus Nicanor, who wrote B.C. 300) is quoted in proof that at his time such incarnations were already held. But the passages in Megasthenes, by the very fact that he identifies Vishnu with Hercules, tend only to demonstrate a belief in a different kind of manifestation of Divine power. Those who labour most to prove that the Brahmanical idea of incarnation preceded the Christian have to allow that it was only subsequently to the spread of Christian teaching that it was fully developed. Thus Lassen writes, " I have, therefore (i.e. in consequence of the allusions in Megasthenes), no hesitation in maintaining that the dogma of Vishnu's incarnations was in existence 300 years before the birth of Christ; still, however, it only received its full development at a subsequent period [1]." And in another place, speaking of the *Avatâra* (incarnations) of Vishnu, in the persons of the heroes of the epic poems, he adds, "this dogma is unknown (*fremd*) to the Vêda, and the few allusions to such an idea existing in some of its myths, and which were later reckoned among the incarnations of Vishnu, show that in the earliest ages the recurring appearance in man's nature of ' the preserving god' for the destruction of evil was not yet invented." And even of the early epic poems he writes, that though such ideas are introduced, yet the heroes still maintain their individuality. They are actuated and indwelt by Vishnu, but they are not he. This, it will be seen, is very different from the Christian dogma of the Incarnation.

Whether the extremely interesting and ancient tradition be genuine (as maintained by Tillemont) or not, that Abgarus, king of Edessa, sent messengers to our Lord in Judæa, begging Him to come and visit him and heal him of his sickness, and that our Lord in reply sent him word that He must do the work of Him Who sent Him and then return to Him above, but that after His Ascension He would send an Apostle to him, and that in consequence of this promise St. Thomas received the far East for the field of his labours—and, however much be chronologically correct of the mass of records and traditions which tell that this Apostle travelled over the whole Asian continent, from Edessa to Tibet, and perhaps China—it would appear to be intrinsically probable and as well attested as most facts of equally remote date, that both this Apostle and Thaddæus, one of the seventy-two disciples, preached the Gospel in countries east of Syria, and that his successors, more or less immediate, extended their travels farther and farther east. It is mentioned in

---

[1] Lassen, ii. 1107.   [2] Lassen, i. 488.

Eusebius (Book v. c. 10), that S. Pantæus, going to India to preach the Gospel early in the 3rd century (Eusebius himself wrote at the end of the same century), met with Brahmans who showed him a copy of the Gospel of St. Matthew in Hebrew, which they said had been given to their forerunners by St. Bartholomew[1]. Lassen himself allows, that in all probability certain Brahmans, at a very early date, fell in with Christian teachers, and brought them back home with them. Further, that the idea of there being any merit in *bhakti*, or pious faith, and a development in the teaching concerning the duty of prayer may be traced to this circumstance. Nor does he deny that when in 435, Eustathius, Bp. of Antioch, with the help of Thomas Kama, a rich local merchant, went to found a mission at Mahâdevapatma (Cranganore), he found Christians who dated their conversion from St. Thomas living there. His further efforts to disprove that St. Thomas himself penetrated very far east, and that the early Christian establishments at Taprobane and Ceylon were founded by Persian Christians, though far from conclusive, tend as far as they go but to support all the more the theory of an admixture of Christian with Brahmanical and Buddhist teaching; because, the less pure the source of teaching the more likely it was to have resulted in producing such an admixture in place of actual conversion. Nor does the circumstance on which he lays much weight, that the Brahmans resented the inroads of Christian teaching on their domain, even with severe persecutions, at all afford any proof that there were not Brahmanical teachers, who either through sincere admiration (for which they were prepared by their early monotheistic tradition), or from a conviction of the advantage to be derived in increase of influence by its means, or other cause, may have thought fit, or been even unconsciously led to incorporate certain ideas of the new school with their own.

I have only space left to touch upon two of the most important of these identifications. And first the imitation of the doctrine of the Holy Trinity. Lassen (i. 784 and iv. 570) fixes as late a date as 1420—1445 for the introduction of the *Trimurti* worship, or, as he expresses it, the bootless attempt to unite various schools by propounding the

---

[1] A great number of early authorities are quoted in Butler's "Lives," vol. xii., pp. 329—334. The subject has also been handled by Gieseler, *Lehrbuch der Kirchengeschichte*; Wilson's "Sketch of the Religious Sects of the Hindus;" Swainson's "Memoir of the Syrian Christians;" most ably by A. Weber, and by many others.

equality and unity of the three great rival gods, Brahma, Vishnu, and Shiva, who were the chief gods favoured by each respectively. Devarâja of Vigajanagara erected the first temple to the *Trimurti* about this date. Ganesha, the god of wisdom and knowledge, appeared to his minister Laxmana and bid him build a temple on the banks of the Penar to the *Hiranjagarbha*, called Brahma, Vishnu, and Shiva; this is the first example of any inscription of honour paid to the *Trimurti* [1].

Secondly, the worship of the god Crishna, whose name and attributes as well as his substitution for Vishnu, the second god of the *Trimurti*, present so many analogies with the teaching concerning our Divine Lord [2]. Whatever difficulty there may be in fixing the date of the origin of the great Pânkarâtra sect, there appears none in affirming that the full development of its teaching in the direction of these analogies was subsequent to the establishment of Christianity. This is how A. Weber speaks of it [3]. Brahmans, who had travelled to Alexandria, and perhaps Asia Minor, at a time when Christianity was in its first bloom, brought back its teaching respecting a Supreme God and a Christ whom they identified with and fastened upon their sage or hero, who had already in some measure received Divine honours—*Crishna Devakiputra* (Son of the divine woman). He also dwells on the influence exercised by the teaching of Christian missionaries. The importance given to *Devaki* would point to an incorporation of Christian teaching concerning the Virgin Mary. Weber, in a paper entitled "*Einige Data auf das Geburtsfest Krishna's*," instances many passages in the Bavrishjottara-Purana (one of the latest Puranas), which it is impossible to read without being reminded of the place of "the Virgin and Child" in Christian tradition, and which find no counterpart in earlier Indian writings. Similarly it was the later schools which dwelt on the fact of his having Nanda the herdsman for his father, seemingly suggested by our Lord's character of "the good Shepherd," because in the earlier Crishna

---

[1] In note 2 of p. 182, vol. iv., Lassen quotes several authors on the meaning of the word and its identity with the *triratna*, as Wilson calls the Buddhist Trinity of Buddha, Dharma, and Sangha. See also infra, n. 1, Tale XVII.

[2] At the same time it presents also, of course, many frightful divergencies, and of these it may suffice to mention that the number of wives ascribed to Crishna is not less than 16,000. Lassen, vol. i. Appendix p. xxix.

[3] *Indische Studien*, i. 400—421, and ii. 168.

Legends[1] this fact is sunk in the view that (though sprung from the herdsmen) he was a warrior and a hero. Nor was the teaching concerning this character of Crishna at all rapid in its extension. Its chief seat, according to Lassen[2], in what he expresses as "the earliest times," was Madura; but the first date he mentions in connexion with it is 1017, when a Crishna temple was destroyed by Mahmûd of Ghazna, Lalitâditja, king of Cashmere, built him a temple containing a statue of solid silver, and he reigned from 695 to 732; but the gold armour the image bore would point to his warrior character still prevailing down to this time. Lassen even finds[3] the introduction of the worship of Crishna[4] a subject of opposition by certain Brahmans as late as the tenth century. The great epic poem concerning him, the *Gitagovinda*, by Gajadeva (still sung at the present day at the Resa festival), was not written till the end of the 12th century[5]. In an inscription at Gujanagara, not very far from Madura, Crishna is mentioned as an incarnation of Vishnu, but the date of this is 1288; and the idea does not seem to have reached Orissa till the end of the 15th century[6].

2. From this exordium we must plainly gather that the original collector of these Tales was himself a Madhjamika, since he begins his work with an invocation of Nâgârg'una, founder of that school. He calls him "second teacher" because his undertaking was, not to supersede, but to develope and perfect the teaching of Shâkjamuni, whom he himself reverenced as first teacher[7].   [Nâgârg'una

---

[1] The very earliest, however, do not go very far back; he was never heard of at all till within 200 B.C., and seems then to have been set up by certain Brahmans to attract popular worship, and to counteract the at that period rapidly-spreading influence of the Buddhists. See Lassen, i. 831—839. See also note 1, p. 335, supra.

[2] Lassen, iv. 575.

[3] Lassen, p. 576.

[4] "On trouvera plus tard que l'extension considérable qu'a prise le culte du Krishna n'a été qu'une réaction populaire contre celui du Buddha; réaction qui a été dirigée, ou pleinement acceptée par les Brahmanes." Burnouf, *Introd.* i. p. 136, n. 1.

[5] Lassen, iv. 815—817.

[6] Lassen, iv. 576.

[7] The best account of his life and teaching is given by S. Wassiljew, of St. Petersburg, "*Der Buddhismus; aus dem Russichen übersetzt*," to which I have not had access.

Nâgârg'una was the 15th Patriarch in the Buddhist succession, born in South India, and educated a Brahman; he wrote a Treatise, in 100 chapters, on the Wisdom of the Buddhist Theology, and died B.C. 212 (Lassen, "*Indische Alterthumskunde,*" ii., Appendix, p. vi.); but at p. 887 of the same volume, and again at p. 1072, he tells us he lived in the reign of Abhimanju, king of Cashmere, and that it was by the assistance of his sage advice that the Buddhists were enabled for a while successfully to withstand opposition dictated by the Brahmanical proclivities of this king, whose date he fixes at 45—65 A.C. The difference between the two dates arises out of that existing between the computations of the northern and southern Buddhists[1]. In the *Raga-Tarangini*, ii. v. 172—177 (a chronicle of Cashmere, written not later than A.D. 1148) Nâgârguna is thus alluded to: "When 150 years had passed by, since sacred Shâkjamuni had completed his time in this world of sufferers, there was a Bodhisattva[2], who was supreme head of all the earth. This was Nâgârg'una, who possessed in himself the power of six Archats[3]. . . . . Protected by Nâgârg'una the Buddhists obtained the chief influence in the country."

Among the Chinese Buddhists he is called Luug-shu, which name Abel Rémusat tells us was given him because after death he was taken up into the serpent-Paradise[4].

The following legend has been told concerning the manner of his conversion from Brahmanism; but it is probable that what is historically true in it belongs to the life of another and much later Buddhist patriarch.

A Samanaer[5] came wandering by his residence. Seeing it to be nobly built, and pleasantly situated amid trees and fountains, and provided with all that was needful and desirable for the life of man, made up his mind to obtain admission to it. Nâgârg'una, before admitting him, required to know whence, and what manner of man he was. On his declaring himself a teacher of Buddhism the door was immediately closed against him. Determined not to be so easily repulsed the Samanaer knocked again and again, till Nâgârg'una, provoked by his pertinacity, appeared on the terrace above, and cried out to him, "It is useless for you to go on knocking. In this house is nothing."

---

[1] See supra, p. 332. [2] See infra, Note 1, Tale XI.
[3] See supra, p. 330.
[4] Concerning Serpent-worship see infra, Note 1, Tale II.
[5] Travelling Buddhist teacher. Lassen.

"Nothing!" retorted the Samanaer; "what sort of a thing is that, pray?"

Nâgârg'una saw by this answer the man must be of a philosophical turn of mind, and was thus induced to break his rule, which forbid him intercourse with Buddhists, and let him in that he might have more discourse with him. The Samanaer by degrees fascinated his mind with the whole Buddhist doctrine, and ultimately told him that Buddha had left a prophecy, saying, that long years after he had departed this life there should arise a great teacher out of Southern India, who by the wisdom of his teaching should renew the face of the earth; that this prophecy he was destined to accomplish. Nâgârg'una believed his words, and subsequently fulfilled them.

His peculiar school received the name of Mâdhjamika, because of three prevailing interpretations of the earlier Buddhist teaching he chose the one which steered its course midway (*madhjana*) between two extremes, one of which held that the Buddhist *nirvâna*, implied the return and absorption of the soul at death into the creative essence whence it had emanated; and the other, its total annihilation.

He left his ideas to posterity in a treatise, bearing the name of *Kârikâ*, denoting an exposition of a theory in verse[1]. Some idea of its intricacy may be formed from the fact that the shortest edition of it contains eight thousand sections; while the most complete has a hundred thousand. His teaching was followed up by two chief disciples, Ârjadeva, a Cingalese, and Buddhapâlita, and still holds sway in the higher schools of Tibet, which accounts for the homage of the editor of these Mongolian tales. He is honoured almost everywhere where Buddhism is honoured; near Gajâ is a *kaitja*, or rock-cut temple, called Nâgârgunî, probably commemorating some visit of his to the shrine of Shâkjamuni.

3. The whole of Buddhist literature is spoken of by its followers as contained in three "vessels," or "baskets"—*tripitaka* (Wassiljew, p. 118, quoted by Jülg); in Tibetian called *samatog* (Köppen, *Die Lamaische Hierarchie*, p. 57).

4. *Madhjamika.* See above, Note 2.

5. *Paramârtha* (true, exact, perfect understanding), and *sanvrti* (imperfect, dubious understanding), were party words, arising out of the philosophical disputes of the *Madhjamika* and *Jogâtschârja* schools. Wassiljew, pp. 321—367.

---

[1] Burnouf, *Introduction à l'Histoire du Buddhisme*, ii. 359.

6. *Magadha*. The legend is in this instance more precise than often falls to the lot of works of this nature. Instead of transferring the scene of action to a locality within the limits of the country of the narrator however, he makes Nâgârg′una to have lived on the borders of Magadha[1]. Lassen, speaking in allusion to the *kaitja* named after him, mentioned above, says there is no allusion in any authentic account of him to his ever being in this part of the country; this Mongolian tradition however corroborates the local tradition of the *kaitja*. I have already had occasion to mention how Magadha came to receive its modern name of Behar[2].

The word Magadha is also used to designate a bard; as this meaning rests on no etymological foundation, it is natural to suppose that it arises from the fact of the country being rich in *sagas*, and that successful bards sprang from its people. The office of the Magadha, also called *Vandin*, the Speaker of praises, consisted chiefly in singing before the king the deeds of his ancestors. In several places the Magadha is named along with the *Sûta*[3]. It is quite in accordance with this view that Vjâsa's[4] mother was reckoned a daughter of a king of Magadha.

It is curious that the poetical occupation of bard came to be combined with the sordid occupation of pedlar, or travelling trader, who is also called a Magadha in *Manu* x. 47, and other places.

7. *Krijâvidja*. Writings concerning the study of magic.—Jülg.

8. Bede = Bhota, or Bothanga, the Indian name of Tibet. See Schmidt's translation of the "History of the Mongols," by the native historian, sSanang sSetsen.

Before proceeding farther it is necessary to say a few words concerning the history, religions, and customs of Tibet and Mongolia, to illustrate the local colouring the following Tales have received by passing into Mongolia.

Buddhism nowhere took so firm a grasp of the popular mind as in Tibet, where it was established as early as the 7th century by its greatest king, *Ssrong-Tsan-Gampo*. No where, except in China, was its influence on literature so powerful and so useful, for not only have we

---

[1] "Southward in Bede." See Note 8.

[2] Spence Hardy, "Legends and Theories of the Buddhists," p. 243, when mentioning this circumstance, makes the strange mistake of confounding Behar with Berar.

[3] See Note 4, "Vikramâditja's Throne discovered."

[4] See supra, p. 241.

thus preserved to us very early translations from the Sauskrit of most of the sacred writings, but also original treatises of history, geography, and philosophy. Nowhere, either, did it possess so many colleges and teachers; it was by means of these that it was spread over Mongolia in the 13th century; the very indistinct notions of religion there prevailing previously, with no hierarchy to maintain them, readily yielding at its approach. Mang-ku, grandson of Ginghis Khan[1], added to the immense sovereignty his warlike ancestor had left him, the whole of Tibet about the year 1248. His brother and successor, *Kublai Khan*, who reigned from 1259 to 1290, occupied himself with the internal development of his empire. He appears to have regarded Christ, Moses, Muhammed, and Buddha as prophets of equal authority, and to have finally adopted the religion of the last-named, because he discerned the advantages to be derived in the consolidation of his power from the assistance of the Buddhist priests already possessing so great influence in Tibet. He was seconded in his design by the eager assistance of a young Lama, named *sSkja Pandita*, and surnamed *Matidhvaga* = "the ensign of penetration," whom he not only set over the whole priesthood of the Mongolian empire, but made him also tributary ruler of Tibet, with the grandiloquent titles of "King of the great and precious teaching; the most excellent Lama; King of teaching in the three countries of the Rhagbân (empire)." Among other rich insignia of his dignity which he conferred on him was a precious jasper seal. He is most commonly mentioned by the appellation, *Phagss-pa* = "the most excellent," which has hence often been taken erroneously for his name; his chief office was the coronation of the Emperor. The title, Dalai Lama[2], the head of Tibetian Buddhism, is half Mongolian, and half Tibetian. *Dalai* is Mongolian for "ocean," and Lama Tibetian for "priest;" making, "a priest whose rule is vast as the ocean."

Of the four Khânats or kingdoms into which the Mongolian Empire was divided, that called Juan bordered on Tibet, and to its Khâns consequently was committed the government of that country; but they interfered very little with it, so that the power of the people was left to strengthen itself. The last of them, *Shan-ti*, or *Tokalmar-Khân*, was turned out in 1368 by *Hong-vu*, the founder of the Ming dynasty, who sought to extend his power by weakening that of the Lamas. In order to this he set up four chief ones in place of one. *Jong-lo* who reigned

---

[1] According to Abbé Huc's spelling, *Tchen-kis Khan.*

[2] According to Abbé Huc's spelling, *Talê Lama.*

from 1403 to 1425, further divided the power among eight; but this very subdivision tended to a return to the original supremacy of one; for, while all bore the similar title of Vang = "little king," or "sub-king," it became gradually necessary that among so many one should take the lead, and for this one the title of *Garma* or patriarch was coined ere long.

The Tibetians and Mongolians receiving thus late the doctrines of Shâkjamuni received a version of it very different from his original teaching. The meditations and mystifications of his followers had invested him with ever new prerogatives, and step by step he had come to be considered no longer in the light of an extraordinary teacher, or even a heaven-sent founder of religion, but as himself the essence of truth and the object of supreme adoration. Out of this theory again rami-fied developments so complicated as almost to defy condensation. Thus Addi-Buddha, as he was now called, it was taught was possessed of five kinds of *gnâna* or knowledge; and by five operations of his *dhjâna* or contemplative power he was supposed to have produced five *Dhjâni-Buddhas*, each of which received a special name, and in process of time became personified and deified too, and each by virtue of an emanation of the supreme power indwelling him had brought forth a *Dhjâni-Bodhisattva*. The fourth of these, distinguished as *Dhjâni-Bodhisattva-Padmapâni*, was the Creator, not only of the universe, but also of Brahma and other gods whom Shâkjamuni or his earlier followers had acknowledged as more or less supreme. And as if this strange theogony was not perplexing enough, there had come to be added to the cycle of objects of worship a multitude of other deifications too numerous even to name here in detail.

Among all these, Dhjâni-Bodhisattva-Padmapâni is reckoned the chief god by the Mongolians. The principal tribute of worship paid him is the endless repetition of the ejaculation, "*Om Manipadmi hum*" = "Hail Manipadmi O!" Every one has heard of the prayer-machine, the revolutions of whose wheel set going by the worshipper count as so many exclamations to his account. "The instrument is called *Tchu-Kor* (turning prayer)," writes Abbé Huc. "You see a number of them in every brook" (in the neighbourhood of a Lamaseri) "turned by the current. . . . The Tartars suspend them also over the fireplace to send up prayer for the peace and prosperity of the household;" he mentions also many most curious incidents in connexion with this practice. Another similar institution is printing the formulary an immense number of times on numbers of sheets of paper, and fixing them in a barrel similarly turned by running water. Baron Schilling de Kanstadt has given us (in

"Bulletin Hist. Phil. de l'Ac. des Sciences de S. Petersburg," iv. No. 22) an interesting account of the bargain he struck with certain Mongolian priests at Kiakhtu, on the Russo-Chinese frontier. It was their great aim to multiply this ejaculation a hundred million times, a feat they had never been able to accomplish. They showed him a sheet which was the utmost reach of their efforts, but the sum total of which was only 250. The Baron sent to St. Petersburg and had a sheet printed, in which the words were repeated seventy times one way and forty-one times the other, giving 2870 times, but being printed in red they counted for 25 times as many, or 71,750; then he had twenty-four such sheets rolled together, making 1,793,750, so that about seventy revolutions of the barrel would give the required number. In return for this help the Mongolian Lama gave him a complete collection of the sacred writings in the Tibetian language; Tibetian being the educated, or at least the sacred, language of Mongolia.

Concerning the meaning of this ejaculation, Abbé Huc has the following:—"According to the opinion of the celebrated Orientalist Klaproth, the 'Om mani padme houm' is merely the Tibetian transcription of a Sanskrit formula brought from India to Tibet with the introduction of Buddhism and letters. . . . This formula has in the Sanskrit a distinct and complete meaning which cannot be traced in the Tibetian idiom. Om is among the Hindoos, the mystic name of the Divinity, and all their prayers begin with it. It is composed of A, standing for Vishnu, O, for Siva, and M, for Brahma. This mystic particle is also equivalent to the interjection O! It expresses a profound religious conviction, and is a sort of act of faith; mani signifies a gem, a precious thing; padma, the lotus, padme, vocative case. Lastly, houm is a particle expressing a wish, and is equivalent to the use of the word Amen. The literal sense then of this phrase is

" Om mani padme houm."
O the gem in the lotus. Amen.

In the Ramajana, where Vasichta destroys the sons of Visvamitra [1] he is said to do so by his hungkara, his breathing forth of his desire of vengeance, but literally by his breathing the interjection 'hum.'

" The Buddhists of Tibet and Mongolia, however, have tortured their imagination to find a mystic interpretation of each of these six syllables. They say the doctrine contained in them is so immense that a life is

---

[1] See the story in Note 8 to " Vikramâditja's Youth."

insufficient to measure it. Among other things, they say the six classes of living beings[1] correspond to these six syllables. . . . . By continual transmigrations according to merit, living beings pass through these six classes till they have attained the height of perfection, absorbed into the essence of Buddha. . . . . Those who repeat the formula very frequently escape passing after death into these six classes. . . . . The gem being the emblem of perfection, and the lotus of Buddha, it may perhaps be considered that these words express desire to acquire perfection in order to be united with Buddha—absorbed in the one universal soul: "Oh, the gem of the lotus, Amen," might then be paraphrased thus:—"O may I obtain perfection, and be absorbed in Buddha, Amen!" making it a summary of a vast system of Pantheism.

Buddhism, however, received its greatest and most remarkable modification in this part of the world from the teaching of an extraordinary Lama, named *bThong-kha-pa*, who rose to eminence in the reign of *Jong-lo*, and is regarded with greatest veneration among not only the Tibetians and Mongolians, including the remotest tribes of the Khalmouks, but also by the more polished Chinese, and more or less wherever Buddhism prevails.

Though subsequently pronounced to be an incarnation of Shiva he was born in the year 1357, in the Lamaseri of *ssKu-bun* = "a hundred thousand images," on the Kuku-noor, or Blue Lake, in the south-west part of the Amdo country, several days' journey from the city of Sining-fu. In his youth he travelled to gTsang-Ischbn, or Lhassa, in order to gain the most perfect knowledge of Buddhist teaching, and during his studies there determined on effecting various reforms in the prevailing ideas. He met with many partisans, who adopted a yellow cap as their badge, in contradistinction from the red cap heretofore worn, and styled themselves the *dGe-luges-pa* = "the Virtuous." Besides introducing a stricter discipline his chief development of the Buddhist doctrines consisted in teaching distinctly that Buddha was possessed of a threefold nature, which was to be recognized, the first in his laws, the second in his perfections, the third in his incarnations.

The supreme rule of the Buddhist religion in Tibet also received its present form under the impulse of his labours. His nephew, *dGe-dun-grub-pa* (born *circa* 1390, died 1475), was the first Dalai Lama. He built the celebrated Lama Palace of *bKra-schiss-Lhun-po*, thirty miles N. of Lhassa, in 1445. Under him, too, was established the institution

---

[1] See Note 4 to "Vikramâditja's Throne discovered."

of the *Pan-tschhen-Rin-po-tsche* (the great venerable jewel of teaching), or Contemplative Lama. *Tsching-Hva*, the eighth Emperor of the Ming Dynasty, established their joint authority as superior to all the eight princely Lamas set up by *Jo-long*[1].

Abbé Huc, in the course of his enterprising missionary travels, visited all the places I have had occasion to mention, spending a considerable time at some of them. By local traditions, collected by word of mouth and from Lamaistic records, he gives us a most fantastic and entertaining narrative of Tsong-Kaba, as he calls the Buddhist reformer: of the fables concerning his birth ; of the marvellous tree that grew from his hair when his mother cut it; of his mature intelligence in his tenderest years; his supernatural call to Lha-sa (Land of Spirits); and of the very peculiar mode of argument by which he converted Buddha Chakdja, the Lama ot the Red Cap. More important than all this, however, is the light he throws on the mode in which the great incorporation of Christian ideas and ceremonial into Buddhist teaching came about. During his years of retirement Tsong-Kaba became acquainted with a mysterious teacher "from the far West," almost beyond question " one of those Catholic missionaries who at this precise period penetrated in such numbers into Upper Asia." The very description preserved of his face and person is that of a European. This strange teacher died, we know not by what means, while Tsong-kaba was yet in the desert ; and he appears to have accepted as much of his doctrine as either he had only time to learn or as suited his purpose, and this in the main had reference " to the introduction of a new Liturgy. The feeble opposition which he encountered in his reformation would seem to indicate that already the progress ot Christian ideas in these countries had materially shaken the faith in Buddha. . . . . The tribe of Amdo, previously altogether obscure, has since this reformation acquired a prodigious celebrity. . . . . The mountain at the foot of which Tsong-Kaba was born became a famous place of pilgrimage ; Lamas assembled there from all parts to build their cells[2]; and thus by degrees was formed that flourishing Lamasery, the fame or which extends to the remotest confines of Tartary. It is called Komboun, from two Tibetan words, signifying ten thousand images. He died at the Lamasery of Khaldan ('celestial beatitude'), situated on the top of a

---

[1] Consult C. F. Köppen, *Die Lamaische Hierarchie.*

[2] According to Huc's version of his history he was not born in a Lamasery, but in the hut of a herdsman of Eastern Tibet, in the county of Amdo, south of the Kouku-Noor.

mountain about four leagues east of Lha-Ssa, said to have been founded by him in 1409. The Tibetians pretend that they still see his mar-vellous body there fresh and incorruptible, sometimes speaking, and by a permanent prodigy always holding itself in the air without any support.

"Mongolia is at present divided into several sovereignties, whose chiefs are subject to the Emperor of China, himself a Tartar, but of the Mantchu race. These chiefs bear titles corresponding to those of kings, dukes, earls, barons, &c. They govern their states according to their own pleasure. They acknowledge as sovereign only the Emperor of China. Whenever any difference arises between them they appeal to Pekin and submit to its decisions implicitly. Though the Mongol sove-reigns consider it their duty to prostrate themselves once a year before the 'Sun of Heaven,' they nevertheless do not concede to him the right of dethroning their reigning families. He may, they say, cashier a king for gross misconduct, but he is bound to fill up the vacant place with one of the superseded prince's sons. . . . Nothing can be more vague and indefinite than these relations. . . . In practice the will of the Em-peror is never disputed. . . . All families related to any reigning family form a patrician caste and are proprietors of the soil. . . . They are called Taitsi, and are distinguished by a blue button surmounting their cap. It is from these that the sovereigns of the different states select their ministers, who are distinguished by a red button. . . . In the country of the Khalkhas, to the north of the desert of Gobi, there is a district entirely occupied by Taitsi, said to be descendants of Tchen-kis-Khan. . . . They live in the greatest independence, recognizing no sovereign. Their wealth consists in tents and cattle. Of all the Mongolian regions it is this district in which are to be found most accurately preserved patriarchal manners, just as the Bible describes them, though every where also more or less prevailing. . . . The Tartars who are not Taitsi are slaves, bound to keep their master's herds, but not forbidden to herd cattle of their own. The noble families differ little from the slave families . . . both live in tents and both occupy themselves with pasturing their flocks. When the slave enters the master's tent he never fails to offer him tea and milk; they smoke together and exchange pipes. Round the tents young slaves and young noblemen romp and wrestle together without distinction. We met with many slaves who were richer than their masters. . . . Lamas born of slave families become free in some degree as soon as they enter the sacer-dotal life; they are no longer liable to enforced labour, and can travel without interference." He further describes the Mongols in general as a hardy, laborious, peace-loving people, usually simple and upright in their dealings, devout and punctual in such religious faith and observances as they have been taught, caring, however, little for mental studies, occupied only with their flocks and herds, and continually overreached by the Chinese in all their dealings with them.

9. *Citavana*, a burying-place.—Jülg.

10. *Siddhî-kür*, a dead body endowed with supernatural or magic powers (*Siddhi*, Sanskr., perfection of power).

11. Mango-tree, *Mangifera indica.* Lassen (*Indische Alterthumskunde*, i. 276) calls it "the Indians' favourite tree; their household companion; rejoicing their existence; the cool and cheerful shade of whose groves embowers their villages, surrounds their fountains and pools with freshness, and affords delicious coolness to the Karavan-halt: one of the mightiest of their kings (Ashôka, 246 B.C.) makes it his boast (in an Inscription given in "Journal of Asiatic Soc. of Bengal," vi. 593) that besides the wide-spreading shade of the fig-tree he had also planted the leafy mango." In Sanskrit, *âmra, kûta, rasâla* (rich in juice). Crawford (Ind. Arch. i. 424) says the fruit is called in Sanskrit *mahâphala*, "the great fruit," whence the Telingu word *Mahampala* and the Malay *Mamplans* and *Manga*, whence the European *Mango*. It grows more or less all over India from Ceylon to the Himâlajas, except perhaps in the arid north-east highland of the Dekhan, but it reaches its most luxuriant development in Malabar and over the whole west coast. Besides its luxuriant shade its blossoms bear the most delicious scent, and its glorious gold-coloured fruit often attains a pound in weight, though its quality is much acted upon by site and climate. In Malabar it ripens in April; in Bengal, in May; in Bhotan, not till August. There are also many kinds—some affording nourishment to the poorest, and some appearing only on the tables of the opulent. Bp. Heber ("Journey," i. 522) pronounces it the largest of all fruit-bearing trees. To the high regard in which this tree was held it is to be ascribed that the story makes the Siddhî-kür prefer giving himself up to the Khan rather than let it be felled.

12. Gambudvîpa, native name for India. See infra, Note 6, Tale XXII., and Note 6 to "Vikramâditju's Birth."

13 Only magic words of no meaning.

14. The "white moon," designated the moon in the waxing quarter; meaning that the axe had the form of a sickle.—Jülg.

TALE I.

1. Songs commemorating the deeds of the departed, were sung at their funeral rites, often instead of erecting monuments to them; the fixing their acts in the memory of the living being considered a more lasting memorial than a tablet of stone.   Probably the custom originated before the discovery of the art of writing; it seems, however, to have been continued afterwards.   *Gâthâ* was the name given to these songs in praise of ancestry, particularly the ancestors of kings, usually accompanied by the lute.   Weber, *Indische Studien,* i. p. 186, gives specimen translations from such.

2. The elephant is the subject of frequent mention in the very oldest writings of India.   He is mentioned as a useful and companionable beast just as at the present day, in the Vêda, and the Manu (e. g. Rig-Vêda, i. 84, 17, "Whoso calls upon Indra in any need concerning his sons, his elephants, his goods and possessions, himself or his people, &c.").   In the epic poems, he is constantly mentioned as the ordinary mount of warriors.   There is no tradition, however, as to his being first tamed and brought under the service of man, though the art penetrated so little into the islands of Borneo and Sumatra, that the inhabitants used to smear themselves and their plants with poison as the best protection against being devoured by him as a wild beast.

The elephant is distributed over the whole of India from Ceylon to China, wherever there is sufficient growth of foliage.   In a domestic state he may live to 120 years, probably nearly double that time when left wild; he is reckoned at his strongest prime in his sixtieth year. His habit is to live in herds.

A beast so intelligent and available as an aid to man, and particularly to a primitive people, naturally took an important place in the mythology of the country.   We find this saliently impressed on the architectural decorations of the country; constantly he is to be seen used as a karyatyd; the world is again seen resting on the backs of four huge elephants, or the king of gods carried along by one.   It is a curious instance of appreciativeness of the acuteness of the sensibility of the elephant's trunk, that Ganesha, the god who personifies the sense of touch, is represented gifted with such an appendage.   It is among the Buddhistic peoples we find him most especially honoured. In Ceylon the white elephant (a variety actually found in the most easterly provinces) is regarded as a divine incarnation; "Ruler of the white elephant," is one of the titles of the Birmese Emperor; in Siam also it is counted sacred. In war he was an invaluable ally: they called him the Eightfold-armed one, because his four tramping feet, his two formidable tusks, his hard frontal bone and his tusk supply eight weapons. The number of elephants a king could bring into the field was counted among his most important munitions of war and constituted one principal element of his power.

The derivation of the word elephant does not seem easy to fix, but the best supported opinion is that it is a Greek adoption of the Sanskrit word for ivory *ibhadanta*, compounded with the Arabic article *al* from its having been received along with the article itself through Arabian traders; the transition from *alibhadanta* to ʼΕλέφας, ʼΕλέφαντος, is easily conceived [1].

Among the Brahmanical writers the most ordinary designation was *gag'a*; also *ibha*, probably from *ibhja*, mighty, but they had an infinite number of others; such as *rág aváhja*, "the king-bearer;" *matanga*, "doing that which (he) is meant (to do); *dvirada*, "the two-toothed;" *hastin* or *karin*, "the handed" (beast), or beast with a hand, for the Indians, like the Romans, call his trunk a hand; *dvipa, dvipájin, anékapa*, "the twice drinking," or "more than once drinking," in allusion to his taking water first into his trunk and then pouring it down his throat. Among the facts and early notions concerning him, collected and handed down by Ælianus, are the following:—that elephants were employed by various kings to keep watch over them by night, an office which their power of withstanding sleep facilitated; that in a wild state, they frequently had encounters with the larger serpents, whose first plan was to climb up into the trees and then dart upon and throttle them. But the most curious remark of all is, that they were endowed with a certain kind of religion, and that when wounded, overladen, or injured, it was their custom to look up to heaven, asking why they had been thus dealt with. (Ælianus, *De Nat. Anim.* v. 49 and vii. 44; also Pliny, viii. 12. 2.) There are also legends about their paying divine honours to the sun and moon, and in the Indian collection of fables called the Hitopadesha, there is one of an elephant being conducted by a hare to worship the reflection of the moon in a lake.

In peace they were equally serviceable as in war, and were employed

---

[1] This elaborate derivation, however, has been disputed, and it is more probable the name is derived from two words, signifying " the Indian ox." In Tibet it has no name but " great ox."

not only for riding, but for ploughing. A beast so useful was naturally treated with great regard, and we read of Indian princes keeping a special physician to attend to the ailments of their elephants, and particularly to have care of their eyesight (Ælianus, *De Nat. Anim.* xiii. 7).

3. The office of the *erliks* or servants of Erlik-Khan, (see next note) was to bring every soul before this judge to receive from him the sentence determining their state in their next re-birth, according to the merits or demerits of their last past existence. (Schmidt's translation of sSanang sSetsen, 417—421, quoted by Jülg.)

4. Erlik-Khan is the Tibetian name of Jama (Sanskrit), the Judge of the Dead and Ruler over the abode of the Departed; he is son of *Vivasvat* or the Sun considered as "the bringer forth and nourisher of all the produce of the earth and seer of all that is on it." *Vivasat* has another son, Manu, the founder of social life and source of all kingly dynasties. (Lassen, *Indische Alterthumskunde,* i. 19, 20.) As with all mythological personages or embodiments, however, the characteristics of Jama have undergone considerable modifications under the handling of different teachers and peoples in different ages, and in some Indian writings he is spoken of as if he were the personification of conscience. Thus, in the ancient collection of laws called the Manu (viii. 92) occurs the following passage, "Within thine heart dwells the god Jama, the son of Vivasvat: when thou hast no variance with him, thou hast no need to repair to the Gangâ, nor the Kuruxêtra;" meaning clearly, "If thou hast nothing on thy conscience, thou hast no object in making a pilgrimage." *Muni,* "who keepeth watch over virtue and over sin," however, more properly represents conscience. Sir William Jones, in quoting the above passage, inserts the words "subduer of all" after "Jama," probably not without some good reason or authority for assigning to him that character.

Lassen finds early mention of a people living on the westernmost borders of the valley of the Indus (iii. 352, 353) who paid special honour to Jama as god of death, deprecating his wrath with offerings of beasts; and he connects with it a passage in Ælianus, who wrote on India in the 3rd century of our era, making mention of a bottomless pit or cave of Pluto, "in the land of the Aryan Indians," into which "every one who had heard a divine voice or met with an evil omen, threw a beast according to the measure of his possessions; thousands of sheep, goats, oxen and horses being sacrificed in this way. He says further that there was no need to bind or drive them, as a supernatural power constrained them to go without resistance. He appears also to have believed that notwithstanding the height from which they were thrown, they continued a mysterious existence in the regions beneath.

" To walk the path of Jama," is an expression for dying, in the very early poems; and a battle-field was called the camp of Jama (Lassen, i. 767). In the Vêda, the South, which is also reckoned the place of the infernal regions, is spoken of as the kingdom of Jama (i. 772).

5. *Mandala,* a magic circle. (Wassiljew, 202, 205, 212, 216, quoted by Jülg.)

TALE II.

1. Dragons, serpents, serpent-gods, serpent-dæmons (*nâga*), play a great part in Indian mythology. Their king is Shesa. Serpent-cultus was of very ancient observance and is practised by both followers of Brahmanism and Buddhism. The Brahmans seem to have desired to show their disapproval of it by placing the serpent-gods in the lower ranks of their mythology (Lassen, i. 707 and 544, n. 2). This cultus, however, seems to have received a fresh development about the time of Ashoka, *circa* 250 B.C. (ii. 467). When Madhjantika went into Cashmere and Gandhâra to teach Buddhism after the holding of the third Synod, it is mentioned that he found sacrifices to serpents practised there (ii. 234, 235). There is a passage in Plutarch from which it appears the custom to sacrifice an old woman (previously condemned to death for some crime) in honour of the serpent-gods by burying her alive on the banks of the Indus (ii. 467, and note 4). Ktesias also mentions the serpent-worship (ii. 642). In Buddhist legends, serpents are often mentioned as protecting-patrons of certain towns (ii. 467). Among the many kinds of serpents which India possesses, it is the gigantic Cobra di capello which is the object of worship (ii. 679). (See further notice of the serpent-worship, iv. 109.)

It would seem that the Buddhist teachers, too, discouraged the worship at the beginning of their career at least, for when the Sthavira Madhjantika was sent to convert Cashmere, as above mentioned he was so indignant at the extent to which he found serpent-worship carried, that it is recorded in the Mahâvansha, xii. p. 72, that he caused himself to be carried through the air dispersing them; that they sought by every means to scare him away—by thunder and storm, and by changing themselves into all manner of hideous shapes, but finding the attempt vain,

A a 2

they gave in and accepted the teaching of the Sthavira, like the rest of the country. Under which last image, we can easily read the fact that the Buddhist teacher suffered his followers to continue the worship, while he set limits to it and delivered them from the extreme awe in which they had previously stood of the serpents. See also note 4 to Tale XXII.

2. Strong drink. See note 8 to Tale V., and note 3 to Tale VI.

3. *Baling*-cakes. See notes 6 and 9 to Tale IV.

4. On the custom adopted by priests of hiding precious objects in the sacred images of the gods, see Lassen, *Indische Alterthumskunde*, iii. 351.

TALE III.

1. Milk-broth is mentioned by Abbé Huc repeatedly in his travels as a staple article of food in Mongolia.

2. *Schimnu* or *Schumnu* (in Sanskrit, Kâma or Mâra) is the Buddhist Devil, or personified evil. He is also the God of Love, Sin, and Death, the Prince of the third or lower world. Sensuality is called his kingdom. The Schumnus are represented as tempters and doing all in their power to hinder mortals in their struggle after perfection, and in this view, take every sort of forms according to their design at the time. They as often appear in female as in male form. Schmidt's translation of sSanang sSetsen.

3. As an instance of the migration of myths, I may mention here, that I met in Spain with a ballad, which I am sorry I have mislaid and cannot therefore quote the verse, in which the love-lorn swain in singing the praises of his mistress, among other charms enumerates, that the flowers spring from the stones as she treads her way through the streets.

The present story, too, reminds forcibly in all its leading details of the legend I have entitled " The Ill-tempered Princess," in " Patrañas," though so unlike in the dénouement.

4. I have had occasion to speak in another place of the early Indian's belief in the dwelling of the gods being situated among the inaccessible heights which bound his sight and his fancy. The mountain of Meerû was a spot so sacred that it was fabled the sun might not pass it. Consult Lassen, i. 847, &c. &c.

5. *Churmusta* = Indra. The ruler of the lower gods, king of the earth and of the spirits of the air; his heaven is the place of earthly pleasures. Dæmons often go to war with him to obtain entrance into his paradise, and he can only fight them through the agency of an earthly hero (Brockhaus, *Somadeva Bhatta*, i. 213); hence it is that he calls Massang to fight the Schimnu-Khan for him.

According to Abbé Huc's spelling, *Hormoustha.*

TALE IV.

1. Here is one of the numerous instances where the Mongolian tale-repeater introduces into the Indian story details drawn to the life from the manners and customs around him of his own people. Compare with it the following sketch from personal observation in Mongolia, given in Abbé Huc's "Travels:"—"You sometimes come upon a plain covered with animation; tents and herds dotted all over it. . . . It is a place whither the greater supply of water and the choicer pastures have attracted for a time a number of nomadic families; you see rising in all directions tents of various dimensions, looking like balloons newly inflated and just about to take flight; children with a sort of hod upon their backs run about collecting argols (dried dung for fuel), which they pile up in heaps round their respective tents. The women look after the calves, make tea in the open air, or prepare milk in various ways; the men, mounted on fiery horses, armed with a long pole, gallop about, guiding to the best pastures the great herds of cattle which undulate over the surrounding country like waves of the sea. All of a sudden these pictures, anon so full of animation, disappear. Men, tents, herds, all have vanished in the twinkling of an eye. You see nothing left behind but deserted heaps of embers, half-extinguished fires, and a few bones of which birds of prey are disputing the possession. Such are the sole vestiges that a Mongol tribe has just passed that way. The animals having devoured all the grass around, the chief gives the signal for departure, and all the herdsmen, folding their tents, drive their herds before them, no matter whither, in search of fresh pastures."

This nomadic life, characteristic of the Mongols, would seem never at any time to have entered into Indian manners and customs. Though in early times pastoral occupations so engrossed them that they have left deep traces in their language (e. g. *gotra*, meaning originally a breed of cows, came to stand for a family lineage; and *gópa*, *gópala*, originally a cowherd, for a prince), and the hymns of the Rig-Véda are full of invocations of blessings on the herds (Rig V. 1. 42, 8. 67, 3. 118, 2); yet wherever they came they occupied themselves with agriculture also, and settled themselves down with social habits which early led to the foundation of cities. Consult Lassen, i. 494, 685, 815, &c.

2. Abbé Huc incidentally mentions also this practice of carrying the produce of the flocks and herds stored in sheep's paunches, as the present common usage of the Mongolians, and adopted by himself among the provisions for his journeyings among them (vol. ii. chap. iii., and other places).

3. *Marmot.* The sandy plains of Tibet are frequently inhabited by marmots, who live together in holes, and whose fur is at the present day an important article of the Tibetian trade both with India and China. It is now generally allowed that it must be these beasts which were intended in the marvellous accounts of the old Greek writers of the gold-digging ants. Though the Indians themselves gave them the name of ants, *pipílika* (e. g. Mahâ Bhârata, i. p. 375, v. 1860), the description of them would pass exactly for that of this little animal—in size somewhat smaller than a fox, covered with fur, in habits social, living in holes underground in the winter.

4. See note 3 to "The False Friend."

5. The number five is a favourite number in Buddhistic teaching, ritual and ceremonies. (Wassiljew, quoted by Jülg.) To Bodhidsarma, the last Indian patriarch, on his removal to China, is ascribed this sentence: "I came to this country to make known the law and to free men from their passions. Every blossom that brings forth fruit hath *five* petals, and thus have I fulfilled my undertaking." (Abel Remusat, Mel. As. p. 125.) One of Buddha, or at least, Âdi-Buddha's titles, particularly in Tibet, is *Pankagnânâtmaka*, or "him possessed of five kinds of *gnâna*" or knowledge (Notices of the Religion of the Bouddhas, by B. Hodgson), and this formed the basis of the complicated system of the later Buddhists.

The Brahmans, too, had five sacred observances which they aimed at exercising; the study of their sacred books, to offer sacrifice to the manes, the gods and all creatures, hospitality, and thereby increase as well their own virtue and renown as that of their fathers and mothers. The five necessary things are clothes, food, drink, coverlets for sleeping, and medicine.

The five colours are blue, white, green, yellow, and red. (Köppen, ii. 307, note 3.)

6. Baling-cakes are figures made of dough or rice paste, generally pyramidal in form, covered with cotton wool or some inflammable material smeared over with brown colour and then set fire to. (Jülg.)

7. *Râkschasas,* Bopp (note to his translation of the Ramajana) calls them giants. In the mythology they are evil demons inimical to man; vampires in human form, generally of hideous aspect, but capable of assuming beautiful appearances in order to tempt and deceive.

There is no doubt, however, it was the Raxasas, the wild people inhabiting the country south of the Vindhja range at the time of the immigration of the Aryan Indians, whose fierce disposition, and cruel treatment of the Brahmans gave rise to the above conception of the word. Consult Lassen, *Ind. Altert.* i. 535, where passages giving them this character are quoted; also pp. 582, 583.

8. *Manggus,* Mongolian name for Râkschasas. (Jülg.)

9. The present mode of treating the sick in Mongolia would seem much the same. Abbé Huc thus describes what he himself witnessed :—" Medicine is exclusively practised by the Lamas. When any one is ill the friends run for a Lama, whose first proceeding is to run his fingers over the pulse of both wrists simultaneously. . . . All illness is owing to the visitation of a *tchatgour* or demon, but its expulsion is a matter of medicine... He next prescribes a specific ... the medical assault being applied, the Lama next proceeds to spiritual artillery. If the patient be poor the *tchatgour* visiting him can only be an inferior spirit, to be dislodged by an interjectional exorcism ... and the patient may get better or die according to the decree of *Hormoustha*... But a devil who presumes to visit an eminent personage must be a potent devil and cannot be expected to travel away like a mere sprite; the family are accordingly directed to prepare for him a handsomes suit of clothes, a pair of rich boots, a fine horse, sometimes also a number of attendants.... The aunt of Toukuna was seized one evening with an intermittent fever.... The Lama pronounced that a demon of considerable rank was present. Eight other Lamas were called in, who set about the construction of a great puppet (*baling*) which they entitled ' Demon of Intermittent Fevers,' and which they placed erect by means of a stick in the patient's tent. The Lamas then ranged themselves in a circle with cymbals, shells, bells, tambourines, and other noisy instruments, the family squatting on the ground opposite the puppet. The chief Lama had before him a large copper basin, filled with millet and some more little puppets. ... A diabolical discordant concert

then commenced, the chief Lama now and then scattering grains of millet towards the four quarters of the compass . . . ultimately he rose and set the puppet on fire. As soon as the flames rose he uttered a great cry, repeated with interest by the rest, who then also rose, seized the burning figure, carried it away to the plain, and consumed it. . . The patient was then removed to another tent. . . . The probability is that the Lamas having ascertained the time at which the fever-fit would recur meet it by a counter excitement."

10. The respective occupations of men and women seem to remain at the present pretty much the same in Mongolia as here introduced by the tale-repeater. Abbé Huc writes : " Household and family cares rest entirely upon the women ; it is she who milks the cows and prepares the butter, cheese, &c. ; who goes no matter how far to draw water ; who collects the argols (dried dung for fuel), dries it and piles it round the tent. The tanning skins, fulling cloth, making clothes, all appertains to her. . . Mongol women are perfect mistresses of the needle ; it is quite unintelligible how, with implements so rude, they can manufacture articles so durable ; they excel, too, in embroidery, which for taste and variety of design and excellence of manipulation excited our astonishment. The occupations of the men are of very limited range ; they consist wholly in conducting flocks and herds to pasture. This to men accustomed from infancy to the saddle is a mere amusement. The nearest approach to fatigue they ever incur is in pursuing cattle which escape. They sometimes hunt ; when they go after roebucks, deer, or pheasants, as presents for their chiefs, they take their bow and matchlock. Foxes they always course. They squat all day in their tents, drinking tea and smoking. When the fancy takes them they take down their whip, mount their horse, always ready saddled at the door, and dash off across the broad plains, no matter whither. When one sees another horseman he rides up to him ; when he sees a tent he puts up at it, the only object being to have a gossip with a new person."

TALE V.

1. Kun-Snang = " All-enlightening." (Jülg.) The Mongolian tale-repeater here gives the Khan a Tibetian name (Tibetian being the learned and liturgical language of Mongolia), making one of the instances of which the tales are full, of their transformation in process of transmission.

2. Sesame-oil is mentioned by Pliny in many places as in use in India for medicinal purposes: as, xiii. 2, 7: xv. 9, 4: xvii. 10, 1, &c.

3. *Baling*-cakes.—See note 6, and note 9 to Tale IV.

4. The Brahmanical system of re-births was followed to a great extent by Buddhists, notwithstanding that it had been one chief aim and object of Shâkjamuni's teaching to provide mankind with a remedy against their necessity. (See Lassen, *Indische Alterthumskunde*, ii. 60, and other places. Burnouf, *Introd. à l'Hist. du Buddh. Ind.* i. 153.) By its teaching, every living being had to be born again a countless number of times, leading them to higher or lower regions according to their dealings under each earlier form. The gods themselves were not exempt from the operation of this law.

5. Serpent-god. See note 1 to Tale II., and note 4 to Tale XXII.

6. Tiger-year. The Mongols reckon time by a cycle of sixty years, designated by a subdivision under the names of five necessary articles, and twelve beasts with the further adjuncts of male and female. The present cycle began in 1864 and will consequently go on till 1923.

The following may serve as a specimen : —

1864, male Wood-mouse-year, *Mato khouloukhana po.*
1865, female Wood-bullock-year, *Moto oukhere mo.*
1866, male Fire-tiger-year, *Gal bara po.*
1867, female Fire-hare-year, *Gal tole mo.*
1868, male Earth-dragon-year, *Sheree lou po.*
1869, female Earth-serpent-year, *Sheree Mokhee mo.*
1870, male Iron-horse-year, *Temur mori po.*
1871, female Iron-sheep-year, *Temur knoui mo.*
1872, male Water-ape-year, *Oussou betchi po.*
1873, female Water-fowl-year, *Oussou takia mo.*
1874, male Wood-dog-year, *Moto nokhee po.*
1875, female Wood-pig-year, *Moto khakhee mo.*
1876, male Fire-mouse-year, *Gal khouloukhana po.*
1877, female Fire-bullock-year, *Gal oukhere mo.*
1878, male Earth-tiger-year, *Sheree bara po.*
1879, female Earth-hare-year, *Sheree tolee mo.*
1880, male Iron-dragon-year, *Temur lou po.*
1881, female Iron-serpent-year, *Temur mokhee mo.*

And so on to the end. The date always being quoted in connexion with the year of each sovereign reigning at the time, to make the distinction more definite.

7. Nothing can be much more revolting to our minds than the idea of

human sacrifices. Nevertheless, one of the grandest episodes of the great epic poem called the *Ramajana*, is that in which King Asbokja goes all the world over in search of a youth possessing all the marks which prove him worthy to be sacrificed : " wandering through tracts of country and villages, through town and wilderness alike, holy hermitages also of high fame." When at last he has found one in the person of Sunasepha, son of Ritschika, a great prince of seers, Visvamitra, the great model penitent, calls on his own son to take his place, crying up the honour of the thing in the most ardent language. " When a father desires to have sons," he says to him, "it is in order that they may adorn the world with their virtue and be worthy of eternal fame. The opportunity for earning that fame has now come to thee." And when his son refuses the exchange, he pronounces on him the following curse, " Henceforth shalt thou be for many years a wanderer and outcast, and despised like to a dealer in dog's flesh."

Concerning the serpent-cultus in general, see note 1, Tale II., and note 4, Tale XXII.

8. Rice is the most ancient and most widespread object of Indian agriculture; it is only not cultivated in those districts where either the heat or the means of natural or artificial irrigation do not suffice for its production; and in easternmost islands of the Archipelago, where the sago-palm replaces it. (Ritter iv. 1, 800.) The name, coming from *vrih*, to grow, to spread (whence also *vrihat*, great), suggests that it was regarded as the principal kind of corn. All the Greek writers on India mention that an intoxicating drink was made from rice, and the custom still prevails.

TALE VI.

1. *Brschiss.* I know not what country it is which is thus designated, unless the word be derived from *brizi*, the ancient Persian for rice, and is intended to denote a rice-producing territory.

2. Palm-tree. India grows a vast number of varieties of the palm-tree; the general name is *trinadruma*, " grass-tree " (Ritter iv. 1, 827). The date-palm was only introduced by the Arabians (Lassen, iii. 312). The fan-palm (*borassus flabelliformis*) is called *trinaråga* = " the grass-king," in Sanskrit also *tåla ;* the Buddhist priests in Dekhan and also in China and Mongolia use its leaves as fans and sunshades, and hence are often called tâlapatri, palm-bearers. *Tålánka* and Tâladhvaga are also

titles of Krishna, when he carries a banner bearing a palm-tree in memory of a legend which makes him the discoverer of the means of utilizing the fruit of the cocoa-nut palm. " The mountain Gôvardhana on the banks of the Jamunâ was thickly grown over with the cocoa-nut palm, but it was kept in guard by a dæmon, named Dhênuka, in the form of an ass, at the head of a great herd of asses, so that no one could approach it. Krishna, however, in company with Rama, went through the wood unarmed, but when they would have shaken down the fruit from the trees, Dhênuka, who was sitting in its branches, kicked them with his hoofs and bit them. Krishna pulled him down from off the tree, and wrestled with him till he had crushed him to death ; in the same way he dealt with the whole herd. A lurid light gleamed through the whole wood from the bodies of the dead asses, but from that time forward, all the people had free use of the trees." (*Hari*, v. 70, v. 3702 et seq. p. 577.)

3. The brandy spoken of is, probably, *koumis*, distilled from mare's milk, and makes a very intoxicating drink. Concerning its preparation, see Pallas, *Sammlung historischer Nachrichten über die Mongolen.*

TALE VII.

1. Compare note 10, Tale IV.

2. Legends of transformed maidens being delivered from the power of enchantment and married by heroes and knights are common enough, but we less frequently meet with stories presenting a reversed plot. I have met with one, however, nearly identical with that given in the text, attached to a ruined castle of Wâlsch-Tirol.

3. The Buddhist idea of the soul is very difficult to define. In other legends given later in the present volume (e. g. the episode of the burying of Vikramâdtja's body and the action of the fourth youth in " Who Invented Women ?") we find it, just as in the present one, spoken of as a quite superfluous and funtastic adjunct without which a man was to all intents and purposes the same as when he had it. Spence Hardy affirms as the result of conversations with Buddhists during half a life passed among them in Ceylon, as well as from the study of their writings, that " according to Buddhism there is no soul."

4. Compare note 7 to " Vikramâditja's Birth."

5. *Obö.* " A heap of stones on which every traveller is expected of

his piety to throw one or more as he goes by." (Jülg.) Abbé Huc describes them thus : " They consist simply of an enormous pile of stones heaped up without any order, surmounted with dried branches of trees, while from them hang other branches and strips of cloth on which are inscribed verses in the Tibet and Mongol languages. At its base is a large granite urn in which the devotees burn incense. They offer besides pieces of money which the next Chinese traveller, after sundry ceremonious genuflexions before the *Obö*, carefully collects and pockets. These Obös are very numerous."

6. The sacred mountain of Meerû. See note 4, Tale III.

TALE VIII.

1. *Kun-smon*, all-wishing (Tibetian).
2. *Kun-snang*, all-enlightening (Tibetian).
3. *Chamuk-Ssakiktschi*, all-protecting (Mongolian).   (Jülg.)
4. *Ananda*, gladness (Sanskrit).
5. *Kun-dgah*, all-rejoicing (Tibetian).
6. *Chotolo* has the same meaning as *Chamuk*, the one in Kalmuck and the other in Tibetian.
7. See note 4 to Tale V., and note 7 to "Vikramâditja's Birth."
8. *Kun-tschong* = all-protecting (Tibetian). (Jülg.)

TALE IX.

1. Heaven-gods, sky-gods, *devas*. They hold a transition position between men and gods, between human and Buddha nature. Their etherial body enables these lowest of gods, or genii, to withstand the effects of age better than mortals ; also they can assume other forms and make themselves invisible, powers seldom allotted to mortals, but they are subject to illusion, sin, and metempsychosis like every other creature. (Schott, *Buddhaismus in Hoch-Asien*, p. 5, quoted by Jülg.)

2. *Garudâ.—Garut'man* (whence Garudâ), means *the winged one*. In the epic mythology of India Garudâ was son of Kashjapa and Vinatâ, daughter of Daxa, king of the Suparn'a ("beautiful winged ones"), divine

birds, whose habitation was in the lower heavens. They were the standing foes of the serpent-gods, on whose flesh they fed. In the Vêda it is spoken of as a bird with beautiful golden wings. A *Gaudharba* of high degree, bearing shining weapons, was placed over the higher heaven. It is said that inhaling the balmy vapours, he gave birth to the refreshing rain; and that when gazing through space with his eagle eye he broods over the ocean, the rays of the sun pierce through the third heaven. From this it may be gathered that the Garudâ originally represented the morning mist preceding the sunrise over land and sea. The *Garudâ* was also the bearer of Vishnu, as the following legend from the Mâha Bhârata tells:—"Mâtali, Indra's charioteer, had fixed his eyes on Sumuka, grandson of the serpent-god Arjaka, to make him his son-in-law by marrying his daughter, Gun'aka'shi, to him. *Garudâ*, however, had already devoted him for his food, purposing to kill him in a month's time; but at Mâtali's request Indra had given promise of long life to Sumukha. When *Garudâ* heard this he went and stood before Indra and told him that by such a promise he had destroyed himself and his race; that he *Garudâ*, alone possessed the strength to bear him up through all worlds, even as he bore up Vishnu, and that by his means he might become lord of all and as great as Vishnu. But Vishnu made him feel the weight of (only) his left arm, and straightway he fell down senseless before him. After this he acknowledged that he was only the servant of Vishnu, and promised not to talk rebellious words any more."

The descriptions of him do not give him entirely the form of a bird, but rather of some combination with the human form; in what he resembles a bird he seems to partake of the eagle, the vulture, and the crane. (Schlegel, *Ind. Bibl.* i. 81.)

TALE X.

1. That the Indians were apt to yield to the temptation of drink is asserted by the Greek writers on India, who also mention that, in spite of the prohibition of their religion, wine was an article of their import trade. See Lassen, ii. 606; iii. 50, and 345, 346.

2. That the wife should give herself to be burned with the body of her husband was a very ancient custom, as it is alluded to as such by the Greek writers on India. Nevertheless it was far from universal.

3. Comp. *Mânu, dh. sh.* viii. 29, concerning the punishment of the false witness.

4. Shaving off the hair was reckoned the most degrading of punishments. (Lassen, vi. 344.)

TALE XI.

1. *Chongschim Bódhisattva.* Chongschim is probably derived from the Chinese, *Kuan-schi-in,* also by the Mongols, called *Chutuku niduber usek tschi* (He looking with the sacred eye), the present representative of Shâkjamuni, the spiritual guardian and patron of the breathing world in general; but, as Lamaism teaches, the *Particular* Protector of the northern countries of Asia; and each succeeding Dalai Lama is an incarnation of him. (Schott, *Buddhaismus,* and Köppen,'*Die Religion des Buddha,* i. 312; ii. 127.) *Bódhisattva,* from *Bódhi,* the highest wisdom or knowledge, and *Sattva,* being. It is the last but one in the long chain of re-births. (See Schott, *Budhaismus,* quoted by Jülg.; also Köppen, i. 312 et seq., 422—426, and ii. 18 et seq.; Wassiljew, p. 6, 106, 134.)

It designates a man who has reached the intelligence of a Buddha and destined to be re-born as such when the actual Buddha dies. This intermediate time some have to pass in the Tushita-heaven, and none of those thus dignified can appear on earth so long as his predecessor lives. (Burnouf, *Introduction à l'Histoire du Buddhisme Ind.* i. 109.)

2. *Suvarnadhari* (Sanskr.), possessed of gold. (Jülg.)

3. *Chutuktu,* holy, consecrated, reverend, honourable—the Mongolian designation of the priesthood in general. (Schott, *Buddhaismus,* p. 36.)

4. It requires nothing less than the creative power of an Eastern imagination first to see a difficulty in a situation simple enough in itself, and then set to work to remove it by means of a proceeding calculated to create the most actual difficulties: it is a leading characteristic of Indian tales. It would seem much more rational to have made the poor man keep up the original story of Buddha having designated him for the girl's husband, which the people at the mouth of the stream would have been as prone to believe as those at its source, than to resort to the preposterous expedient of leaving her buried in a box.

TALE XII.

1. *Küwón-ojótu*, of child intellect. (Jülg.)

2. Sandal-wood is a principal production of India. The finest grows on the Malabar coast. Among its many names *goshirsha* is the only one in use in the Buddhistic writings, being derived from a cow's head, the smell of which its scent was supposed to resemble. (Burnouf, *Introd. à l'Hist. du Buddhisme* i. 619.) *Kandana* is the vulgar name. It was also called *valguka* = beautiful, and *bhadrashri* = surpassingly beautiful. Its use, both as incense in the temples and for scent in private houses, particularly by spreading a fine powdering of it on damp mats before the windows, is very ancient and widespread.

3. *Gegén uchátu*, of bright intellect. (Jülg.)

4. Cap woven of grass. Probably the *Urtica* (*Bœhmeria*) *utilis*, which is used for weaving and imported into Europe under the name of China-grass. See *Revue Horticole*, vol. iv. ann. 1855.

TALE XIII.

1. *Shrikantha*, "one whose cup contains good fortune" = born with a silver spoon in his mouth.

2. The merchant class acquired an important position in India at an early date, as the *Manu* concerns itself with laws for their guidance. The *Manu*, however, distinctly defines trading as the occupation of the third caste (i. 90), "The care of cattle, sacrifice, reading the Véda, the career of a merchant, the lending of gold and silver, and the pursuit of agriculture shall be the occupation of the Vaishja." Similarly in the Jalimálá legend given in Colebrooke's "Miscellaneous Essays," it is said "The Lord of Creation viewing them (the various castes) said, ' What shall be your occupation ?' These replied, ' We are not our own masters, O God. Command what we shall undertake.' Viewing and comparing their labours he made the first tribe superior over the rest. As the first had great inclination for the divine sciences (*brahmaveda*) it was called *Brahmana*. The protector from ill was *Kshatriga* (warrior). Him whose profession (*vesa*) consists in commerce, and in husbandry, and attendance on cattle he called *Vaisga*. The other should voluntarily serve the three tribes, and therefore he became *Sudra*." That a Brahman's son, therefore, should condescend to engage in trade must be ascribed either to the

degeneracy of later times or to the ignorance of or indifference to Brahmanical peculiarities of the Buddhist tale-repeater; or else his parents
were of mixed castes.

In legendary tales *Banig* is a typical merchant, and the name ultimately came to designate the subdivision of the Vaishja caste, in which
trading had become hereditary. The word is derived from *pani*, which
means both to buy and to play games of hazard, and *ga*, born or descended;
hence Banig meant, literally, merchant's son. This designation later became corrupted into Banyan.

It is not possible to learn very much about the merchant's early status,
as the subject of trade would naturally seem unworthy of frequent mention in the great epic poems; nevertheless the *Ramajana* (ii. 83, v. 11)
speaks of "the honourable merchants" (*naigamâh*). Mercantile expe-
ditions, especially by sea, however, partook of the heroic, and as such
find a place even in the Mâha Bhârata; and there is a hymn in the
Vêda (Rig. V. i. 116, 5) praising Asvin for protecting Bhugju's hun-
dred-oared ship through the immeasurable, fathomless ocean, and bringing it back safely to land.

3. Apes enter frequently not only into the fables but into the epic
poetry of India. The *Ramajana*, narrating the spreading of the Aryan
Indians over the south and far-east, speaks of the country as inhabited
by apes, and of Rama taking apes for his allies; also, on one occasion, of
his re-establishing an ape-king in possession of his previous dominions.
Consult Lassen, *Indische Alterthumskunde*, i. 534, 535. Megasthenes
mentions various kinds of apes and monkeys, with, however, scarcely re-
cognizable descriptions, in his enumeration of the wild animals of India
(Fragm. x. p. 410). Kleitarchos tells that when Alexander had reached
a hill in the neighbourhood of the Hydaspes, he came upon a tribe of
apes arranged in battle array, looking so formidable that he was about to
give the signal for attacking them, but was withheld by the representa-
tions of Taxiles, king of the neighbouring country of Taxila, who accompanied him (Fragm. xvi. p. 80). The Pantcha-Tantra contains a
fable in which the King of Kamanapura establishes an ape for his body-
guard as more faithful and efficient than man; a thief, however, brings
a serpent into the apartment, and at sight of the mortal enemy of his
kind, the ape runs away. Another fable of the same collection tells of a
Brahman who, having succeeded in rearing a flourishing garden of melons,
found them all devoured as soon as ripe by a party of apes, nor was he
able by any means to get rid of them. One day he laid himself down
hid amid the leafage as if he had been dead, but with a stick in his hand

ready to attack them when they approached. At first they indeed took him for dead and were venturing close up to him, when one of them espied the stick and cried to the others, "Dead men do not carry arms," and with that they all escaped ; and it was the same with every trap he laid for them, by their wariness they evaded them all.

4. The Indian world of story abounds in tales in which the low notion of expecting some advantage to accrue in this life is proposed as the object and reward of good actions. Instances will doubtless occur to the reader. The *Pantcha-Tantra* Collection contains one in which an elephant is caught by a Khan out hunting, by being driven into a deep dyke. He asks advice of a Brahman who passes that way, as to how he is to extricate himself. "Now is the time," answers the Brahman, " to recall if you have ever done good to any one, and if so to call him to your aid." The elephant thereupon recalls that he once delivered a number of rats whom a Khan had hunted and caught and shut up in earthen jars by lifting the earthen jars with his trunk and gently breaking them. He accordingly invokes the aid of these rats, who come and gnaw away at the earth surrounding the dyke, till they have made so easy a slope of it that the elephant can walk out.

Christianity fortunately proposes a higher motive for our good actions, and the experience of life would make that derived from results to be expected from gratitude a very poor one.

5 A story, with a precisely similar episode of the recovery of a jewel by ancillary beasts, comes into the legend of another ruin of the Italian Tirol.

6. See note 4 to " Vikramâditja's Throne discovered."

TALE XIV.

1. I know not whether this placing together of lions and tigers is to be ascribed to unacquaintance with their habits, or to idealism. Though both natives of parts of India they have not even the same districts assigned them by nature. So inimical are they also to each other, and so unlikely to herd together, that it has been supposed the tiger has exterminated the lion wherever they have met. (Ritter, *Asien*, vol. iv. zweite Hälfte, 689, 703, 723.) Indian fable established the lion as the king of beasts—*Mrigarâga*. Amara, the Indian Lexicographer, places him at the head of all beasts. The ordinary Sanskrit name is *Sinha*, which some translate "the killer," from *sibh*, to kill. The same word (*sinhanâda*) stands for the roaring of the lion and for a war cry. *Sinhâsana,*

B b

literally a lion-seat, stands for a throne; for the lion was the typical
ruler. The fables always make him out as powerful, just, temperate, and
willing to take the advice of others, but often deceived by his counsellors.
The lion also gave its name to the island of Ceylon, which to the Greeks
was known as Taprobane, from Tâmbapanni or Tâmrapani, the capital
built by Vigaja, its first historical settler (said by the natives to come
from *tâmra*, red, and *pâni*, hand, because he and his companions being
worn out with fatigue on their arrival lay down upon the ground and
found it made their hands red ; but *tamra* (neut.) means also red sandal-
wood, and *parna* is a leaf, which makes a more probable interpretation,
but there is also another deriving from " a red swamp "). But this name
passed quite out of use both among native and Greek writers in the
early part of the first century. Ptolemy calls it Σαλικὴ, the Indian word
being *Sinhala*, the Pali, *Sihala* = "resting-place of the lion " (i. e. the
courageous warriors, the companions of Vigaja). Kosmas has Σιελεδίβα
= *Sinhaladvipa*, " the island Sinhala." In the writings of the Chinese
pilgrims it is called Sengkiolo, which they render " lion's kingdom." In
the southern dialects of India *l* is often changed into *r*, and thus in Mar-
cellinus Ammianus we find the name has become Serendivus. Out of this
came *zeilan* and our Ceylon. In our word "Singhalese" we have a
plainer trace of the lion's share in the appellation.

The writers of the time of Alexander do not appear to have come across
any authentic account of the tiger, and his people seem to have known it
only from its skin bought as merchandize. Nearchos and Megasthenes both
quite overstate its size, as "twice as big as a lion," and "as big as a horse."
Augustus exhibited a tiger in Rome in the year 11 B.C., and that seems
the first seen there. Claudius imported four. Pliny remarks on the extreme swiftness and wariness of the tiger and the difficulty of capturing
him. His place in the fable world is generally as representative of un-
mitigated cruelty. The Pantcha-Tantra contains a tale, however, in
which a Brahman, wearied of his existence by many reverses, goes to a
tiger who has a reputation for great ferocity and begs him to rid him of
his life. The tiger in this instance is so moved by the recital of the
man's afflictions that he not only spares his life, but nurtures him in his
den, enriching him also with the jewelled spoil of the many travellers who
fall victims to his voracity. In the end, however, the inevitable fox
comes in as a bad counsellor, and persuades him the Brahman is intending
to poison him, and thus overcoming his leniency, induces him to break
faith with the Brahman and devour him.

2. *Dakinis* were female evil genii, who committed all sorts of horrible

pranks, chiefly among the graves and at night. In this place it is more probably *Raginis* that are intended, beautiful beings who filled the air with melody. (Schmidt, trans. of sSanang sSetsen, p. 438, quoted by Jülg.)

3. *Nûpuras*, gold rings set with jewels, worn by women of rank, and also by dancing girls.

4. The custom of wearing quantities of jewelled ornaments seems to have passed into Rome, along with the jewels themselves, and to such an extent that Pliny tells us (book ix.), that Roman women would have their feet covered with pearls, and a woman of rank would not go out without having so many pearls dangling from her feet as to make a noise as she walked along. The long-shaped pearls of India, too, were specially prized for ear-rings; he particularly mentions their being made to bear the form of an alabaster vase, just as lately revived in Rome. They particularly delighted in the noise of two or more of these pendants together as a token of wealth, and gave it the name of *crotalia*, which, however, they borrowed from the Greeks. They also wore them pendant from their rings. The Singhalese pearls are the most esteemed. The dangerous fishery of these forms the occupation of a special division of the *Parawa* or Fisher-Caste of the Southern Indians. The pearl-oysters were said to swim in swarms, led by a king-oyster, distinguished by his superiority in size and colouring. Fishers aimed at capturing the "king," as then the whole swarm was dispersed and easily caught; as long as the king was free, he knew how to guide the major part of his swarm of subjects out of danger (Pliny, ix. 55, 1). They thought the pearl was more directly under the influence of the heavens than of the sea, so that if it was cloudy at the time of their birth, they grew dull and tinted; but if born under a bright sky, then they were lustrous and well-tinted; if it thundered at the time, they were startled and grew small and stunted. Concerning the actualities of pearl-fishery, see Colebrook's "Account" of the same in Trans. of R. As. Soc. ii. 452, et seq.

Megasthenes, Diodorus, Arrianus, and others (quoted by Lassen, 1, 649, n. 2), tell a curious legend by which Hercules as he parted from earth gave to his young daughter Pandaia the whole of Southern India for her portion, and that from her sprang the celebrated hero dynasty of the Pândava; Hercules found a beautiful female ornament called pearls on his travels, and he collected them all and endowed his daughter's kingdom with them.

5. It is impossible not to be struck by the similarity of construction

B b 2

between this tale and that of the Spanish colonial one I have given in
"Patrañas" with the title of "Matanzas," thus bringing the *sagas* of
the East and West Indies curiously together.

6. Lama, Buddhist priest : the tale-repeater again grafts a word of
his own language on to the Indian tale.

7. *Tîrtha*, from *tri*, to cross a river. It denoted originally a ford ;
then, a bathing-place on the borders of sacred streams; later its use
became extended to all manner of pilgrimage-places, but more frequently
those situated at the water's edge. They were the hermitages of Brahmans who gave themselves to the contemplative life before the rise of
Buddhism, while to many of them also were attached legends of
having been the dwellings of the mysterious Rishi, similarly before the
rise of Brahmanism. The fruits of the earth and beasts brought to them
as offerings at these holy places, as also the mere visiting such spots, was
taught to be among the most meritorious of acts. "From the poor can
the sacrifice, O king, not be offered, for it needs to have great possessions,
and to make great preparations. By kings and rich men can it be
offered. But not by the mean and needy and possessing nothing. But
hear, and I will tell thee what is the pious dealing which is equal in its
fruits to the holy sacrifice, and can be carried out even by the poorest. This
is the deepest secret of the Rishi. Visits paid to the *tîrtha* are more meritorious than even offerings" (made elsewhere). "He who has never fasted
for three nights, has never visited a *tîrtha*, and never made offerings of
gold and cows, he will live in poor estate" (at his next re-birth). "But
so great advantage is not gained by the *Agnishtoma* or other most costly
sacrifice as by visiting *tîrthas*." (Tîrthagâtrâ, iii. 82, v. 4055 et seq.) In
other places it is prescribed that visits paid to some one particular *tîrtha*
are equal to an offering of one hundred cows; to another, a thousand. To
visiting another, is attached the reward of being beautiful at the next re-
birth; a visit to another, cleansed from the stain of murder, even the
murder of a Brahman ; that to the source of the Ganges, brings good
luck to a whole generation. Whoso passes a month at that on the
Kanshiki, where Vishvamitra attained the highest perfection, does
equivalent to the offering of a horse-offering and obtains the same
advantage (*phala* = fruit). Several spots on the Indus or Sindhu,
reckon among the holiest of *tîrthas* pointing to the course of the immigration of the Aryan race into India. Uggana on its west bank is named
as the dwelling-place of the earliest Rishis and the scene of acts of the
gods. A visit to Gandharba at its source, or Sindhûttama the northern-
most *tîrtha* on its banks, was equivalent to a horse-offering.

The Puranas are full of stories and legends concerning *tirthas* note-worthy for the deeds of ancient kings and gods. They tell us of one on the Jumna, where Brahma himself offered sacrifice. At the Vârâha-*tirtha* Vishnu had once appeared in the form of a wild boar. The Mahâ Bhârata and other epic poems speak of these visits being made by princes as a matter of constant occurrence, as well as of numbers of Brahmans making the occasion of their visits answer the purpose of an armed escort, to pay their devotions at the same time without incurring unnecessary danger by the way. The *Manu* also contains prescriptions concerning these visits. In consequence of the amount of travelling they entailed the *tirthánusartri* or *tirtha*-visitor was quoted as a geographical authority.

The Horse-sacrifice mentioned above was part of the early Vedic religion. In the songs of *Dirghatamas, Rig-Veda* i. 22, 6 and 7, it is described with great particularity. And instances are mentioned of horse-sacrifices being performed, in the *Ramajana*, i. 13, 34, and *Mahâ Bhârata*, xiv. 89 v. 2644. There is also a medal existing struck by a king of the Gupta dynasty, in the 3rd century of our era, commemora-tive of one at that date. There do not appear altogether to be many instances named however. The Zendavesta (quoted by Burnouf, *Yacna*, i. p. 444) mentions that it was common among the Turanian people, on the other hand, to sacrifices horses to propitiate victory.

TALE XV.

1. "Diamond kingdom." It is probably Magadha (now Behar) that is here thus designated (Julg.); though it might stand for any part of Central India : "Diamonds were only found in India of all the king-doms of antiquity" (Lassen, iii. 18), and (Lassen i. 240), "in India between 14° and 25° ;" a wide range, but the fields are limited in extent and sparsely scattered. The old world only knew the diamond through the medium of India. In India itself they were the choicest ornaments of the kings and of the statues of the gods. They thus became stored up in great masses in royal and ecclesiastical treasuries ; and became the highest standard of value. The vast quantities of diamonds made booty of during the Muhammedan invasion borders on the incredible. It was thus that they first found their way in any quantity to the West of Europe. Since the discovery of the diamond-fields of Brazil, they have been little sought for in India. In Sanskrit, they were called *vag'ra*,

"lightning;" also *abhédja*, "infrangible." It would appear, however, that the Muhammedans were not the first to despoil the Eastern treasuries, for Pliny (book ix.) tells us that Lollia, wife of Claudius, was wont to show herself, on all public occasions, literally covered from head to foot with jewels, which her father, Marcus Lollius, had taken from the kings of the East, and which were valued at forty million sesterces. He adds, however, this noteworthy instance of retribution of rapacity, that he ended by taking his own life to appease the Emperor's animosity, which he had thereby incurred. -

Hiuen Thsang, the Chinese pilgrim who visited India about A.D. 640, particularly mentions that in Maláva and Magadha were chief seats of learned studies.

2. *Abaraschika ;* magic word of no meaning. (Jülg.)

3. Astrologers. Colebrooke ("Miscellaneous Essays," ii. 440) is of opinion that astrology was a late introduction into India. Divination by the relative position of the planets seems to have been in part at least of foreign growth and comparatively recent introduction among the Hindus; (he explains this to refer to the Alexandrian Greeks). "The belief in the influence of the planets and stars upon human affairs is with them indeed remotely ancient, and was a natural consequence of their early creed making the sun and planets gods. But the notion that the tendency of that supposed influence and the manner in which it is to be exerted, may be foreseen by man, and the effect to be produced by it foretold through a knowledge of the position of the planets at a given moment, is no necessary result of that belief; for it takes from beings believed divine their free agency." See also Weber, " *Geschichte der Indische Astrologie,*" in his *Indische Studien,* ii. 236 et seq.

TALE XVI.

1. *Tabun Minggan* = "containing five thousand." (Jülg.) The tale-repeater again gives a name of his own language to a town which he places in India.

2. Cows and oxen were always held in high estimation by the ancient Indians. The same word that stood for "cow" expressed also "the earth," and both stand equally in the Véda for symbols of fruitfulness and patient labouring for the benefit of others. The ox stands in the Manu for "uprightness" and "obedience to the laws." In

the Ramajana (ii. 74, 12) Surabhi, the cow-divinity (see the curious accounts of her origin in Lassen, i. 792 and note), is represented as lamenting that over the whole world her children are made to labour from morning to night at the plough under the burning sun. Cows were frequently devoted to the gods and left to go whithersoever they would, even in the midst of towns, their lives being held sacred (Lassen, i. 298). Kühn (Jahrbuch f. w. K. 1844, p. 102) quotes two or three instances of sacrifices of cows but they were very rare; either as sacrifices to the gods or as *rigagna* ("sacrifices to the living") i. e. the offerings of hospitality to the living. The ox was reckoned peculiarly sacred to Shiva, and images were set up to him in the temples (see Lassen, i. 299). Butter was the most frequent object of sacrifice (ib. 298). The Manu (iii. 70) orders the *Hóma* or butter-sacrifice to be offered daily to the gods, and the custom still subsists (see Lassen, iii. 325). Other names for the cow were *Gharmadhug* = "giver of warm milk;" and *Aghnjâ* = "the not to be slain;" also *Kâmadhênu* or *Kâmaduh* = "the fulfiller of wishes," and (in the Mahâ Bhârata) *Nandunt* = "the making to rejoice" (Lassen, i. 721). See also the story of Sabala, the heavenly cow of the Ramajana, in note 8 to "Vikramâditja's Youth." Oxen were not only used for ploughing, but also for charioteering and riding, and were trained to great swiftness. Ælianus (*De Nat Anim.* xv. 24) mentions that kings and great men did not think it beneath them to strive together in the oxen-races, and that the oxen were better racers than the horses, for the latter needed the spur while the former did not. An ox and a horse, and two oxen with a horse between them were often harnessed together in a chariot. He also mentions that there was a great deal of betting both by those whose animals were engaged in the race and by the spectators. The Manu, however (d. p. c. ix. 221—225), forbids every kind of betting under severe penalties. Ælianus mentions further the *Kâmara*, the long-haired ox or yak, which the Indians received from Tibet.

3. The "Three Precious Treasures" or "jewels" of Buddhism are *Adibuddha, Dharma,* and *Sangha,* which in later Buddhism became a sort of triad, called *triratna,* of supreme divinities; but, at the first, were only honoured according to the actual meaning of the words (Schmidt, *Grundlehre der Buddhaismus,* in *Mém. de l'Ac. des Sciences de S. Petersbourg,* i. 114), viz. *Sangha,* sacred assembly or synod; *Dharma,* laws (or more correctly perhaps, necessity, fate, Lassen, iii. 397), and *Buddha,* the expounder of the same. (Burnouf, *Introd. à l'Hist. du Budd.* i. 221.)

Consult Schott, *Buddhaismus*, pp. 39, 127, and C. F. Köppen, *Die Religion des Buddha*, i. 373, 550—553, and ii. 292—294.

4. See note 2, Tale IV.

5. Abbé Huc describes the huts of the Tibetian herdsmen as thus constructed with a hole in the roof for the smoke. The Mongolians live entirely in tents which, if more primitive, seem cleaner and altogether preferable.

TALE XVII.

1. Probably it was some version of this story that had travelled to Spain, which suggested to Yriarte the following one of his many fables directed against ignorant writers and bad critics.

1.
Esta fabulilla,
　Salga bien ó mal,
Me he occorrida ahora
　Por casualidad.

2.
Cerca de unos prados
Que hay en mi lugar,
Passaba un borrico
　Por casualidad.

3.
Una flauta en ellos
Halló que un zagal,
Se dexó olvidado
　Por casualidad.

4.
Acercóse á olerla,
El dicho animal
Y dió un resoplido
　Por casualidad.

5.
En la flauta el ayre
Se hubo de colar
Y sonó la flauta
　Por casualidad.

1.
This fablette I know it
　Is not erudite;
It occurr'd to my mind now
　By accident quite.

2.
Through a meadow whose verdure
　Fresh, seem'd to invite,
A donkey pass'd browsing
　By accident quite.

3.
A flute lay in the grass, which
　A swain over night
Had left there forgotten
　By accident quite.

4.
Approaching to smell it
　This quadruped wight
Just happen'd to bray then
　By accident quite.

5.
The air ent'ring the mouthpiece
　Pass'd through as of right,
And gave forth a cadence
　By accident quite.

6.

"O!" dixó el borrico
"Que bien sé tocar!
Y diran que es mala
La musica asnal."

7.

Sin reglas del arte
Borriquitos hay
Que una vez aciertan
Por casualidad!

6.

"Only hear my fine playing!"
Cries Moke in delight,
"That dull folks vote my braying
A nuisance, despite."

7.

It may happen some once, thus
Although they can't write,
Human asses may hit off
By accident quite!

2. The woman invents a name to frighten, and also as a trap for, her husband. " *Súrja*, is Sanskrit, and *Bagatur*, Mongolian for a 'Hero.' Such combinations are not infrequent." (Jülg.)

" *Shura* means a Hero in Sanscrit, agreeing not only in sense with the Greek word ἥρως, but also in derivation; thus revealing a primeval agreement in the estimation in which hero-nature was held. It is more properly written *Sura*, because it comes from *Svar*, heaven, and means literally 'heavenly.' It is used in that form as an appellation of the Sun. Heroes are so called, because when they fell in battle, *Svarga*, the heaven of deified kings, was given them for their dwelling-place. 'Indra shall give to those who fall in battle the world where all wishes are fulfilled, for their portion. Neither by sacrifices, nor offerings to the Brahmans, nor by contemplation, nor knowledge can mortals attain to *Svarga* as securely as do heroes falling in battle.' Mahâ Bhârata, xi. 2, v. 60." (Lassen, i. 69.)

3. "The women of Tibet are not indeed taught the use of the bow and the matchlock, but in riding they are as expert and fearless as the men, yet it is only on occasion that they mount a horse, such as when travelling; or when there chances to be no man about the place to look after a stray animal." (Abbé Huc's "Travels in China and Tibet," vol. i. ch. iii.)

4. A very similar story may be found in Barbazan's, " *Fabliaux et Contes des Poètes Français des XI—XV Siècles*," in 4 vols., Paris 1808, vol. iv. pp. 287—295. (Jülg.)

TALE XVIII.

1. Shanggasba is possibly a Tibetian word, *bsang, grags, pa* = "of good

fame," but more probably it is compounded from the Mongolian *sSang*, "treasure." (Jülg.)

2. Garudâ: see note 2, Tale I. The allusion in this place is to an image of him over a shrine.

3. Silk was cultivated in India at a very early date, probably much earlier than any records that remain to us can show; there are twelve indigenous species of silkworm. That of China was not introduced into India before the year 419 of our era (Ritter, vol. vi. pt. 1, 698). The indigenous silkworms fed upon other trees besides the mulberry and notably on the *ficus religiosa*. The Greeks would seem to have learnt the use of silk from the Indians, or at least from the Persians. Nearchos is the first Greek writer in whom mention of it is found; he describes it as like the finest weft of cotton-stuff, and says it was made from fibre scraped from the bark of a tree; an error in which he was followed by other writers; others again wrote that the fibres were combed off the leaf of a tree; yet Pausanias had mentioned the worm as the intermediary of its production (C. Müller, Pref. to his Edition of Strabo, and notes). The Romans also carried on a considerable trade in silk with India, and Pliny, vi. 20, 2, mentions one kind of Indian silk texture that was so fine and light, you could see through it, "*ut in publico matrona transluceat.*" Horace also alludes to the same, *Sat.* i. 2, 101. Pliny also complains of the luxury whereby this costly stuff was used, not only for dresses, but for coverings of cushions. Vopiscus, in his life of the Emperor Aurelian, tells us that at that time a pound weight of silk was worth a pound weight of gold. In India itself the luxurious use of silk has restrictions put upon it in the Manu. It was also prescribed that when men devoted themselves to the hermit life in the jungle, they should lay aside their silken clothing; and we find Râma (*Râmajana*, ii. 37, 14) putting on a penitential habit over his silken robe. The *Mâha Bhârata* (ii. cap. 50) contains a passage in which among the objects brought in tribute to Judhishthira is *kitaga*, or the "insect-product," a word used to designate both silk and cochineal.

4. A similar episode occurs in a tale collected in the neighbourhood of Schwaz in North Tirol which I have given under the name of "Prince Radpot" in "Household Stories from the Land of Hofer." The rest

---

[1] Virgil, Georg. ii. 121, "Velleraque ut foliis depectant tenuia Seres;" and Pliny, H. N. vi. 20, 2, "Seres, lanicio silvarum nobiles, perfusam aqua depectentes frondium canitiem." Also 24, 8; and xi. 26, 1.

of the story recalls that called "The three Black Dogs" in the same collection, but there is much more grace and pathos about the Tirolean version.

TALE XIX.

1. See note 2, Tale XVII.

2. The fox plays a similar part in many an Eastern fable. The first book of the *Pantscha Tantra* Collection is entitled *Mitrabheda*, or the Art of Mischief-making. A lion-king who has two foxes for his ministers falls into great alarm one day, because he hears for the first time in his life the roaring of an ox, which some merchants had left behind them because it was lame and sick. The lion consults his two ministers in this strait, and the two while laughing at his fears determine to entertain them in order to enhance their own usefulness. First they visit the ox and make sure he is quite infirm and harmless, and then they go to the lion, and tell him it is the terrible Ox-king, the bearer of Shiva, and that Shiva has sent him down into that forest to devour all the animals in it small and great. The lion is not surprised to hear his fears confirmed and entreats his ministers to find him a way out of the difficulty. The foxes pretend to undertake the negotiation and then go back to the ox and tell him it is the command of the king that he quit the forest. The ox pleads his age and infirmities and desolate condition, and the foxes having made him believe in the value of their services as intermediaries bring him to the lion. Both parties are immensely grateful to the ministers for having as each thinks softened the heart of the other, but the foxes begin to see they have taken a false step in bringing the ox to the lion, as they become such fast friends, that there is danger of their companionship being no longer sought by their master. They determine, therefore, the ox must be killed; but how are they to kill so disproportioned a victim? They must make the lion do the execution himself. But how? they are such sworn friends. They find the lion alone and fill his mind with alarm, assure him the ox is plotting to kill him. They hardly gain credit, but the lion promises to be on his guard; while they are on the watch also for any accident which may give colour to their design. Meantime, they keep up each other's courage by the narration of

fables showing how by perseverance in cunning any perfidy may be accomplished. At last it happens one day that a frightful storm comes on while the ox is out grazing. He comes galloping back to seek the cover of the forest, shaking his head and sides to get rid of the heavy raindrops, tearing up the ground with his heavy hoofs in his speed, and his tail stretched out wildly behind. "See!" say the foxes to the lion; "see if we were not right. Behold how he comes tramping along ready to devour thee; see how his eyes glisten with fury, see how he gnashes his teeth, see how he tears up the earth with his powerful hoofs!" The lion cannot remain unconvinced in presence of such evidence. "Now is your moment," cry the foxes; "be beforehand with him before he reaches you." Thus instigated the lion falls upon the ox. The ox surprised at this extraordinary reception, and already out of breath, is thrown upon the defensive, and in his efforts to save himself the lion sees the proof of his intention to attack. Accordingly he sets no bounds to his fury, and has soon torn him in pieces. The foxes get the benefit of a feast for many days on his flesh, besides being reinstated in the full empire over their master. In one of the fables, however, the tables are cleverly turned on Reynard by "the sagacity of the bearded goat." An old he-goat having remained behind on the mountains, one day, when the rest of the herd went home, found himself suddenly in presence of a lion. Remembering that a moment's hesitation would be his death, he assumed a bold countenance and walked straight up to the lion. The lion, astonished at this unwonted procedure, thinks it must be some very extraordinary beast; and instead of setting upon it, after his wont, speaks civilly to it, saying, "Thou of the long beard, whence art thou?" The goat answered, "I am a devout servant of Shiva to whom I have promised to make sacrifice of twenty-one tigers, twenty-five elephants, and ten lions; the tigers and the elephants have I already slain, and now I am seeking for ten lions to slay." The lion hearing this formidable declaration, without waiting for more, turned him and fled. As he ran he fell in with a fox, who asked him whither he ran so fast. The lion gives a ridiculous description of the goat, dictated by his terror; the fox recognizes that it is only a goat, and thinking to profit by the remains of his flesh perfidiously urges him to go back and slaughter him. He accordingly goes back with this intention, but the goat is equal to the occasion, and turning sharply upon the fox, exclaims, "Did I not send thee out to fetch me *ten* lions for the sacrifice? How then darest thou to appear before me having only snared me *one*?" The lion thinking his reproaches genuine, once more turns tail and makes good his escape. It has much similarity with the episode of the hare and the wolf in the next tale.

3. *Svarga.* See note 2, Tale XVII.

TALE XX.

1. *Hiranjavati,* "the gold-coloured river," also called *Svarnavati,* "the yellow river," both names occurring only in Buddhist writers: one of the northern tributaries of the Ganges, into which it falls not far from Patna, and the chief river of Nepaul. Its name was properly Ganda-kavatî = "Rhinoceros-river," or simply Gan'da'kî, whence its modern name of the Goondook, as also that of Kondochates, into which it was transformed by the Greek geographers. In its upper course it often brings down ammonite petrifactions, which are believed to be incarnations or manifestations of Vishnu, hence it has a sacred character, and on its banks are numerous spots of pilgrimage.

2. Concerning such distributions of alms, see Koppen, i. 581 et seq.

3. The story affords no data on which to decide whether this cynical speech is supposed to be a serious utterance representing the actual motives on which the mendicant life was actually adopted under the teaching of Buddhism, affording a strong contrast from those which have prompted to it under Christianity, or whether it is intended as a satire on the Bhixu. (For Bhixu, see pp. 330, 332.)

4. I know not how the tufts of wool could have got caught off the sheeps' backs on to ant-heaps, unless it be that the marmots being as we have already seen (note 3, Tale IV.) called ants, the tale-repeater takes it for granted there are marmot-holes in Nepaul like those familiar to him in Mongolia, which Abbé Huc thus describes (vol. i. ch. ii.), "These animals construct over the opening of their little dens a sort of miniature dome composed of grass artistically twisted, designed as a shelter from wind and rain. These little heaps of dried grass are of the size and shape of mole-hills. Cold made us cruel, and we proceeded to level the house-domes of these poor little animals, which retreated into their holes below, as we approached. By means of this Vandalism we managed to collect a sackful of efficient fuel, and so warmed the water which was our only aliment that day."

5. "Though there is so much gold and silver there is great destitution in Tibet. At Lha-Ssa, for instance, the number of mendicants is

enormous. They go from door to door soliciting a handful of *tsamba* (barley-meal), and enter any one's house without ceremony. The manner of asking alms is to hold out the closed hand with the thumb raised. We must add in commendation of the Tibetians that they are generally very kind and compassionate, rarely sending the mendicant away unassisted." (Abbé Huc, vol. ii. ch. v.)

6. Indian tales often remind one of the frequent web of a dream in which one imagines oneself starting in pursuit of a particular object, but another and another fancy intervenes and the first purpose becomes altogether lost sight of. This was particularly observable in the tale entitled "How the Schimnu-Khan was slain," in which, after many times intending it, Massang never goes back to thank his master at last. The present is a still more striking instance, in its consequence and repeated change of purport. In pursuing the mendicant's life, the search for the man's parents is forgotten; and the man and his wife are themselves lost sight of in the episode of the lamb.

7. Concerning the combination of the Moon and the hare, see Liebrecht, in Lazarus and Steinthal, *Zeitschrift*, vol. i. pt. 1. The Mongols see in the spots in the moon the figure of a hare, and imagine it was placed there in memory of Shâkjamuni having once transformed himself into a hare out of self-sacrifice, that he might serve a hungry wayfarer for a meal. (Bergman, *Nomadische Streifereien unter den Kalmüken, in* 1802–3, quoted by Jülg.)

8. See note 5, Tale III.

TALE XXI.

1. Compare this story with the "*Wunderharfe*" in the "*Mährchensaal*" of Kletke. (Jülg.) Its similarity with the story of King Midas will strike every reader.

2. *Chara Kitad* = Black China; the term designates the north of China.

3. *Daibang* (in Chinese, Tai-ping = peace and happiness), the usual Mongolian designation for the Chinese Emperor. (Jülg.)

4. See note 9, Tale IV.

TALE XXII.

1. *Bagatur-Ssedkiltu,* " of heroic capacity." (Jülg.) See Note 2, Tale XVII.

2. The Three Precious Treasures, see note 3, Tale XVI.

3. Pearls. Arrianus (*Ind.* viii. 8) quotes from Megasthenes, a legend in which the discovery of pearls is ascribed to Crishna. The passage further implies that the Greek name μαργαρίτης was received from an Indian name, which may be the case through the Dekhan dialect, though there is nothing like it in Sanskrit, unless it be traced from *markará,* a hollow vessel. The Sanskrit word for pearls is *muktá,* "dropt" or "set free," "dropt by the rain-clouds." (See Lassen, *Indische Alterthumskunde,* i. 244 n. 1. See also note 4, Tale XIV.) How the Preserver of mother-o'-pearl shells comes to live up a river, I know not, unless in his royal character he was supposed to have an outlying country-villa. However Megasthenes (quoted by Lassen, ii. 680, n. 2) tells us not only that there were many crocodiles and alligators in the Indus, but also that many fishes and molluscs came up the stream out of the sea as far as the confluence of the Akesines, and small ones as far as the mountains. Onesikritos mentions the same concerning other rivers.

4. The serpent-gods are spoken of sometimes as if they were supposed to wear a human form and as often as in their reptile form. In the present place in the text there is a strange confusion between the two ideas, the "son" whom the White Serpent-king comes to seek evidently wore a reptile form, as when he was in the owl's mouth he resembled the Tamer's girdle, yet the king himself and his companion are said to be riding on horses; as it is also said they come out of the water it was probably a crocodile that the story-teller had in his mind's eye, and which might fancifully be conceived to be a serpent riding on horseback, as a centaur represents a man on horseback. The serpent-gods generally would seem to be more properly termed reptile-gods, as not only ophidians and saurians seem to belong to their empire, but batrachians also; in this very story the gold frog is reckoned the actual daughter of the White Serpent-king, probably even emydians also, though I do not recall an example. Water-snakes, however, are common in Asia, and there is also there a group of batrachians called cœliciæ, which are cylindrical in form, without feet and moving like serpents, and considered to form a link between that family and their own. I do not know if this in any way

explains the symbolism whereby a creature that had any right to be reckoned a frog could be called the daughter of a serpent-king.

When the stories of encounters of heroes with huge malevolent serpents, or crocodiles, passed into the mythology of Europe, these were generally replaced by " dragons," or monsters, such as " Grendel" in our Anglo-Saxon " Lay of Beowulf." There are some, however, in which a *bond fide* serpent figures. In parts of Tirol, a white serpent is spoken of as a "serpent-queen" and as more dangerous than the others; various are the legends in which the release of a spell-bound princess depends on the deliverer suffering himself to be three times encircled, and the third time, kissed by a serpent; the trial frequently fails at the third attempt. Sir Lancelot, if I remember right, accomplished it in the end.

Every collection of mediæval legends contains stories of combats with dragons, the groundwork probably brought from the East, and the detail made to fit the hero of some local deliverance; the mythology of Tirol is particularly rich in this class, almost every valley has its own; at Wilten, near Innsbruck, the sting of a dragon is shown as of that killed by the Christian giant Haymon; the one I have given in " *Zovanin senza paura,*" from the Italian Tirol (p. 348, " Household Stories from the Land of Hofer "), has this similarity with Tales II. and V., that it is actually the water supply of the infested district which is stopped by the dragon. There is this great difference, however, between the Eastern and later Western versions of serpent myths. The Indians having deified the serpent, their heroic tales have no further aim than that of propitiating him. On the other hand, it was not long before the religious influence under which the Christian myths were moulded had connected and by degrees identified the serpent-exterior, under the parable of which they set forth their local plague, with that under which the adversary of souls is named in the sacred story of the garden of Eden; and thus it became a necessity of the case that the Christian hero should destroy or at least vanquish it.

Though the Indian serpent-gods seem to have been generally feared and hated, we have instances—and that even in this little volume—of their harmlessness also and even beneficence. An innocuous and benevolent phase of dragon-character seems to have been adopted also in the early heathen mythology of Europe. Nork (*Mythologie der Volks-sagen*) tells us the dragon was held sacred to Wodin, and its image was placed over houses, town-gates, and towers, as a talisman against evil influences; and I have met with a popular superstition lingering yet in Tirol that to meet a crested adder (the European representative, I believe, of the Cobra di capello, which is, as we have seen, the species specially worshipped in India) brings good luck. I have said I do not remember an instance in Indian mythology in which any member of the emydian family comes under the empire of the serpent-god; I should expect there are such instances, however, as the counterpart exists in Tirol, where there are stories of mysterious fascination exercised by sacred shrines upon the little land-tortoises and which have in consequence been regarded by the peasantry as representing wandering souls waiting for the completion of their purgatorial penance. See also concerning the serpent-gods, note 1 to Tale II.

5. *Mirjalaktschi.* Jülg says, " *Fettmacher* " (fat-maker) is the best equivalent he can give, but he is not convinced of its correctness, and then exposes what he understands by " *Fettmacher* " by two German expressions, one, meaning " pot-bellied," and the other not renderable in English to ears polite. It would seem more in accordance with the use of the name in the text to understand his own word *Fettmacher*, as " he giving abundance," " he making fat."

6. *Gambudvîpa.* I have already (page viii.) had occasion to explain this native name of India; otherwise spelt *Dschambudvîpa* and *Jambudvîpa* and *Jambudîpa.* But as I only there spoke of the actual species of the gambu-tree, one of the indigenous productions of India, I ought further to mention that the name is rather derived from a fabulous specimen of it, supposed to grow on the sacred mountain of Meru. Spence Hardy (" Legends and Theories of the Buddhists," p. 95) quotes the following description of it from one of the late commentaries of the Sutras : " From the root to the highest part is a thousand miles; the space covered by its outspreading branches is three thousand miles in circumference. The trunk is one hundred and fifty miles round, and five hundred miles in height from the root to the place where the branches begin to extend; the four great branches of it are each five hundred miles long, and from between these flow four great rivers. Where the fruit of the tree falls, small plants of gold arise which are washed into one of the rivers." Earlier descriptions are less exaggerated; details remaining in this one suggest that it has not been invented without aid from some lingering remnant of an early tradition of the Tree of Life and the four rivers of Paradise, " the gold of " one of which " is good."

The great continent of India being called an island is explained in a parable from the Jinâlankâra, given at p. 87 of the same work, likening the outer Sakwala ridge or boundary of the universe to the rim of a

C C

jar or vessel; the vessel filled with sauce representing the ocean and
the continents, like masses of cooked rice floating in the same.

At p. 82, he quotes from the first-mentioned commentary a description
of the mountain of Meru itself, illustrative of the habitual exaggeration
of the Indian sacred writers. "Between Maha Méru and the Sakwala
ridge are seven circles of rocks with seven seas between them. They are
circular because of the shape of Maha Méru. The first or innermost,
Yugandhara, is 210,000 miles broad; its inner circumference is 7,560,000
miles, and its outer, 8,220,000, miles; from Maha Méru to Yugandhara
is 840,000 miles. Near Maha Méru, the depth of the sea is 840,000
miles, &c.," the seven circles being all described with analogous dimensions. Also p. 42, "Buddha knows how many atoms there are in Maha
Méru, although it is a million miles in height."

TALE XXIII.

1. "The five colours," see note 5, Tale IV.

"The seven precious things," are variously stated. Sometimes they
are gold, silver, lapis lazuli, crystal, red pearls, diamond and coral.
Sometimes gold and silver are left out of the reckoning, and rubies and
emeralds substituted. See Köppen, i. 540 et seq. The extravagant and
incongruous description in the text is not artistic.

2. The month *Pushja*. Before the time of Vikramâditja astronomy
was not studied in India as a science; the course of the heavenly bodies
was observed, but only for the sake of determining the times and seasons
of feasts and sacrifices. The moon was the chief subject of observation
and of the more correct results of the same. Her path was divided
into twenty-eight "houses" or "mansions" called *naxatra*. This
division was invented by the Chinese, and India received it from them
about 1100 B.C. The *naxatravidjá* or the knowledge of the moon-
mansions, is set down in one of the oldest *Upanishad* as a special kind of
knowledge. In the oldest enumeration extant of the moon-mansions
only twenty-seven are mentioned, and the first of them is called *Krittiká*,
and *Abhigit*, which is the 20th, according to the latest enumeration, is
wanting; other lists have other discrepancies. It is worthy of notice
that *Kandramas*, the earliest name by which the moon is invoked in the
Vêda, is composed of *kandra*, "shining," and *mas*, "to measure," because
the moon measured time, and the various names of the moon in all the

so-called Indo-European languages are supposed to come from this last word. There were also four moon-divinities invoked, as *Kuhú, Sinivali, Rákâ,* and *Anumati,* in the Rig Vêda hymns; these are all feminine deities. *Soma,* the later moon-divinity, however, was masculine, and had twenty-seven of the fifty daughters of Daxa for his wives. *Kandramas* was also a male divinity. The worship of the four goddesses I have named was afterwards superseded by four (also feminine) deifications of the phases of the moon. There seems a little difficulty, however, about fitting their names to them. *Pushja,* with which we are more particularly concerned, would properly imply " waxing," but she presided nevertheless over the last quarter; *Krita,* meaning the " finished " course, over the new moon; the appellations of the others fit better. *Drapura* (derived from *dva,* two) designated the second quarter, and *Khârvâ,* "the beginning to wane," the full moon. In the list given by Amarasinha of the moon-mansions, *Pushja* is the name of the eighth, in the Mahâ Bhârata it stands for the sixth.

The month Pauscha answers to our December. (Lassen, iii. 819.)

3. We have many early proofs that India possessed an indigenous breed of hunting-dogs of noble and somewhat fierce character. They were much esteemed as hunting-dogs by the Persians, and formed an important article of commerce. Herodotus (i. 192) mentions their being imported into Babylon; whether the mighty hunter Nimrod had a high opinion of them, there is perhaps no means of ascertaining. Strabo (xv. i. § 31) says they were not afraid to hunt lions. In the *Ramajana,* (ii. 70, 21) Ashvapati gives Rama a present of " swift asses and dogs bred in the palace, large in stature, with the strength of tigers, and teeth meet to fight withal." Alexander found them sufficiently superior to his own to take with him a present of them offered him by Sopeithes. Aristobulos, Megasthenes, and Ælianus mention their qualities with admiration. Their strength and courage led to the erroneous tradition that they were suckled by tigers (see Pliny, viii. 65, 1). Plutarch (*De Soc. Anim.* x. 4) quotes a passage from an earlier Greek writer, saying they were so noble, that though when they caught a hare they gladly sucked his blood, yet that if one lay down exhausted with the course, they would not kill it, but stood round it in a circle, wagging their tails to show their enjoyment was not in the blood, but in the victory.

The house-dog and herd-dog, however, was rather looked down upon ; it and the ass were the only animals the Kandala or lowest caste were allowed to possess (Manu, x 51), and it is still called Paria-dog (Bp Heber's " Journey," i. 490).

4. A functionary invented by the Mongolian tale-repeater. The idea evidently borrowed from his knowledge of the paramount authority of the Talé Lama of Tibet, leading him to suppose there must exist a corresponding dignity in India.

5. *Barin Tschidaktschi Erdektu*, " The mighty one at taking distant aim." (Jülg.)

6. Gesser Khan, the great hero of Mongolian tales; called also " The mighty Destroyer of the root of the seven evils in the seven places of the earth." (Jülg.)

7. Tschin-tâmani, Sanskrit, " Thought-jewel,"is a jewel possessing the magic power of producing whatever object the possessor of it sets his heart upon. (Böhtlingk and Roth, Sanskrit Dict.) See infra, note 2, to " The False Friend," and note 8 to " Vikramâditja's Youth."

8. *Barss-Irbiss*, " leopard-tiger." (Jülg.)

HISTORICAL NOTICE OF VIKRAMADITJA.

1. Professor Wilson.

2. Reinaud, *Fragments relatifs à l'Inde.*

3. See a most extraordinary instance of this noticed in note 11 of the Tale in this volume entitled "Vikramâditja makes the Silent Speak."

4. Thus Reinaud (*Mémoire Géographique sur l'Inde*, p. 80) speaks of a king of this name who governed Cashmere A.D. 517, as if he were the original Vikramâditja.

5. The honour of being the first to work this mine of information belongs to H. Todd; see his "Account of Indian Medals," in Trans. of As. Soc.

6. The art of coining at all was, in all probability, introduced by the Greeks.—Wilson, *Ariana Antiqua*, p. 403; also Prinsep, in Journ. of As. Soc. i. 394.

7. In the list of kings given by Lassen, iv. 969, 970, there are eight kings called Vikramâditja, either as a name or a surname, between A.D. 500 and 1000.

8. The kingdom of Malâva answers to the present province of Malwa, comprising the table-land enclosed between the Vindhja and Haravatî ranges. The amenity of its climate made it the favourite residence of the rulers of this part of India, and we find in it a number of former capitals of great empires. It lay near the commercial coast of Guzerat, and through it were highways from Northern India over the Vindhja range into the Dekhan. It is also well watered; its chief river, the Kharmanvati (now Kumbal), rises in the Vindhja mountains, and falls into the Jumna. At its confluence with the Siprâ, a little tributary, was situated Uggajini = "the Victorious," now called Uggeni, Ozene,

and Oojein, and still the first meridian of Indian astronomers. It also bore the name of Avantî = "the Protecting," from the circumstance of its having given refuge to this Vikramâditja in his infancy.

9. This length of reign is actually ascribed to him in the Chronological Table out of the Kalijuga-Râgakaritra, given in Journ. of the As. Soc. p. 496.

10. This resolution was quite in conformity with the prevailing religious teaching. In the collection of laws and precepts called the Manû, many rules are laid down for this kind of life, and were followed to a prodigious extent both by solitaries and communities; e. g. "When the *grihastha* = 'father of the house,' finds wrinkles and grey hairs coming, and when children's children are begotten to him, then it is time for him to forsake inhabited places for the jungle." It is further prescribed that he should expose himself there to all kinds of perils, privations, and hardships. He is not to shrink from encounters with inimical tribes; he is to live on wild fruits, roots, and water. In summer he is to expose himself to the heat of fierce fires, and in the rainy season to the wet, without seeking shelter; in the coldest winter he is to go clothed in damp raiment. By these, and such means, he was to acquire indifference to all corporeal considerations, and reach after union with the Highest Being. Manû, v. 29; vii. 1—30; viii. 28; x. 5; xi. 48, 53; xvii. 5, 7, 24; xviii. 3—5, &c., &c. It is impossible not to be struck, in studying such passages as these, with a reflection of the inferiority which every other religious system, even in its sublimest aims, presents to Christianity. If, indeed, there were a first uniform limit appointed to the hand of death at the age of threescore years and ten, then it might be a clever rule to fix the appearance of wrinkles, grey hairs, and children's children as the period for beginning to contemplate what is to come after it; but, as the number of those who are summoned to actual acquaintance with that futurity before that age is pretty nearly as great as that of those who surpass it, the maxim carries on the face of it that it is dictated by a very fallible, however well-intentioned, guide. Christianity knows no such limit, but opens its perfect teaching to the contemplation of "babes;" while, practically, experience shows that those who are called early to a life of religion are far more numerous than those in advanced years.

11. Given in W. Taylor's Orient. Hist. MSS., i. 199.

12. "The Indians have no actual history written by themselves." (Lassen, *Indische Alterthumskunde*, i. 357, note 1.)

13. Klaproth, *Würdigung der Asiatischen Geschichtschreiber.*

14. *Indien*, p. 17.

15. *Examen Critique*, p. 347.

16. But only committed to memory. See supra, p. 333.

17. Burnouf, *Introduction à l'Hist. du Buddh.*, vol i.

18. Concerning the late introduction of this idea, see supra, pp. 337-8.

19. *Indische Alterthumskunde*, i. 839.

20. Lassen, iii., p. 44.

21. Mommsen (History of Rome, book iv., ch. viii.), writing of Mithridates Eupator, who died within a few years of the date ascribed to Vikramâditja's birth, says, "Although our accounts regarding him are, in substance, traceable to written records of contemporaries, yet the legendary tradition, which is generated with lightning expedition in the East, early adorned the mighty king with many superhuman traits. These traits, however, belong to his character just as the crown of clouds belongs to the character of the highest mountain peaks; the outline of the figure appears in both cases, only more coloured and fantastic, not disturbed or essentially altered."

22. The legend from which the following is gathered has been given by Wilford, in a paper entitled "Vikramâditja and Salivâhâna, their respective eras."

23. See Lassen, *Indische Alterthumskunde*, ii. 49—56.

24. Wilson, in Mackenzie Collection, p. 343.

25. A *vetâla* is a kind of sprite, not always bad-natured, usually carrying on a kind of weird existence in burial-places. "They can possess themselves of the forms of those who die by the hand of justice, and assume them. By the power of magic men can make them obedient, and use them for all manner of difficult tasks above their own strength and sufficiency." Brockhaus' Report of the R. Saxon Scientific Soc. Philologico-historical Class, 1863, p. 181. "The *Vetâlas* were a late introduction among the gods of popular veneration." (Lassen, iv. 570.) "They came also to be regarded as incarnations of both Vishnu and Shiva." (Lassen, iv. 159.)

26. Two interesting instances of the way in which traditionary legends become attached to various persons as they float along the current of time, have been brought to my notice while preparing these sheets for the press. I cannot now recall where I picked up the story of "The Balladmaker and the Bootmaker," which I have given in "Patrañas," but I am sure it was told of a wandering minstrel, and as occurring on Spanish soil, as I have given it. I have since met it in "The Hundred Novels" of Sacchetti (written little after the time of Boccacio) as an

episode in a no less celebrated life than that of Dante, thus : " . . . Going out and passing by Porta S. Piero (Florence), he (Dante) heard a blacksmith beating on his anvil, and singing ' Dante ' just as one sings a common ballad; mutilating here, and mixing in verses of his own there; by which means Dante perceived that he sustained great injury. He said nothing, however, but went into the workshop, to where were laid ready many tools for use in the trade. Dante first took up the hammer and flung it into the road ; took up the pincers and flung them into the road; took up the scales and flung them out into the road. When he had thus flung many tools into the road, the blacksmith turned round with a brutal air, crying out, ' *Che diavol' fate voi?* Are you mad ?' But Dante said, 'And thou; what hast thou done?' 'I am busied about my craft,' said the blacksmith; 'and you are spoiling my gear, throwing it out into the road like that.' Said Dante, 'If you don't want me to spoil your things, don't you spoil mine.' Said the smith. ' What have I spoilt of yours ?' Said Dante, ' You sing my book, and you say it not as I made it; poem-making is my trade, and you have spoilt it.' Then the blacksmith was full of fury, but he had nothing to say ; so he went out and picked up his tools, and went on with his work, And the next time he felt inclined to sing, he sang Tristano and Lancellotte, and left Dante alone." " . . . Another day Dante was walking along, wearing the gorget and the *bracciaiuola*, according to the custom of the time, when he met a man driving an ass having a load of street sweepings, who, as he walked behind his ass, ever and anon sang Dante's book, and when he had sung a line or two, gave the donkey a hit, and cried ' *Arrri !*' Dante, coming up with him, gave him a blow on his shoulder with his armlet ('con la *bracciaiuola* gli diede una grande batacchiata,' literally ' bastonnade :' *bracciaiuola* stands for both the armour covering the arm, and for the tolerably formidable wooden instrument, fixed to the arm, with which *pallone*-players strike the ball), saying, as he did so, ' That "*arrri*" was never put in by me.' As soon as the ass-driver had got out of his way, he turned and made faces at Dante, saying, ' Take that !' But Dante, without suffering himself to be led into an altercation with such a man, replied, amid the applause of all, ' I would not give one of mine for a hundred of thine !' " (2.) It was lately mentioned to me that there is a narrow mountain-pass in the Lechthal, in Tirol, which is sometimes called Mangtritt (or St. Magnus' step), and sometimes Jusalte (Saltus Julii, the leap of Julius), because one tradition says Julius Cæsar leapt through it on horseback, and another that it opened to let St. Magnus pass through when escaping from a heathen horde.

27. Quoted by W. Taylor, in Journ. of As. Soc. vii. p. 391.

28. Quoted by Wilford, as above.

29. Quoted in Wilford's "Sacred Isles of the West."

30. Lassen.

31. Roth, *Extrait du Vikrama-Charitram*, p. 279.

32. Lassen, ii. p. 1154.

33. Lassen, ii. 1122—1129.

34. Abbé Huc narrates how enthusiastically the young Mongol tool-holos, or bard, sang to him the Invocation of Timour, of which he gives the refrain as follows:—"We have burned the sweet-smelling wood at the feet of the divine Timour. Our foreheads bent to the earth, we have offered to him the green leaf of tea, and the milk of our herds. We are ready: the Mongols are on foot, O Timour!

"O Divine Timour, when will thy great soul revive?

Return! Return! We await thee, O Timour!"

35. See Note 11 to "Vikramâditja makes the Silent Speak."

THE BOY-KING.

1. *Ardschi-Bordschi* is a Mongolian corruption of King Bhoga. (Jülg.)

The name of Bhoga (also written Noe, Nauge, and Noza; the *N* having entered from a careless following of the Persian historian Abulfazl, *n* and *b* being only distinguished by a point in Persian writing; and the *z* through the Portuguese, who habitually rendered the Indian *g* thus) seems to have been almost as favourite an appellation as that of Vikram-âditja itself, and pretty equally surrounded with confusion of fabulous incident.

The Bhoga were one of the mightiest dynasties of ancient India, and the name was given to the family on account of their unbounded pros-perity; being derived from *bhug* = enjoyment. The most celebrated king of the race bore a name which in our own day has become associated with prosperous rule, Bhoga Bismarka, or Bhismarka, is celebrated in ancient Sagas for his resistless might in the field, and was also accounted the type of a prudent and far-sighted sovereign. Many glories are fabled of him which I have not space to narrate, and even he only reigned over a fourth part of the Bhoga.

The individual Bhoga, however, who is probably the subject of the present story, and the details of whose virtues and wisdom present par-ticular analogies with the life of Vikramâditja is, comparatively speaking, modern, as he reigned from A.D. 1037 to 1093 according to some, or from 997 to 1053 according to others. He was likewise originally King of Maláva or Malwa, and fabulous conquests and extensions of dominion are likewise ascribed to him.

He was the greatest king of the Prâmâra dynasty, one of the four so-called *Agnikula,* or " from-the-god-Agni-descended," or " fire-born " tribes, and traced up his pedigree to a certain Paramâra, " The destroyer of adversaries," born at the prayer of the Hermit Rishi Vasichta on the lofty mountain of Arbuda (Arboo).

The story of this Bhoga is contained in two somewhat legendary accounts, called (1) the *Bhogaprabandha,* or poetical narrative concerning Bhoga; and (2) the *Bhogakaritra,* or the deeds of Bhoga. The first was written or collected by the Pandit Vallabha about 1340. The first part relates the circumstances concerning Bhoga's mounting the throne, and the second part is a history of the poets and learned men who flocked from all parts of India to his court. It tells an intricate fable about his having been persecuted in youth by a treacherous uncle who preceded him on the throne, but who afterwards came to repentance, while a supernatural interposition delivered Bhoga from all his machinations and made him master of Gauda or Bengal, and many other parts of India. Other legends mention his discovery of the throne of Vikramâditja, and make the figures on the steps *Apsarasas,* or nymphs, who were delivered and set free by him when he took possession of it and removed it to Dhara, whither he had transferred his capital from Uggajini. An Inscription (given at length, viii. 5, 6, in Journ. of As. Soc. of Bengal, v. p. 376) speaks thus of him :—" The most prosperous king Bhogadeva was the most illustrious of the whole generation of the Prâmâra. He attained to glory as great as that of the destroyer (Crishna) and traversed the universe to its utmost boundaries. His fame rose like the moonbeams over the mountains and rivers of the regions of the earth, and before it the renown of the inimical rulers faded away as the pale lotus-blossom is closed up." The Persian historian Abulfazl testifies in somewhat more sober language, that he greatly extended the frontiers of his kingdom.

His career was not one of unchecked prosperity however. According to an Inscription he was at last subdued by his enemy, and it thus gently tells the tale of his reverse :—" After he had attained to equality with Vâsava (Indra) and the land was well watered with streams, his relation Udajâditja became Ruler of the earth." His adversary being a relation, and a Prâmâra like himself, the feud between them was considered a scandal, and the inscription avoids perpetuating the details of it. A

legend in the *Bhogakaritra* supplies some. A hermit had been rather
severely judged by King Bhoga for a misdemeanour, and condemned
to ride through the streets of the capital on an ass. To punish the king
for this scandal he went into Cashmere till he had acquired the power of
making the soul of a man pass into another body. Then he came back
and constrained the soul of the king to pass into the body of a parrot while
he made his own soul pass into the king's body; then he issued a decree
commanding the slaughter of all the parrots in the kingdom. The royal
parrot, however, who was the object of the decree, effected his escape and
came to the court of Kandrasena, where he became the pet bird of the
princess his daughter; to her he revealed the story of his transformation.
At her instigation the hermit-king was persuaded to come to Kandrasena's court to sue for her hand, and there, by means of an intrigue of
hers he was put to death. Bhoga thus regained his original form and
his kingdom.

Abulfazl celebrates his moderation and uprightness, as well as his
liberality and the encouragement he gave to men of learning, of whom he
had not less than five hundred at one time lodged in his palace. This similarity of pursuits helped so to foster the tendency of which I have already
spoken, to confuse the deeds of one hero with another, that one poet at
least (Vararuki by name), who flourished under Bhoga, is reckoned
among the nine "jewels" of Vikramâditja's court! Kalidasa, who was
not very much, if at all later, is also put among the protégés of Bhoga
in the Bhogaprabandha. The actual writers of any note belonging to
Bhoga's age, whose names and works have come down to us are
chiefly Subandhu and Vâna, authors of two poems entitled respectively
Vâsavadattâ and *Kâdambari*, of which a reprint was issued at Calcutta
in 1850. Dandi, who wrote a celebrated drama called *Dashakumâraka-
ritra*, affording a useful picture of the manners prevailing in Hindustan
and the Dekhan in his time; he also left a treatise on the art of poetry,
called *Kâvjadarshâ*. Another poet of this date, named Shaukara, has
often been confounded with a philosophical writer of the same name in
the eighth century. The Harivansha, a mythological poem in continuation of the Mâha Bhârata, also belongs to this reign. Among numerous
other works ascribed to it, many of which have not yet been examined
into by Europeans, are several treatises of mathematics and astronomy.
Bhoga himself is entered in a list of the astronomers of his time, and he
was said to be the author of a treatise on medicine, called *Vriddha Bhoga*,
and of one on jurisprudence, called *Smritishâstra*. ●

2. *Boddhisattva.* See p. 342 and p. 365.

THE FALSE FRIEND.

1. Compare this story with that given Nights 589—593 of Arabian Nights. (Jülg.)

2. That the jewel-merchant had no written proof of the trust he had committed to his friend would appear quite in conformity with actual custom, at least in primitive times. Megasthenes has left testimony (Strabo xv. i. 53, p. 709), quoted by Schwanbeck (Megas. *Ind.* p. 113), in favour of the general uprightness of the Indians and their little in-clination to litigation, which he bases on the fact that it was the custom to take no acknowledgment under seal or writing of money or jewels en-trusted to another, or even to call witnesses to the fact; that the word of the man who had entrusted another with such sufficed; also Ælianus, V. H. iv. i. This, notwithstanding that the Manu (*dh. c.* viii. 180) con-tains provisions for regulating such transactions in due form and order; the man accordingly does not think of denying that he received the jewel, which would seem the easier way of concealing his fraud, because he knew the word of the jewel-merchant would be taken against his.

3. *Stupa*, a shrine; often a natural cave; often one artificially hewn; containing relics, or commemorating some incident considered sacred in the life of a noted Buddhist teacher. We read of *stupas* instituted at a spot where there was a tradition Shâkjamuni had left a foot-print; and another at Kapilvastu, his native place, over the spot where, as we saw in his life, he was led to devote himself to serious contemplations by meeting a sick man, &c. When of imposing proportion it was called a *mâhastûpa*. When such monuments on the other hand were put to-gether with stones (usually pyramidal in form) they were called *dhâtu-gopa*, whence Europeans give them the name of *Dagobas*. The word *Pagoda*, with which we are familiar, is probably derived from the Sans-krit *bhâgavata* = "Worthy to be venerated." The syllable *ava* was transformed in Prakrit into *o*, and the *ta* into *da*. The Portuguese took the word as applied to religious edifices as distinguished from the *kaitja* [1], or rock-hewn temples. The word *pagoda*, however, is usually reserved for Brahmanical temples. The word *stupa* has now become corrupted into *tope*, by which word you will find it designated by modern writers on India. The etymology of the word makes it mean much the same as *tumulus*, but *kaitja* conveys further the meaning that it was a sacred place.

4. The notion of jewels being endowed with talismanic properties is

---

[1] See infra, note 2 to "Vikramâditja's Birth."

common iu Eastern story. Ktesias (Fragm. lvii. 2, p. 79) mentions a celebrated Indian magic jewelled seal-ring called *Pantarba*, which had the property when thrown into the water of attracting to it other jewels, and that a merchant once drew out one hundred and seventy-seven other jewels and seals by its means.

THE PRETENDED SON.

1. *Schimnu.* See supra, note 2, Tale III.

2. Diamond, Sanskrit, *vadschra*, originally the thunderbolt, Indra's sceptre ; then the praying-sceptre of the priests ; the symbol of durability, immovability, and indestructibility. (Köppen i. 251, and ii. 271, quoted by Jülg.) It was permitted to none but kings to possess them. (Lassen, iii. 18.) See also note 1, Tale XV.

ARDSCHI-BORDSCHI DISCOVERS VIKRAMÂDITJA'S THRONE.

1. We read of a silver statue in one of the many temples founded by Lalitâditja, King of Cashmere, whose bright golden cuirass " gave forth a stream of light like a river of milk." Mentioned in Lassen, iii. p. 1000, and iv. 575.

2. It will be perceived the story is not without a certain meaning. It inculcates regard for the example and experience of the ancient and wise—the wisdom of the hero Vikramâditja (typified by his throne) was to be the model and guide of other kings and dynasties.

3. Sounding of trumpet-shells. The *shankha* or *concha* seems to have been the earliest form of trumpet used in war. It often finds mention in the heroic poems. Crishna used one in his warrior character ; and Vishnu, from bearing one, had the appellation *shankha* and *shankhin.* To the present day it is used in announcing festivals in Mongolia.

4. *Sûta*, bard. To this order it is that we are indebted for the preservation of so many myths and heroic tales. He was also the charioteer of the kings.

5. The six classes, states, or stages of living beings, by passing through which *Buddhahood* was to be attained—(1) Pure spirit or the devas gods (Skr. *Surâs ;* Mongolian, *Tegri ;* Kalm. *Tenggeri*) ; (2) the unclean

spirits, enemies of the gods (Skr. *Asurâs*); (3) men; (4) beasts; (5) *Pretâs*, monsters surrounding the entrance of hell; (6) the hell-gods. (Köppen, i. 238, et seq., quoted by Jülg.)

VIKRAMÂDITJA'S BIRTH.

1. Udsesskülengtu-Gôa-Chatun, a heaping up of synonyms of which we had an example, note 2, Tale XVII. Both words mean "beautiful," "charming." *Gôa* is a Mongolian expression by which royal women are called (as also *chatun*). Thus we sometimes meet with *Udsessküleng*, sometimes *Udsesskülengtu* (the adjunct *tu* forming the adjective use of the word); *Udsesskülengtu-Goa, Udsesskülengtu-Chatun,* or *Udessküleng-Gôâ-Chatun.* (Jülg.)

2. *Kaitja* or *Chaitga* is a sacred grotto where relics were preserved, or marking a spot where some remarkable event of ancient date had taken place. We are told that King Ashokja (246 B.C.) caused kaitjas to be built, or rather hewn, in every spot in his dominions rendered sacred by any act of Shâkjamuni's life [1]; as also over the relics of many of the first teachers (p. 390). The number of these is fabled in the Mahâvansha (v. p. 26) to have been not less than 84,000! He opened seven of the shrines in which the relics of Shâkjamuni were originally placed, and divided them into so many caskets of gold, silver, crystal, and lapis lazuli, endowing every town of his dominion with one, and building a *kaitja* over it. These were all completed by one given day at one and the same time, and the authority of the *Dharma* (law) of Buddha was proclaimed in all. In process of time great labour came to be spent on their decoration, till whole temples were hewn out of the living stone, forming almost imperishable records of the earliest architecture of the country, and to some extent of its history and religion too. The most astonishing remains are to be seen of works of this kind, with files of columns and elaborate bas-reliefs sculptured out of the solid rock.

3. Abbé Huc tells us that the Mongolians prepare their tea quite differently from the Chinese. The leaves, instead of being carefully picked as in China, are pressed all together along with the smaller tendrils and stalks into a mould resembling an ordinary brick. When required for use a piece of the brick is broken off, pulverized, and boiled in a kettle until the water receives a reddish hue, some salt is then

---

[1] Burnouf, i. 265.

thrown in, and when it has become almost black milk is added. It is a great Tartar luxury, and also an article of commerce with Russia; but the Chinese never touch it.

4. An accepted token of veneration and homage. (Jülg.)

5. Sesame-oil. See note 2, Tale V.

6. Kalavinka = Sanskrit, *Sperling*, belongs to the sacred order of birds and scenes, in this place to be intended for the *Kokila*. (Jülg.)

The *Kokila*, or India cuckoo, is as favourite a bird with Indians as the nightingale is with us. For a description of it see "A Monograph of Indian and Malayan Species of Cuculidæ," in Journal of As. Soc. of Bengal, xi. 908, by Edward Blyth.

7. You are not to imagine that by "four parts of the universe" is meant any thing like what we have been used to call "the four quarters of the globe." The division of the Indian cosmogony was very different and refers to the distribution of the (supposed) known universe between gods of various orders and men, to the latter being assigned the fourth and lowest called Gambudvîpa [1].

8. Concerning such religious gatherings, see Köppen, i. 396, 579—583; ii. 115, 311.

At such a festival held by Aravâla, King of Cashmere, on occasion of celebrating the acceptance of the teaching of Shâkjamuni as the religion of his dominion, it is said in a legend that there were present 84,000 of *each* order of the demigods, 100,000 priests, and 800,000 people.

9. The parrot naturally takes a prominent place in Indian fable, both on account of his sagacity, his companionable nature, and his extraordinary length of days. He did not fail to attract much notice on the part of the Greek writers on India; and Ktesias, who wrote about 370 B.C., seems to have caught some of the peculiar Indian regard for his powers, when he wrote that *though he ordinarily spoke the Indian's language*, he *could* talk Greek if taught it. Ælianus says they were esteemed by the Brahmans above all other birds, and that the princes kept many of them in their gardens and houses.

10. Bodhisattva. See p. 346 and note 1, Tale XI.

11. Concerning the serpent-gods, see supra, note 1 to Tale II.; and note 4, Tale XXII.

12. A legend containing curiously similar details is told in the Mahâvansha of Shishunâga, founder of an early dynasty of Magadha (Behar). The king had married his chief dancer, and afterwards sent

---

[1] See supra, p. 351 and p. 385.

her away. Partly out of distress and partly as a reproach she left her infant son exposed on the dunghill of the royal dwelling. A serpent-god, who was the tutelar genius of the place, took pity on the child, and was found winding its body round the basket in which it was cradled, holding its head raised over the same and spreading out its hood (it was the Cobra di capello species of serpent, which was the object of divine honours) to protect him from the sun. The people drove away the serpent-god (Nâga) with the cry of *Shu! Shu!* whence they gave the name of Shishunâga to the child, who, on opening the basket, was found to be endowed with qualities promising his future greatness. In this case, however, the serpent-god seems to have borne his serpent-shape, and in that of Vikramâditja, the eight are spoken of as in human form.

VIKRAMÂDITJA'S YOUTH.

1. *Nirvâna.* See supra, p. 330, note, p. 334, and p. 343. The word is sometimes used however poetically, simply as an equivalent for death.

2. *Kütschün Tschindaktschi* = "One provided with might." (Jülg.)

3. "The custom of requiring women to go abroad veiled was only intro-duced after the Mussulman invasion, and was nearly the only important circumstance in which Muhammedan influenced Indian manners." See Lassen, *Indische Alterthumskunde*, iii. p. 1157. In Mongolia, however, Abbé Huc found that women have completely preserved their indepen-dence. "Far from being kept down as among other Asiatic nations they come and go at pleasure, ride out on horseback, and pay visits to each other from tent to tent. In place of the soft languishing physiognomy of the Chinese women, they present in their bearing and manners a sense of power and free will in accordance with their active life and nomad habits. Their attire augments the effect of their masculine haughty mien."

In chapter v. of vol. ii., however, he tells of a custom prevailing in part of Tibet of a much more objectionable nature than the use of a veil :—"Nearly 200 years ago the Nome-Khan, who ruled over Hither-Tibet, was a man of rigid manners. . . . To meet the libertinism prevailing at his day he published an edict prohibiting women from appearing in public otherwise than with their faces bedaubed with a hideous black varnish. . . . The most extraordinary circumstance connected with it is that the women are perfectly resigned to it. . . The women who bedaub their faces most disgustingly are deemed the most pious. . . . In country places the edict is still observed with exactitude, but at Lha-Ssa it is not unusual to meet women who set it at defiance, . . . they are, however, unfavourably regarded. In other respects they enjoy great liberty. Instead of vegetating prisoners in the depths of their houses they lead an active and laborious life. . . . Besides household duties, they concentrate in their own hands all the retail trade of the country, and in rural districts perform most of the labours of agriculture."

4. *Schalú.* In another version of the legend he is called Sakori, the soothsayer, because he made these predictions. (Journal of As. Soc. of Bengal, vi. 350, in a paper by Lieut. W. Postans.)

5. The wolf-nurtured prince has a prominent place in Mongolian chronicles. Their dynasty was founded by *Bürte-Tschinoa* = the Wolf in winter-clothing. See I. J. Schmidt's *Die Völker Mittel-Asiens, vorzüglich die Mongolen und Tibeter*, St. Petersburg, 1824, pp. 11—18, 33 et seq.; 70—75; and sSanang sSetsen, 56 and 372.

6. I cannot forbear reference to notices of such sudden storms and inundations in Mongolia made from personal experience by Abbé Huc "Travels in China and Tartary," chapters vi. and vii.

7. The persistent removal of the child after such tender entreaties and such faithful unrequited service carries an idea of heartlessness, but in extenuation it should be mentioned that while the Indians honoured every kind of animal by reason of their doctrine of metempsychosis, the wolf was just the only beast with which they seem to have had no sympathy, and they reckoned the sight of one brought ill-luck, a prejudice probably derived from the days of their pastoral existence when their approach was fraught with so much danger to their flocks. In Mongolia, where the pastoral mode of life still continues in vogue, the dread of the wolf was not likely to have diminished. Thus Abbé Huc says, "Although the want of population might seem to abandon the interminable deserts of Tartary to wild beasts, wolves are rarely met, owing to the incessant and vindictive warfare the Mongolians wage against them. They pursue them every where to the death, regarding them as their capital enemy on account of the great damage they may inflict upon their flocks. The announcement that a wolf has been seen is a signal for every one to mount his horse . . . the wolf in vain attempts to flee in every direction; it meets horsemen from every side. There is no mountain so rugged that the Tartar horses, agile as goats, cannot pursue it. The horseman who has caught it with his lasso gallops off, dragging it behind, to the nearest tent; there they strongly bind its muzzle, so that they may torture it securely, and by way of finale skin it alive. In summer the

wretched brute will live in this condition several days; in winter it soon dies frozen." The wolf seems fully to return the antipathy, for (chapter xi.) he says, "It is remarkable wolves in Mongolia attack men rather than animals. They may be seen sometimes passing at full gallop through a flock of sheep in order to attack the shepherd."

8. Tschin-tâmani, Sanskrit, "thought-jewel," a jewel having the magic power of supplying all the possessor wishes for. Indian fable writers revel in the idea of the possession of a talisman which can satisfy all desire. The grandest and perhaps earliest remaining example of it occurs in the Ramajana, where King *Visvamitra* = the universal friend, who from a *Xatrija* (warrior caste) merited to become a Brahman, visits *Vasichtha*, the chief of hermits, and finds him in possession of *Sabala*, a beautiful cow, which has the quality of providing *Vasichtha* with every thing whatever he may wish for. He wants to provide a banquet for Visvamitra, and he has only to tell *Sabala* to lay the board with worthy food, with food according to the six kinds of taste and drinks worthy of a king of the world. She immediately provides sugar, and honey, and rice, *maireja* or nectar, and wine, besides all manner of other drinks and various kinds of food heaped up like mountains; sweet fruits, and cakes, and jars of milk; all these things *Sabala* showered down for the use of the hosts who accompanied Visvamitra. Visvamitra covets the precious cow, and offers a hundred thousand cows of earth in barter for her. But *Vasichtha* refuses to part with her for a hundred million other cows or for fulness of silver. The king offers him next all manner of ornaments of gold, fourteen thousand elephants, gold chariots with four white steeds and eight hundred bells to them, eleven thousand horses of noble race, full of courage, and a million cows. The seer still remaining deaf to his offers the king carries her off by force.

The heavenly cow, however, in virtue of her extraordinary qualities, helps herself out of the difficulty. It is her part to fulfil her master's wishes, and as it is his wish to have her by him she gallops back to him, knocking over the soldiers of the earthly king by hundreds in her career. Returned to her master, the Brahman hermit, she reproaches him tenderly for letting her be removed by the earthly king. He answers her with equal affection, explaining that the earthly king has so much earthly strength that it is vain for him to resist him. At this *Sabala* is fired with holy indignation. She declares it must not be said that earthly power should triumph over spiritual strength. She reminds him that the power of Brahma, whom he represents, is unfailing in might, and begs him only to desire of her that she should destroy the Xatrija's host.

He desires it, and she forthwith furnishes a terrible army, and another, and another, till Visvamitra is quite undone, all his hosts, and allies, and children killed in the fray. Then he goes into the wilderness and prays to Mahâdeva, the great god, to come to his aid and give him divine weapons, spending a hundred years standing on the tips of his feet, and living on air like the serpent. Mahâdeva at last brings him weapons from heaven, at sight of which he is so elated that "his heroic courage rises like the tide of the ocean when the moon is at the full." With these burning arrows he devastates the whole of the beautiful garden surrounding *Vasichta's* dwelling. *Vasichta*, in high indignation at this wanton cruelty, raises his *vadschra*, the Brahma sceptre or staff, and all Visvamitra's weapons serve him no more. Then owning the fault he has committed in fighting against Brahma he goes into the wilderness and lives a life of penance a thousand years or two, after which he is permitted to become a Brahman.

9. Those who can see one and the same hero in the Sagas of Wodin, the Wild Huntsman, and William Tell [1], might well trace a connexion between such a legend as this and the working of the modern law of conscription. There is no country exposed to its action where such scenes as that described in the text might not be found. There have been plenty such brought under my own notice in Rome since this "tribute of blood," as the Romans bitterly call it, was first established there last year.

10. I have spoken elsewhere in these pages of the question of re-birth in the Buddhist system. Though not holding so cardinal a place as in Brahmanism the necessity for it remained to a certain extent. All virtues were recommended in the one case as a means to obtaining a higher degree at the next re-birth, and in the other the same, but less as an end, than as a means to earlier attaining to *Nirvâna*. Of all virtues the most serviceable for this purpose was the sacrifice of self for the good of the species.

11. Sinhâsana, lit. Lion-throne; a throne resting on lions, as before described in the text.

12. At the exercise of such heaven-given powers nature was supposed to testify her astonishment, and thus we are told of sacrifices and incense offered for the pacification of the same. (Jülg.)

---

[1] See Max Müller's "Chips from a German Workshop."

VIKRAMÂDITJA ACQUIRES ANOTHER KINGDOM.

1. Concerning such sacrifices, see Köppen, i. 246 and 560, and Trans. of sSanang sSetzen, p. 352.

VIKRAMÂDITJA MAKES THE SILENT SPEAK.

1. The Kalmucks make the 8th, 15th, and 30th of every month fast-days ; the Mongolians, the 13th, 14th, and 15th. (Köppen, i. 564—566; ii. 307—316, quoted by Jülg.)

2. *Dakini.* See note 2, Tale XIV., infra.

3. *Dakini Tegrijin Naran* = the Dakini sun of the gods. (Jülg.)

4. *Aramâlâ,* a string of beads used by Buddhists in their devotions.

5. Abbé Huc mentions frequently meeting with such wayside shrines, furnished just as here described.

6. *Chatun.* See note 1 to "Vikramâditja's Birth."

7. This beautiful story, which does not profess to be original, but a re-production of one of the *sagas* of old, is to be found under various ver-sions in many Indian collections of myths.

8. Compare note 3, Tale VII.

9. This story also holds a certain place among Indian legends, but is not so popular as the last.

10. Cup. No one travels or indeed goes about at all in Tibet and Mongolia without a wooden cup stuck in his breast or in his girdle. At every visit the guest holds out his cup and the host fills it with tea. Abbé Huc supplies many details concerning their use. They are so in-dispensable that they form a staple article of industry ; their value varies from a few pence up to as much as 40*l*.

11. Tai-tsing = the all-purest, the name of the Mandschu or Mantschou dynasty (or Mangu, according to the spelling of Lassen, iv. 742), who, from being called in by the last emperor of the Ming dynasty to help in suppressing a rebellion, subsequently seized the throne (1644). This dynasty has reigned in China ever since, while the Mantchou nationality has become actually forced on the Chinese.

Previously, however, the Mantchous were a tribe of Eastern Tartars long formidable to the Chinese. The introduction of a king of the Mantchous, therefore, as identical with Vikramâditja, presents the most remarkable instance that could be met with of what may be called the confusion of heroes, in the migration of myths.

12. Tsetsen Budschiktschi = the clever dancer. (Jülg.)

THE WISE PARROT.

1. "At any former time," i. e. in a previous state of existence, according to the doctrine of metempsychosis.

2. "The day will come"—similarly on occasion of a subsequent re-birth.

3. Tsoktu Ilagukssan = brilliant majesty. (Jülg.)

4. Naran Gerel = sunshine. (Jülg.)

5. Ssaran = moon. (Jülg.)

GLOSSARY-INDEX.

GILBERT AND RIVINGTON, PRINTERS, ST. JOHN'S SQUARE, LONDON.